ELIZA HOPE-BROWN

Muse

First edition

ISBN: 9798859004522

Editing by Daisy Jean Hollands

This book was professionally typeset on Reedsy.
Find out more at reedsy.com

Two souls intertwined across time
Always destined to find each other
No matter what it takes
Or the consequences

Even in their darkest moments
They're fated to find each other
Like pieces of a beautiful cosmic puz‐
zle
That always find a way to click into
place

One of them always knowing
Understanding the sweet inevitabil‐
ity
Particles of the stars once blown
apart
Always finding their way home

~ EHB

Foreword

Sweet Inevitability Series

Different universes. Different timelines. Different iterations of the same people.

Can Dan and Laura find their matching pieces in every world?

The same hearts, different lives. Will love find a way?

Books in this series:

Sanctuary
Colours
Muse

Acknowledgement

As an author, this is always by far the hardest part for me to write.

I should start by thanking everyone who has read my previous two books, for their wonderful feedback. It really does add fuel to the fire to keep going. I hope you love this story as much.

Again, to my test readers, Gee and Julie, whose time and insights during the process have been invaluable, thank you so much for giving up your time to read this story and help me shape it in the way I have done. I'm sorry I've made you cry so much.

And finally, no acknowledgement would be complete without me thanking Daisy who is the keystone of all my work. This story has been a hard one for us to tell and has been revised and revisited regularly over the past months. Without her guidance and love, the book you are about to read simply would not exist.

The Playlist

I have always been a lover of music from a very young age.
    As cliched as it sounds, music is regularly the soundtrack to my
    life and you'll often find me plugged into something listen-
ing
    to my favourite songs.

Large portions of this story you're about to read were written
    to specific songs that I listened to on repeat.

I have collected them into a single randomised Spotify playlist
    for you to listen to and enjoy while you read.
    Enjoy!

I

Part One

Part One

Taking a deep breath, he knelt in front of her. Like a Cheshire Cat, she grinned at him expectantly, her eyes crinkling at the corners.

"Yes?"

"You're going to make this difficult for me, aren't you?" He asked.

"Oh yes. Very much so."

Pulling a small box from his pocket, he opened and presented it to her, his hands trembling slightly.

"Yes?"

His voice shook as his nerves threatened to overrule him. "Will you marry me?"

"Oh I bet you ask all the girls that." She fluttered her eyelashes at him, as he squirmed uncomfortably in front of her.

"I promise you, you'll be the only woman I'll ever ask to marry me. So will you?"

"Will I what? Sorry, I *completely* forgot what you asked me." She smirked at him.

"Natalie!"

"Oh, my God Dan! What?"

"Will you marry me?"

She grinned and nodded enthusiastically.

* * *

"Do you believe in fate?"

Dan Muir lowered his phone and looked over at his wife who was smiling sweetly back at him, knowing full well she'd just lit the touch paper on a deep conversation that was almost certainly about to catch fire.

Letting out a mock sigh, he adjusted himself on the sofa in anticipation of the abyss he was about to tumble into with her.

"What?"

"Do you believe in fate?"

"That's a pretty big question for a Tuesday evening, baby."

"Well yeah, but do you?"

He thought for a moment. There was so much in his life he couldn't explain and over the years he'd tried to reconcile his understanding of it all with concepts of God and fate and so on.

"I dunno. It's a pretty tricky notion, isn't it? Why? Do you?"

"I don't think I do quite as much as I believe that we are given predetermined choices in life that lead us in different directions with a myriad of options."

"Jesus, Natalie! What have you been watching on YouTube?"

She smiled. He loved seeing that. There was something homely in her smile that would radiate warmth and comfort to those around her. It was one of the things he'd fallen in love with on their very first meeting.

"Like, if we'd not met, do you think you'd have ended up being a published author or do you think you'd be doing

4

something else now?"

A dull ache radiated from Dan's rapidly furrowing brow and he considered his answer carefully.

"I guess I get the *choices* idea. I certainly like that more than the thought of *destiny*. The idea that I'm not in control of anything at all feels a bit shit, to be honest. I like that I have an element of choice in it. But what are you saying? That life is one big ever-changing puzzle, that shifts with every choice we make?"

"Woah Dan, now who's getting deep?!" The loving wink she gave him prompted a smile in return. "So every choice, even the small ones, matter?"

"Erm. No. I highly doubt that my choice to have coffee in one cup over another particularly affects the path of my life. But I guess I like the idea that at points in my life, when something or someone feels I'm ready for that next step, that I'm provided with choices and whatever I decide kind of unlocks the next stage of life."

"Like you deciding to start writing?"

"Yeah, I suppose. That day when I first wrote, it was on a random whim and I could have easily ignored it and carried on watching TV. But that choice opened up this path of my life."

"You could have met any girl but me."

"Exactly, but we made choices that led us to each other and now I love you more than anything else in my life."

"Now you're just trying to be sweet."

"I mean, aren't I always sweet?"

Natalie nodded thoughtfully and rose from the sofa. Dan looked up at her curiously as she held out her hand.

"Come on. Time for bed."

"It's a bit early isn't it, baby? I'm not really that tired 'cos I napped after lunch."

She took his hand and pulled him up, leading him towards the stairs, her smile growing bigger.

"Mhmm. I'm fully aware you're not tired, don't worry."

* * *

Natalie smiled as Dan walked back across the quiet pub, a cup in each hand.

"For the lady," he said, setting a tea down in front of her.

"Such a gent."

"Always the tone of surprise, baby." He joined in with her teasing, even though it was an effort.

He always managed to make her smile, even on the days when he was struggling with something himself.

Having picked up from his body language that he wasn't having the best morning, she'd suggested they go out for a late breakfast, to get him out of the house. Dan had spent the early part of the day struggling to hold a conversation and he'd looked drawn and tired. Wondering if he'd been awake in the night again, Natalie had encouraged him to come out for some fresh air and pleasant company; two things she knew from experience would help.

They'd come to their usual brunch spot at The Wheatsheaf and were tucking into plates of cooked breakfast when Dan put his cutlery down and spoke.

"Thank you."

"What for, my love?"

"You know what."

"Hmm, humour me." She winked at him.

"For doing what you do, for getting me out of the house and out of my head for a bit."

"Were you awake in the night again?"

"Mhmm. Around 3 am. I tossed and turned for ages. Just couldn't seem to settle."

"I figured this morning, when I asked you twice if you wanted a coffee and you didn't answer either time, that something was up."

"Sorry, baby. I didn't hear you."

"Don't be sorry, it's fine. You were fully zoned out so I knew something wasn't right and didn't want to push you on it."

"I hate days like these when I feel like a zombie."

"I know you do, they're brought on by bad nights and that's something we can fix today. You can grab a nap later and then get an early night tonight. Hopefully, that'll right your body clock again. Just don't have a coffee after this one." She pointed to her husband's half-drunk cup of black life-giving liquid, "or it'll sit in your system too late into the evening."

"Thank you. I don't know what I'd do without you."

"Oh, you'd be on the streets, staring longingly into cute little coffee shops desperate for caffeine, if you didn't have me."

Natalie laughed and it warmed Dan better than any heat source ever could. He knew that no matter what, she was his gravity and she kept his world in orbit, allowing him to spin effortlessly around with her at the centre, never letting him fly away and lose himself.

* * *

"Right, come on then, What's this big news? Got another book deal?

Martin France placed his best friend's pint down in front of him and slid into the booth opposite.

That morning, Dan had called unexpectedly but not unwontedly, to ask him if he fancied a beer at lunchtime as he had some news to share. Martin hadn't seen the point in pussyfooting around after they'd arrived, he wanted to hear whatever it was Dan was wanting to share.

"It's not a book deal, no. I'm gonna need a few more months yet to finish the manuscript I'm working on. This news is... something else."

Dan and Martin had known each other for years, having met through friends at university. Time and shared experiences had forged their relaxed and easy relationship, each of them leaning on the other in times of crisis.

As Dan sat opposite his closest friend, he knew there was no one else in his life with whom he'd rather be sharing this news.

"Okay, so if it's not work, then what is it?"

Martin looked confused as he carefully worked the foam off the top of his pint.

"I'm going to be a dad."

"Fuck off!"

Dan just smiled and nodded.

"That's amazing news!"

"Thanks, mate!"

"When?"

"I'm not telling you when it happened, that's all kinds of wrong!"

"No, you twat! When is she due?"

"November time."

"Does Issy know?"

"Well, if our plan is working correctly, Natalie is telling her as we speak."

"Ah, I'm so happy for both of you."

"There's something else."

Martin paused, unsure what else there could be.

"We want you and Issy to be godparents."

"Fuck off! Me, a godfather?"

Dan laughed, knowing that *The Godfather* was one of his best friend's favourite films.

As if on cue, Martin squinted his eyes and relaxed his jowls, holding his hand out in front of him.

"I'm gonna make him an offer he can't refuse."

"Alright Don Corleone, save it for when the kid is here!"

"Ha!" Martin slapped his hand down on the table in excitement, causing an old couple nearby to almost jump out of their seats in shock. "Whiskey. We're having whiskey to celebrate!"

Watching Martin, who raced to the bar like an ID-clutching eighteen-year-old keen for his first legal pint, Dan smiled. Life was starting to slowly come together for him and his wife after years of struggle.

* * *

Natalie pulled the blanket over her bare feet and leaned back into the rocking chair. Her newborn son Max, was fast asleep in the bassinet next to her after his mid-afternoon feed and was making soft baby noises as he slept. All they had ahead of them was his nap and her book, which now rested in her lap, eager to be opened.

"Whatcha reading?"

"Shhh! I just got him back to sleep." She gently placed her finger to her lips, making a quiet gesture.

Dan continued in a whisper as he slowly entered the room. "Sorry."

"It's okay. He's had his feed but he didn't want to sleep, he just wanted to look around the room and take it all in, so he's only just gone back down."

"That's my inquisitive son." Dan squatted next to the crib just to be close to him.

"Don't you dare! You wake him up and you can deal with him."

"I'm just looking." Dan lowered his voice a few more decibels just to be safe.

Natalie smiled. He'd been besotted with his newborn son from the moment he'd been born. She was sure without any doubt that there were now two things in this world that Dan loved equally above all else and without question; her and Max. *He'll make a good dad*, she decided as she looked over at him.

"So whatcha reading?"

"It's the latest book from that series I started when I was pregnant."

"Any good?

"Yeah, it's really lovely."

Dan looked over at his wife, reclined in her chair which sat by the window in their bedroom. It was her favourite spot to read and relax, had been ever since she had restored it just after they'd moved in, years before. She could happily while away the hours in that chair, curled up under a big blanket reading a book or napping; she'd even taken to sleeping upright in it for a few nights during the latter stages of her pregnancy when she couldn't get comfortable lying down.

"Want me to take him downstairs so you can read in peace?"

Natalie knew exactly what that meant; that her husband had every intention of waking the newborn up to play but she also knew that it was coming from a place of love. He wanted to spend time with his son while also giving her a rest.

"No, he's fine. If he wakes up and doesn't want to settle you can take him for a bit but otherwise, just let him sleep."

Dan rose and walked the few steps to where she sat.

"You want anything?"

"A kiss and then for you to bugger off so I can read my book?" She grinned at him.

"Your wish is my command, my love."

He leant down to kiss her and let it linger for a moment. Dan relished every opportunity to show her that she was both loved and wanted, something Natalie would happily let him do. His kiss left her smouldering as he turned and headed back downstairs. Deciding to cool her jets, she shook her head clear and picked up her book, losing herself in delicious words.

* * *

She yawned as she flicked the kettle on before rubbing her tired eyes.

It had been a rough night. Max had colic and between them, his parents had been tag-teaming all night, taking turns caring for him. By 5 am the little one had finally tired himself out, having been awake most of the night and Dan had let Natalie get a few more hours of precious sleep, while he stayed up to keep an eye on their ailing son.

Just after 8 am, she'd come downstairs to see how the boys were, to find them fast asleep together on the sofa, Max lying completely sparked out on Dan's chest; both snoring softly. Her heart melted a little.

Deciding to let them sleep a little longer, she moved quietly through to the kitchen to make herself a much-needed cup of tea.

Opening the cupboard door she reached up to the top shelf for her favourite oversized mug, perfect for mornings like this when the first drink of the day was about quantity, not quality. Pulling it down she found a piece of sticky yellow paper, folded in half inside. Familiarity brought a smile to her lips.

Unfolding the little yellow Post-It note, she read.

I love the way
Your eyes sparkle
When you laugh
Or smile

I love the way
When you're in view
That you shy away
And hide

I love the way
That without even trying

You have me hopelessly
In love with you.

"Hey, you're awake. What time is it?"

"Just gone eight." She smiled at a sleepy-looking Dan, standing in the kitchen doorway.

"Hmm okay."

"Where's Max?"

"I put him down in his basket for a bit, he's still asleep."

"Is his monitor on?"

Dan yawned wide enough to swallow a ship. "Yeah. Why?"

" 'Cause I'm going for a shower."

"Oh okay. Want me to finish making your tea for you?"

Natalie walked past Dan and took him by the hand, dragging him behind her. "No, you're coming with me."

She led her husband upstairs to the small family bathroom as he followed behind her, stumbling and groggy, baby monitor in hand. Shutting the door behind him, he set the white plastic speaker down near the sink. Her lips were on his before his mind was fully caught up with what was happening.

It only took a few moments before her soft but purposeful kiss was replaced with a sense of urgency and she bit his lip; Dan's fingertips hooking into the waistband of her knickers. The steam had built up in the small room so quickly that it was hard for them to see each other clearly.

Under the hot shower head, her husband had her pinned against the shower wall; his left hand between her legs as she sank her teeth into his shoulder, her desire becoming uncontrollable.

"Ow!"

Natalie chuckled, "not even a little sorry."

Teasing her, he removed his hand and she pouted, looking up flirtatiously. Yeah, he looked tired but he was still hot, his skin glistening with rivulets of shower water. "Sorry."

Dan couldn't withhold any longer, that pout of hers would be the death of him.

Natalie's hands began to move south, drawing an involuntary growl from him, as she held his gaze and raised her eyebrows, her smile growing wider.

A crackle from the baby monitor made them both pause briefly. Max was awake.

"He might go back off, baby." Dan softly pleaded, while methodically leaving a trail of kisses along her collarbone.

But when another cry rang through the mini speaker, she called time on their fun.

"Sorry, stud."

Stepping out, she wrapped a big towel around her body, her husband staring after her lustfully.

"Finish your shower and come down for breakfast. I'll start it when I've settled him back down."

"It's not food I'm hungry for!"

Natalie turned and blew him a kiss before disappearing downstairs to tend to Max, with Dan left to turn the shower dial to cold in a feeble effort to calm himself down.

* * *

Staring through the kitchen window, out over the garden, he pondered his next move as steam rose gently from the freshly brewed cup of coffee in his hand. He breathed in the strong aroma emitting from it as he lost himself to his thoughts.

Dan had always loved words. At school, he'd always found himself creating comics or writing short stories when he found it hard to pay attention in class. While his ability wasn't ever encouraged by his teachers, with one even telling him he wasn't very good at all, writing had always been a part of him growing up.

He'd decided to go to university after school, to do an English degree in the hope that he'd slip effortlessly into a career as an author but the reality he'd found had been very different. His classes had quickly become a drag and acted more as an inconvenience than an inspiration, leaving him to work tirelessly on his stories in his own time.

Fortune somehow smiled on him when one of his cohort told him that their father worked as a literary agent. After weeks of pestering, Dan managed to convince his friend to share his current manuscript with their dad. It had paid off, however, and within months, Dan was fervently working on his first proper book, a deal secured by his new agent.

Now, looking out at the washing hanging on the line, the life of a full-time writer was anything but the romantic notion he had fantasised about as he'd grown up.

The reality was that he'd fumble through his days, trying to expand on ideas and finish chapters for the current book he was working on, while wondering if in fact, he had any business being a writer at all. Self-doubt and sickly imposter syndrome gnawed at the edges of his confidence on a daily and relentless basis.

His current project, a prequel to the fantasy fiction series that had brought him a modicum of success and helped to pay the bills, was stuttering along on the laptop behind him.

It wasn't that he'd lost the love for writing or for this story, not at all. It was just that he wasn't excited by it anymore. That heady buzz he used to get from writing had gone and he wasn't sure how to bring it back. The story he was writing was good and would sell some copies, he was sure of that, but it wasn't gripping. It felt more like work and less like a story he desperately needed to get out of him.

Taking a sip of his coffee, he wondered if he had any ideas in him that could bring that excitement back.

* * *

"God, bedtime stories are lame!"

Dan plonked himself on the sofa next to his wife after putting four-year-old Max to bed and being made to endure three decidedly boring bedtime stories.

"You're so judgmental." Natalie grinned at him. He was ever the wordsmith and she knew he loathed boring stories, even if they were only ten pages long and printed on cardboard.

"I swear if I have to read about dinosaurs being friends one more time, I might need to see what cutlery we have in the kitchen that I can take my eyes out with. Do we still have that melon baller your mother gave us for Christmas? I'm sure she'd be happy to know it was getting put to good use!"

His wife playfully hit him on the arm and shook her head.

"That was not why my mother gave that to us and you know it but knowing how she feels about you, she'd probably be all for it."

Natalie's mum, Chloe, had never really warmed to her, as she would tell people, *artist* son-in-law. She would say artist but the disdain in her voice ensured it was anything but complimentary.

"Maybe it's in the back of the drawer by the sink?" Dan dramatically made to get up from the sofa.

"Or..." she said, grabbing his arm gently, "you could write your son a bedtime story you'd both enjoy."

Dan thought about it for a moment.

He could, he knew, spin a story pretty easily when inspired but it had been a few months since he had written properly now that some of his works had started to receive some more commercial success.

"I've never written a short story before."

"So?"

"So, it's different isn't it?"

"What, in that it's *shorter*?"

"Ha fucking ha. You know what I mean."

"Look, yeah okay so you haven't done short stories before but we're talking about one little story for your son. There's no pressure to make it literary gold: his eyes light up when you pull a face at him for goodness sake! Just think about it. Let that big, beautiful brain do what it does best."

"Yeah maybe. But no fucking dinosaurs."

"Fine. No fucking dinosaurs." She chortled at him.

Within a few days, Dan had a completed story and Max had made him retell the tale of *Max and the Loud Lion* every night for the rest of the week.

Natalie had watched on from their son's bedroom doorway with tears of pride in her eyes as father and son bonded in a way that was breathtaking to see.

* * *

Natalie knelt in front of Max and flattened down his collar.

"Right, my big boy. Go have a lovely time."

"Bye Mum!" He turned to leave.

"Oi! Don't I get a kiss?"

Max rushed back and threw his arms around her neck, kissing his mum's face.

"Sorry, Mum. Bye!"

Her little four-year-old son turned again and excited, hurried into his new class.

"Don't worry he'll be fine."

She felt Dan at her back as she stood.

"I know he will. But it's his first day and I'm his mother so I'm allowed to worry."

They walked out of the school gates, hand in hand, alongside a gaggle of other parents, all wondering how they were meant to spend their days now that their offspring wouldn't be keeping them busy.

"What time do you need to leave for work?"

"Around two."

"So we have some time?" Dan raised his eyebrows at his wife.

"Yeah. Why? What's in that big, beautiful brain of yours?"

"Fancy going for brunch somewhere?"

"Oh Dan, are we going on a date?" Natalie cooed as she let go of his hand, linked her arm through his and snuggled into him.

"Maybe, but you can pay. I'm a struggling writer don't you know?"

"You'll be single if you say something like that again don't you know?"

Laughing, the pair made their way to their favourite local pub, The Wheatsheaf.

A few hours later, Natalie sat on the edge of the bed, pulling her top back on, Dan lying naked behind her. After brunch, they'd spent the early part of the afternoon in bed enjoying the alone time with each other.

"Are you sure you're okay to pick him up?"

"Yeah of course, baby."

"I hate that I have to work on his first day of school. I really wanted to be able to pick him up today."

"I know. One day, when I'm rich and famous you'll be able to quit your job and pick him up every day."

"That's the dream."

She leaned back and kissed him.

"You could call in sick..." Dan stroked her thigh as he tried to kiss her neck.

"Easy there, tiger. We still have bills to pay for now. So less trying to feel me up and more writing!"

He smiled. "I'm on it. I'll pick Max up and then I'll get a few hours in this evening. This manuscript is nearly done. Got a good feeling about it."

While it wasn't always easy, they had found a steady rhythm of balancing child care and her work schedule at the hospital where she worked as a nurse. Dan, for his part, made sure he was putting the time in looking after Max and trying to get that lucky break with his writing that would allow her to quit work and just be a stay-at-home wife and mum, the one thing she truly wanted more than anything.

* * *

Natalie pushed herself back into her husband as he dozed quietly. Instinctively, as if his hands knew she was there even while asleep, Dan pulled her to him sliding his hand over her tummy. She purred.

"Happy Valentine's Day, baby."

She smiled. He wasn't dozing. *Fucker!*

"Happy Valentine's Day. I thought you were sleeping."

"I am. This is me, asleep."

His lips found her neck and his hand moved from her tummy, pulling gently but purposefully at her hip causing her to feel him behind her.

"Down cowboy. We have a little boy to get ready for school."

"What time is it?"

"Just gone seven."

"We have time." His hands and lips persisted, making her fizz with excitement and her belly tense.

Grabbing his hand as he hooked his fingers into the waistband of her underwear, she stopped him. "No, we don't."

She couldn't help but smile. She always felt wanted and desired by her husband. Some days, he just couldn't seem to get enough of her company whether that was cute walks with takeaway coffees, snuggling on the sofa with a movie or taking her to bed in the middle of the afternoon.

She reached over to her nightstand and lifted the envelope with his name on it, handing it to him.

Reluctantly, Dan took it. He didn't want to do cards just yet, he wanted something else. But smiling, he opened her card.

To my first love.

Your love sees me through every day, good or bad.
Happy Valentine's Day.

All my love.
N xxx

"Thank you, baby."

He rolled away and produced his own card for her and an accompanying gift.

"Hey! I thought we said we weren't doing presents this year!"

"I can take it back?"

Natalie smacked his hand away as he reached out for the small velvet box she was now holding.

"Try it and you'll lose a finger!"

Smiling, she opened the navy blue lid to find a little silver locket inside.

"Dan!"

As she opened it gently, he explained. "It has pictures of me and Max inside. I thought you might like it."

With tears filling her field of vision, she stared at the

21

pictures of her boys in her hand. "It's perfect. Thank you."

Dan watched as she placed it back in the box and put it on her nightstand, along with the unopened card before she turned and kissed him.

"I love you, Mrs Muir."

Natalie smirked as she climbed on top of him. "I love you too, now shhhh or we'll be really late."

"What do you....ohhhhhh."

* * *

"Daddy!"

Dan snapped back into focus at hearing his son. *How long had he been sitting there?*

"Daddy. Where did you go?"

"Nowhere Maxxy. I'm right here."

Even at six years old, such was his growing emotional intelligence, Max knew his dad was different and could sometimes be there but not fully present. He snuggled back against his dad's chest and continued to tell him about the cartoon they were both watching.

They had a very close bond. With his wife working forty hour weeks at the hospital, Dan had become Max's primary caregiver and it was a role he loved. They were the best of friends; father and son enjoyed nothing more than sitting on the sofa together, watching cartoons and laughing along at the banal stupidity.

He would often do the school runs, help with homework and if Natalie was working a late shift, sort dinner for the two of them. Max was a bright boy and they loved talking about everything and anything as they walked home from school or sat eating fish and chips at the table.

Later in the kitchen, Natalie pulled Dan to one side while Max ate his dinner.

"Don't be too hard on yourself, baby."

"I hate when I zone out around him like that."

"Where did you go?"

"I started thinking about work stuff and then before I knew it, I was gone and he was calling me."

"Baby."

"I hate it."

"You're struggling to sleep again, aren't you?"

Dan hung his head, partly in shame and partly in exhaustion.

"Yeah. I can't seem to regulate myself at the moment."

"Okay, so we need to get you back into a routine. This can stop for starters." She lifted the half-drunk cup of coffee from his hands which she suspected was at least his fifth of the day. The hurt on Dan's face was evident. "No coffee after 3 pm remember? I know you're tired but this won't help tonight."

"No, I know."

He watched with loss and regret as she poured the inky liquid away down the drain.

"I know this is tough Dan and when you're struggling everything seems dark and heavy, but it's times like this that you need to try and focus on Max. If you're finding it hard to stay on top of the basics, then do it for him because I know how much it hurts you when you aren't present for him."

"It's literally one of the worst feelings."

"Then use it to help you stay present with him. He loves you dearly baby, so let him help you in his own way."

"Yeah, I guess."

"Look, let's focus on the basics for a few days and get you back in a better routine and that might help your mind slow down a little, yes? We'll do it together."

She hugged him, instantly feeling him relax against her.

"Okay?"

"Okay. Thanks, baby. I'm not sure what I'd do without you."

"I know we've talked about this before and you weren't ready but maybe now we could think again about you getting tested?"

Dan sighed and looked from Natalie to Max. He couldn't keep walking through life blindly trying to cope with his undiagnosed symptoms. He owed it to both of them to take this seriously.

"I know. Let's see about getting me a diagnosis."

* * *

Dan folded the letter back up and placed it carefully on the coffee table in front of him.

"How do you feel?"

Natalie sat on the edge of the coffee table, wanting to be with him but at the same time allowing him to have some physical and mental space.

"Erm...I don't know to be honest."

"It doesn't have to define who you are, baby."

He thought about it. One of the things the therapist had said when they'd first met with her, was that it was likely that he'd always had ADHD and had just spent a lifetime masking it so he could fit in. So he knew in a way that his condition did define him. What he had now, written on creme hospital paper in front of him, was confirmation.

"I think it already does."

"This is just validation for what we've believed for a while. That's all. Nothing needs to change."

"No, I know. It's just...you know."

"I know, baby." She held out her hand for him to take. The trembling slowed as his skin touched hers.

"I don't want to be medicated. I don't want a life on tablets Natalie, I can't."

"I know but they might help."

"They might but I don't want to be dependent on them. It feels like too much pressure."

"Okay, then we'll find a way to help you manage without them; there's plenty of stuff I've read online about food and exercise that can help to manage your symptoms."

"God, that just makes it sound like I'm broken."

"You are as far from broken as you could possibly be. Dan, this condition is why you have your gift. This is the reason you can write the way you do with all its glory and emotion. My love, you, and that big beautiful brain of yours are not broken."

"It'll be okay, won't it? I'll be enough, even with this?"

"Of course, you will baby, you have always been enough. This doesn't change a thing."

She'd moved to the sofa next to him and held him for the rest of the morning while they both came to terms with the validation this news gave them both.

* * *

Issy picked up her phone as it buzzed on the kitchen counter.

"Hey, Natalie. You alright?"

"Yeah, I am. Have you got a few minutes?"

"Sure! What's up? Everything okay?"

"Yeah, everything's fine. We heard from the doctors that's all."

Issy had been expecting this when they'd first shared with her and Martin that they were going to try and get Dan diagnosed.

"I'm guessing it's a yes?"

"It is. They say it's mild, which is kind of what we expected."

"How's he feeling about it?"

"He's okay. I don't think he's quite shellshocked, but I still think it's big news for him."

"It's just validation, isn't it really?"

"Yeah, that's what we've said. It's not going to change anything particularly but at least we know now for sure that it's definitely ADHD."

"Has he thought about medication? The therapist said it could make a big difference, didn't she?"

"Yeah, he doesn't want to go onto tablets at the moment. I think he's scared he'll get dependent on them and then not be sure who he'd be without them. So for now we're going to work on habits and lifestyle changes to help and then see where we end up."

"Okay well, I can understand that."

"He'll be alright."

"Of course, he will. He has you!"

Natalie smiled to herself knowing that there was much more to her husband's support network than just her.

"Hey, you three want to come over for dinner? Was going to do a lasagna."

"Yeah, I think that would be lovely actually."

"Cool okay, well look pop over whenever but I'll dish up around five."

"Thanks, Issy. Love you."

"Love you too."

With his wife's help, they figured out what triggered him and what he could do to manage his condition to make the day-to-day easier, without having to resort to medication. She would often say that it was his superpower and gave him the ability to change people's lives with his words. But they both knew it also came with downsides.

He suffered a lot with energy dropouts brought on by low levels of dopamine, after having bouts of mental hyperactivity where his brain just wouldn't stop. Natalie also knew he suffered horribly with rejection sensitivity, so it sometimes would take a lot of time and energy on her part to keep his head up when things weren't going to plan.

* * *

"Whatcha doing?"

Bored, Natalie plonked herself down on the sofa next to her husband who was scribbling notes into his black notebook. It was a fresh one, with his latest constant companion recently filled with words and thoughts and added to the pile by his desk.

A few months prior, Dan had found a notebook he'd fallen in love with and seeing how much he'd used it, Natalie had found a UK distributor who kindly shipped her a box of ten. *That should keep him happy for a while!*

"I'm just working on an idea."

"Anything you want to share?"

Dan scratched a few more words on the page and put his pen down in the fold.

"Erm, you know that new story I did for Max? The one with the school bully?"

"Yeah. Max and his eight friends take on the school bully and win. What about it?"

"Well, does it seem a bit... tame?"

"Tame? Dan, it's a kid's short story. Shouldn't it be tame by nature?"

"Well yeah."

"Unless you're planning on doing an adult version that's more gory?"

She watched the cogs grinding, showing in his face as his focus drifted away from her.

"Dan?"

He often did this. Part of his condition was that he had a wonderful ability to hyper-focus on something but it meant when his mind went somewhere, it was hard for him to pay attention to anything else, even if that meant her and Max.

Taking a breath, Natalie gave him a moment to process what he was seeing in his mind.

"It could be gory." He spoke mostly to himself.

"Okay?"

"Maybe not kids at all, but adults."

"Right, okay?"

"And set in the past. Like maybe medieval? Kings and

28

queens of old but less Pride and Prejudice and more Robin Hood, Prince of Thieves."

"So more, working people fighting against a great foe?"

"Yeah."

Dan's gaze shifted again as he watched the movie of his thoughts play out in his mind.

"Nine Kings defeat an evil power spreading throughout the kingdom."

His eyes widened.

This was a look Natalie had seen before. The seedling of a big idea had been planted and he was frantically trying to water it to make it grow. She watched as he mentally tumbled through ideas and plots.

"Dan. Look at me."

He shook himself from his musings and looked at his wife. It felt as though she'd suddenly appeared from nowhere in front of him.

"Write it down. Don't think about it. Write it."

He nodded, as if he were dazed and confused and coming to after being in shock.

"Dan, stay with me. You need to write this down now while it's still in your head."

Natalie knew what to do in this situation. She had to just let him immerse himself in the thoughts rushing through his mind's eye. But she also had to encourage him to take notes as he did it; too many times in the early days he'd had a great idea and lost it due to not making notes of it anywhere. Between them, they'd developed robust systems for him so he could take notes anytime, anywhere. It had proved invaluable.

She watched him as he frantically scribbled page after page of notes; his new idea pouring out of him like a flash flood.

29

Max bounced down the stairs a while later, pulling her from her happy observations.

"Hey Mummy, can..."

Natalie smiled at her son and pushed her finger to her lips as she quickly rose from the sofa. She scooped her happy little boy up into her arms and carried him through to the kitchen.

"We need to let Daddy work for a bit, I think he's got a good idea, so how about you and I do some baking for a while out of his way?"

"Maybe Daddy would like some cookies for after he's had his idea?"

"Oh, Maxxy, you are a clever little boy! I was just thinking the same." Winking at him, she set about making cookies for the afternoon with Max eagerly *helping*.

* * *

For the next eight months, Dan worked doggedly on his story.

The words and ideas flowed out of him effortlessly as he typed out page after page. When he wasn't looking after Max or sleeping, he was writing. Even on the tough days, when he'd bin a whole chapter because it just didn't fit anymore, he always felt like he was moving it in the right direction.

While Natalie knew that trying to get her husband to stop in this hyper-focused state was pretty futile, she did encourage him to sit next to her in the evenings while she watched TV, so they could at least be together as he worked.

Many a show was routinely interrupted as he shared his thought process or a current paragraph he was working on, continuing aloud a conversation he had started with himself in his head, often causing Natalie to ask him to rewind his thoughts so she could understand what the hell he was going on about.

By December of that year, she watched him close his laptop lid and sit back, as she repositioned a bauble on the Christmas tree.

"Natalie, I think it's done."

"Really?"

She moved away from the shiny decorations and went to stand next to him by his writing desk.

"Mhmm. I think so."

"Wow. How does that feel?"

"Big. But I think it's ready."

"Are you going to send it off?"

"Yeah."

She could tell that while he was happy to have finally completed the story of the nine kings, something wasn't sitting right with him.

"Baby, what's wrong?" She asked, moving behind him, sliding her hands over his shoulder as she hugged him.

"It's out of my hands now. Months of work, all done. Feel nervous now. I really want this one to be the one you know? I have such a good feeling about the idea and the publishing house loves it, but what if it doesn't sell?"

"Then we'll try something else but I don't think we need to worry about it right now. It's a wonderful piece of writing Dan, you know it is. Let the pieces fall where they may and we'll see what the future brings."

The Sanctuary of Nine was published a few months later and after a slow start, began to sell modestly. Dan was unable to hide his disappointment at it not becoming the huge success he'd dreamed it would be. It became just another book to add to the pile, which helped to keep the wolves from the door for a while longer.

* * *

"What? You're kidding right?"

Natalie looked on, intently trying to figure out what the hell was going on. When the call came moments before, they'd both looked curiously at each other at the unknown and unexpected number showing on his phone screen.

"Right. So what happens now?" Dan asked, looking shocked, the not-knowing driving his wife crazy with worry.

"Okay. I'll keep an eye out for the email then I guess. And thanks. It really is amazing news."

His wife was on him before he could disconnect the call.

"What's going on? What amazing news? What's happened? What email are you going to get?"

He just looked at her in shock. It was just a random Tuesday. Things like this weren't meant to happen to people like him and certainly not on a Tuesday, this felt more like a Friday thing. His usually overactive brain was having trouble catching up and processing the last few life-changing moments.

"Erm, someone wants to buy the book?"

"Which book?"

"The Sanctuary of Nine."

"What, they want to buy a copy?"

"No. They want to buy all of it."

"Huh?"

"Somehow, and I'm fucked if I can figure it out, a production company has gotten hold of a copy and they now want to buy the rights to it and make it into a TV series."

Natalie clasped her hands to her face. "You're shitting me?!"

"Baby, trust me, right now I'd love this to just be a simple prank. But no, apparently they want to buy the rights to the whole thing and start writing a script as soon as possible."

Neither of them could quite believe it. For years, they'd struggled along financially like most couples do, making ends meet. Dan's books had been selling relatively well, granted not well enough to impress Natalie's mother, but they were paying bills and it was helping them get by month to month.

But this was the first time something really big had happened. The disbelief they shared was as profound as it was shocking.

His phone chimed.

"An email?" Natalie was curious.

"Yeah. They said they're sending an offer over."

"Well open it then!"

Dan realised he was just standing there, immobile.

"Yeah. Sorry." He looked down and unlocked his phone, his thumb hovering over the email notification.

"I can't." He said, passing it to her.

Taking the phone from him, she opened the email and began to skim-read. Natalie knew that she needed to do this for him.

"Dear Mr Muir, Further to our conversation...yada yada... buy the exclusive rights for usage and distribution for the amount of...Dan oh my god..."

"What?"

She read it again over and over in her head just to be sure.

"Natalie! What?"

"They want to buy the rights for half a million pounds with the possibility of future royalties!"

"What? No, that's got to be a typo." He pulled the phone out of her hands to read himself.

"Fuck!"

"Baby, you did it!"

"No."

Natalie was surprised both by his reply and his tone. He seemed calm; she was as far removed from calm at that moment as she could ever possibly feel.

"What do you mean?"

"I didn't do it. We did. I couldn't have done this without you."

She hugged him, nearly knocking the phone out of his hand. "I love you, Mr Muir. I'm so proud of you."

* * *

"It's here!"

Natalie opened the door to a delivery driver in a high-vis jacket.

"Parcel for you, love. Can you just sign here for me?" He thrust a small digital pad into her hands, onto which she quickly scrawled haphazardly.

"Oh it's not for me. It's a boy toy." She couldn't help but smile.

The driver, nonplussed, thanked her as she handed the signed pad back; he leant the tall thin box up against the doorframe before making his way back out the front gate to his delivery van.

As she brought it in and shut the door behind her, Natalie heard Dan's feet rushing down the stairs.

"Oh, this isn't for you. I just signed for it, so that makes it mine."

"You're funny." He laughed at her.

"I'm not completely sold on you having another woman in the house you know." Her hand was resting on the upright box, tapping gently.

"Baby, you will always be my favourite girl but this particular woman is special and you're just going to have to accept that."

He kissed his wife on the lips, sliding his hand over the box to hers as he did so.

"Hmm, we'll see." She joked and let Dan take control of his delivery.

Once unboxed, with the packaging strewn across the entranceway of their home, he rested the large metal flight case carefully on the coffee table. There were two loud clicks as he flicked the latches at either end of the case and reverently lifted open the lid.

"Oh, she's pretty."

"She is. I'll give you that." Natalie stood over her husband with her hand gently on his shoulder. She wanted to be a part of this exciting moment for him; he deserved this.

In front of them lay an ebony Gibson 355-style guitar with gold trim, commonly known all around the world as *Lucille*. Whilst only a replica, and an expensive one at that, the guitar certainly was beautiful.

"You earned this, baby. I'm very proud of you."

Dan lifted it carefully out of the case and sat it in the playing position on his lap.

"I feel that as an author, I should probably have treated myself to something more writing specific."

"Okay cool. Let's send her back then and we can get you a fountain pen instead."

Natalie leaned down to kiss him lovingly on the head.

"Yeah, let's not." Dan smiled but never took his eyes off the *BB King Signature Lucille* he not only held in his hands but actually owned. He could scarcely believe it.

"You gonna play me something then?"

"God, I don't know if I'm ever gonna be good enough to play something like this, baby."

"Then get good 'cause otherwise it's going to become a very expensive dust magnet!"

Without even bothering to plug it in, Dan nervously played a few simple blues licks over the neck of *Lucille,* making the guitar tentatively sing. He'd played guitar sporadically over the years, owning and ultimately selling acoustic guitars when he got bored of them or when there was a big bill to be paid and no other way of paying it. This one, however, was one he'd always dreamed of owning.

Smiling with a mixture of pride in her husband and exasperation at the idea of boys and their toys, Natalie brushed her fingers through Dan's hair and left him to play.

She listened to him playing for over an hour that first day, getting himself used to the new instrument in his hands. Dan was by no means an accomplished guitarist. He was an author and an incredibly talented one at that, but music was a creative outlet that allowed him to work his brain in a different way.

But like the silly little love poems Dan would compose and leave around the house for her, she loved how he expressed himself in a variety of different ways that only he could.

* * *

"Right, they're here."

Natalie looked at the text Dan had just sent her from the driveway. He, along with Martin, had taken Max to watch his first premiership rugby match for his 7th birthday and now phase two of the little boy's big day was about to begin.

"Everything's ready, don't worry." Issy watched Natalie make final adjustments to everything before moving to the door to greet them.

"Mummy! Mummy! We won!"

Max sat on Martin's shoulders beaming with joy, kitted out in his new jersey shirt. "And look, Mum! Emily Scarratt signed it for me after the game!"

"She did? Aren't you a lucky boy!" She eyed her husband with suspicion. He just winked in return.

"We waited around at the end of the game and were lucky enough that she came to our end of the line of fans first. She even wished him a happy birthday."

"Yup. Your husband did good suggesting we stay on! I think he deserves a medal or something for that!"

"No one asked you, Martin," Natalie smirked at him, knowing full well that Dan did indeed deserve a medal for pulling this off.

Issy drew Max down from her husband's shoulders and carried him through to the kitchen.

"Wow, Maxxy you're getting so heavy now!"

"Maybe I feed him too much?" His mum smiled knowing

how much her growing son loved his food and no matter how well she fed him, it never seemed to be enough.

His eyes lit up when he saw the table prepared for him. Between the two of them, Natalie and Issy had made a huge gooey chocolate cake which was the centrepiece of a spread of party food fit for a king; or in Max's case, a young prince.

"Woah dude! Look at that cake!" Martin leaned down to talk to his godson, who was giddy just trying to take it all in.

"Thank you, Mummy!" Max rushed to hug his mum who was trying to hide the happy tears in her eyes.

"You're welcome, my big beautiful boy. Issy helped too."

"Hey yeah, I helped! Where's *my* hug?!"

Max laughed at Issy's mock indignation and went to give his godmother a similarly affectionate hug.

Dan moved behind his wife and slid his hand around her waist while kissing her temple.

"Good job, baby."

"I just hope he loves it."

"He will."

"It's nice having us all together. It doesn't matter the occasion, it just makes my heart happy to have all my favourite people here together."

* * *

Max sat at the dining table building Lego, a new set that had been a favourite birthday gift, while his mum boiled the kettle for her first cup of tea of the morning. Wrapped in a fluffy dressing gown, the feeling of Dan's lips still on her skin, she watched her son sitting in his pyjamas building his Lego with gusto. *This is what weekends are about,* she thought to herself.

Pouring hot water over a teabag, she heard her son's belly grumble.

"Don't worry Maxxy, Dad will be back from the shop any second now and I'll get breakfast started as soon as he walks through the door."

"Thanks, Mum. Can I just have cream cheese on my bagel please?"

"Of course you can!"

Within minutes of Dan returning from the shop weighed down in complex carbohydrates, two halves of a soft white bagel popped out of the toaster causing Max to pause his building.

"There you go, my big boy!" Natalie lovingly placed a plate of bagels smothered in pure white cream cheese in front of her son, who gratefully took it, rammed one bagel in his mouth and carried on with his Lego.

"Dude!"

Dan smiled at his hungry son who seemed to be as content as any child could be.

Natalie moved to her husband and wrapped her arms around him.

"Ah, he's fine. Gets it from you."

Dan mockingly stuck a large piece of doughnut-shaped bread into his mouth, filling his cheeks with it.

"I take offence at that."

"Sure you do."

They'd been awake together for a few hours and had made love in the quiet of the morning before Max had woken up; Dan was still feeling playful. Scooping up a fingerful of cream cheese from the half-eaten bagel still on his plate, he kissed

Natalie on the nose, holding his surprise out of her field of vision.

"What?" She knew he was up to something; he had that mischievous glint in his eye which she knew meant something was coming.

Without warning he smeared his finger down the side of her face and grinned like an idiot. "Love ya!"

She looked at him in mock outrage. "You can clean that off now!"

"Take yourself upstairs and I will."

Natalie pushed him away flirtatiously. Putting the leftover bagels away in the bread bin, she picked up the empty cream cheese tub, throwing it in the bin as she made her way out of the kitchen.

"Max, we're going to go get dressed. Stay down here and finish your breakfast."

Leaning back into the pillows fifteen minutes later, after their playfulness had quickly dissolved into a heated tangle of limbs, Dan's phone beeped on the nightstand next to her.

Picking it up, she saw it was a text message from an unknown number. She was usually hugely respectful of her husband's personal space and his privacy. They didn't have secrets from each other and her trust in him and his love for her left Natalie feeling no desire to snoop or pry as she fervently believed he had nothing to hide.

With Dan in the shower, she would usually have left his phone alone but the message preview made her heart stop.

I love you, can't wait till we can be together...

Natalie felt sick. He was cheating on her. The father of her child was keeping the worst kind of secret.

Dan walked back into the bedroom, unsuspecting and unprepared for the fury that was about to explode out of the love of his life.

"You fucking arsehole!"

It took him a few minutes to establish what had happened in the time he'd been taking a shower as she hastened to get dressed, screaming at him the whole time.

"Natalie! Calm down!"

"Who is she, Dan?"

"She isn't anyone! She's just some crazy-obsessed fan!"

"Sure she is!" Natalie was shaking as every ounce of self-doubt she had bubbled to the surface.

Since the TV show had become a hit, her husband had received a lot of attention as a writer and it was something that they had both had to learn to come to terms with. She knew it was part of the role that was hard for Dan. He didn't want the attention, which is why he'd always kept his persona out of the proverbial limelight; people only really knew his name rather than his face. For the most part it had worked and they'd continued to live in anonymity.

But the growing notoriety of her husband had left Natalie with her own growing self-doubts. *Would he still want her now that he was famous? Would she be enough? Would he leave her for someone less plain and boring?*

While they weren't loud obtrusive thoughts, their quiet whispers in her psyche were a slow abrasive torture she couldn't escape from.

She stormed out of the bedroom and downstairs, her husband in hot pursuit.

"Natalie. Baby, come on. I don't even know who she is." Dan chased her down the stairs, trying to reason with her.

"But she says she's messaged you before!" She thrust the phone towards Dan, showing the disgusting message for him to read again. He turned away not wanting to see it.

"And I have never replied. I told you that! I deleted the other messages so I could ignore them."

Tears fell on his wife's cheeks as she tried to come to terms with the events as she understood them in her head.

She looked over at Max who sat confused and upset at the table.

"Max, go get dressed please," she said through her tears.

As the boy ran to his room, Dan tried again to reason with her.

"Baby, please. It's you I love. I have never even spoken to this woman."

"I feel like there's something that you're not telling me Dan! If you want someone else just say so! If you don't want me anymore, then fine!"

Her voice broke the more she spoke. Dan tried to move closer to comfort her in her pain.

"No! I don't want you near me right now!" Her fury was palpable.

"Natalie!"

"No, Dan! I don't know what to think at all!"

"What's there to think about? She's clearly unhinged. I haven't ever spoken to her. Come on, please don't be like this."

"I think I have every right, don't you?"

"What's that supposed to mean!?"

"Well you're this big success now, aren't you? Maybe you need some blonde bimbo hanging off your arm."

"I don't want anyone else but you. You know that, don't you?"

She stared back at Dan in silence; the lump in her throat, coupled with the anvil sitting on her chest made it hard for her to breathe, let alone reply. Eventually, she was able to take a deep centering breath.

"I need some space right now. I need to decide if I still want this life."

"What does that mean?!"

"It means I don't think I can do this anymore! I need to go!"

Natalie grabbed her coat and slammed the door behind her leaving Dan to stare around the empty living room.

* * *

II

Part Two

Three years later...

Part Two

Dan Muir's grey MacBook Air sat where it had for the last three years, gathering dust on his desk under a pile of assorted books and papers. He'd intentionally forgotten about it in the early days when Max had been his entire focus but the longer he left it, the bigger the gap became between who he used to be and who he was now. The idea of opening it up again and possibly feeling nothing filled him with a deep sense of dread.

Staring at it, he thought back to earlier that morning as they'd walked to school.

"Why don't you try writing again, Dad?" Typical nine-year-old. Random conversations from nowhere that hit out of the blue.

"I don't have anything to write these days Maxxy. I think the gift I had is gone."

"You used to love writing when mum was around."

Just thinking about her at times was hard, no matter how many years had passed. Max was right though. It had always been good when he wrote, even if it was stupid little love poems on a PostIt note that he'd stick somewhere in the kitchen for her to find.

"I know mate, but it's different now."

"Why?"

"Because to write like I did, in the way I used to write, I'd have to have my head in a certain place. And it isn't really in that place anymore." He didn't want to say *happy place.* The last thing he wanted was for his son to think he wasn't happy.

"So don't write those things? Write something different."

"It's not that easy."

They stopped at the school gate and hugged.

"Okay. I love you, Dad. See you later."

"Love you too, Maxxy. Have a good day!"

Dan's beloved boy wandered happily into school, stronger and happier than his dad could ever hope to be.

For the rest of the morning, he thought about his son's words. *You used to love writing when Mum was around.*

Natalie had always been the biggest supporter of Dan's work. Even in the tough times, when as a writer he was barely earning enough to afford a cup of coffee, she would be there for him, keeping him going. Following *Sanctuary of Nine* being made into a hugely successful TV series, commercial success had flooded in and he had slowed the pace of his writing so he could pay his family back for every bit of support they'd given him. He'd become content to lead an easier life. Enjoying the lack of pressure to create, the bulk of his time back then was taken up with replying to emails from his lawyers about royalties and licensing and then spending the rest of his time with his family.

Now, three years later, even the mere idea of writing terrified him. She'd always had faith in him even through the times when he'd lost his own belief in himself; she was no longer here to be his escape route and safety net when it felt like he had nothing to give. *You used to love writing when Mum was around.*

Maybe Max was right. Maybe he should write something, or at the very least, try.

Rising from the sofa on unsteady feet, Dan walked over to his desk and pulled the MacBook out from under the overgrowing pile of books and papers it had cohabited with on the desk. He gently brushed the dust off the lid before opening it and sat back down with the device on his lap.

His old login screen blinked into life in front of him and on instinct, he entered the password. A few minutes later he was staring at a blank document feeling more scared than he had in a long time.

* * *

Dan hit *Move to Trash* on the file and added it to the pile of digital writing junk in his MacBook's Trash Can. Had he been writing old school, he'd have been perfecting his 3-pointers with balls of paper containing his wasted, pointless words clattering off the rim of the metal paper bin in the corner of the room.

He'd been trying to write for two days and nothing was grabbing him. The fear that his gift had vanished, gone from his life like Natalie years before, lingered in his mind like fog clinging to the forest floor at sunrise.

49

In the past forty-eight hours, Dan had done a lot of walking around the living room, a lot of staring at the laptop from different angles and a lot of throwing his old souvenir NFL ball from hand to hand in an attempt to still his restless mind.

But nothing was working.

He would dither as soon as he dropped Max at school, letting the resistance win over his want to write again, busying himself unnecessarily around the house. When he would eventually sit down, a few badly constructed sentences would ultimately find their way to the trash, leaving him deflated.

Max had looked at his blank page on the laptop at the end of the second day after dinner and asked what the problem was.

"I've got no ideas Maxxy. I can't seem to get started because I don't know what to write."

"What do you want to write about?"

Dan had pulled him in a hug on the sofa which had made the boy giggle.

"That's the problem, mate. I don't know. I need some inspiration."

An ensuing tickling fight, with squeals of delight filling the house, distracted him from his lack of creativity for a few precious minutes.

By the end of the week, he still had nothing and was fast giving up hope, wondering what other washed-up writers did when they gave up. *Maybe I should take up golf?*

Everything he started to write seemed forced and awkward. The one character he did manage to come up with, a marketing executive working in Japan, felt utterly trite and unbelievable, leaving the struggling author feeling decidedly meh.

Taking the weekend off, like some kind of regular nine-to-fiver, he took Max to the park for a while, hoping the fresh air might do him good and that some quality time with his favourite person would somehow unlock the words he prayed silently were still buried away in his psyche. But even that hadn't seemed to do the trick.

Sitting on the sofa on Sunday evening, with Max bathed and ready for school in the morning, they sat watching reruns of old cartoons, the boy's favourite.

Maybe I don't need to write anymore. Maybe this is all I need.

Max had been his whole life for the last three years and once they'd navigated the first few months of hurt, they managed to find an easy rhythm which bonded them together, closer than they had ever been before. Dan's son was more than just his son, he was his little buddy and without him, he knew he'd never have made it out of the misery of the last few years alive. Max was his reason for getting out of bed in the morning, for filling his lungs with air and for carrying on.

They had both struggled at times but with the love and care of his best friend Martin and his wife Issy, Max's godparents, they'd managed to find their way out of the pain and suffering. Now they were as inseparable as fish and chips, Max's favourite treat.

The show they were watching came to an end, signalling the boy's bedtime.

"Right, go brush your teeth and I'll come up in a few minutes to tuck you in."

Max paused as he stood up.

"Dad?"

"'S'up mate?'"

"Are you still struggling to come up with an idea for your new book?"

"Sadly, yeah. There's no new book yet Maxxy, just can't seem to find anything I want to pour my heart into. I know that doesn't probably make sense."

To Max, it made perfect sense. He wandered over to the large bookcase on the back wall of their living room, his dad watching on curiously. As he looked, Dan saw him heading to the middle shelf where some of Natalie's books resided still, covered in dust in her absence. It didn't take the boy long to find what he was looking for and soon he was back in front of his dad with a smile on his face.

"Mum's favourites. Maybe they might give you an idea or two because she always liked what you wrote, even when it was just stuff for us and not even your proper books...I dunno..." Max Muir knew and in fact knew very well, what he was doing.

"Wow, I haven't seen these for a while." Memories of Natalie, curled up in the rocking chair in their bedroom under that old grey blanket, bathing herself, as she often put it, *in delicious words*, brought a sad smile to Dan's face and a sad ache to his heart.

Ten minutes later, Max was in bed with clean teeth and a kiss goodnight, while Dan was sitting back on the sofa turning the thicker of the two books over in his hands. She'd read this one so many times, he'd had to buy her a second copy but to look at it you'd never have known; it was as worn and dog-eared as the first copy, it was that loved and well-read.

Simply called *Colours,* it was a love story about two people apparently destined to be together, but that was pretty much all he knew, having never actually read it himself. Dan had always preferred to stick to the exciting action-based stories that would fuel his own creative writing, so had generally stayed away from this kind of storyline.

Turning off the paused TV, he leant back into the comforting embrace of the sofa cushions and opening the book, was met by the inscription he'd long since forgotten that he wrote for her.

To my favourite reader, treat this with love and care. Love you
always. Dan x

He'd earned an extra kiss for that, the memory of her soft lips on his cheek and her fingers in his hair made him miss her even more.

Deciding to trust Max's judgement, he turned to the first chapter and began to read.

* * *

At a little after 2 am, Dan read the final line and sighed, an emotional lump swelling in his throat. He could see now why his wife had loved this story so much. It was beautiful. From what he understood of the series, it was based around the concept that two hearts will always find each other, if they're destined to be together for eternity.

It really had something.

For the past few hours, the book had taken him through the wringer, with heartache and happy moments dragging him hurriedly from beginning to end.

This book was good. On top of just being a beautiful story,

it was really clever too; something that really appealed to the author in him.

Placing the book on the coffee table in front of him, next to his now-closed MacBook, Dan wondered for a moment.

What if I write a love story?

He only had one experience of true love. Natalie. They'd fallen in love so young, still at university and they'd had their share of struggles early on. But he had loved her for every moment of those hard times as much as he did during the good ones. He had known from early on that he would love her always, no matter what happened to them in the future.

It gave him an idea.

Pulling the laptop open, he loaded a blank document and began to type quickly, words flowing from his fingertips with ease as he rapidly tried to get his ideas out of his head and onto the page. He wasn't trying to write for anyone to read, just simply to get the words down before his brain lost them in the jumble of hyperactivity that was its usual state.

A few minutes later he hit *save* and sat back, looking at the screen in front of him.

It wasn't much but it was a start. Dan knew from experience, the way he worked best was not to have a plan but to find a jumping-off point, from where he could launch himself and from there, the story would tell itself.

His best work came when he would weave the story around what he'd written in the first tsunami of ideas, rather than trying to write a story from start to finish. That way he could be flexible and bold, not being afraid to change or lose things if they didn't feel right. His process was something unique to him and he knew that, but it worked and when everything was clicking into place like a puzzle, he knew he could create magic.

Reading his outpouring back, he knew he had something and was filled with the smallest sense of hope.

A part of him didn't want to go up to bed, scared that the ethereal nature of his good idea could vanish as he slept but he knew he couldn't be a zombie in the morning for Max on the school run. Routine was an important part of managing his brain, so reluctantly he dragged himself off the sofa and up to his bed.

* * *

The following morning he woke, half expecting the idea to have gone or the worst critic in his mind to have completely torn the premise of his story to bits while he slept. But his heart leapt as he remembered the idea hastily typed words on his MacBook downstairs on the coffee table. That was a good sign.

Checking his phone screen for the time, he saw he had about an hour before Max was likely to wake up and rather than dozing under the warmth of his covers, decided to get up, make a coffee and have some writing time before he would need to make breakfast and a packed lunch for a growing, hungry boy.

By 7:30 am Max stumbled into the living room, bleary-eyed

with hair resembling a bird's nest.

"Dad, what are you doing up so early?"

"I, Maximus Martin Muir, have a story idea and I have you and your cunning plan to thank for it!"

"I had a cunning plan?"

"Are you telling me mate, that you giving me your mum's favourite books last night was not part of some elaborate scheme you dreamed up to help me start writing again?"

"Well, yeah," he spoke through yawns, "but I didn't really think it would work." Max grinned.

He moved to sit with Dan on the sofa, the glow from his dad's computer feeling bright so early in the morning.

"Thanks, Maxxy," Dan said, pulling him into a big hug. "You may well have just saved the day."

"Does this mean we can have eggy bread for breakfast?" He grinned hopefully.

"You, young man, can have two slices of the finest eggy bread in the universe. And chocolate milk!"

Dan heaved Max up, threw him over his shoulder and marched into the kitchen, holding his squealing, laughing son by the legs.

* * *

He felt nervous as he stood outside the shop, a ten-minute walk from Max's school; somewhere he'd often driven past but never stopped and visited. Noting the sign above the door he paused and smiled to himself before stepping inside.

What greeted Dan was a small cafe-style coffee shop that could probably only hold around twenty customers when at full capacity. It was made up of a random collection of tables and chairs, none of which matched, giving it the feel of some vast Christmas dinner, where everyone sits on a chair different to that of the person next to them. Each table was also covered with a tablecloth; those all seemed to have some sort of floral pattern but looked as though they'd been chosen for their singular look rather than being part of a set.

Around the walls hung plastic vines and fake flowers that gave the room a soft, bright feel which was enhanced by the large floor-to-ceiling windows that made up the front of the shop. It felt, for want of a better word to Dan, welcoming; something that a lot of public places did not.

Making his way to the counter, he was met by a woman slightly taller than him, who he estimated could be in her late twenties, wearing a name tag, handwritten with *Sarah* in gold letters. She had dark hair and a genial face that felt like she'd be a friend to many.

"Hey! What can I get you?"

Dan had been so busy taking in the shop and his surroundings, that he'd forgotten to look at the list of drinks on offer on the wall behind the counter. He panicked.

"Erm."

"Don't worry, take your time. What do you usually have?"

"I usually like a black coffee to be honest."

"Good choice. We can do Espresso, Long Black or Americano."

"You do a Long Black?" Not many places did Dan's favourite coffee so it was often a surprise when he saw it was available.

"We do."

"I'll take a Long Black then please."

"You sitting in or taking away?"

"Sitting in please if that's okay?"

"Of course!" Sarah was smiling. Often in coffee shops, servers have fake smiles that are designed to be repeated on every new customer throughout the day. But Dan felt that hers was a genuine one; as if she was actually pleased that he was choosing to stay and drink his coffee rather than leaving with it.

"That'll be £2.50 then please."

He tapped his phone on the terminal by the till to pay.

"Go take a seat and I'll bring it over for you."

"Okay. Thanks."

Dan turned around and was immediately faced with too much choice.

With only three other people sitting in the coffee shop enjoying their drinks and quiet conversations, he had five tables to pick from and each had up to four chairs to sit at. For someone like him, he knew that was a lot of options and he could start to feel the familiar paralysis of it all setting in.

Picking safety over comfort, Dan placed himself with his back against the wall at a two-seater table in the corner of the room, putting his black messenger bag down on the floor beside him. He still wasn't yet sure that this was a good idea, so wasn't quite ready to commit.

Within a few minutes, Sarah approached with his coffee. Dan appraised the cup she carried. For him, one of the defining things with coffee was it being made correctly and that included cup size. A few years previously, one winter when Max was a baby, he'd become hyper-focused and had learnt all there was to know about coffee. Now as he looked at the cup she held, he knew he'd like this place.

She placed the small white cup, full of delicious black coffee, in front of him and stood back like she was waiting for his approval.

"Looks good," he said. "Not many people get this one right."

"Well, I'm one of those people."

Sarah smiled at him and noted that he didn't quite meet her eye and that the smile he gave back was forced in a slightly uncomfortable way.

"Sugar or sweetener?"

"Sugar please?"

"White or brown?"

"Brown, if you have it. But it's fine if not. Don't worry. Sorry." Dan tried to hold her attention and her gaze while talking to her. Talking to new people could sometimes be difficult but Natalie had always encouraged him to try and look at new people when he first met them.

"I'll bring you some over. Enjoy!"

Sipping his black coffee, Dan started to relax in his surroundings. This could work. A few minutes from Max's school so he could drop his son off in the morning, walk back here and write for a few hours if he ever wanted a change of scenery from working at home.

While he'd brought his laptop and notepad with him, he decided not to get them out for this visit. He'd be too distracted by the new environment to focus completely on what he was writing, so instead decided to just have a coffee and get used to the new place. Tomorrow he could then come back and try working; hopefully at this very table which seemed to be ideally placed in the shop for him to work in privacy, without people looking over his shoulder but also afforded him a line of sight to the door; something he always found comfort in.

Yeah. This could work nicely.

* * *

A day later, Sarah Miller ran a clean cloth around the inside of the metal milk jug she held in one hand, and looked over at the newcomer seated on the far side of her cafe and wondered.

When she had first been handed the keys to her new business years before, she had hoped that the small coffee shop would one day become a hive of creative activity; a deluge of creatives, busily working away.

In reality, it was oftentimes filled with OAPs, all hoping for a quiet spot to enjoy a pot of tea and a nice cake, away from the hustle and bustle of the increasingly busy high street. But she didn't mind, she was content to just have a special place to call her own.

The town, while busy with the introduction of the larger chain stores to its dilapidated streets, was almost exclusively uninspiring, where little to nothing exciting ever happened. The place was on the whole, pretty boring.

Watching him making notes in his black, leather-bound notebook and occasionally typing onto his laptop, Sarah couldn't help but wonder if he may be one of the very few creatives to ever frequent her little cafe. He certainly gave off that vibe, although she also felt like he was uncomfortable.

As she studied him, she suspected that discomfort was more about the skin he was in, than the place he was sitting.

Deciding that the milk jug was perfectly dry now she turned and placed it on the shelf, still mulling over things in her head.

"Erm, could I get another coffee please?"

She quickly pulled herself out of her thoughts and realised that the newcomer was now standing at the counter in front of her, awkwardly avoiding eye contact.

"Yeah, sorry about that. Miles away. Long Black?"

He nodded. "Please."

"No worries. Give me a few minutes and I'll bring it over."

As she placed his coffee down at the table moments later, carefully not to disturb his workspace, he looked up.

"Thank you." He smiled but still didn't make eye contact; seeming to look past her, to the counter behind.

"My pleasure." Sarah loitered at his table, curiosity getting the better of her. "You were here yesterday, weren't you?"

"Yeah. I popped in after dropping my son at school. I was looking for a quiet place to work, so I can get out of the house for a bit."

"Always happy for people to work from here. What do you do if you don't mind me asking?"

"Erm."

In the pause that lasted for only a fraction of a second, she realised that this wasn't a simple question to be answered; that it probably asked a lot of him as a person and whatever words he spoke next would more than likely be a tiny glimpse into his heart.

"I'm a writer."

"Very cool! What sort of thing?"

"Oh, this and that. Nothing much really."

It felt like he was holding back and Sarah got the sense that he wasn't the sort of person who'd respond to inquisitive digging for information. She decided to back off a bit.

"Well, you're more than welcome to use my cafe anytime to write. I'm Sarah, by the way."

"Hi Sarah. I'm Dan."

For the first time, he looked at her fully and held her gaze for a moment, smiling a half smile. The uncomfortableness of the skin he wore seemed to wane in front of her ever so slightly and she thought he seemed like one of life's good people.

"It's lovely to meet you, Dan."

Walking away, she had the feeling he was probably a little different to most.

Dan sat noodling out ideas in his notebook, fleshing out the late-night brain dump he'd had a few days before. There wasn't much to go on in reality but it was enough for him to sink his writing teeth into and that was important. He knew a good idea when it came.

Over the years, when he'd had a good idea and he had shared it with Natalie, he'd always been able to tell simply from her reaction if it was a good idea or not. She wouldn't heap praise on him but instead, just tell him to get going with it and let it write itself. She always knew that getting in his way with a million questions and suggestions wouldn't help the process.

Now, with a fresh black notebook in front of him, the last of the ones Natalie had bulk-bought for him, the idea of starting anew was both exciting and terrifying. However, on the screen in front of him was the first good idea he'd had in years and he was sure it had something, he just had to go with it.

Dan knew one thing for sure; he trusted his gut and when it felt like something was good, it was nearly always right.

He kept working until Sarah came to collect his empty coffee cup.

"How's it going?"

"Yeah, it's getting there. It's very early days really. I've just got lots of ideas that I'm trying to shape into something that works."

"So it's a book?"

"Yeah. I'm a fiction writer, of sorts."

She nodded in understanding.

"What's it going to be about?"

"Erm." There was that pause again. "It's too early to say really at the moment. The initial idea could really become anything at this stage."

Sarah could tell he was keeping his cards close to his chest.

"You said you had a son, right?"

"Yeah. He's nine. Goes to the school round the corner."

"Well, you should bring him in some time. We make a very good hot chocolate, even if I do say so myself, very popular with our younger clientele."

Dan smiled. *Max would love that and it had been a little while since they'd been out for a treat together.*

"Thanks, Sarah. I will. He'd like that. In fact, it's nearly time to go pick him up!"

"Well crack on or you'll be in trouble."

Her laugh was gentle, Dan noticed, it felt musical, not forced or fake.

63

Walking through the school gates fifteen minutes later, Dan smiled as Max came running out of class, bag and coat in hand and with one shoe untied.

"Dad!"

"Max! You okay?"

"Yeah, I missed you!"

"Missed you too, mate."

Dan helped his son on with his coat, "Hey Maxxy, you want to go for hot chocolates on Friday for your inset day? Apparently, they do really, really good ones at this place I've been working from these last couple of days."

"Yes, please! And I can see where you're working!"

Max positively skipped up the street as they headed home, making Dan feel that for the first time in a long time, he could finally step out into the world again.

* * *

Max sat giddily squirming in his seat as he watched the server bringing it over.

He'd thought his dad was kidding when he'd said he could have anything he wanted, so being the bright kid he was, he tested that theory out. Much to his surprise, his dad hadn't batted an eyelid and now making its way to Max was a vision of pure childhood joy.

"Coffee for the young man and our biggest and best hot chocolate for Dad? Did I get that right?" The waitress beamed, inviting him to share in the joke.

"Noooooooo." Max laughed. "Gimme gimme gimme."

"Max, manners!"

"Ah, Dan he's fine. He's just excited. If I was being allowed

64

to drink that, I would be exactly the same."

He ruffled his son's hair. "Still, we use our manners."

"Thank you!" Max grinned, his eyes trying to take in the massive mug of steaming hot chocolate, topped with thick, white foamy cream, mini pink marshmallows and a chocolate flake thrown in for good measure.

"Max, this is Sarah. I've met her a few times lately when I've been here, working."

Looking up as he grabbed a spoon and started shovelling squirty cream into his mouth, he smiled at her. "Hi! I'm Max."

"It's very lovely to meet you, Max."

"Thanks, Sarah." Dan took a sugar sachet from her as she stood smiling at the boy, who was ramming the flake sideways in his mouth.

"You feed him, right?"

"Yeah, apparently not enough."

"Not writing today?" She asked, tilting her head to the side. Sarah hadn't really seen Dan without a laptop or notepad since he'd first started working out of her coffee shop.

"Not today. Father and son day 'cos this one" he jerked his head in Max's direction, "has an inset day at school."

"Yup!" Max piped up without being asked. "I wanted to see where Dad was writing and he promised me a hot chocolate."

"Ah, I see. So Max, tell me, has your dad told you what he's writing about? He won't share his secrets with me."

"It's a love story."

Dan blushed and wanted the ground to swallow him up. "Max, come on. Sarah's probably busy and doesn't want to hear you going on."

Ignoring Dan, she pulled up a chair next to Max and kept up

her amusing conversation with the boy.

"Is that right?"

"Yup. It's different from what he used to write...that made him famous."

"Max! I'm not famous. Will you stop telling people that?"

"Why is your dad famous, Max? I had no idea." Sarah was basking in the enjoyment of watching Dan wanting to sink into the depths of the earth in front of her, playfully disregarding his protests.

"He used to write like fantasy stuff."

"Oh? Anything I would have read?"

Without looking up from his hot chocolate and as if it was a perfectly normal thing to announce to a stranger, Max answered, "*The Sanctuary of Nine.*"

"What?!"

"Thanks for that Max. Much appreciated buddy."

Sarah was stunned.

"What?! Your dad wrote T*he Sanctuary of Nine*?! I love that book! And the TV show."

"Mhmm, that's my dad's book. Good, right?" Max grinned at a shocked Sarah who was flabbergasted to learn that she was sitting in the company of one of her favourite authors.

Sarah turned to look at him. "Dan Muir! I had no idea!"

In return, he just shrugged. While he thought it was cool that his book had been made into something that lots of people had watched on a Monday evening for the last few years, he still felt awkward talking about it. Self-doubt was a companion that never truly left him alone.

"Why didn't you say?"

"It's not something I really talk about. Plus it's a part of my past now."

"But why?"

"He stopped writing when Mum went."

The atmosphere shifted. Sarah gave Dan a compassionate look, while his mouth pulled to the corner of his face in a show of awkwardness that was mirrored in his vacant look towards his coffee cup.

"Dan. I'm sorry."

"It's okay. You didn't know. It was hard to write after...you know...So *anyway*, now I'm just Dad to this pain in my ass, he's my world and that's enough for me" He smiled affectionately at his son who was looking sheepish, realising he'd just put his foot in it.

After a few silent moments, Sarah sighed quietly and turned back to Max.

"Max, I think another flake is needed don't you?"

The boy's eyes lit up and he nodded enthusiastically, as she rose, winking at him and went off to get the promised chocolatey treat.

"Sorry."

"Hey, no. You have nothing to be sorry for Maxxy. It's absolutely okay. Promise."

"Thanks, Dad. I love you," he said, taking his dad's hand in his own.

"Love you too, mate."

* * *

67

Sarah smiled as the door to her coffee shop opened a little after 9 am. "Ah! Hi Dan!"

"Hey."

"What can I get you?"

"The usual, please." Dan smiled a little awkwardly.

"One Long Black coming right up."

He headed over to his usual spot by the wall and started to unpack his things. Even though a few days had passed since Max had essentially outed him to Sarah, he was still concerned that things could be uncomfortable with her now knowing his true identity. Dan hated feeling uncomfortable.

"There you go!" She placed the coffee next to his open laptop.

"Thanks, Sarah."

"Look Dan, about the other day..."

"What, when my son gave away my not-so-secret, secret identity?"

She laughed and relaxed, glad things weren't going to be awkward with her new regular customer. "Yeah, that's the one. I just wanted to say, I don't want you to feel uncomfortable. I am a big fan but you don't come here for me to heap praise on you I guess, so I'll happily respect your privacy and let you work."

"Thank you. Not many people know about it really, any of it. I just like being that guy who flies under the radar you know?"

Sarah nodded. She could tell that Dan wasn't the type of person to seek the limelight and would probably actively avoid attention where possible.

"No, it's okay I get it. My lips are sealed!"

He chuckled. It was nice to not have a fuss made of it, as was usually the case whenever anyone found out.

Writing for him was about creating and threading stories together to surprise and delight people. It wasn't to win awards and sign autographs.

"This," he pointed to his laptop, "is the first piece of proper writing that I've done since everything..."

"Can't be easy?"

"It's not been, to be honest. Like learning to walk again."

"I think he's proud of you, you know?"

"Who Max? I guess so. He's only really been used to me creating short bedtime stories for him."

"Jesus, that's sweet!"

Dan smiled. "He loves them. We have a collection of ones I've written for him over the years, called *Stories for Max.* They're like *Aesop's Fables* where I try to teach him something in a fun way but I haven't written any new ones for quite a while, although we still read a few old ones together."

"I bet he loves that."

"He does. It was his mum's idea in the beginning." Dan half chuckled as he described how Natalie was so fed up with hearing him whinge about lame bedtime stories for Max that she suggested he write one himself.

Sarah sat across from Dan and listened as he described how his son had loved *Max and the Loud Lion.*

"So now we have quite a few and I've updated the older ones over the years to make them more applicable to him. He's nine now but he still loves them."

"So is it like a real book?"

"What do you mean? Printed? Published?"

"Yeah."

"No no. Maybe one day when he's older and has a family of

his own, I'll have them all put together in a book but for now, they're just printed out on loose pages at home."

"He's a lucky boy."

She cursed herself for her insensitivity. There was no way Max would ever feel lucky without his mum around and it was only after the words left her lips did she realise.

"Sorry, Dan."

"Hey, it's okay. In terms of having short stories written all about him, yeah he is a lucky boy. He's been through a lot but he's got godparents who absolutely adore him and he's got me."

A silence grew between them for a moment.

"Max seems to be a lovely little boy." Sarah smiled weakly.

"He is and he likes you."

"He does?"

"Of course! You gave him extra chocolate!"

They laughed together. Dan felt as though she was one of the rare people in life whom he could relax around a little and he knew it was seldom that he encountered those kind of people.

"So I have to ask. The name?"

Sarah smiled and nodded. "Yup."

As a big fan of his book and the resulting TV show, she had named her coffee shop Sanctuary, feeling like it was fitting, giving the quiet, comforting vibe she wanted for her customers.

"I like it." Dan couldn't help but feel a smidgen of pride at the fact.

"That makes me very happy to hear!" To Sarah, he seemed like a really nice guy who had clearly been dragged through the mill.

"The whole thing came out of a short story for Max, you know?"

"What? That's crazy!"

"Yup. One of his stories is about how he stood up to school bullies with eight of his friends. I felt it was a bit tame after I wrote it. Between me and his mum, we came up with an idea to work it for a more mature reader and so it became the book you know now."

"I never knew that!"

"No one does. It's not something I've ever really told anyone. Max doesn't even really know because he's never seen the show."

"I mean that's understandable given the themes." Sarah pulled a look of mock disgust at the violent nature of the storyline.

He couldn't help but laugh at her. "Yeah, not something you'd want your nine-year-old watching. He will one day I'm sure though."

"Curiosity will get the better of him someday, no doubt."

"Definitely."

"So, is what he says true? You're working on a love story?"

"Trying to, yeah."

"That must be a bit different?"

"Yeah, it is. It's tough too because I'm trying to find my writing rhythm again at the same time."

"Well, me chewing your ear off isn't going to help that, is it?" She rose. "So, want another coffee while I leave you to get some work done?"

"Yes please."

"Coming right up!"

As she turned to head over to the counter, Dan called her back, "Sarah?"

"Mhmm?"

"Thanks."

She tilted her head to the side inquisitively. "For what?"

"For listening. And for understanding. I appreciate it."

She knew there weren't any words needed in reply, so she just nodded and went off to make his coffee, as he pulled his laptop closer to him and began to type.

* * *

Dan parked himself in his usual spot by the window and opened his laptop. He had a good feeling; it felt like it would be a good writing day.

With Max going to Dylan's after school for a sleepover, Dan had plans to just while away the hours working on his ever-growing manuscript, with the buzz of the little coffee shop for company.

Sarah brought him a long black coffee as he started a tab for the day and got to work.

He already had his really good ending, so now Dan was trying to work his way back through the story, filling in the gaps as he went. To look at the timeline of events as he constructed them would have confused just about anyone as he always wrote in a nonsensical order, working on ideas as they came to him, until finally he had a finished story.

So now, with the end of his story pretty much in place, for most of the week, Dan had been working on developing some ideas for earlier in the book which would help to bring some of the main characters to life.

Sipping his sweet rich coffee and letting the words flow, he felt a calmness settling in for the day. The only time he spoke to anyone was when he went to order another drink or a piece of cake and then he chatted casually to Sarah at the counter. He was glad of a friendly face amongst the to-ing and fro-ing of customers.

At lunch, he ordered a sandwich and closed his laptop while he ate; the opportunity to rest his eyes from the screen was a welcome one. Rather than typing during his lunch break, he jotted down notes by hand in the black notebook.

While making a quick note of a line he had in his head regarding *the falling sands of time,* Dan looked up and saw Sarah pulling a microphone stand and wooden stool to a corner of the shop where there was normally a table and four chairs. Busy working that morning, he hadn't noticed that small space being cleared and now, with a mouthful of brie and cranberry on wholewheat, he looked on curiously.

Noticing his interest, she headed over to him, carrying a handful of flyers.

"We sometimes have artists come and sing on Friday and Saturday evenings." She handed Dan a leaflet. "If you're around you should come see. This one's good. She's a friend of mine."

He glanced down at the leaflet in front of him.

Laura Gray: Singer/Songwriter/Guitar tutor.

"Looks interesting. But I dunno. Max is having a sleepover at his best friend's house so it was kinda going to be a takeaway for one and some TV."

"How's that feel?" Sarah pulled out the chair opposite Dan and sat down.

"Okay I guess, just not sure what takeaway I fancy."

"You know what I mean."

Dan sighed. Max's sleepover, while exciting for his son, was terrifying for him as his parent.

"Weird. It's the first time we've been apart for a night since..." He trailed off. Some things are always hard to say, no matter how long or how often you've had to say them. Sarah nodded in sympathy.

"He'll be fine."

"To be honest, it's not Max I'm worried about."

"Hey look, then distraction might be just what you need tonight. So why not carry on working till my friend does her set, stay for some entertainment and then you can head home to your takeaway for one? It's got to be better than sitting in a quiet house alone all evening, hasn't it?"

"Yeah I guess."

"Think about it and I'll get you another coffee."

He checked his watch. "Better make it a decaf."

She looked back at him surprised.

"I have a rule to not have caffeine after 3pm. It's not good for my head and stops me sleeping at night."

"One decaf coming up! And you'll stay for the music?"

"Yeah maybe. Let's see how I get on working this afternoon." Dan put the flyer carefully down on the table next to his notepad and stared at it for a few moments as Sarah walked away. He felt a strange pull to stay for the evening and wasn't sure where it was coming from.

Socialising wasn't his thing at all. Growing up, he'd always been awkward and uncomfortable in social settings but had been told that he was just an odd kid and assumed that was the truth. But it was only when he was diagnosed with Adult ADHD did that awkwardness he'd known all his life finally make sense.

It wasn't so much that the penny had dropped and he finally understood the little things; it was more like the *whole bank* had come falling down and he could see his entire life in crystal clear clarity.

He really wasn't sure he had the mental energy for staying tonight, but something in him made him want to stay. It was as if he was meant to be there. He couldn't quite explain it. So rather than trying to work out why, he finished his sandwich and fell back into working on his story.

* * *

Around 6 pm, with the coffee shop darkening around him as he wrote, Dan's attention was brought out of the chapter he was working on by the shop door opening and closing. Looking up from his laptop he wondered who had walked in, not that he particularly cared but he was curious that his subconscious was alert to something.

Walking in, carrying a guitar in a case over her right shoulder, was a young woman Dan had never seen before. Her blonde hair fell softly onto her shoulders, spilling over the strap of the guitar case. As she greeted Sarah who was behind the counter, Dan noticed that her blue eyes seemed to shine as she smiled; the corners of her mouth caused her cheeks to fill, in a way that made him smile to himself.

Watching Sarah hug the newcomer, he felt oddly drawn to the woman whom he assumed was tonight's musician, Laura Gray. He was unsure why; it was a weird feeling.

An hour or so later, Dan was out of words having been struggling with the same sentence for nearly twenty minutes. He gave up fighting against it, saved out his work and closed his laptop. Looking around, he could see that the little coffee shop was busier now and that a white acoustic guitar had been leant up against the wooden stool in the faux stage area.

After grabbing himself a Coke and paying off his tab for the day at the till, Dan packed his things away and made himself comfortable, waiting to see if Sarah's friend was any good.

When Laura finally settled herself onto the stool a few moments later and pulled her six-string guitar across her lap, he saw her take a deep calming breath and look out into the small intimate audience in front of her.

She was beautiful.

As Dan looked at her, he felt a disconcerting tightness in his chest and a strong desire to turn and run, but something in his psyche was holding him there, focusing on the woman.

She tucked her hair behind her ear and time seemed to slow for a heartbeat. It was only when she started to talk that Dan realised that he wasn't breathing and as his brain caught up, he relaxed, trying to clear the fog rapidly building in his head.

"Hi, I'm Laura. I'm going to play a few covers for you tonight. I hope you like them. This one's called *Use Somebody.*"

Before she started to play, Laura smiled at the crowd as she rested her fingers on the fretboard for the first chord. For a fraction of a second that seemed to last a lifetime, it felt to Dan like her smile lingered on him before she dropped her gaze and started to play.

While he was muddled up watching her, Dan couldn't deny that she was very talented. The covers she played were stripped back and soulful, and she floated soft melodies over the top of her guitar playing with her gentle voice. There was no showmanship in Laura's performance, making it seem like she could easily have been playing alone at home as much as in a room full of people. She made the whole thing look effortless and Dan couldn't pull his eyes from her for the better part of fifteen minutes.

Pausing in between songs to sip at her drink gave Dan enough time to panic and decide that it was time to leave. Watching her felt wrong. Thinking she was beautiful felt wrong. Feeling drawn to her felt very wrong.

Grabbing his bag, he made a quick but quiet exit from the coffee shop as Laura started singing through her version of *This Year's Love* by David Gray. Not even waving goodbye to a surprised Sarah, he promised himself he would apologise the next time he saw her.

Outside in the fresh air, Dan hurried away down the street heading for home; each step taking him further and further away from a problem he hadn't known he would have when the day began.

He pulled out his phone and messaged Max. He needed something to hold onto that felt solid.

Dan: Hey mate. Hope you're having a great time. Miss you. Dad.

x

He knew the chances of his son paying enough attention to his phone to notice his cry for help were pretty slim but he needed that connection for a moment, even if it was one-sided.

Walking past the local takeaways he decided he wasn't in the mood for food anymore. The only thing he longed for was the familiarity of home and the comfort of knowing that once the door shut behind him, the world and everyone in it could be distanced; the only person able to breach his sanctuary would be a returning Max in the morning.

* * *

Shutting the front door behind him, Dan stepped into the dark and quiet of home, fighting the tightness in his chest. The adrenaline that had coursed through his veins since the second she had looked at him, caused the blood to thud loudly in his ears. He leaned against the wall next to the coat rack and tried to slow his whole body down. It was as if the beautiful, curvy blonde had shaken him like a bottle of pop and now the resulting pressure was causing his whole existence to fizz out of control.

Jesus, who the hell is she? And why am I being like this?

He pushed himself from the wall and took a deep breath before making his way into the kitchen, carelessly dropping his bag on the kitchen table, nearly knocking over the vase of fake flowers that sat at its centre. Remonstrating with himself, Dan straightened up the offended bouquet and moved to the sink to get a glass of water, which he downed without thinking in one, burping loudly when he'd finished.

Calmer now, he fought between the idea of heading for bed

to attempt sleep, or staying up to wait until his brain slowed down. Without much deliberation, Dan decided on the latter, starting to unpack his bag, mainly to have something to do with his hands.

After putting his laptop on charge on the kitchen side, he pulled his black notepad out of the inner sleeve of his bag and went to place it on the table. As he did this, he noticed that without thinking, he'd picked up the leaflet Sarah had given him about tonight's acoustic performance.

Laura Gray: Singer/Songwriter/Guitar tutor.

Her name stared back up at him as the already quiet house felt suddenly eerily silent. A familiar, if not slightly odd, feeling bubbled away under the surface; as if pieces of a puzzle he had no notion of were beginning to form. The only time he'd felt this way previously was with Natalie when she had announced that she had fallen pregnant with Max. Amidst the joy and tears of that day, Dan had felt like everything was beginning to come together in his life and that it was all as it was meant to be.

Looking down at the leaflet in his trembling hand, he felt a similar feeling. *But surely that was impossible?*

He noticed her social media account name at the bottom of the page. For a second, his heart leapt with excitement before he quickly shoved the leaflet back into his bag, thrust the bag down onto the chair next to him and pushed it forcibly under the table. *Out of sight, out of mind.* He knew how his condition worked; he could easily become hyper-fixated and attached to things very quickly if he wasn't careful and the last thing he needed or even wanted to do was to get caught up in feelings for someone else. He couldn't do that. To Natalie or to Max. It wasn't fair.

Leaving Laura's leaflet hidden away, he went to bed, hoping a new day would clear his head of stupid ideas and thoughts.

When he stood in the kitchen the following morning brewing coffee, Dan's skin crawled agonisingly as he tried to ignore the fact that hidden under the table was the leaflet.

He knew that as was often the way with his personality, he could sometimes get a bit obsessed and so he felt like following Laura Gray online was a recipe for disaster. But something bigger than his body was pulling him back to that A5 piece of paper.

He felt like an addict, desperately trying to avoid taking that hit even though his resolve was crumbling faster as each second passed.

What harm could really come from following her on Instagram? The devil sat on his shoulder pouring sweet and sickly ideas incessantly in his ear.

Deciding to let the mysterious pull win over, Dan moved back to his bag and retrieved Laura's leaflet before quickly pulling out his phone and opening his social media app.

He had two accounts saved into his phone. One was personal, containing a lot of photos of family, especially Max, and the other was his more public-facing account for his past life as an author. It showed book covers and scenes from the show, but precious little about Dan personally and that was the way he liked it. While he didn't really use it much anymore, he chose to follow Laura's account using that one. Something about the anonymity of it right now felt secure. He hit follow and began to scroll through her grid to see the things she shared with the world.

Most of her content was pictures of her playing her white acoustic guitar in cafes and bars, as well as a few video clips of her practising at home.

As he clicked on the first video to listen to her play, a notification popped up on his phone telling him he had a new message in the app. It was from Laura! *That's odd.* Opening it, he read:

Hi. Thanks for following my account. If you would like to book me please reply to this message and I'll get back to you as soon as I can. Thanks. Laura x

Dan's heart sank a little as he realised it was just an automated message, most likely for all new followers but it didn't stop him feeling a tiny bit disappointed.

With the timer for his brewing coffee sounding on his smart speaker, he pulled himself away from her Instagram feed and poured his first cup of coffee for the day.

Then it hit him. He'd just followed her from his professional account, one that had well over 100,000 followers due to his fanbase, something that he always shied away from. If she noticed he'd followed her from *that* it would probably draw more attention to the follow than if he had just randomly done it from his nondescript personal account.

Fumbling with his phone, he quickly unfollowed her from his professional account and hoped to God she hadn't seen yet and quickly switched accounts to follow her again. *It was still early, he might have gotten away with it.*

Dan's brain was spinning faster than a top as he scrambled to fix his mistake. He felt a mess. He wasn't a particularly extroverted person but he usually had enough confidence to be able to interact with people without second-guessing himself, however something about this girl was tying him up in knots and he hadn't even spoken to her.

His phone pinged in his hand. *Fuck, it had to be her!*

Max: Hey Dad! Can you pick me up at ten, please?

Dan let out a breath. Max had saved him countless times in the years since Natalie had been gone and here he was again, saving his dad again from a morning of ineffable mental anguish.

* * *

Max tiptoed quietly into the bedroom and made his way to the left-hand side of the bed. It used to be his dad's side but since his Mum was gone his dad had started sleeping on her side surrounded by her plethora of pillows. Now, the left was Max's way in on a quiet Sunday morning.

Sliding himself under the heavy duvet, he scooched himself up to Dan and savoured the warmth for a few minutes, throwing his small arm over him.

"Hmpf what time is it?"

"Morning."

"Max, you're a bright lad, you know morning isn't actually a time."

Dan kept his tired eyes shut, letting his mind slowly wake

up as his son snuggled closer into him.

"Yeah but you say morning time, so technically morning *is* a time."

"I can tell you for sure, whatever time it is, that it's too early for your brain to be this kind of smart."

He rolled onto his back and dragged his arm over his eyes. It was definitely not too early, given by the amount of light in the bedroom.

"You sleep okay?" He asked.

"Yeah. It's nice to be back in my own bed."

"You mean it's nice to be in *a* bed."

"Yeah." Max laughed. While the sleepover at Dylan's was fun, sleeping on the floor was not.

"We can have a nice, lazy day today, ready for school in the morning. Go on, let your dad wake up and I'll come make some breakfast in a minute."

Max took his cue to leave. "Love you, Dad."

"Love you too, Maxxy."

When Max had gone, Dan sat up against the pillows and allowed himself to fully enter the conscious world.

A pain sat around his eye sockets which made it hard to focus on the dimly lit room around him. The discomfort it caused pulled the muscles in his forehead tight making his head feel like a heavy weight on his neck, which was already aching from the effort.

He swung his legs out of bed and took a gulp from the glass of water on his nightstand. The stale taste did nothing to rob him of the pain.

It felt like a hangover, even though he knew it had nothing to do with alcohol. He hadn't touched a drop for months. This, he knew, was guilt and shame manifesting in a sickly feeling that was consuming his body.

The thoughts of Friday night lingered quietly in the back of his mind and had done since he stepped out of the coffee shop thirty-six hours before.

This is not the time.

Taking himself out of bed, he pulled on the jumper he'd previously slung carelessly over the unused rocking chair in the corner of the room and went downstairs.

Max and Dan spent the rest of the morning together, filling their Sunday with relaxed easy nonsense that only a father and son can share. They made pancakes for brunch and proceeded to turn the kitchen into a disaster zone, which Dan had ended up cleaning while his son watched YouTube videos on the TV in the front room.

But no matter how much distraction he managed to have, his headache didn't seem to want to shift. It wasn't so much that he was constantly thinking about the girl with the white guitar, but more something inside him was struggling with the notion of her very existence and it was making his brain ache in a way that he couldn't rationalise.

Max had noticed the distance in his dad's eyes later, watching him staring off into nothing, a cup of coffee in front of him.

"Dad? Your coffee's going cold."

"Sorry mate. Miles away."

Dan pulled his attention back to his son, sitting across the table doing homework. He knew Max didn't deserve an absent father; the fog that was building in his head was threatening to consume him.

"How much you got left to do?"

"Just this page and then I'm finished. Why?"

"Want to get out of the house? Maybe go see Issy and Martin?"

"Yes! Please? I can finish this later!" The excitement in his son's eyes was shining so brightly Dan felt like he needed sunglasses to look at him.

Within the hour, the pair had relocated themselves a few miles down the road to Martin's and Issy's house. While Martin was Dan's best friend, they were also Max's godparents and so had been a rock for them both in ways that they never imagined they would need.

Despite having her own troubles to deal with, Issy had recognised that in order for Dan to get through the ordeal and for her beloved godson to handle the upheaval caused by his mother's absence, she needed to be the glue that held it all together.

In the early days, she made sure to call every day on the pretext of checking on her godson but also very much aware that Dan needed a link back to the outside world and away from the darkness that was most likely consuming him. Issy was patient; working on their relationship and the one with Max, slowly and gently. With Martin's unwavering support, she'd helped the pair to assimilate back into some semblance of normal life after everything that had happened.

"How was his sleepover at Dylan's?" She asked as they sat at the dining table in their open-plan kitchen, dining room and living room. Max and Martin were watching rugby highlights from the previous day's games, comfortably rooted on one of the two huge sofas that filled the space.

"He loved it, I think."

"And how did you find it?"

"Yeah. It was fine."

"It's okay for it to be *not* fine Dan. It was his first night away from you since…everything. It's bound to have been challenging for you."

"I took myself out and worked a bit, then just came home and went to bed."

"I'm glad you're writing again. Max seemed really excited about it when I spoke to him on the phone the other day."

"It's early days, Issy. And it's much harder than I thought it would be."

"It's going to be hard. Jesus, the things you've been through were always going to make this next part of life hard in every area. You know that. And if you're writing again and it brings you a little slice of happiness, then I'm all for it."

She smiled and tried to get him to hold eye contact with her, something she knew was hard for Dan, even more so with the grief that clung to his heart.

"I'm not sure what I'm writing is the right thing, though."

"What do you mean?"

"It's a love story, Issy."

"Oh wow."

"Yeah. It's a stupid idea."

"Whoa! No. I didn't say it was a stupid idea, I just said wow. Because in all the years I've known you and your ability to tell wonderful stories, I've never known you to write a love story. Sure, you've incorporated love into a much bigger story, but to tell a story just about love? That's new and different. And I, for one, am very proud of you for that."

"Thanks."

"Dan, look at me."

She knew that she had to ask for eye contact at times with him. It was an unspoken rule between them that he had also shared with Natalie; that when he was struggling in a conversation and couldn't maintain eye contact, if they felt what they needed to say was important that they could ask and he would force himself to look. There would be no judgement. It was a rule that also meant he was guaranteed safety in their words.

Issy had taken the rule very seriously and had only ever used it sparingly, and only in situations like this, a handful of times.

Dan took a shallow breath and met her gaze.

"Tell the story your heart wants to tell. We will both support you and love you regardless of what you do."

"Thank you."

"Always. So what's caused you to go in that direction?"

He nodded over towards the brown-haired boy sitting on the sofa.

"He did. I was struggling with trying to get back into writing and then Max suggested I read some of the books Natalie used to read. So I did and it gave me the idea to write a love story based loosely on us. But I'm really struggling with the characters. I can write the male character like me, and that seems to be fine. But I can't seem to get the female lead at all. Making it Natalie is just something I can't seem to do. I can't get it to work."

"Then base it on someone else."

87

"Issy, I can't."

"Of course you can. You're writing fiction. It's not an accurate retelling of your relationship with Natalie. If it was, you'd be including a chapter about that night you two spent in the Cotswolds, right? You know, that time you had too much red wine and it was...a bit of a letdown." She giggled.

"You knew about that?!"

"Dan! Of course I knew. Natalie and I didn't keep secrets from one another!" Issy carried on laughing quietly, so as not to draw attention from the boys in front of the TV.

"Fuck sake!" He couldn't shook his head and chuckled. A night of debauchery had been ruined by him having too much wine and struggling to step up when needed.

Issy gently put her hand on his.

"Seriously, let the story tell itself. It doesn't have to actually *be* Natalie even if you're basing it on the two of you. It's okay."

Max came running over, saving Dan further embarrassment.

"Dad, can we stay for tea? Please?"

Issy smirked. "Oh Maxxy, we're having fish and chips tonight. I'm not sure you'd like it."

"Dad! Please!"

* * *

Standing at the door, Dan took a deep breath.

Half of him wanted to just turn around and go home, leaving the awkward confrontation for another day. The other half of him really wanted a coffee.

88

But deep down and for a reason he didn't fully understand, he felt like he needed to show his face and apologise to Sarah. The look she had given him as he rushed out of Sanctuary on Friday night, halfway through Laura Gray's set, was one of surprise and hurt. Dan knew he had to put that right.

Pushing the door open, the small bell above his head tinkled merrily.

He looked up to see her smiling at him from behind the counter as if nothing had happened.

"I was wondering if you were ever going to come in, or just stand out there all morning."

"Hey."

"You okay?"

"Mhmm."

"Coffee?"

"Please."

"Okay, go grab a seat and..."

"Sarah, I'm sorry!" The apology exploded out of him like a firework, the tension that had been building all morning becoming too much when he finally saw her. He knew that he needed to just bite the bullet and say it, but his subconscious had blurted it out before the sensible part of his brain had had a chance to engage.

"I was worried. You looked distressed when you ran out of here on Friday."

"I know. I'm sorry. My social anxiety just got the better of me and I had to go." *It wasn't a complete lie, but it lacked enough details to be the full truth.*

"Look, it's fine. As long as you're okay. That's all that matters."

89

Dan's shoulders relaxed visibly.

"Go and get to work, I'll bring your coffee over in a minute."

As he settled down in his usual spot, Dan still felt like a bit of a dick but at least he'd apologised. The rest of the feelings were on him now and he'd just have to work through that on his own.

While he worked, or tried to, he spent the morning trying to avoid staring at the spot in the corner where Laura had played her guitar and sung like an angel the previous week. Working with his AirPods in, music playing away, Dan tried to just get into the writing zone but no matter how hard he tried to focus, his arms and hands trembled. It seemed like the adrenaline that had overwhelmed him on Friday night, simmered under the surface and his senses were heightened.

* * *

Over the next few weeks, Dan struggled to reconcile the confusion going around in his head with the need to keep working on his ever-growing manuscript.

While working out of Sanctuary was something that had gradually gotten easier with visits, it still had its challenges. He was able to work and focus more each time he dropped by, but the hope he'd had that he'd miss Laura by strategically only going in first thing in the mornings had been proved wrong.

After a few days of thinking he'd gotten away with it, she'd come to see Sarah and had spent about half an hour standing at the counter chatting to her. Dan was sitting at the back of the coffee shop and would have to pass right by her if he'd chosen to leave; so he'd been effectively pinned in place and had to endure it. But by the time she'd left, the visceral reaction in his body to being in the same room as he was, had begun to fade. She no doubt had an effect on him, but it wasn't anywhere as shocking as the first time he'd seen her playing guitar.

He saw her in passing a few times as they both went about their lives, ebbing and flowing out of Sanctuary but they never said more than a casual hello; two people who didn't really know one another but recognised the other's face in a familiar environment.

As time passed, Dan even made the decision, spurred on by Sarah's endless friendly and above all else, gentle nagging, to stay for another performance. He'd been unsure at first but when she'd handed over the reins to her assistant and sat herself down at his table with a cup of tea, Dan knew he was probably going to have to endure it.

He couldn't really remember what Laura had played that afternoon but he remembered watching her intently while his heart hammered in his chest. This time he didn't want to flee. He wanted to stay and bask in her talent with a guitar, even with the gnawing sense of guilt burning away deep inside of him. He'd excused himself as soon as she'd finished, however, sensing that she'd come over and speak to Sarah and there was no way he could be that close to her.

There was still no way he could interact with her, that would be too much for him to cope with, but over the weeks, he found he could at least be in her presence, albeit from a distance, and not run.

* * *

The soft light of a quiet Saturday morning sunrise, spread gently through the Muirs' living room blinds, as Dan sipped tentatively at his first hot cup of coffee of the day. He enjoyed these moments of solitude at the very start of the day as they eased him slowly into the hours ahead. School mornings could, at times, be fraught with chaos with Dan following Max upstairs and down in an attempt to get him ready to be out the door in a timely fashion.

Today, however, was going to be anything but hectic. He and Max had nothing to do but relax and watch the hands of the clock tick by.

He had written well during the week and felt like his creative brain deserved an easy day off; as did his son.

When Max bounced downstairs later that morning, his dad was ready for his second cup of black goodness and so he wasted no time in making breakfast for them both.

A little later, Max dropped his spoon into his empty bowl of cereal, where it rang out like a bell and declared he was going to read his book for a while. Once Dan had cleared their bowls away, he flicked open his phone and scrolled through Instagram as he often did when he had bored hands. After a few seconds of said scrolling, he was greeted by a video of Laura showing off one of the songs she had played the previous afternoon.

He smiled as he watched the video back on his phone. She'd played really well and he was actually able to sit and enjoy the experience. The initial visceral reaction he'd had the first time he'd seen her play had gone and while he still tried his best to avoid any sort of social interaction, he could at least now watch her perform without having a panic attack.

The post she'd uploaded that morning looked as if it had been shot by Sarah's assistant from somewhere near the counter. It consisted of a verse and the chorus of a song he hadn't heard before but that she'd performed as if it was her own.

When the video had played through, he hit reply to send her a direct message.

Dan: You were really good yesterday.

He wasn't expecting a reply immediately, if at all, so he placed his phone in his pocket, made another coffee from his machine, and tried to forget about Laura for a bit. Stirring sugar into his drink a few minutes later, he turned to see Max sitting quietly, reading on the sofa and decided to go sit with him for a while.

Around an hour later, Dan's phone pinged with a new message.

Laura: Thanks Dan!

He knew it was silly but he couldn't stop the grin that spread across his face. It wasn't one of triumph or achievement, more akin to the smile of a teenager getting to talk to their crush for the first time. Not something befitting a grown man. Or a single dad for that matter!

He pondered on a sensible response in an effort to engage

her in conversation.

Dan: Was it an original song? In the video?

He stared at the screen for a moment but the realisation he might get caught out by Max who was sitting engrossed in his book next to him, caused him to put his phone face down on the arm of the sofa. Guilt churned gently inside of him.

The quiet morning turned easily into afternoon and the boys broke from their loafing to grab a bite to eat for lunch. Rather than resuming his book, Max suggested a movie. For ten minutes they deliberated the best options available before Dan managed to convince his son that he needed to begin his education on the *Back to the Future* franchise.

Later that afternoon, with Marty racing towards the clock tower at the end of the movie, Dan's phone vibrated gently on the sofa arm. Hope rose as he moved to pick it up.

Laura: I wish I could write things like that! Haha! No it's an old song from the late 90s called Feels like Home.

Dan sighed inwardly at the basic, relaxed interaction with her. This is all he wanted. To just be able to chat to her, to smile and laugh. To talk about random stuff. *Maybe this was the start of things? Maybe this was the conversation that would ease them into a friendship.*

Dan: Well I really liked it! Obviously, it was better live but it was nice to watch it back this morning.

Placing the phone back down on the arm of the sofa, doubt built in Dan's head. He wasn't sure if he'd closed the conversation off inadvertently. *Should I have ended it with a question?* His head hurt a little as he wondered if he'd made an error. One thing he knew for sure was that it was too late now, it would just come across as being too much if he replied again. He had to let her respond before he could send another message.

As the afternoon drew to a close; they paused their time-travelling movie marathon and made dinner. While Max had complained when his dad said no to a takeaway, they still enjoyed bowls full of steaming spaghetti bolognese and soft, warm garlic bread.

The urge to check his phone had scratched quietly away in the back of his mind throughout the rest of the day, until later that evening, with Max tucked up in bed and Dan sat watching some show on Netflix he'd seen a hundred times before, the phone finally buzzed in his waiting hand.

Opening the app expectantly he saw a new notification from Laura. *Why am I fucking nervous for Christ's sake!* His thumb anxiously pressed onto the chat they were sharing.

Nothing.

She hadn't replied.

The notification was just her liking his last message, effectively killing the conversation. He knew there was no way to reply now, that would just make him feel like he would seem too needy for her attention. He was, he knew it, but Dan didn't want Laura to know it. His heart sank.

He just wanted to talk to her. He just wanted to spend some time with her, albeit digitally, just to be in her world for a while. The idea of them laughing together over some stupid joke hung heavy in his mind as he pictured her, tears welling in her eyes as she fought back a fit of giggles. But the idea, as sweet as it was, left him hollow. For every nice feeling it gave him, it was as though it simultaneously robbed him of something else, although of what exactly, he was unsure.

Dan spent the next hour staring blankly at the TV wondering how he could have played the conversation differently, drawing it out to have more of her time and attention. For a time, he wondered if he'd said something wrong but after going over the messages a few times, he felt like he'd not misspoken. *Was he really that hard to talk to?*

Begrudgingly he pulled himself away from the sofa to bed where he lay for a while, just letting his mind swirl with thoughts of Laura. He felt defeated from a battle he hadn't known he'd been a part of and that he'd made no effort to win. Without noticing the transition, his thoughts of her became dreams he wouldn't remember in the morning as he fell into a restless sleep.

* * *

Sitting down to write that lunchtime, after a morning of procrastinating, Dan had tried to work on his female lead character but still nothing felt right. Flashes of the girl from the coffee shop kept firing into his overactive mind and no matter how much he tried to focus on his book, he couldn't get her out of his head.

Instead of the words he needed to write to move his story on, all that seemed to be reverberating around his head was the start of a poem; something that hadn't happened in years.

All your glitter and flaws
I see the beauty that lies within too
Deeper than the surface
You leave me breathless

He quickly scribbled it down in his black notepad and tried to forget about it.

Minutes passed and thoughts of guitar-playing Laura with her blonde hair and the soft freckles on her cheeks seemed to be blocking his ability to write anything good for his story.

Dan's eyes drifted to the notepad on the table in front of him. Even with the cover closed and the elasticated band holding it shut, he knew he was actually looking directly at the handwritten words he'd just marked onto the page.

His ears were ringing.

Instinctively he reached out, pulling the pad towards him, unfastening it and taking out the pen held against the spine of the book. Sitting back against the sofa with his feet up, he began writing, using his legs as support.

The rush of creativity took him and in less than three minutes he had a completed poem. It had effortlessly written itself.

You don't see me
I'm just someone

97

in the background, behind the page
But I see you

All your glitter and flaws
I see the beauty that lies within too
Deeper than the surface
You leave me breathless

And you can't see
I wish you could
But you can't
And without you, I feel like nothing

What worried him wasn't that he'd just written a love poem about another woman, it was also that it had poured out of him with such ease. Dan knew that feeling when it came to writing and it only meant one thing. That he had real inspiration. And that, as exciting as it might have been in any other situation, was terrifying right now.

He needed to get out of the house and try to clear his head. Every thought and feeling was muddling him up and making his thinking fuzzy around the edges. He put his AirPods in, pulled his hood up and stepped out of the front door, shutting the world out for a little while.

Dan walked for over an hour, just letting his feet guide him until he found himself at Max's school just before the end-of-the-day bell. It was as if his body knew where he needed to be even though his head was struggling with the guilt that he felt.

"Dad!"

Same thing. Every day. It was as if Max was relieved and excited to see his dad every time he picked him up. Dan pulled him into a huge hug.

"Hey, mate. Are you okay? How was school today?"

"It was good. I got a headteacher's award!"

"You did? Maxxy that's amazing! What's it for?"

"For being awesome, obviously!" He winked at his dad.

"I mean of course, yeah, what *else* could it possibly be for?!"

They laughed as they headed out of the playground, Max's hand in his father's.

Walking home, they talked over everything about Max's day at school and for a time Dan felt like he had all he could ever want in the world.

"Did you write today?"

"Yeah, some. Got a bit of writer's block again but I'm sure I'll be fine by tomorrow."

"I like to see you writing, Dad."

"You do? Why's that, mate?"

"It's your thing."

"My thing?"

"Yeah! Like, Dylan's dad works at the council. Other kids in my class, their dads all do different jobs. But my dad is a writer."

"Thanks, mate. It means a lot for you to say that."

"I want to be like you when I grow up."

Max was repeatedly hitting his dad squarely in the feels and Dan was on the verge of tears from it.

"You do? What, a writer?"

"No, not really a writer but just really good at what I do.

Like you are. I'm proud of you."

"I'm proud of you too, Max."

His son looked up the street and saw they were nearing their house.

"Race you!"

He shot off, his school bag bouncing on his back, zips jangling.

"Hey, no fair! False start!"

The pair raced each other up the street and the weight of the world and the pain in his heart fell off Dan with every foot strike. Max was the right tonic for any ailment he had and he knew that as long as they had each other, everything else would be okay.

* * *

The black ink pen landed heavily on the wooden coffee table and came to rest next to a half-drunk cup of cold coffee; dark liquid spilling from the nib onto the tabletop.

"Argh!"

Dan was frustrated. Leaning back against the sofa with his hands holding his head, he let out a loud exclamation of annoyance.

For the whole day, he'd been trying to work on his storyline but all he could come up with were poetic lines that seemed to flow beautifully into one another like vines around a tree. It was as if the words needed to get out of him like a sickness leaving his body; the urge to just expel them from his heart was greater than his ability to focus on his love story.

Some days are harder than others
'Cos what keeps me awake
Is the love that's keeping you awake

Wanting you to be happy
Isn't as easy some days as it is others
But it's the only truth I hold on to

The words stared back up at him from the white page of his notebook which now rested in his lap. He couldn't shake Laura Gray out of his head and it left him feeling like he was drowning in an emotional mixture of guilt and infatuation.

Turning the page, he read the other poem he'd had to rid his soul of earlier that morning.

For so long I've been drifting away
from everything I knew,
tail spinning out of control,
losing myself
but when I finally found some gravity,
it was you at the centre
that I was orbiting around.

He needed to work on his story, not lose himself in the distractions of confusing poetry; he knew this but no matter how much he tried to concentrate, his brain wanted to go in another direction. It was as if his head contained a weight that was causing his focus to yaw towards poetry and away from fiction.

Rising from the sofa, hoping to leave his frustration behind, he went to the kitchen to get a fresh coffee and something to clean up the ink now splashed over the table.

When he came back and set the freshly filled cup of dark coffee down, Dan noticed that next to his notebook, his phone had silently lit up with a text message.

Martin: Are you home?

Dan: Yeah why? Everything okay?

Martin: Not really mate. Had a big fight with Issy and just need to be anywhere but around her right now.

Half an hour later, Martin France sat angrily opposite his best friend, recounting the fight he'd had with his wife only an hour before and all the terrible things she'd done.

"And then she said, if I didn't like it then I knew where the door was and I could just go! Can you believe that?"

"She's just upset, mate. You know what people can be like when they're upset. They say things they don't mean in the heat of the moment."

"Yeah well, maybe I just shouldn't go back and then she'd maybe think better of the words she uses."

"That wouldn't be a good thing and you know it."

"You just don't want me crashing on your sofa."

"You're always welcome, you know that. But you're overre-acting right now."

Martin's shoulders slumped at the realisation that it would actually be a stupid idea. "No, you're right. I do love her. We're great. But sometimes I envy you and the peace you have when Max is at school and you have the joy of an empty, quiet house."

Dan looked away, unsure of what to say, thoughts of hurt words lingering in his mind.

"Shit, Dan. I'm sorry mate. I didn't think."

"It's okay. I was just remembering our last fight, that's all."

Sitting in the living room with Martin, Dan could still hear the echo of the door slamming behind her and how the sound seemed to punch him in the heart.

Even now, years later he still longed to hear her key in the lock and her lilting voice asking where her favourite boys were. The memories of that fight, some of the last words they'd ever spoken, broke his heart every day.

Missing her was a pain that never truly went away.

"I'm sorry. I shouldn't have said that." Martin felt sick at his thoughtlessness.

Dan took a moment to choose his words carefully, wanting to keep his tone as light and as steady as he could.

"Martin. I'm saying this with love. But you're a dick. Go home and apologise."

"But I didn't do anything wrong!"

"Mate, do you want to be right or do you want to be happy? For what it's worth I don't think either of you did anything wrong but one of you needs to cross the floor to make it right."

Martin stared into his coffee cup, guilt hitting him like a cold shower. His fight with Issy was stupid in reality, born out of tiredness and frustration; nothing they'd shouted at each other that morning was really true. All the while, his best friend was sitting in front of him wishing he could take back the stupid fight he'd had all those years ago and see his wife again.

He departed shortly afterwards, tail between his legs and an apology on his lips, leaving Dan sitting on the sofa staring at his notebook.

He missed her more than anything. Natalie had been the cornerstone of his life for so long and she'd left him and Max picking up the pieces of a shattered home. He longed to hear her voice again, to see her face in the morning when he woke up or to see a message from her on his phone.

Picking it up, he opened his voicemail messages and pressed play on the only one he had saved.

Natalie: Hey baby it's me. Just heading back from my mum's. I'll be back in about twenty minutes. Want to open that bottle of wine when I'm back? Feel like I could do with it. I love you.

Dan struggled to hold the emotions at bay. Her voice sounded more like home than the bricks and mortar around him ever did. He'd give anything for her to come back.

* * *

Word couplings seemed to be stuck in his head as he worked, even though they were of no use to his slowly growing storyline. Out of habit, he made notes of them anyway, on a page in his black notebook and wondered if they'd work elsewhere.

Within twenty minutes, he had abandoned all thoughts of this other work and was focusing on another short poem which seemed to need to escape from his head and his suffering heart.

"Hey! What's that?"

He hadn't noticed that Sarah had moved past him, clearing the neighbouring table of its empty plates and cups. Instinctively he covered the page with his hand.

"Nothing."

Sarah immediately felt guilty for her intrusion.

"Sorry Dan, I caught a glimpse of it as you were zoned out. I shouldn't have. It was rude of me. Forgive me?"

He slid his hand off his secret shame and looked away.

"It's okay, Sarah. Don't worry."

"It's beautiful. Is that for the book?"

For a heartbeat, he wondered if he could concoct a lie and just say it was part of the story but not wanting to be tripping over one another any further with apologies and half-truths, he thought better of it. He sighed.

"No. It's just a poem."

"Oh wow. I didn't realise you did poetry too! But now I come to think of it, it would make sense as it's all writing, isn't it?" Sarah was rambling.

"Well, to be honest, I've never really done poetry as a writer. I mean, I did it for a term at uni as part of my course but that was only because we had to, it wasn't by choice. It's never been something that I've really ever done of my own volition. Yet, this is the fourth one I've written in as many days. I'm not really sure where they're coming from."

"Maybe beginning to write again has unlocked you a little bit and now your brain is trying to work through that on a different level?"

Dan shrugged. "Yeah, maybe."

"May I?" She gestured to the now uncovered page, open between them. He nodded and let her read.

You wrung my heart out
until it was empty
Left me bruised and battered
And without a word of condolence

"It's beautiful, Dan. Truly."

"Thanks."

He felt wildly exposed. It was as though she was looking directly into his soul and the energy needed for him to stay in the moment and not run was draining.

With his other writing it had become easier to share snippets of chapters; the confidence of being a published author, while not completely liberating him from his self-doubt, enabled him to at least let people read his works in progress. But this was different. This was new and he had no confidence in it.

Standing next to him, Sarah knew that he was feeling vulnerable. The energy he was giving off, simply sitting quietly while avoiding her gaze was like a heat haze in summer, shimmering around him.

"The confidence will come." She spoke without thinking. "If you write more poems, you'll feel more comfortable with letting people see them. It's probably just because it's a new way of writing for you."

He screwed his face up awkwardly and watched helplessly as

his hand, seemingly with a mind of its own, turned the pages of his notebook to show Sarah the other poems he'd written. As she read he hung his head.

"Dan!"

She stood flabbergasted at the depth of emotion he had written into each and every stanza. This was nothing like the books she'd previously loved reading with his name on the cover. The poetry that flowed across the pages in front of her, was deep, meaningful and beautiful. It was hard to breathe.

Not knowing what to say, Dan felt conspicuous.

"They're not very good really but they're in my head and I can't seem to do anything but write them at the moment."

"Then don't fight it."

"Huh?" He asked, confused and a little taken aback.

"Look," Sarah sat down opposite him as she spoke gently, "these are a creative outlet right?"

He nodded, unsure of where she was going with this.

"So maybe let them be a sort of a warm-up for you writing your story. Surely writing these is better than writing nothing and staring at a screen? Maybe you could use the act of writing poems as a stepping stone back to writing fiction. When did you even write last?"

"Properly? Before Natalie..." Dan's heart caught in his throat as he tried to find the words. "Just over three years."

"Then maybe poetry, if that's where your creativity is going, is a way back in? Like warming up your writing muscles."

"Yeah, maybe."

As she moved away a few minutes later, Dan felt that Sanctuary was fast becoming the place he needed to be to write again. Being here, with Sarah's encouragement and company, felt safe.

Yet, it didn't feel perfect. For all its positives, a seed of confusion had been planted in him and the anxiety around what it meant was troubling.

* * *

Martin picked his wife up and spun her around as they danced to an old love song playing on the radio. He had a wonderful habit of pulling Issy into his arms and dancing her around the kitchen whenever a good song came on, which she delighted at.

"I bloody love you, Issy France."

Wrapping her arms around his neck she kissed him, taking a bite of his bottom lip as she pulled away. "Love you too, stud."

The guitar solo kicked in and he spun her again, causing her to squeal and laugh.

He loved moments like this with his wife and was grateful that they had returned after everything that had happened during the last few years. Issy had been heartsore for such a long time. While on the outside she was always there for Dan and her godson, Martin would often pick up the pieces of her emotional exhaustion in the quiet of their home.

So now, being able to spend a happy Saturday morning dancing her off her feet and kissing her whenever the mood struck, was a precious treasure he was glad to have back.

As they danced, Martin grabbed Issy's hips and drew her

closer to his body, letting his lips find the soft skin on her neck in a way he knew drove her crazy.

"No. No no no. Don't start. That's not fair; we're meant to be going out in a few minutes."

She might as well be trying to reason with someone who didn't understand a single word of the English language. Attempting to keep her eyes from closing, she tried to reason with him. "Martin we can't! We need to go! Isn't twice before 11 am enough?!"

Her husband just chuckled.

An hour later Issy rang the doorbell of Dan's house and was greeted by Max.

"You two are late!"

"Sorry Maxxy, something... came up. We didn't miss lunch did we?" She blushed as she apologised.

Dan called through from the kitchen, "no, it's fine. You're just in time, don't worry about my little timekeeper of a son!"

Max was scooped up by Martin as he came through the door, who then proceeded to tickle him furiously.

"Martin for God's sake he's nine! Can't you talk football with him or something without the need to play-fight all the time?" Issy shook her head as she spoke to the pair who both looked back at her incredulously at her mention of the round ball game.

"Maxxy, she's got a point mate. Stick the rugby on, there's a good lad." As he spoke, he unceremoniously dropped his godson from about six feet in the air, straight onto the bouncy sofa below.

"Martin!"

Dan walked out of the kitchen with a tray full of buffet

snacks, chuckling.

"Issy, he's fine. Take a breath."

"Sod off telling me to take a breath when he ends up in A&E, Dan!" She laughed at him. It was good to see them both.

After he'd put the tray down on the coffee table, they hugged as they did every time they saw each other.

"You doing okay?" She would always ask him quietly as they embraced, giving him the chance to confide in her privately if needed. He didn't often but those times when he was struggling, he'd tell her no as they held each other and she'd understand the tone for the day.

"I'm good, Issy."

It was going to be an okay day at least, she thought.

"So, how's the writing going?" Martin asked, chomping down on a large piece of pork pie.

"Yeah, slow and steady."

"I guess it's like riding a bike?"

"Erm, a little bit but it's a confidence thing, I think. Like, I know how to ride the bike, I'm just building up the confidence to lean into the corners again."

He didn't really want to say he felt less like a nervy cyclist and more like Bambi on ice but he hoped they'd understand.

"Just go slow Dan and take your time. It'll come." Issy smiled, her godson leant up against her, eating crisps from a tube.

"With the story or on the bike?"

"Both?" That made him laugh and she was glad to see it, as she always was when he seemed happier.

"Dad's writing most days at the moment, aren't you?"

"Mhmm. Little by little."

"Are you helping, Maxxy?" Issy pulled him into her side. Max knew he was loved.

"I'm staying out of the way," he chuckled.

"The boy knows best!" Martin howled as he reached for another piece of meat pie.

"So guys, it's Max's birthday coming up," He winked at his boy. "Maybe we could go out before coming back here for a birthday tea?"

"Yeah sounds good! Did you have anything in mind?"

"No, not really, It's a Wednesday so Max will have school and you two will be at work but maybe we could do something and then come back for dinner here afterwards?"

"We could go for hot chocolate at that coffee shop you go to, Dad?" Max's eyes lit up at the prospect of Sarah's extra flakes.

"Ah I don't know, mate." Dan's thoughts immediately turned to Laura.

"That could work," Martin added, "I can take a half day if we want to go straight after school for Max."

"Guys..."

"Yeah, okay I can probably wrap my meetings up by three and come and meet you guys there." Issy was thinking through the logistics, talking out loud.

"Wait...maybe we could..."

"Dad! Come on. The hot chocolates are *so* good."

"I just thought maybe we might like to go somewhere else, that's all." Dan was desperately trying to get them away from the idea of going to Sanctuary for a birthday outing but he could see he was losing the battle. He also knew if he defended his position too strongly, Martin and Issy might start asking

111

difficult questions that he wasn't ready or able to answer.

"No, I think that works for all of us. Unless you have a particular reason to want to go somewhere else?" Issy looked at him curiously. She could feel something was making Dan uncomfortable but she wasn't sure what that could be.

Dan realised that if he wanted an out, this was his opportunity. He turned the idea over in his mind quickly. He didn't want to disappoint Max and he didn't want to arouse any kind of suspicion.

"No, it's okay. Let's go to Sanctuary. Max is right; the hot chocolates are the best around."

Later that afternoon, after everyone was stuffed full from lunch, Dan put a now clean serving plate back in the cupboard as Issy dried up cutlery from the draining board next to him.

"About the coffee shop? If you'd rather we do something else, we can." She was concerned that they'd possibly backed him into a corner.

"No, it's okay. I just didn't think you'd all want to go where I'm working out of that was all." He tried to hide the truth in his eyes but suspected he wasn't doing a great job of it.

"You sure?"

"Sure as sure can be."

Placing a spoon into the drawer, she asked, "Did you figure out your leading lady?"

A flash of Laura's smile shone brightly in Dan's mind for a second.

"Not quite, no."

"It's okay, you know?"

"What is?" Guilt flared in him.

"That your female character isn't Natalie."

"She was for so long, it feels odd for her not to be."

"Maybe it's time for a new leading lady, Dan."

* * *

The birthday boy woke to find his dad sitting quietly on the end of his bed.

"Dad?"

"Happy Birthday Max."

Dan happily handed over a small wrapped box to his sleepy son.

Once he had sat himself up in bed and rubbed the sleep out of his eyes, he began to unwrap the gift.

"Dad!"

Max was surprised and delighted with a brand new phone. His first. It had been something he'd been asking of his dad for a while, ever since Dylan had been given an iPhone a few months earlier.

"Thank you!" He threw his arms around Dan, tears welling in his eyes.

"You're welcome, Maxxy."

Dan held his son for a few moments, thinking how much Natalie would have protested him getting a phone at his age. She was the sort of mum who would want to bury her son in books sooner than put an addictive device in his hands.

"I wish Mum was here."

"I know mate. Me too."

Max sat up and dried his eyes, marvelling at the shiny box in his hands.

Dan felt ground rules were needed early. "I don't want you on it all the time and you ask me before you install games and apps, okay?"

The boy nodded. His dad could have set him any rules at all; at that moment, he didn't care. He had a phone and he was made up.

"Right, come on. Let's get you ready for school, then we can open more presents over breakfast and I can help set up your phone before we have to leave."

* * *

After school, Max sat squirming in his seat as he waited. The boy had been a bundle of excited energy all day and the walk in the sunshine from school to Sanctuary hadn't seemed to take the edge off. Dan sat across from his son, smiling. He loved Max so much and being able to see his face lit up like this, today of all days, was something that warmed his heart.

"When are they getting here?"

"Soon, Maxxy. Soon."

The overly large birthday badge on his chest sparkled in the tungsten spotlights hanging from the ceiling of the coffee shop as they waited. As the birthday boy, he had requested a big hot chocolate and a slab of thick chocolate cake, which was being prepared at the counter. Dan could see the candle waiting to be added once Issy and Martin had arrived and glanced at Sarah, who had winked at him to signify it was all ready.

As if on cue, the door to the cafe chimed open and Max spun round to see Issy wearing a huge smile, Martin a few steps behind carrying a concerningly large gift-wrapped box.

"Argh!"

The excited, bouncing child rushed from his seat and flung himself into Issy's arms.

"Happy Birthday Maxxy!"

"Thank you!"

Martin's head appeared over the top of the box. "Happy Birthday little dude."

Max's eyes lit up.

"What. Is. That?"

"Well, let me sit down mate and I might let you have it seeing as it's your birthday."

The troupe sat around the table as Dan's eyebrows furrowed.

"Erm, I thought we said no big presents?"

Issy completely ignored him, turning to Max. "For the birthday boy."

Max tore into the wrapping paper without ceremony.

"ARGGGGGHHHHH!! Thank you!"

A Lego Delorean from the *Back to the Future* movies sat in front of the wide-eyed child, whose mouth was hanging open as if he was trying to catch flies.

"Your dad said you really liked the films so we thought it was a good choice."

"Thank you!"

Dan smiled and shook his head. "Yeah, thanks for that!"

"Right, make way."

Sarah bustled over carrying a tray of hot chocolates and a block of chocolate birthday cake which was adorned with a Happy Birthday candle. As Martin moved the brick set off of the table, she set the tray down with a flourish.

"Yours is the one with the extra flake Max, obviously."

For the next little while, they all sat around the table laughing and joking; occasionally wiping hot chocolate and cream from around their lips.

"I have to concur with the childbeast, these hot chocolates are good." Martin said with a wink at his godson who giggled back, his mouth full of cake.

Dan laughed. "I'll get us another round."

As he approached the counter, Sarah pulled herself away from washing up to come and talk to him.

"How's my favourite customer enjoying his birthday?"

"Wait! I thought I was your favourite customer?"

"I don't think I ever said that, now did I?"

"True. And he's fine. I think he's had a lovely day."

"Good. I'm glad. I wasn't sure how days like this would be for him."

"Yeah, today is definitely the best one so far. It's not always been easy, especially in the early days but aside from a little blip this morning, he seems to be doing okay."

They chatted for a while before they heard the door opening behind them which caused Sarah to look up. But Dan didn't join her. Something inside told him without question who'd just walked through the door and he didn't need to turn around to have it confirmed.

"Hey babe! What you doing here at this time of day? Aren't you teaching?"

He felt his chest tightening when he heard Laura reply over his shoulder.

"Just popped in for a tea to go. On my way to a lesson."

The ground stubbornly refused to swallow him and the counter whole, as he tried to hide his face.

"Hello, Dan."

He turned slightly, trying to mask the anxiety that was already fighting to bubble over.

"Hey, you. I mean...erm...hi Laura."

The smile on her face did nothing to calm his rapidly rising panic. He just wanted to become invisible.

"How are you?"

"I'm okay. Erm. I'm good. It's Max's birthday. So we're here for some hot chocolate and cake." *OMG, Dan shut up and stop talking now! She doesn't even know who Max is!*

From the other side of the counter, Sarah noticed her slightly awkward friend tripping over himself and decided to intervene.

"Medium tea, babe?"

"Please."

Before he could slip away from the counter, Dan was confronted by Max.

"Dad! Issy says get some more cake."

Dan was flustered; his mind distracted from the boy in front of him by the woman standing next to him, who he felt sure was staring. It took a few seconds of Dan replaying the interaction in his head to work out what his son was saying now.

"Hi! I'm Max!"

He watched in disbelief as Max approached Laura with a huge smile on his face and an outstretched hand.

Her eyes danced as she held in a giggle, accepting the

handshake. "Hi Max. I'm Laura. I hear it's your birthday."

"Mhmm. Yup!" The boy proudly brandished his birthday badge at her.

"Well, happy birthday. Did you get anything nice?"

Max launched into recalling a detailed list of the presents he'd been given already today as Laura listened intently. As Dan stood by helplessly with this playing out in front of him, he was struck by the feeling that she actually wanted to hear all about his son's day and his gifts. It was odd. A behaviour so far removed from his own experiences with her that he couldn't quite make sense of it.

Max grinned as he ran out of both breath and items on his gift list.

Laura half-whistled in appreciation. "Wow".

"Come on Max. Let's leave Laura and Sarah to chat. Issy and Martin will be getting bored without you."

"I'll bring your drinks over with the extra cake."

He nodded to Sarah and averting his gaze, made his way back to their table where he proceeded to surreptitiously watch Laura out of the corner of his eye until she left a few moments later, tea in hand.

* * *

Max gently brushed over the strings and they sang out beautifully. Even though he couldn't play, the boy knew that this was a special thing and being allowed to touch it was a privilege, something to be done with care and attention.

"It won't bite Maxxy, don't worry."

"I just don't want to break it, that's all, Dad. I know what this means to you."

Every family has that one precious item that you're not supposed to mess around near, let alone touch without permission. For some, it's a priceless antique or family heirloom that causes Grandma to glare at anyone who goes anywhere near it. And while Dan wasn't the kind of father to be paranoid about his son being near his things, the boy knew the importance and significance of this permanent fixture in their living room.

Max Muir understood that his dad's ebony Gibson *BB King Signature Lucille* guitar was very special. Bought as a celebratory gift for himself when his book, *Sanctuary of Nine* was made into a TV show, it had been like a faithful dog in their family; ever-present and much loved.

Even though Dan wasn't much of a guitar player himself, he loved blues music and to him, BB King was a god amongst men, so it was only fitting that when he could treat himself, he did so with an exact replica of the famous *Lucille.* It would occasionally be played. Dan would take to noodling out some pentatonic solo in A minor, or rock out some bluesy licks that would always make Natalie smile. It was as much a work of visual art as it was a playable instrument.

"Do you want to have a play?"

Max's eyes opened as wide as saucers. "Really?"

"Mhmm." Dan smiled and walked over to the guitar, lifting it from its stand in the corner of the room. Max quickly stepped towards the small tweed practice amp and flicked the switch that made it hum as it fired up. He sat gently on the edge of the sofa as Dan lowered the guitar into his lap.

"Remember to keep one hand on it, okay?"

Max nodded excitedly as his dad sat opposite him, perched on the coffee table.

"Go on then."

He nervously strummed his fingers over the strings, holding down basic chord shapes he'd been shown. To the ten-year-old, it didn't really matter that he wasn't actually playing a tune, it was more just the simple joy of getting it to make a sweet noise. In Max's eyes, his dad was a really good guitarist, such was the naivety of youth, but he still loved the rare times that he was allowed to just play it himself.

When he'd finished his turn, Max beamed. "Thanks, Dad!"

"You're welcome. We might need to get you some lessons one day, if you wanted."

"Yes please!"

"Okay, let me look into it and we can see."

"Dad? Will you play something now?"

Dan hefted the guitar from Max and settled it in his own lap.

"Flick the channel, buddy."

Max stepped back over to the amp and pressed the little black button marked OD which made it sound like a rock guitar.

Dan adjusted the volume control slightly and then slid his fingers down the neck of the guitar along the strings and began to somewhat clumsily play a solo, an attempt at the opening bars to Gary Moore's *I'm Still in Love with You*; not that Max would have known or recognised the song. As he bent the strings, making the guitar sing and wail, Dan wished he played more often. It was something of an out-of-body experience when he would play, brought on by the complete focus and concentration needed to make it sing out. It was as if everything else faded away and he could just exist.

Max made an excited squeal as his dad finished and dialled the volume pot back to zero, silencing the guitar. Dan chuckled and moved to gently place the instrument back on its stand.

"Can I get a drink?"

"Yeah, go for it Maxxy."

He rushed off to the kitchen, leaving Dan to turn off the amp. Next to *Lucille* and the amp sat his vinyl record player and he decided he needed a little blues to pass the afternoon. Picking the record he wanted and placing it on the turntable, he flicked the vintage player on and it crackled into life as the record began to wobble and spin, expectantly waiting for the needle, which Dan dutifully dropped into place. After more popping and cracking BB King himself came to life through the little speakers and *The Thrill Has Gone* began to play out through the room.

When Dan turned to sit on the sofa and listen, he noticed that a ray of sunshine was sliding silently through the front room blinds, bathing the resting guitar in slotted light.

Dan grabbed his phone and opened Instagram, adding an arty photo of *Lucille* to his story for the day, sitting back to enjoy his music.

On the other side of town, relaxing at home, Laura Gray was coincidentally scrolling through social media and was greeted by a picture of a beautiful ebony guitar washed in sunlight. Hitting the message tab on the picture, she sent Dan a message. *He probably won't mind, we've been following each other for a few weeks now.*

Laura: Beautiful guitar.

Dan: She's stunning isn't she?

Laura: Yeah. Do you play?

Dan: A little bit yeah. Only for fun really. The guitar is more of a piece of art at home than something I play a lot. It's a BB King Lucille.

Laura: Cool.

And that was that.

Dan was confused about how the conversation had gone flat so quickly. *Did I say something wrong?* He reread the exchange. *It doesn't seem like it.* It was so weird.

While not great in social situations, he knew that with written words he was okay and could keep conversations light and flowing when needs be. Reading their brief messages back once more, he felt that it had been relaxed and easy, so he didn't understand why she'd turned so short with him, so quickly. Glancing up, his eyes rested again on *Lucille*.

As Dan stared at the guitar, sat in the shade, with the short burst of sunlight now long gone, he wondered how he could have acted differently with Laura. He longed for a protracted conversation with her, just to get to know her and build some kind of rapport but his social awkwardness had so far gotten the better of him in person.

Deciding that if he wasn't careful, he was going to spend the rest of the day incessantly checking his messages, he instead called through to Max.

"Come on, buddy. Let's go to the shop and get some treats for after tea."

Five minutes later they were heading out the door, Dan's phone left behind quietly on the coffee table as he closed the heavy front door behind them.

* * *

Watching her packing her guitar away, Dan felt a sudden and unusual wave of confidence rising up in him and went over to talk to her.

"Hey."

"Hi!" She looked up at him, smiling brightly, prompting him to smile back.

"Lovely set tonight. You're really good."

"Thanks! I'm really glad you enjoyed it. I've seen you here before, right?"

Dan blushed a little, realising that she'd noticed him at least once previously when he'd watched her perform. He liked feeling seen.

"Yeah. I work out of here a little and Sarah's encouraged me to stay on for the music nights a few times now. I can't say I'm not grateful to her for that."

"Oh? Why's that?"

"As I say, you're good. I've always appreciated creative talent."

"Is that right?"

She really was beautiful and for a few seconds, Dan basked in it, enjoying the warmth that radiated from her.

"Yeah. From one creative to another."

123

Laura had stopped packing her things away now and was completely focused on the conversation with the man in front of her.

"A fellow artist. Very nice. Let me guess." She looked him up and down with a mock appraising look on her face. "You're too clean-cut to be a musician, even if you do have the coolest guitar I've ever seen and you don't have that dead look behind the eyes so you can't be anything as mundane as a photographer, that must mean you're a writer."

Dan grinned at her. "I'm impressed!"

She smirked. "What can I say, I'm not just a pretty face."

God, she was pretty though.

They both laughed and it felt as comfortable as a warm blanket on a winter's day.

"Can I buy you a drink?" It was a calm request, which was completely out of character but he was running with it. "A fair payment for such good entertainment."

"Whoa! My singing is only worth a drink?" She was being openly playful with him. He was cute and Laura was enjoying the attention.

"Fine, let's make it one of those big hot chocolates then!"

A little while later, they were sitting in the almost deserted coffee shop with two sizable hot chocolate mugs, long-finished and empty on the table between them.

Sarah busied herself, cleaning and upturning chairs on tables around them.

The conversation had been pleasant; relaxed and easy with a welcome side dish of flirty and neither of them really wanted it to end.

Dan had told her all about his writing and Laura had told him her dream of recording her own acoustic album, as they both seemed uncharacteristically to want to be open and vulnerable with the other.

A few times the conversation had slowed and they'd sat comfortably making flirtatious eye contact. The world and the coffee shop around them had melted away and what was left were two souls who could happily revolve around each other for eternity, never wanting to be pulled apart.

"So, can I call you sometime?"

"Ah, I don't think so Dan. It's time to wake up." Laura smiled at him, her blue eyes twinkling in the evening light of the room that seemed to be swirling around her.

"What?"

"Dan, you need to wake up."

Her face started to fade slightly and he shook his head feeling like he was about to pass out. A blinding pain shot through his temples and he screwed his eyes shut, trying to fight it off.

When he woke Dan realised that it hadn't been real at all but just a dream, as fictional as the words he used to construct stories. He cursed every stupid pointless piece of prose he'd ever written for fuelling his subconscious with beautiful lies like that, wishing the whole thing had been real.

He lay perfectly still in the inky black of night; the covers pulled up over his head, wishing that he could be consumed by the darkness and left alone forever.

What hurt the most wasn't that he was falling in love with someone who couldn't love him back. It was that he seemed to have no control of his mind running all over his heart, even when he didn't want it. He just wanted to be free of this and not think about her or how she made him feel.

Dan shut his eyes, not to sleep, more to try and close himself off from the pain of it all. Guilt and shame boiled inside his head, along with his heartbreaking feelings for Laura, creating a perfect storm of emotions that he wished he could just drown in, never resurfacing.

Hours passed as he stared into the emptiness of it all, trying to reconcile himself through the confusion of his heartache of losing Natalie and his growing love for a woman he'd barely spoken to. Dan just wanted it all to stop. His head was ringing with a high-pitched whine which he knew was a sign of his mind being hyper-focused and there was nothing he could do to stop it.

He eased the covers off and slipped out of bed in a haze, his mind elsewhere as his body went into autopilot drawing him to where he needed to be. A few minutes later he found himself sitting on the sofa, pen in hand with his AirPods in his ears listening to the playlist he'd created of songs from her sets, which he'd simply called *Muse*.

Six lines found their way through his pen and onto the pages, effortlessly flowing out of his aching heart and when he was done he couldn't help but lose tears to his words.

Days like today suck
While I drown in the misery of my love for you

I know you're living your life and I'm living mine
But I hate the pain I didn't choose

So I drown out the noise
With songs of love and hurt hoping it all goes away

* * *

When Saturday rolled around, the boys decided to go out for hot chocolate and cake. Max stared excitedly at the neon orange poster in the front window of Sanctuary.

Open Mic.

Sing a song. Read a poem. Tell a story.

Entertain us and get a free drink.

"Ah Dad, come on!" Max pleaded.

Dan knew exactly what his son was getting at and it wasn't happening. Certainly not here.

"Dude! I can't do that!

"Yes, you can! You're really good!"

"Maxxy..."

"Don't you Maxxy me." The boy was full of laughter knowing full well that his father would most likely relent if he kept up this emotional pressure. "Let me show you how to be a kid for a change."

"I think you'll find, young man, it's my job to teach *you* how to be a grown-up! Lessons don't go in both directions. That's not how this works."

"Well, today school's in session. Please, Dad! You'd be awesome."

The boy took his dad's hand and practically dragged him into the little coffee shop which was fast becoming one of their favourite places on the weekends. A cheery wave from Sarah caused Max to let go and run over to say hello, while Dan went to claim a table. As he dropped his jacket into a chair, he spotted Laura in the corner tuning her guitar.

Wearing blue jeans and a pink top, she looked up, spotted him and smiled before going back to what she was doing. Dan's heart fluttered with palpations, but he showed a half smile in return before she looked away.

Seeing Dan take a seat, Sarah wandered over with Max and greeted him warmly.

"Hey, you!"

Max beamed as he sat down. "Tell Dad he should have a go today."

She looked at Max, confused and then over at Dan who was trying to busy himself, moving menus around the table.

"But what would he do, Max?"

"You don't know?"

"Know what?"

The boy grinned like a Cheshire cat, holding on to the best secret he held against his chest.

"Dad plays the guitar."

"Max, why is it every time I bring you here you rat me out to Sarah about something!?"

"Shhh, you!" Sarah smiled at Dan and gave Max her full attention. "What sort of things does he play? He's kept that one quiet from me."

"Like electric guitar. Blue stuff."

"Blues," Dan said quietly, staring at the floor. If his son

was going to spill his father's secrets, he might as well do it correctly.

"Right young Max, I'm going to get you a nice big hot chocolate with an extra flake and then we can work on your dad, okay?" And with that, she turned and headed back to the counter full of mirth and delight.

He'd hoped that they'd just let it go and leave him be, but an hour later Sarah and Max were still trying to nudge him, albeit gently, into giving it a go.

"You just need to play to Max and me. Don't worry about anyone else."

Dan thought about it. A part of him had always wanted to be up there, performing in front of others. surprising and delighting them but fear had always kept him playing small. It had taken a few months for him to play in front of Natalie for the first time, even though every time she visited his uni flat she would comment on his old, battered black Stratocaster guitar.

The creative part of his soul, however, yearned to play for others. While he might not be a virtuoso, he knew he could pull off a tune if he paid enough attention to what he was doing.

"Guys, I don't know. I've never done that sort of thing."

Sarah smiled. "Always a first time."

"But I don't even have my guitar with me."

"Oh no! Whatever will you do..." Sarah was smirking, tilting her head in the playful way she did when she was having fun.

"Well unless you can magic one up, I can't really just go and play air guitar, can I?"

"Dad. There's a guitar up there. Look!"

Dan turned curiously to see a black acoustic guitar, tucked back behind the stool for performers to sit on.

For fucks sake!

Watching the realisation on his face, Sarah smiled. "Reckon you could use that?"

"I mean, yeah probably. But guys..."

It was too late, she was gone and moving towards the mic.

No no no!

"Ladies and gentlemen. Our next performer is going to play us some blues. Give a big hand for Dan!"

He stared at her, trying to muster as much menace in his look as possible but he couldn't manage it.

"Go on, Dad. I believe in you."

He turned to Max who was smiling at him proudly, even though he'd not done anything yet.

Feel the fear and do it anyway.

The words rang in his head as he rose as if possessed by a force outside of himself and moved to the mic, picking up the guitar as he sat down. Subconsciously he cast an eye over to see if Laura was looking but mercifully she had left her table and he couldn't see her.

Dan's hands trembled as he played through the chord progression to the introduction and resolved to never listen to Max again. *What the hell am I doing?*

As he looked out across the very small crowd of people assembled around the mismatch of chairs in Sanctuary, a curious thing happened. All he could see was Max. Everything and everyone else in the cafe he'd spent so many hours in of late, seemed to fade away and it was as if he was sitting back on the sofa; his enthralled son looking on with glee.

When I'm driving down the highway when I want to let up
There's an angel on my shoulder with
Sweet tea driving in her old grey one
Saying play this song, but the heart is a road that don't give up

So I could sell my soul to rock and roll
So I could sell my soul to rock and roll
She made a deal with the angels and then never let go
So I could sell my soul to rock and roll

Even with a nervous energy causing him to have to really focus on each chord and lick, Dan began to feel something akin to joy as he sang to Max, who sitting with Sarah, smiled back at him with nothing but love.

He didn't care if it was any good, he was just enjoying the pleasure of feeling like a kid again, with Max's permission.

A small smattering of applause broke out when he finished and placed the guitar back onto its stand behind him. Sarah and Max were whooping and banging on the table making him smile as the room slowly came back into stark focus. And there, leaning against the counter, was Laura with a look of apathy on her face.

His heart sank.

She must have been watching when he was playing and he hadn't noticed. The all too familiar feeling of anxiety tightened his chest as he tried to calmly stand and return to his table.

Confusion settled in him as Dan sat down with an excited and proud Max, who proceeded to hug him so hard he was literally squeezing the air out of his dad's lungs.

Why did she look so disinterested? Was he really that bad?

Doubt and hurt swirled around his head as he tried to listen to what Max was saying.

"I'm impressed, Dan! That was ace! Now about that free drink?"

Hearing Sarah's voice pulled him from his reverie.

"Dad, you were amazing! I'm so proud of you"

"Thanks, guys. I think I'll stick to writing though, eh?"

* * *

Max bounded into his Dad's bedroom at exactly 7 am and started yelling.

"Dad! Wake up! It's your birthday!"

Aside from Dan being terrified at being violently awoken from a deep sleep, he couldn't help but be happy for having such a sweet caring boy to greet him on his birthday.

"Thanks, mate. Sleep okay?"

Pulling his son into a hug while still half asleep, he tried to engage his brain enough to make conversation and not fall back to sleep. He had been having a pretty good dream about a blonde girl and he could definitely remember lots of laughing.

"Yeah! Dad, open your presents!"

"Alright alright, take a breath."

With Max extricating himself to the foot of the bed where there lay a carrier bag of clumsily wrapped presents, Dan sat himself up against the pillows and waited, trying to keep his tired eyes open.

Stopping short of creating a mess, Max upended his bag of gifts and cast the plastic carrier aside, looking at his Dad as though single-handed, he'd pulled off the most amazing thing ever. In front of Dan lay an array of small gifts and one large present, all wrapped in multi-coloured paper, held together by what Dan could only assume was a whole roll of sellotape.

"Happy Birthday Dad!" The 10-year-old beamed, handing his father a birthday card in a blue envelope.

To the Best Dad in the world. Have a brilliant day. Love always.
Maxxy. Xxx

Dan's heart nearly melted down through his stomach and onto the bed.

"Love you, mate."

"Love you too, Dad!"

They spent a few minutes unwrapping with Max deciding which present Dan should open next. When the bed was covered in pieces of torn gift wrap, he'd ended up with a pretty good haul and knew he would have to thank Martin and Issy later for helping Max to pick out and pay for the presents in front of him. He was pretty enamoured by the T-shirt Max had gotten him, with a picture of a guitar on it.

But as he sat on the bed with his son, Dan felt torn. On the one hand, he felt grateful for Max and everything he'd done for him that morning. He didn't really need much else in life aside from his infectious, loving son but a part of his heart still felt empty and he longed for it to be made whole again. Dan wondered how it would feel if Laura was sat on the bed with them, sharing in the moment and he ached for something that didn't feel right as a result.

He needed to keep his focus on real life, and not in the make-believe of his emotions.

"Shall we go get some breakfast? Your old man needs a coffee."

Max bounced off the bed with a smile.

Before he gathered up his gifts to take them downstairs, Dan removed the shreds of torn paper from the pile and snapped a quick photo which he shared on his Instagram story. It wasn't much and he knew on a deeply selfish level he was only doing it for attention but he let himself do it all the same, before following Max down into the kitchen.

The two spent the day hanging out.

Max helped make breakfast while Dan took control of the coffee-making duties. They had pancakes and maple syrup and felt too stuffed to move by the end of it, so had a relaxed morning on the sofa watching superhero movies.

He periodically checked his phone for notifications, replying to wishes of happy birthday from friends and family, while one notable potential well-wisher remained silent.

Logically, Dan knew the likelihood of Laura even being aware that today was his birthday, was remote and the idea of her feeling like she could or should wish him well was even more remote but a part of him still longed to be connected with her, even briefly, today. He hated himself for wanting it. It felt like he was a kid at Christmas, who desperately wanted a gift that never seemed to appear, no matter how many presents he opened. He had to fight against his rejection sensitivity and waves of despondency to keep focused on following the movie in front of them.

After skipping lunch caused by overzealous morning pancake eating, they went for a walk in the park. While Max rode the zip line repeatedly until his dad thought the thing might actually wear out from overuse, Dan thought about how it would feel if Laura was sitting with him on the bench, chatting and watching Max swing by in front of them, upside down. Every thought of her was making his heart heavy.

"Dad?"

"Yeah?"

"Your fish and chips are going to go cold."

Max looked sympathetically at his dad, who seemed to be lost in his head as they sat together watching TV.

"Sorry mate. Just a bad head day."

"Have you not had a nice day?"

Guilt crashed over him like a falling wave.

"Of course I have Maxxy. It's been a really lovely day. Thank you. My brain is just a bit wobbly today but that's nothing you've done or not done. Just one of those days."

The boy smiled but Dan could tell he was a little hurt that it hadn't been a completely perfect day.

"I'm very lucky to have you, Max. Even on my hard days, I never forget that. It's been a really good birthday, you did a great job. Promise.

Max smiled and rammed more chips in his mouth sideways as they watched the flickering coloured lights in front of them.

As he climbed into bed a few hours later, Dan checked his phone one more time.

Nothing.

Curiously he checked the app to see who'd viewed his story that morning, scrolling through the collection of round profile pictures and towards the bottom of the list he saw it. Her picture. Laura had seen that it was his birthday and had chosen not to say anything.

He sighed and put his phone on charge on his nightstand.

Lying in the dark, staring up at the ceiling, Dan wondered why. Had he seen it was *her* birthday, he would have said something out of politeness, just to be nice but for whatever reason she hadn't.

He didn't understand it. *She was a nice person from what he could tell so why wouldn't she say a casual happy birthday to him? Had he done something wrong?*

He felt the tension in his shoulders building as he thought about it and couldn't shake the feeling that he was getting too invested and that actually he was falling in love with the idea of her.

Rolling over he shut his eyes, hoping the darkness that seemed to be creeping into his heart would take over his head and lull him into a painless sleep.

* * *

Dan stared again at the picture on his screen and wondered what the fucking point of it all was. She wasn't interested and she never would be. She had the man of her dreams and he just had to accept it for better or worse. It was just the way it was.

136

His eyes drifted from the screen as he got lost in thought.

Things had been going pretty well of late and he'd written loads of really good words, albeit poetry rather than fiction, bundling up his feelings for her in a way he could convey to others. His creativity was flowing easily again after years of it hardly making an appearance. But blinkered, he'd walked into today without recognising the real significance of it and as a result, had gotten blindsided. And it tore him up.

Opening his Instagram app earlier that morning, his heart leapt as he saw she'd posted something new. He knew it was wrong and he shouldn't be that invested but curiosity got the better of him and clicked on the new notification symbol. But as soon as he did, his heart sank as he realised what he was looking at. There in front of him, in all his refined, smug fucking glory was her fiancé, smiling in the appreciation post for Valentine's Day she'd shared.

Fuck this!

He could feel himself spiralling as soon as he closed the app and put his phone on the side. It wasn't even that Dan felt he was better for her. Chris was probably a really decent guy and loved her without question but that didn't seem to stop another crack from appearing in his heart. Laura was happy. That's all he ever wanted for her but that didn't mean seeing her being so vocal about her love for another man would sting any less.

He closed his laptop and locked his phone. He was done

writing for the day. There weren't any good words left in him now, just hurt and pain for the loss of something he'd never had.

On the quieter, less important days, he could convince himself she was single and that eventually, they'd find a way to each other like stardust reforming. But on days like this? When the whole world was in love? It felt like he was destined to drift alone and the weight of that knowledge was crushing.

The last thing he wanted to do was to declare his love to her and fuck up something good that she had. That felt worse than loving her from afar. But today he'd have given anything to wish her Happy Valentine's Day even if it was from a distance. Roses and chocolates would have been one thing, but just being able to wish her a happy day would have made his year.

He needed to get out of the house to try and clear his head. Every thought and feeling was muddling him up and making his thinking fuzzy at the edges. He put his AirPods in, pulled his hood up and stepped out through the front door.

A while later, Dan found himself sitting in a chain coffee shop, staring into a half-filled, poorly made cup of Americano. There was a profound ache in his body that he knew wasn't anything to do with muscle soreness, but was radiating out of his bruised heart. What accompanied it was a dark brooding which left him feeling like the world was a shitty place to be, and aside from Max, there was no good in it.

Sulking into his cup, Dan wished he could just escape this life with Max and get away from all of it. Without his son needing a formal education, he knew he could have just packed them both up and moved away that day. Away from the hurt, away from the pain, and away from the deep sense of loss he felt every day.

It was really the worst kind of torture.

Maybe it's meant to just be me and Max. We can shut the world out and just be happy, the two of us. We don't need anyone else.

Leaving his untouched coffee on the dirty table, Dan left to collect Max from school, resolving to shut the world out and focus on his son. No one would really care if they disappeared, he knew that, so deciding that everyone else would be happier, he figured it was time to cut themselves off from the world.

Fuck this!

* * *

Issy sighed.

"Babe? What's up?"

"I just keep getting Dan's answerphone."

"Did you try texting him?"

"Yeah. He just said they were fine and just busy with school and stuff. Martin, I'm worried. We've seen neither hide nor hair of either of them for weeks. Something's wrong."

Her husband looked on, sharing her concern.

"Listen, I'm sure everything's fine. Maybe they really are just busy."

"Yeah. Maybe." She wasn't convinced. Something didn't feel right at all.

Martin excused himself to go to the toilet but instead sat on the top of the stairs and pulled out his phone.

Martin: We're genuinely worried, mate. I'm sure you're both just busy but Issy's getting upset by it all thinking something is wrong. You know what she's like! Can we just go for a coffee and a catch-up or something? It would make my life immeasurably better if we could? Text me."

* * *

He woke on Saturday morning with a dull feeling in his head that he put down to not drinking enough water the day before. Another reason to be annoyed at himself. With Max still in bed asleep, Dan lay back and let the world seep in around him as he breathed deeply, trying to ignore the intense longing he felt in his core.

It wasn't long until the reality of the day settled into focus in his mind. He'd avoided Issy and Martin for weeks, keeping them at arm's length in an attempt to hide his shame and guilt from them but now they had pushed the issue of coffee and Dan felt he was running out of excuses.

It was hard. He didn't have the energy to work through his own stuff, let alone relay it all back to them and mask his feelings from them. He knew he had to just see them though or it could create much larger problems down the road.

He just wished they'd picked somewhere different. Sanctuary, with its good coffee and convenient location, had been the obvious choice but Dan wanted to be anywhere else instead.

Not today.

Issy and Martin weren't the only people he had intentionally removed himself from of late. Sarah and her lovely little coffee shop had shared in the effects of his feelings and he'd purposely avoided working anywhere other than home. It all felt too much to process. If it wasn't for Max, Dan knew he would have shut himself away from the world completely and taken to sleeping his days away. The conflict between his heart and his head was exhausting both emotionally and physically.

But now he was going back, surrounded by people who cared, to the source of his weakness and failings. His hands shook slightly as he sat himself up in bed, thinking about it.

He hoped desperately that they'd be able to meet and catch up and everything would be fine, then slip out before it got too late. He couldn't see her. Not today. He screwed his eyes closed trying to rid her from his thoughts. Her gentle smile and beautiful face haunted him in ways he didn't realise were possible, breaking his resolve down little by little.

He'd intentionally taken a break from everything related to Laura Gray after the Valentine's Day debacle, in an effort to purge her from his head. It hadn't really helped but he felt that at least he'd made some kind of attempt for the better. Writing at home, had allowed him to avoid seeing her. He had even made an attempt to remove all of his social media from his phone, just so that he didn't have constant reminders of her face and could try to stay away from his fast-developing drug of choice.

But all it did was hurt. Laura was his disease and his cure.

Writing was becoming some form of painful solace, where he could keep pouring out his emotions while maintaining some flimsy grasp on his notion of her. Although it wasn't the type of work he was used to, the words were flowing and he was creating again.

But he knew it wasn't right. Dan was starting to feel like some obsessed stalker and he hated how the whole sorry situation was making him feel.

Feeling the need to move, he climbed out of bed and headed to the bathroom. Leaning against the sink with his eyes closed in an attempt to quieten his racing mind, he let the shower run. It was only when the small room was full of dense steam, did he realise that he'd lost himself to a hundred, fast-paced, potential conversations he'd have if he saw her later that day.

Removing the t-shirt and shorts he'd slept in, Dan stepped under the hot running water hoping that it would somehow wash away the pain he was feeling, loving a woman who barely knew he existed. For over ten minutes he stood under the water, staring mindlessly into the steam.

The reality of the situation was stark and cut like a knife. Even if Laura actually saw him for who he truly was, not just some random face in the crowd, but someone who wanted to love her until the end of her days, there was still so much that would make it impossible. She wasn't single. From the little he knew, she seemed happy in a long-term relationship with a guy who probably loved her just as much as he did. Dan didn't want to spoil that for her. He just wanted her to be happy. Even if she was single, she'd never go for a guy like him anyway. He was older, probably by more than ten years and while that maybe didn't seem like a lot, the difference in where they were in their individual lives was vast.

And then there was Max. Beautiful, bright and brilliant Max. Dan had no idea how he would ever explain it to his son. There were no clues on how to bring some random, woman home without the boy worrying that his mum was being forgotten and replaced. Max was his everything and the guilt of wanting happiness for himself felt just as hard as the guilt of having feelings for Laura.

Realising that he'd been in the shower for an overly long time, and unsure if he'd washed himself or not, he shut off the water, stepped out and wrapped a towel around his waist.

It felt like his head was in a million different places at once and the effort of keeping everything together felt like something Dan couldn't manage.

He went to get dressed and start his day, hoping that doing something, anything, would distract him for a while.

"You okay with me meeting Issy and Martin later Maxxy?" Dan had asked, as he sat with his son over ham and cheese sandwiches at lunchtime.

"Of course, Dad."

"Make sure you call me as soon as you want to come home from Dylan's okay?"

"We're just gonna play xBox and eat sweets. You take your time." He winked and it drew out a smile, something that had been distinctly lacking in his dad of late.

Dan busied himself with Max for the rest of the afternoon, trying not to stare at the walls as he waited for his time to leave. When it was the two of them he could easily keep himself busy.

It was only when the house was quiet, with Max at school

or in bed, that the loudness of his thoughts of Laura filled his head.

She'd never been interested in a guy like me; older and with a kid at home. Her life on the surface looked like a happy one so there was no reason for Dan to think that what he had and who he was, would ever be enough.

* * *

As he walked into town that afternoon, having dropped Max at his best friend Dylan's, he hoped he'd just be able to focus on spending time with Issy and Martin and not have to think about her, far less see her. He knew that was virtually impossible given the circumstances but he could hope, so foolishly, hope he did.

Arriving outside, he took a deep breath as he pushed open the door to Sanctuary, and praying silently to himself for everything to be okay, walked inside.

He hadn't realised how much he'd missed the smell of this place. The aroma of good coffee. Or that feeling of warm, welcoming air on his face. It was a good place to be. But it was also the source of so much emotion and pain.

He made a beeline straight for a table near the back of the shop where he could see his best friend was sitting.

"Hey."

Martin looked up from scrolling through his phone as Dan pulled out a chair. "There he is! We were getting worried we might never see you again." The joke was made gently but there was an underlying touch of seriousness.

"Sorry, I've been so busy lately. Just trying to be there for Max, you know?"

"You don't need to be sorry, mate. You both been okay?"

"We're fine. Where's Issy?"

"She'll be here in a bit. She's just popped into that charity shop over the road to do a bit of thrifting while we waited for you to get here. I think she wanted to keep herself busy."

Dan knew that feeling.

Martin smiled at his friend. He knew he'd been through hell over the last few years but in the past couple of months, he'd appeared to have been turning a corner. However, in the last few weeks for whatever reason, he seemed to have gone backwards and withdrawn back into a world where only he and Max existed.

"Dan, what is it? What's going on with you?"

Martin had been watching his best friend staring off into the distance for a moment and knew he was struggling to find the words for something.

He just couldn't do it anymore. It was eating him up inside and the simple act of holding it all together was becoming too much. It felt like he was slowly coming undone at the seams and he was having to fight harder to cover up the holes that were being created in his emotional stitches.

The pressure of the secret he was keeping was becoming so hard to manage that the stress of it was starting to wreak havoc in his life. He was painfully short on sleep, something he knew he needed to maintain with his condition. His body was in a constant state of aching and he hadn't been able to eat properly for weeks.

Dan knew it wasn't good and things were starting to reach

a point where he couldn't carry the burden any longer.

Realising that there was a level of safety in Martin's company, he decided it was time to open up a little. "It's the book."

"What about it?"

"Ah mate, this is really fucked up. I need you to promise me that you'll just listen, okay and try to understand. I hate myself for this."

"Okay, relax. Who do you think you're talking to? It's me. Tell me what's going on."

"So you remember me saying a while back that I was struggling to create a female character around Natalie?"

"Yeah. Issy said that you should base it on someone else instead, right?"

"Mhmm. To begin with I couldn't. I took a while to come around to the idea, as it felt like I was dishonouring our story and Natalie in some way. But then something happened. And I kinda let my writing take on a life of its own and now I don't know what to do."

"What is it?"

"There's a girl. I've been coming here to write, just to get me out of the house. She's here too, every so often and she sings here some nights."

Dan paused, struggling to put the feelings in his heart into words that would make sense to his friend but also importantly, to himself. Every thought he'd had in his soul about this had so far been introspective; he'd not vocalised it, not even to himself.

Martin waited. He knew that him speaking could derail this conversation with relative ease and he sensed, rightly so, that Dan needed to get this out.

"Fuck sake." Dan was fighting internally, trying to prevent himself saying something that was ready to burst out of him. He sat absentmindedly itching his fingers with the stress of it all.

"I think I'm in love with her."

"Wow okay...is she pretty?"

"She's beautiful. But it's more than that Martin."

"How d'you mean?"

"I feel drawn to her. I can't figure it out. It's like some weird cosmic pull that wants to draw me to her. A lot of the time I have no control over it. Everything about this is so messed up; she's at least ten years younger than me, she's in a pretty big relationship, and I'm a single dad. It's so fucked up, I know. But I can't help myself. I've tried to fight it; I really have but I can't seem to find a way out. It's like my heart knows even though my head is trying to be rational. The stupid thing is, she's not even my type, not really. Like she's beautiful but she's nothing like Natalie at all. I just can't seem to stop these feelings for her."

Martin let Dan's pause hang in the air between them for a moment, hoping that it would help his best friend collect his raging emotions.

"It's okay that you've fallen for someone. It's actually fucking good if you ask me. I can understand why you're fighting against it though and in no small part that's because of Natalie but that's normal, man. She was such a huge part of your life."

"I know. But I hate that I have these feelings for someone else. It's like I'm cheating on her.

"Fucking hell, mate. You're doing nothing of the sort. Come

on. It's been three years. You deserve to be happy again. It's time to move on."

"Yeah maybe."

"So what's this got to do with the book?"

Dan knew this bit would make him seem like some crazy obsessed stalker and he hated himself more for this part of it than the fact he was in love with someone already in a relationship.

"A few weeks ago, just after I saw this girl for the first time, I was trying to write and I couldn't. I wasn't able to figure the female character out and get her onto the page no matter what I tried. She was in my head and I was feeling horribly guilty that I was letting her be there. But I kept thinking about some lines of something and that ended up becoming a poem. I haven't been writing a story for a while really. It's all just poetry."

"Okay. Has it worked? From a writing point of view, I mean?"

"Erm, yeah. It's like the poems are made for her to be honest. It just seems to be flowing out of me. I can easily write now. But there's no book now. I'm just writing poems."

"So I'm not sure what the problem here is mate?"

"This doesn't sound weird to you?"

"No, not really. You've got feelings for her, sure she's in a relationship but truth be told unless you've met the guy, he could be a little twat for all you know. You're writing poetry and you've based it on her. I'm sure you're not the first writer to do that. Sounds to me like you're overthinking it to be honest."

Martin cringed at his own words. He knew Dan would definitely be overthinking it all, as that's what his brain did.

When they'd first found out from Natalie that he had been diagnosed, Issy had taken to the internet to find out as much as she could about his condition so they could help and support them.

Sitting next to Martin, night after night, she had shared nuggets of information that she found pertinent to Dan. Martin, therefore, knew full well that his best friend's brain was in a near-constant state of hyperactivity and to say to his face that he was overthinking something was really stupid and insensitive.

"Sorry, Dan. I worded that badly."

"Don't be. It's okay. I am overthinking it. I've gotten hyper-focused and I can't seem to step away from my feelings for her, thinking through all of the outcomes and possible conversations we could have. It's exhausting."

"So what are you gonna do?"

"I have no idea."

"To be honest Dan, I don't think this is something to hold onto yourself. I can see it's eating away at you."

As if on cue, Dan awkwardly rolled his head on his shoulders, his skin crawling.

"Talk to Issy. Or at least let me tell her." Martin knew that his wife would be a good ally for Dan to have on his side.

"I don't think I can, Martin."

"Feel the fear and do it anyway, right?"

Natalie's favourite saying when Dan's heart wouldn't let go of his head and he was full of doubt. He smiled to himself at the memory of her saying it to him for the first time at university as he submitted the first draft of his first ever story to his new agent.

"I wish it was that simple."

"Then look, let me talk to her. I won't tell her everything, but I'll introduce her to the idea at least and you can then talk to each other about it."

"Yeah okay. Thanks, Martin."

"Dan, she loves you. If you're in love, Issy will be happy for you and you need to remember how important you are to us. You're still going to be my best mate, Max is always going to be our godson and both of you will always be a part of our hearts."

Dan sighed.

What scared him more than the love he was fighting against, was Issy's possible reaction, upon finding out the truth. She had been a lynchpin over the last few years and had naturally become hugely protective of Max, so the idea of breaking her heart and the resulting rejection he would feel was too hard to imagine.

He felt like he was caught between a rock and a hard place, and the space between them was rapidly decreasing, crushing him at the core.

The shop door opened behind them and in walked Issy holding a blue plastic bag containing, as they both correctly assumed, her charity shop finds.

"Look mate, just don't say anything to her today. Please." Dan lowered his voice, the words coming out in a rush, desperate to avoid that particular conversation with Issy.

* * *

"Hey, you." Dan spoke as Issy approached, forcing a smile, as much to welcome her as to push the previous conversation with Martin from his mind.

"You doing okay?" She asked, as they hugged.

He thought about his answer but realised quickly that this time, a lie was kinder and easier than the truth.

"I'm fine."

Issy sat next to her husband, who lifted the carrier bag from her hand and set it on the floor next to his seat.

"Ordered you a hot chocolate, babe."

"You're a keeper you, aren't you?" She beamed at him whilst trying to read his expression for any hints of how his planned chat with Dan had gone.

"Stuck with me now, unfortunately, my dear."

Dan wished he had that. A close relationship which was as easy out in public as it was at home behind closed doors. Feeling awkward both in himself and with being around the loved-up couple, his eyes drifted away and fell on Sarah who was making her way over to them carrying two large hot chocolates and a big slab of fudge cake on a tray. He noted the two spoons resting together next to the dessert.

"The wandering writer returns." She placed the tray on the table and started to unload its contents.

"Hey, Sarah."

"You okay?"

"Yeah." Dan paused. "Look I'm sorry…"

Sarah cut him off. "Nope. Don't. There's no need. You can come and go from here as much as you like. You're always welcome, you know that. As long as you're okay, that's all I'm worried about."

"I'm okay, thanks. I have to say, to be honest, I didn't realise how much I've missed this place."

She smiled. It was good to see him. "The usual?"

"Yeah. Please. I'd like that."

Dan felt awkward but he knew Sarah wasn't putting on a pretence, she just wasn't that kind of person. Had she been pissed at him, she would have called a spade a spade and said so, regardless of the company he was with.

Tucking the tray under her arm Sarah looked at them all.

"We have live music on a little later. You guys should stay. She's good."

A prickle of anxiety snaked down Dan's chest.

"Ooo yay!" Issy looked delighted. "We'll stay. Thank you!"

Dan quickly moved the conversation onto Issy and Martin, asking how they had been. He needed to connect back to the familiar, rather than the clawing panic that was now growing in his head. He was terrified that his friends would see right through him. His anxiety was redlining just being there. The fewer people that knew about his problem the better, he didn't want to burden the whole world with what felt like an increasingly upsetting obsession. Telling Martin had been hard enough.

The memory of his past hung over him like a cloud and it jarred horribly with his growing feelings for Laura. Just thinking about another woman felt like he was cheating on her; he missed her so much. The irony that Natalie would have known exactly what to do in a situation like this wasn't lost on Dan.

Still, he just couldn't shake Laura from his thoughts, no matter how hard he tried.

As he got up to get the next round of drinks from the counter a little while later, he saw Laura moving across the busy shop, guitar case in hand.

It had been a few weeks since they'd been in the coffee shop at the same time and a few awkward messages online were all they'd exchanged. Dan had tried to engage her in some form of basic interaction in the hope that they could just talk but just when he thought the conversation was starting to flow, she cut it off and went quiet on him.

He could never seem to find a rhythm when he was around her. Everything just made him feel like a self-conscious, sullen teenager.

She looked at him across the crowded room.

While she probably hadn't intended to, Dan felt Laura glaring at him, burning holes into his soul as he stood before her. As she did, he couldn't find the usual weak smile he gave her whenever she would look his way and instead panicked.

For a heartbeat, he wondered if she actually hadn't seen him at all and was just looking in his general direction but he knew in his heart that wasn't true. It was him that Laura was staring down.

Maybe she knew? Maybe she'd figured it out and realised that he'd purposely pulled away. Maybe she just couldn't stand the sight of him?

Doubt swirled in his head as the brief moment of eye contact upended his world. *Fuck.* Dan averted his gaze to his phone and busied himself with that as Laura walked away.

Watching her perform that afternoon was a slow drawn-out torture, with Martin throwing him sympathetic questioning glances throughout the entire set. She only played a handful of songs and as usual, she sang like an angel, however he felt every kind of awful. The smile he had worn in recent months, since first hearing her sing, was gone. It felt too hard to enjoy it now, the nagging feelings in his heart clouding his senses; everything just felt muddled. He hated it. He wanted to be cheering her on and bathing in the experience, but he couldn't bring himself to do it.

The last few weeks had felt like a one-sided breakup that she knew nothing about, where all the hurt was piled solely on Dan.

He just wanted her to see him for who he really was and help take the pain away. But telling her would potentially break her world apart and the last thing he wanted to do was to steal any happiness from her.

So he did the only thing he could think of to do. He swallowed the hurt and the darkness down, burying it deep and used it to help him tap the vein of writing he'd found for the first time since losing Natalie from his life.

When the torture was over and Laura had hopped down from her stool and gone to talk to her own friends, including someone who Dan recognised as her fiancé, Issy announced it was time for them to go.

"Well, that was bloody lovely!"

"Yeah." Dan didn't know what else to say.

"Right. I need to put some dinner in this one," she jerked her head towards her husband sitting quietly next to her, "and I promised him we could have pizza tonight. I swear some days it's like having a 40-something-year-old Max living in my house." She laughed at her own joke.

As they said goodbye, Martin looked knowingly into Dan's eyes. Issy moved away towards the door and Martin pulled his friend close as he passed.

"It'll be alright, mate. I promise. I'll talk to her."

Sarah stood at the end of the counter sorting sugar into dispensers as Dan returned from the toilet before heading off.

"You okay?"

"I'm fine, Sarah."

"You look anything but."

"I said I'm fine."

"How's the writing?" Sarah asked, tightening the lid on a container of Demerara sugar.

"Yeah it's getting there I think. It's hard to know if it's any good because it's so far removed from what I'm used to writing. I'm just going on feel right now."

"The poems you've already let me read are beautiful, Dan. Seriously."

"Thanks."

Just thinking about writing made him want to hide, such was the fragility of his work recently. It was as if he was trying to catch smoke; each wisp escaping his grasp every time he reached out a hand.

"Anyway, I should get going. I need to pick Max up. Hopefully, catch you soon."

"Dan?"

He looked up as she spoke.

"It'll be okay, you know? I know it doesn't feel like it right now, but it will. Keep going."

He responded to her words with a brief smile and made his way out onto the street.

Walking away, he really wished he could talk to Natalie. She always knew what to do in social situations, something his muddled-up neurodivergent brain often couldn't cope with.

Deciding that he needed a bit more time, he turned off down a side street and headed away from the high street. He sent a text to Dylan's parents saying he was on his way but he just needed to do something en route.

* * *

III

Part Three

Part Three

With the winter sun low in the sky, he looked over to where Natalie lay, near the cherry blossom tree and felt so heavy he could have easily sunk into the ground where he stood by the large iron gates that lead into the cemetery.

Dan slowly walked towards her headstone, listening to the birds going about their mindful business. Every step brought him closer to where she lay and simultaneously tightened the grip on his chest. Nearing her grave he saw cherry blossoms scattered peacefully over her, blown down by the breeze from overhanging branches.

"Hey, you," he said looking at her name carved into the marble.

The first few times he'd done this after she died he felt stupid, as though he was talking to himself and was scared that people would think he was crazy. Those fears were long gone now, replaced by a familiar sense of closeness.

"I miss you."

The tears stuck in his throat along with the words he wanted to say but couldn't. Shame for holding feelings for another

159

woman in his heart caused Dan to avert his eyes from her and look out down the hill over the town and for a moment he lost himself.

"It's okay, you know?"

"Natalie?" Dan whipped around and saw her sitting on the nearby bench that he'd bought, chosen with Max as a gift to the cemetery, so they could sit together and be near her when the longing got too much.

She smiled at him.

"Don't worry, you're not losing the plot. I'm just a figment of that big, beautiful brain of yours. But for now, I'm as real as it's going to get."

Dan's heart ached for her to be real, just for one last moment, to be with her, to hold her hand and tell her he loved her. It was the one regret he held, that he hadn't told her before she left the house that day.

"Natalie."

"Your heart looks heavy Dan; like you're carrying too much. Maybe you should let some of it go."

Intuitively he knew what she was talking about; it was his subconscious after all.

"I can't. I'm scared."

"Scared of what?"

"That if I let go, you'll be gone forever."

"Baby, I won't ever go. But that doesn't mean you can't be happy again."

"I don't know if I can."

"You remember what I used to say? About how the universe brings people into our lives for a reason."

"Yeah. I do. But the universe takes them away too, doesn't

it? It took you away."

"Dan, you need to let go of that bitterness. It's eating you up every day. What happened to me was an accident but maybe Laura coming into your life was not."

* * *

That fateful day, they'd spent a lazy Sunday morning at home; Dan dragging down the king-sized duvet from their bed for the three of them to snuggle under and watch cartoons. While Max had laid across his mum, as happy as any seven-year-old boy could ever be, Dan had sipped coffee and made mental notes for a poem he was going to write to his wife when they eventually got off of the sofa and he could get a pen. Just seeing them both sitting there gave him enough inspiration for a lifetime; back then finding words was that easy.

Following their fight the day before, things had gone tentatively back to normal. After a few hours of ranting with Issy, Natalie had calmed down and seen the truth in her husband's words.

They'd decided on waking, that a relaxed family day was in order.

"Right. Who fancies bagels?" She had asked, as one cartoon came to an end. "Babe, do we have any left over from yesterday?"

"Yeah, there's a couple left in the bread bin. But I don't think we have any cream cheese."

A few minutes later, after checking the fridge, she returned pulling on her coat.

"Nope, we're out of cream cheese. I'll nip to the shop and

get some."

"I'll go, baby." Ever the gentleman, Dan hadn't wanted her to leave the house unless she absolutely had to.

"No, it's fine. Got my coat on now." She'd smiled, giving them both upside-down kisses from behind the sofa. "Want anything?" She'd asked Dan as he'd looked up at her.

"No, just a kiss and you coming back."

Natalie had smiled and kissed him again. And then left to go to the shop.

The next time either Dan or Max saw her, she was in a hospital bed barely clinging on to life, surrounded by the wires and beeps of a life support system working overtime to keep her alive.

The taxi that had hit her as she'd crossed the street, had been going at least ten miles over the speed limit and the driver had been checking a text message instead of paying attention to the road. He'd ploughed straight into the unsuspecting woman in the big coat, who was on the pedestrian crossing, just trying to make her way home. As Dan had rushed to the hospital with a distraught Max in the passenger seat, he'd had to be diverted around the high street because of the accident. A glimpse past the barriers as he drove by revealed an upturned shopping bag on the tarmac, cream cheese and goodies scattered and strewn across the road, the shops decked out in all their festive fare.

To this day, he'd never been able to look at the twinkle of Christmas lights in the same way. Memories of that road bathed in the luminescence of Christmas and emergency vehicles simply too much to bear.

By the following morning, the doctors had done all they could for Natalie Muir. Her body was just too badly broken and her head injury too severe for her to survive.

She died at 9:02 on a cold Monday morning. Max should have been starting a school day and listening for his name in the register, but had instead been holding his mum's hand while saying goodbye, something no seven-year-old should ever have to do.

All Dan could do was watch in tears, his wife's little silver locket clasped in his hands. She loved that locket, which contained pictures of both him and Max. Now it sat heavy in his fingers, a coldness to the touch that he'd never felt before.

His heart broke for the loss of his wife and for what his son was having to go through. After a few minutes, Max pulled away and walked around to hug his dad. It felt like neither of them ever wanted to let go as they both sobbed openly.

"It's just you and me now, Maxxy. I've got you. I promise."

* * *

Hearing Natalie say Laura's name, even though it was only in his head, was harder than anything he'd ever heard her say before. It cut through his soul like a knife.

"That's her name, Dan. Don't be afraid of me saying it. She's come into your life for a reason, but if you keep fighting against it then you'll never learn what that reason is."

"Natalie, I can't."

"You need to trust me. Everything in life is about choices. The universe offers you an option and you pick something and move forward before being given the next choice. You

163

picked writing when the mood took you, when you could have easily pushed the thought aside and done something else. You asked me out that night at uni when you could have picked anyone else in the Students Union. You chose me. That's how life works."

Dan understood this. It was something they had discussed at length many times.

"And now the universe is giving you some new things to choose from: to be happy and let Laura be your muse or to stay living in sadness and fear. We don't always realise how our cosmic puzzle will come together; so for me, please, let the pieces fall where they may. It'll be okay."

"I feel like I'm cheating on your memory just thinking about her."

"I've been gone for three years, Dan. If we'd divorced you'd be seeing someone else by now, this is no different. We didn't break up by choice, this was forced on us. But now you do have a choice. I want you to be happy. I want you to be contented. I want Max to have a happy life."

"I'm trying, I really am."

"Oh, I know you are. I see it. You've always been a wonderful father but the journey you've had to take is one nobody should have to go on. Max is our wonderful boy and he loves you dearly but he can see the turmoil you're keeping in your head."

"He misses you. We both do."

Natalie just smiled back at Dan. She seemed so real it was as though he could just walk over and gather her up in his arms and she'd hold him tight like she always did.

"It'll be okay, I promise. Stop fighting it."

Dan took a deep breath and looked back out over the graves and the horizon below the hill, trying to compose himself. When he turned back to tell her he'd try, she was gone and he just stared hollowly at the empty bench. Tears spilled down his face.

Her words echoed in the vast emptiness he'd felt inside ever since the day she was taken away from him.

"Your heart looks heavy Dan; like you're carrying too much. Maybe you should let some of it go."

Standing in front of her white marble headstone, Dan placed his hand on top of it and waited for the tears falling onto the dirt at his feet to subside. He knew he needed to finally let her go and that she had only ever wanted him to be happy but it wasn't an easy thing to do.

But he also understood that letting her go didn't mean she'd be gone, her spirit lived on in their brilliant son and he was grateful for that every day.

He gently squeezed the headstone as he leaned down and kissed it. It was time to let go.

* * *

Issy took a deep breath, which was for as much Dan's benefit as it was for hers. She wanted him to see that she was calm and relaxed so he didn't pick up on any of her nervous energy as they sat on one of her big living room sofas. When Martin had told her everything the night before, she'd been relieved of sorts, knowing that Dan was finally ready to take that final step and move his life on.

"Look I know this will be hard but we need to talk about things. For your sake. Please don't be mad at Martin either; he tried so hard to not tell me everything."

He looked away ashamed. Aside from Max, this was going to be one of the hardest conversations he would need to have.

"Issy, I'm so sorry."

"You have nothing to be sorry for." She reached over and took his hand in hers.

"I do. I feel awful about this."

"Dan, for Christ's sake! You've fallen in love with someone. That's wonderful. I'm very happy for you. We're very happy for you."

"Issy..."

He felt like she was just trying to put on a brave face and really deep down she hated him, such was how his brain worked.

"It's time you moved on Dan. It's okay."

Just the notion of it felt uncomfortable. Trying to hold it all together, he could feel his hands shaking.

"It's not that easy is it though? She's all I've ever really known."

"Dan, she'd want you to be happy. I want you to be happy. It's time for you to move on."

"But it's your sister that's dead and buried in the ground that I'd be moving on from!"

* * *

Natalie had been sitting with two friends the first time he'd seen her. Her brown hair tied up in a high ponytail, she had smiled at him as he looked at her across the crowded students' union bar.

Not usually one for public displays, Dan had tried to be brave, buoyed on by a few too many Snakebite and Blacks. He'd walked over to her table and while she was mid-conversation with her friends had introduced himself.

"Hi, I'm erm, Dan."

Her friends had looked up at him like he'd lost the plot but Natalie had smiled.

"Hi, erm Dan. I'm Natalie."

"Hi."

"Hi."

The pause in conversation now he'd introduced himself grew with each protracted, awkward moment and her friends, sensing that they didn't need to be present for whatever this was, got up and left.

"Would you like to join me?" She'd asked.

Dan had been desperately trying to play it cool, something that didn't come naturally to him, even after a few drinks. She was gorgeous. Brown hair, dark eyes and a friendly face that he wanted to stare at all evening. Realising that he hadn't actually answered, he quickly sat, promptly spilling a bit of his pint on the table as he clumsily took his seat.

That first night they'd talked as the atmosphere had quietened around them until the bar closed at 1 am.

Natalie had told him that she was studying to be a nurse at the local hospital and was taking her classes at the university. It wasn't what she was passionate about but she liked to help people so had figured after school that nursing would be a good career to get into. She really wanted a family and to spend her days being a mum; the only thing she truly wanted in life.

After a few exposing questions, Dan had explained that he was taking an English degree and wanted to be a writer but was getting increasingly frustrated having to attend classes. He just wanted the freedom to write. She had listened with intent interest as he'd talked passionately about story ideas he'd had, with a leaning towards fantasy fiction.

"So can I call you sometime?" Dan had asked, as he walked her back to her uni accommodation, sober now having stopped drinking while they'd talked the night away.

"Yeah, go on then or it'll make falling in love really hard for us, won't it?"

He smiled. Natalie had a lovely soft way about her that felt comforting, something he had always struggled to find in most other people.

"You think we're going to fall in love?"

"Am I not falling in love material, Dan?"

He blushed but he could tell she was only teasing him.

"I think you're the most beautiful girl on campus."

"Then I suggest we swap numbers, so this love story can begin to write itself. Unless you think you have a better story to work on?"

They swapped numbers, each inputting their own into the other's phone, grinning like children sharing a private joke and when that was done Dan had taken her hand. Natalie looked down.

"That feels nice." Nice wasn't the word she wanted to use but she could tell he would probably struggle with the idea of her saying it felt perfect. He seemed fragile under the surface, in a way that made her curious.

"Yeah, it does."

"Dan, you have a thoughtful look on your face. Care to share?"

"Oh, I was just wondering if kissing you would feel as nice, that's all."

"Only one way to find out I guess."

* * *

Issy took a moment. She remembered how her little sister had called her, brimming over with excitement the following morning, gushing about the cute English student she'd met. Dan had meant everything to her Natalie and everyone could tell he was the perfect man for her, even if their mother didn't agree.

The uncomfortable comment drifted slowly away from them like smoke from an old man with a 50-a-day habit. Neither spoke till the air had cleared.

"Sorry."

Issy missed her sister terribly. While they'd bickered a lot growing up, as hormonal teenage girls often do, they'd become the best of friends in the time since they had both left home and started their own lives.

Having to stand alongside her brother-in-law and nephew as they buried her was something she never anticipated. But she knew she needed to step up for them both and had helped to fill the void that had opened up in their lives; she'd become

Dan's rock through the hard times and now she knew it was about time for a new start.

"Look, it's okay. I know this is hard. I know a lot of the angst you're fighting right now isn't about me or Max or even Natalie but about the guilt you feel. But I mean what I say, Dan, she'd want you to move on."

"Oh she does," Dan spoke quietly, realising how ridiculous the admission sounded.

When Issy looked at him sceptically, he went on to explain how he'd gone to the cemetery and spoken to his dead wife as clearly as he was speaking to her now. Finishing, clearly embarrassed, he glanced over to see her smiling at him.

"Sounds like something my sister would do. Come back just to tell you to get on with it."

He half laughed through his nose. "Yeah. She was always one to let me know in her own inimitable way that I needed to crack on with things."

Issy squeezed his hand gently. "It'll be alright, Dan."

"I hope so."

"But you need to tell Max."

"Yeah, I know. I'm going to as soon as I can, I just need to work out what I want to say. I don't want to break his heart."

"You won't. That boy is brilliant and bright. He might be upset to begin with, this is stuff that he's never had to deal with before but if you take your time he'll understand."

"I know. Just scary isn't it?"

"He'll be fine. You'll see. Just give him time."

Dan nodded.

"So this Laura, she's the singer from yesterday? With the white guitar?"

"Mhmm."

Issy nodded. She didn't really want to get drawn into a conversation about her just yet but she wanted Dan to know that she was aware.

"Talk to Max. Then you can figure out what, if anything, happens next."

"Yeah. Thanks, Issy. I'm sorry I didn't say anything sooner."

"Don't be silly, it's fine." She pulled him into a hug and felt him relax.

They heard the front door open as Martin returned with a mud-covered Max, who was wearing the biggest smile ever. When Issy looked at them both in horror, her nephew explained proudly.

"We were practising tackling in the park!"

"You're covered!" Dan said, shaking his head at his son, incredulous.

"I know! Good isn't it?!"

* * *

Dan reached for his phone. 3.10 am. He groaned and unlocked the screen. It wasn't uncommon for his condition to bring on bouts of sticky insomnia where everything seemed to cling to his skin, so he knew he was in for yet another night of wakefulness.

In the first few days and weeks afterwards, whenever these nights would occur, he would reach for Natalie, his eyes not fully open, his arms instinctively seeking her warmth. Those dark, terrible days when time lost all meaning seemed to drag

171

on and on while simultaneously blurring into one. When the cold reality of her absence would hit, the empty space next to him was almost too much to bear. Some nights it felt like losing her all over again.

Lying in the dark he scrolled through his emails, deleting the offers of cheap pizza from places he never went and discount-price flights to places he didn't want to go. When there was nothing else to scroll through, he took to skimming down his suggested videos on YouTube for a while, not really wanting to watch anything but the colours and lights from his phone acting as a distraction from the loneliness of his bed.

After a few minutes of idly flicking his thumb up the screen, a video caught his eye and he stopped to focus on the title. *TedTalk: The Realities of Grief.*

His heart felt heavy reading the words. This was one of those things that seemed like a good idea in the moment but he knew would probably tear open old wounds that weren't even close to fully healed. The impulsive and impetuous decision-making that had played out many times throughout his life seemed to compel him to press play.

The video opened on a middle-aged woman with blonde hair and glasses, standing on a darkened stage with the words TEDx Brighton written across the back in giant red block letters.

When she spoke quietly through his phone speaker, Dan tried hard to focus on her words.

"There is no wrong way to grieve. There is no time limit. There are no rules. Grief is not linear. It is not regulated and it doesn't

care who you are or how over it you think you might be. It is as unique as your fingerprints and will be with you eternally. Once grief arrives, it stays forever. Sometimes it's a boulder, tied to your waist and the effort needed to drag it around with you is immense. Other days it's a tiny, storm-weathered pebble you carry in your pocket, slipping your hand in every so often and rolling it around in your fingers, just to remind yourself that you are still alive".

As he watched and listened, Dan started reading comments left by other viewers who felt the desire to share their stories in the two years since the video had been uploaded. Some of them explained who they were grieving for. Others emptied their hearts about how grief imprinted on their lives.

His breathing shallowed and his eyes felt wet with unshed tears as he took in the sea of words and realised he wasn't alone. While he'd lived this nightmare, he could see that others had gone through their own personal sorrows and had felt the same things as him. His chest was tight as he identified with the emotions being discussed.

He started typing without a clear idea of what he wanted to say. He just needed an outlet.

Dan Muir: 3:20am.

Grief does not define me. Yes, it's changed me but it's not who I am. It's a reminder of who I have lost but also of who I had for a time and how lucky I was to share my life with her.

Grief is the price we pay for love. It's unrelenting and unforgiving and even on the days I think it has gone, it's always there. Sometimes quietly, sometimes roaring. Some days a challenge and some days a comfort.

Grief is about the past we shared together but also about my future. All the things we won't get to do as a family. All the things she will miss out on because she's no longer part of our family.

Grief is feeling empty and full at the same time; desperate for the grief to end but terrified because when it does, what will I be left with?

His tears fell freely as he turned off his phone; unable and unwilling to continue watching.

With the light of his phone now gone, he could see the glimmers of sunrise through the curtains. He'd made it through another lonely night in the dark and been given the gift of another day.

* * *

He sat, drawing in ragged breaths as he heard his dad's footsteps approaching.

"This isn't about my mum!"

Dan couldn't breathe. He'd come downstairs, the weight of expectation of telling Max about Laura sitting heavy on his chest. The boy deserved to know now and the longer he left it before telling him, the worse this was all going to feel.

But walking down the stairs, the choice of timing was taken away from him; he had found his son sobbing his heart out on the sofa, holding a piece of paper.

"Max? What's the matter? What are you doing up so early?"

"This isn't about my mum!"

174

He was holding a piece of notepaper in his small trembling hand, which his dad recognised as something he'd used to scribble down a recent poem about Laura.

Time slowed as he thought through all the permutations of what he could now say and do. At ten years old, his son was a very emotionally bright boy. There was no sense in lying to him or wrapping him up in the comfort of false truths just to stop his tears and Dan knew it.

"Maxxy, we need to talk."

* * *

Max had sat in front of the headstone, tears filling his eyes as the pain of the first few weeks simmered on the surface. While the rawness of her death had begun to fade, his intense longing to see his mum and to hug her again had been growing with each day. He missed her deeply.

Sitting a few feet away, Dan had listened to his son talking to the inanimate white marble headstone about the funeral the day before. He'd been filled with pride for his son, who even while suffering with the effects of grief, was able to understand that he had to accept the situation and that although his mum was now gone, that didn't mean she would need to be forgotten. On the other hand, Dan felt like he himself had been struggling to hold it all together. He had just wanted one more chance to talk to her, to hold her, to kiss her.

Everything had been snatched away in an instant and he felt that he'd left so much unsaid and so much undone that the heaviness of those wasted moments seemed to enclose him in his heartache.

He had rubbed his thumb gently over the locket he held in his palm as he had watched Max wiping his tears away on his sleeve. She was really gone and there was nothing he could do to bring her back. The hurt had been more intense than anything he'd ever experienced.

What made the whole thing worse was that neither of them had caused this. It wasn't as if either of them had walked out on the other; they'd loved each other with every breath until she'd taken her last and Dan just wanted to trade places with her. Max would be better off with his mum around, he knew that but they weren't the cards they'd been dealt.

He had been brought back to the present, as Max stood and walked over to him.

"You okay buddy?"

"No." Tears still glistened on the boy's cheeks. "I miss her, Dad."

He drew his son into a hug and kissed the top of his head. "I miss her too. But we can come back here as often as you need, okay? If you want to come and see her and talk to her, she's right here."

"I still love her."

"I do too, Maxxy and I always will. She's never going to be forgotten because we'll both always love her."

They had cried together as the wind whistled gently through the trees and tombstones that sat on the hillside. Dan was very grateful that her final resting place had been somewhere with such a beautiful view; she'd always loved simple things like that.

* * *

"You said you'd always love my mum! This isn't always! You said you'd never forget her!"

Max was raging against emotions he was too young to under-stand and too immature to control.

"Max, I haven't forgotten about Mum I promise and I haven't stopped loving her, but..."

Dan couldn't find the words to take his son's pain away and make it all make sense. Max stared back at his dad, tears streaming down his anguished face.

"Mate, come sit with me." He moved himself to the edge of the sofa and waited for the boy to join him. "Please?"

Eventually, an emotionally exhausted Max slumped onto the sofa; the guilty shred of evidence still clutched firmly in his hand.

"I haven't forgotten about her. And I haven't and won't stop loving her. That's a promise."

His son looked at him angrily.

"But...it's time for me to move on. I didn't plan for this. It's just happened. It's really hard Max because I don't understand why I feel like this but I know that what my heart is telling me is right. No one is ever going to replace your mum. I promise."

Dan slid along the sofa closer to his son. Inch by inch trying to reclaim the void that had opened up between them. Max looked at him warily.

"I've been struggling to write the story I told you I was working on. It's like it just didn't want to come out of me, but this poem? And the others like it, have flowed out of me without an issue and that's because of Laura."

Max was trembling as he sniffed tears away.

"If I tell her how I feel, and I still haven't fully decided that I will yet, and if she comes into our life, she is not going to replace your mum. Situations like this are really hard and it won't be easy for anyone but I promise, you will always be my first priority. Max, please."

The terror of losing his relationship with his son was crippling. The realisation that the cliche of nothing else matters rang truer to him, sitting with Max, than anything else in his life. Literally, nothing was more important than the boy sitting next to him.

A wave of doubt rushed through him as he wondered if all of this with Laura was worth it, if it meant that his son would hate him as a result.

"I miss her, Dad." The boy wept with the paper still in his hands, so much so that his little body shook. Instinctively Dan pulled him into his arms and was relieved when his son didn't resist.

"I miss her too, Maxxy. I do. I'm so sorry I didn't tell you any of this."

"I knew this was going to happen one day but it's really scary."

"How did you know?"

"Some of the kids in my class said one day I'd get a new mum."

"Max. That's not going to happen. Firstly, I don't want you to have a new mum. But second, no will can ever replace your beautiful, brilliant mum in your heart I promise. She loved you so much."

His son started to relax against him.

"Honestly Maxxy, if you don't want me to do this, I won't. You are singularly the most important thing in my life. I'd like to find love again because I know it's what my heart needs but I won't if it's too hard for you."

He hated putting that much responsibility on his son's shoulders but the words had come out without much consideration.

The ten-year-old paused for a moment.

While the other kids in his class had said he'd get a new mum one day, he knew that wasn't really going to happen but he had realised that maybe his dad might get a new girlfriend at some point. The idea of an evil stepmum, locking him in his room and making him sweep the floors flashed in his head.

"Is she nice?" He quietly asked.

"I think so mate. She seems like a very gentle, lovely person. Why do you ask?"

"I don't want to be like Cinderella."

Dan smiled to himself and pulled his son back against the sofa with him.

"That's never going to happen, buddy. I promise."

They sat there for over an hour, Dan answering every question Max had and both of them sharing their precious memories of Natalie. The chasm that had grown between them slowly vanished and by breakfast time, it was like it had never existed.

As Max stood up to go to the kitchen, he turned back to his dad.

"So there are more poems like this? He handed over the

crumpled, tear-stained piece of paper.

Dan took it and sighed.

"Yeah, there are. But I don't really know what to do with them, to be honest. I'm hoping that soon I'll be able to go back and write this book once they're all out of me."

"Maybe they're meant to be the book."

He looked inquisitively at his son.

"What do you mean, mate?"

"Well, what if the book you want to write is actually a book of poems?"

Max could see Dan starting to zone out, thinking about his suggestion.

"Come on, Dad," he pulled him up by the hand. "You make your coffee. I'll get us some cereal."

* * *

Tearing the last page out of his notebook, he added it to the assortment of scattered poems that now lay on the table in front of him.

All in all, he had almost thirty short poems about Laura and how he felt about her and they were staring back up at him, making him feel like he was on the cusp of something special. He'd had this feeling before in the past.

Max's suggestion of creating a book of poetry had sparked something in him and he'd let the notion of it simmer in him all day until finally, the boy's bedtime had come. Once back downstairs, having tucked his son in for the night, Dan had set to work in earnest.

Clearing the dining table, he'd started tearing pages of poems from his notebook, something that horrified him but he knew it was a necessary evil for the idea in his hyperactive mind. For the poems he had stored digitally on his phone and laptop, he quickly scrawled them out onto blank pages and added them to the ever-growing pile. And then, within twenty minutes he had a jumble of prose in front of him.

As he stared at the pile, his head throbbed. This kind of disorganisation and uncertainty was something he hated and would usually run from. Not today, something inside him was telling Dan this was the way forward.

For hour upon hour, he shuffled the pieces of paper around trying to find an order and some semblance of how these poems were all meant to fit together. When the kitchen clock chimed midnight, he was sitting in his hoodie with the hood pulled up over his head, resting his chin on his hands at the table, lost in thought.

What if she reads these and knows instantly it's me and hates me for it? What if the outpouring of my heart onto the page made no difference at all and she still doesn't see me? What if having this all out of my head and heart means her spell on me is gone and again I will be left with nothing; alone in the world except for Max?

He thought back to seeing Natalie in the graveyard. *Be happy and let Laura be your muse.* As messed up as this seemed, sitting at the family dining table, Dan felt that this was the only way available to him now. Something in the universe was calling him to this and there had to be a reason for that; he just knew it.

Standing, he snapped a picture of the poems on his phone before gathering them up and placing them back into his now-ruined notebook. Even though he knew he'd probably not manage it, sleep felt like the sensible thing to attempt right now, even with his brain going a million miles an hour.

The following morning, outside the school gates, Max looked up at his dad.

"So are you gonna do it?"

"I'm thinking about it. Just got to work out how."

"I believe in you, Dad."

"Thanks, mate. Feels a bit scary, to be honest."

"Feel the fear and do it anyway, right?"

The ten-year-old smiled and reached up to kiss his dad before bouncing happily into school, Dan watching him go, full of pride and emotion.

"You okay, Dan?"

He focused his attention on Max's class teacher, now standing in front of him.

"Yeah, just Max hitting me in the feels first thing in the morning."

"How's he doing? I know this time of year can be difficult with it being close to his mum's anniversary."

"Yeah, he's okay. We're going through some stuff at the moment so maybe keep an eye on him for me please?"

"Of course, Dan. No worries."

Walking away from school, he felt relieved that someone there would be looking out for Max. While everything seemed fine after the talk about Laura the day before, he worried that his son would still be emotionally sensitive to it and although he was a bright kid, Dan knew the next few days might be turbulent.

Arriving at Sanctuary a short walk later; he felt relief at being able to work and think in a comforting environment that reminded him of her, while safe in the knowledge that any awkward interaction wouldn't happen as it was a Monday and she wasn't likely to be there.

"Morning, Dan. How are you feeling today?" Sarah smiled from across the counter. He seemed different this morning. As though an unknown weight had lifted from his shoulders and he was able to hold his head higher.

"Better, thanks. How are you?"

"Ah, you know. Same old, same old." She shrugged and smiled.

He grinned back, happy to see her in less emotionally heavy circumstances than their last encounter.

"Usual?"

"Please, yeah. And maybe some toast too?"

"Sure thing. I'll bring it over."

Watching him walk away, she noticed that he forwent his usual spot against the wall and opted for a bigger table.

Feeling nervous, he unpacked his things. While he knew the larger workspace was needed, he couldn't help feeling adrift at it, anxious about its spaciousness. But he needed the extra room today to move his bits of paper around.

Usually, he'd try to hide things like this away from prying eyes, but today he didn't seem to care; all that mattered was figuring this out.

"One coffee and two rounds of toast. Got enough room?" Sarah was curious about this step away from his normal routine.

"Yeah. Need the extra space today."

"May I ask why, or are you not sharing?"

"Erm. Max gave me an idea. About the poems. And the story I was meant to write. So I need the space to work on it. There's a lot of pages. I need to try and figure it out. I can't seem to get it straight. No matter what I do. But I need it out of my head." He was talking at pace, his mouth trying to keep up with his hyperactive mind.

"Dan, take a breath." She sat down calmly opposite him at the table.

Stopping for a second, he did as she suggested and everything seemed to slow down for a moment.

"Sorry. Max has given me an idea. Rather than me trying to force a story from my head that obviously doesn't want to come out yet; he suggested that I take the poems I have and start to make a book out of them."

"Oh, that's a good idea!"

"Yeah, it is! He suggested that the poems could become the book I'm trying to write; rather than the story I originally had in mind."

"So why the extra space today?"

Dan pulled open his notebook to show her the torn pages.

"Jesus! How many are there?"

He smiled proudly. "About thirty in total. But the final number might change yet; it's just everything I have at the moment. A bit like a band having a bunch of songs they need to whittle down to the final album." His thoughts slipped casually to Laura and her guitar.

"Yeah, that makes sense. Okay. So what do you need? Space and then just time to move it all around until it seems to fit?"

"Yeah, I think so."

"Right. Let me get out of your hair. I'll keep you topped up in caffeine, just wave if you need me."

"Thanks, Sarah."

As she walked away she marvelled at how much Dan had written. He'd only shared a few of his poems with her over the past few weeks but she'd clearly not realised the volume of work he had already created. She felt an exciting buzz in her belly for what she was about to witness.

He worked tirelessly for hours, shuffling scraps of his heart around the table, reorganising and reordering until it was nearly time to collect Max from school.

Sitting back with a contented sigh he surveyed what he felt could be a final order.

"That sounds like the sigh of a man who's done a good day's work."

Dan looked up to see Sarah coming to collect his cold and empty coffee cup.

"Mhmm. Think I'm there with it. There's a few gaps I'd like to fill with poems I still want to write, but I think it's pretty much there. I think anyway. Now I need to figure out what I do next."

"Would your publisher be interested?"

"Nah, I don't think so. They've always just wanted more fantasy fiction out of me. This is very left field for me to pitch to them and I can't see them going for it. And truth be told; this feels too personal to shove in front of a publisher."

"Why don't you self-publish it?"

"Self-publish?" Dan hadn't previously had to consider that as a possibility.

"Yeah. There's plenty of ways to do it. A few of the people who sell their books here self-publish." She waved to the small bookshelf at the back of the shop full of crafters and makers' wares.

"Huh. I didn't think about self-publishing."

He quickly jotted something in his notebook as a reminder and then started to pack up.

"Thanks, Sarah. You've been a big help today."

"Ah, I didn't do anything but feed you."

Dan smiled. *What else was there in the world?*

"Well, it helped a lot!" He smiled.

As he left to pick up his son in the afternoon sunshine, Dan felt like he was lighter for the first time since Natalie's death; as if all of the hurt and loss he was carrying had been let go and he could exist again.

* * *

Dan dropped the carrier bag on the counter in front of Sarah and smiled awkwardly at her.

"So, there's five in here. Not expecting them to sell quickly for you but if you run out just let me know and I can drop some by."

"Thanks, Dan! Honestly, even without your name on the front, it's still such an honour to have anything you've written on sale here in my little shop!"

She could see him becoming shy in front of her but she didn't care. Their easy relationship had risen out of a random coffee order and now she was able to call Dan Muir her friend.

"Stop it you. You'll make me blush."

"Suck it up, pal! I'm riding this little wave for a while."

Dan laughed. It was nice to feel valued as a writer again after so long. So much so that he was able to stand a little bit taller even with the constant storm of emotions that raged in his heart.

"And I got you a little something too. For letting me sit here and write. It means a lot and I wanted you to know that I didn't take it or you for granted."

He lifted the copy he'd been concealing below the counter on his side and handed it to her. Taking it from him reverently, she gazed at the gift in her hands. This was the first time she'd seen what he'd been sitting and working on for months; this was the actual book. It hardly seemed real.

"It's the first off the print run and I've signed it *Max Danielson* and even though the book is not in my name, you'll know it's from me and that's all that matters."

It was such a special gift that she could barely describe how much the simple gesture meant to her. "Dan, I don't know what to say."

He just shrugged.

"Sarah, this might be the last time I'm here for a while. Now the book is done, it's time for me to move on for a bit. I just wanted to say thanks and stuff. You have a lovely coffee shop and if I'm ever passing with Max we might pop in for a hot chocolate. If you need any more books, my number is on a card in the front of your copy."

She always knew that this was probably going to be the case after he'd told her his book of poetry was finished but she'd hoped she might be able to hang out with one of her writing heroes for a little while longer.

"Well, my door will always be open to you Dan, I'm going to miss you."

He smiled an awkward smile and nodded slightly as if he was unsure of the words to say in this social situation but Sarah took it as a good thing, she'd gotten used to his quirky little mannerisms whenever he visited.

"I'm gonna just stay for a bit and maybe listen to the music and then I'll get going."

"Decaf? It's past 3 pm now; I've learnt your rule."

"Please, yeah."

She smiled. "Go grab a seat and I'll bring it over."

* * *

Opening the cover of *Endlessly* a little while later, Sarah found the inscription inside that Dan had written for her.

"Thanks for everything."

She smiled to herself knowing she had a one-of-a-kind copy of something she could barely have imagined months earlier. She pulled out a plain white business card, printed with just a phone number. *If you need any more books, my number is on a card in the front of your copy.*

Looking across at Dan who was gently stirring a spoonful of sugar into his coffee, she wondered what twist of fate had brought her favourite writer into her coffee shop all those months ago. For a moment her mind wandered, the idea that it was something as simple as him just needing a place to write felt pedestrian and oversimplified. There had to be something more compelling.

Shaking her head clear, *I read too many books*, she turned to the first page.

What she found there wasn't what she had expected at all. She'd assumed that the first page would be a poem, maybe one of the ones he'd already shown her but she was wrong. It was much more intriguing than that.

On the first page, Dan had written something entitled, *The Explanation*. Curiously she read on.

This collection of poems was never something I intended to write but came out of the broken pieces of my life.
For so long I've been drifting away from everything I knew, tail-spinning out of control and losing myself but when I finally found some gravity, it was you at the centre that I was orbiting around.
From the first time our eyes met, I've been lost in your smile and its effects on my heart have fuelled every word across these pages. So here, for you, I bare my soul; open and vulnerable in the hopes that one day you'll understand and see me for who I am.
I know like star-crossed lovers from a Shakespearean play, so much has the potential to keep our hearts apart in this reality, which is why throughout the lines that follow, I'm able to suspend disbelief. My heart is yours. And even if I have to love you from a distance for the rest of my life, I know I can, just to see you happy. Be happy. That's all I'll ever ask of you. That's all I need. And it's all I want.
I will love you always and these words I have written because of you will live on long after I am dust in the ground. And so everyone will know. I was here and you were loved.
Endlessly.

Sarah read it again. Her eyebrows furrowed. As Dan had shared snippets of poems with her over the last few weeks and months, she'd assumed that his words were being fuelled by the grief of losing his wife. While he seemed okay on the surface most of the time, she knew that the pain of her loss still weighed heavy on his heart.

But reading this explanation it was clear that he'd actually been inspired to write these heartbreaking lines of poetry by someone else. *But who?* Dan had never alluded to being interested in anyone. He'd come in, drink coffee, and write; occasionally looking out of the window or stopping for some casual conversation with her.

* * *

As the afternoon dragged on, Sarah leafed gently through *Endlessly*, occasionally looking up at the author sitting in the corner of her coffee shop and marvelling at how someone so quiet and awkward could have such a deep well of emotion tucked away inside him.

A little after 6 pm the shop door opened with a clatter.

"Sorry, Sarah!"

Laura bustled in looking stressed.

"Babe, it's okay. You're not late, you've got some time yet."

"Yeah, just wanted to be here a bit earlier, that's all but I got held up. Sorry. Don't want to be rushing in at the last minute."

"Honestly it's fine. You've got time. Take a minute. We can start a bit later than planned if we need to."

Sarah smiled at her friend to reassure her while keeping her thumb in between the pages of *Endlessly* on the counter. Laura looked down.

"What you reading?"

"Ah, just a poetry book." A part of her felt a bit guarded over the pages in her hand and she didn't want to give away their secrets just yet. Not wanting to get drawn into a conversation about it, she verbally nudged the singer along. "Go drop your stuff by the stage and I'll bring you a tea over."

Laura relaxed. "Thanks, babe."

During the lull in service during Laura's set, Sarah continued to devour Dan's poetry, getting herself lost in the effortlessness of his words which seemed to grab onto her heart and repeatedly twist and pull.

She knew that whoever his muse was, was one lucky woman. *Jesus to be loved like that,* she thought as she listened to Laura's beautiful solo rendition of *Watch Over You* By Alter Bridge.

* * *

Watching her zipping her guitar case back up, Dan felt like the time had come. After today, he could very easily never see her again and as much as he hated the idea of an uncomfortable social interaction, he knew he wanted one last opportunity to talk to her before fading away and just becoming one of her memories.

"Hey."

"Hi, how are you?"

"Yeah, I'm okay thanks." Maintaining eye contact felt painful and all he wanted to do was look away as every fibre

191

of his being screamed at him.

"That's good."

Why couldn't she just make conversation with him? It had always been so frustrating.

Dan awkwardly looked away for a moment and then resolved to say what he felt he had to.

"I just wanted to say I've enjoyed watching you play over these past few months. I'm probably not going to be around for a while now so I just wanted to say thanks, I guess."

"Aww thanks, Dan. I hope everything's okay?"

"Yeah, all good."

His urge to fidget was overwhelming but he tried to fight it, as he could feel his heart rate skyrocketing when she smiled at him.

"Anyway, I'll let you finish getting packed up. See you, Laura."

And with that Dan hurried away, out of Sanctuary and into the fresh air. He was going to miss that place. It had been the site of his rebirth as a writer and he'd treasure it for the rest of his life but he knew he couldn't stay. There was too much pain there now.

* * *

Sarah watched him walk away from Laura, with her mouth open. She couldn't quite believe it at first. They'd only talked a handful of times and as far as she was concerned that was all the contact they had with each other. Laura had alluded to a few messages sent here and there on social media, but it wasn't like they had a budding friendship.

She quickly turned back to the explanation at the front of the book she'd been gripping a little too tightly. *And so everyone will know. I was here and you were loved. Endlessly.* Now it was obvious but she'd just never put two and two together.

Laura is his muse!

 The doorbell rang merrily behind Dan as he walked out and she felt panic growing inside her. He was cutting himself off. He was stopping coming to Sanctuary, not because the book was done and he had no reason to work here any longer; no, he was cutting himself off so he didn't have to keep going through the pain which had created the words she held in her hand.

No. She couldn't let this happen. Dan was a lovely guy and if Laura just glanced up from her life once in a while she might just see the nice person that had been standing in front of her. Time to give fate a little nudge.

Sarah watched her friend packing up the last of her things. She grabbed a copy of *Endlessly* from the carrier bag under the counter and quickly scribbled Dan's number down on a serviette, before transferring the business card into the book.

She called out as Laura was walking away from the stage area. "Got a sec?"

* * *

Laura Gray dried her eyes on the sleeve of her top.

She couldn't remember when the tears had started to fall but they didn't seem to want to stop now even as she read the last page.

Taking the book from her bag a few days after Sarah had handed it to her, Laura had thought she'd just have a read of some poems to see what this was all about. Hours later she was lost in the pages, reading and rereading, drowning in feelings and dusk had fallen.

By the time she'd finished, it was early evening and the street lights had come on outside her house; her living room bathed in a soft orange glow.

She quickly grabbed her phone from the arm of the sofa and called her friend.

"Hey babe."

Laura stuttered to get the words out of her mouth as emotions from the pages she'd just read, stuck in her throat.

"Erm hey." She sniffed, tears still very much in her eyes, her body feeling shaky.

"Hey, you. How you doing?"

"I just finished that poetry book. It's beautiful," Laura replied. It was hard to put into words how she felt.

"It really is, isn't it?" Sarah's heart was racing.

"The poems are just so lyrical. It's like the author has looked into my heart and written about how I see love. Whoever they're writing about, they love them selflessly. It's how love should be."

Sarah paused, there was so much she wanted to say.

"I always thought when I saw some of the early poems in this book, that the inspiration for them was someone who the author had loved in another lifetime. They never really hinted that their muse was a real person in the here and now, so I assumed they weren't. But on Friday, when I saw how awkward Dan was, trying to have a conversation with you, the penny finally dropped."

"What?" A sickening feeling struck her like a sledgehammer to the soul as she remembered him coming to talk to her after her set. Laura was trying to put the puzzle together but without a clear picture to work from, she couldn't find edges to make a start. *That can't be right!*

"Laura, I think that *Endlessly* isn't just a collection of poems. I think it's sort of a love letter. One that Dan wrote. For you."

"Wait, what?! Dan wrote these?" She couldn't believe it.

Sarah continued, even though the words cloyed in her throat. "I think, having seen you together, that you're his muse. That introduction at the beginning? I think he wrote that for you and you alone."

Laura's head was spinning and she felt dizzy. This literally made no sense at all. Dan was always shy and awkward around her and conversation had always been hard.

And so everyone will know. I was here and you were loved. Endlessly

"Oh, Dan," she said aloud.

Sarah gave her friend a moment to breathe and gather her thoughts. She didn't know what she'd just set into motion and she was worried, knowing she'd just betrayed Dan's confidence.

"I'm not sure how reading was going to make you feel Laura."

She sighed and let the tension in her shoulders ease, hoping it would help her head stop spinning. "I dunno. I can't believe

195

Dan loves me. He's never shown any interest."

"I know. But from what I've learnt about him over the past few months, he wouldn't. Like the bit at the front says, he just wants to see you happy. And if he thought you were, then he'd have no reason to show you how he truly felt. He's a really good guy though, Laura."

"But I don't really know him."

"I know babe. To be fair – and I'm saying this with love – you have been completely buried in wedding prep lately. Look, take some time to figure out how you feel about this and what, if anything, you want to do about it. The number on the card is his. He doesn't know you have it or that you've read the book, far less that he wrote it. Please just promise me you'll be gentle with him, whatever you decide. Dan is a beautiful soul and he's been through hell these past few years in ways you can scarcely imagine. He's just trying to find his person."

"His cosmic puzzle piece." Laura let out a long sigh and it further eased her body.

"Exactly.I'm always here for you babe, you know that. Love you." Sarah said her goodbyes and hung up the phone.

Laura knew she needed to talk to him. Waiting on this would just make everything more awkward and difficult. Hitting the call button, she stood up. The nervous energy that had been building in her muscles needed to be walked off and all she could do to ease it was to wander around the ground floor of her house while she waited.

She was confused to the point that it was making her head throb.

It wasn't so much the shock that was creating a storm of

what ifs in her mind, it was that she hadn't seen this coming. It just didn't make any sense.

Had she had a vague idea of what was happening, she might have felt as though the obvious becoming clear that afternoon would have been exactly that; obvious. But she was beginning to see now, that what she had looked at many times, she hadn't fully seen and that in itself frustrated her.

While generally quiet and reserved, she still prided herself on having enough emotional intelligence to usually be able to read a situation like this. But with her emotions still drying on the sleeves of her hoodie from the tears of the last few hours, she could see now that she had somehow missed this entirely. She looked back to the book on the arm of the sofa.

How had she not seen? It was all literally right there in front of her and had been for months, apparently.

The call went to voicemail and as she waited for the tone, she took a deep breath.

"Dan? It's Laura."

* * *

"I'm going to see him tomorrow." Laura watched her friend who was silently brewing a takeaway tea for her. The fact that Sarah hadn't say anything worried her. "Do you think I shouldn't?"

"I think you should see him babe. But..." She turned and placed the paper cup on the counter in front of her and secured the plastic lid on top.

"But what?"

"I shouldn't say."

"Yes you should! We're friends. You're meant to tell me stuff! Sarah, please!"

Sarah sighed and met her friend's gaze.

"Have you considered the possibility that this is more than just a random thing that's happening?"

"Don't be silly. You've just read too many romance novels."

"I have yeah but this feels different, doesn't it?"

Laura shook the uncertain feeling out of her head as Sarah touched a nerve she'd been ignoring thus far. "No it doesn't."

"Okay, so what are you going to do?"

"I'm going to go see him and tell him it's lovely but we can only ever be friends. It's the only way."

"Have you told Chris?"

"God no! I love him but he'd lose the plot if he found out. It's fine, I can manage this myself."

"Okay."

Laura tried to silence the nagging doubt resonating somewhere deep inside her that she couldn't quite rationalise. "It'll be fine.

* * *

"Why didn't you tell me?"

Laura sat on a park bench looking out over the playing fields with an anxious Dan fidgeting next to her.

"It's really complicated Laura."

She had assumed when coming to meet him, that she was

going to feel awkward in his presence, the natural defensiveness in her playing its usual tricks. As they sat together, Laura realised it didn't feel that way at all. She wasn't mad, she wasn't upset and she wasn't uncomfortable. She just wanted to understand the man sitting by her side. Yet still, her heart felt heavy.

"Dan, talk to me. I'm not going anywhere." She tried to smile at him gently. Something about his outward behaviour felt familiar.

"I didn't tell you for so many reasons but mostly because you seemed happy and you didn't need me inadvertently changing that."

"Thank you. A lot of people in your position wouldn't have considered that I guess." She noticed he hadn't looked her in the eye once since he arrived.

"If the situation was different, I still wouldn't have said anything. There'd be no point. It's only because of Sarah and the fact you've read my book that you know anything. That's not me trying to lie to you, more that sometimes, some things are better left unsaid."

His hands were sore from the pressure he was applying on them as he spoke, the skin at the back of his neck feeling like it was trying to crawl off his bones.

"I've fallen in love with you Laura and have tried so hard to stop myself but nothing has worked. I'm sorry. I never wanted to confuse you or muddle you up, God knows my brain is muddled up enough for the both of us. I know if you were single and stuff, that anything between us would be pretty much impossible; the differences in our ages, the fact that I'm a dad and that we're at very different stages of life. For months, I've tried to stop how I feel about you but I've not been able to. I'm scared I'm in love with the idea of you."

He seemed like a good guy. He'd only ever been nice to her when they'd spoken, if a bit awkward at times. But he seemed genuine and caring, and seemed to spend a lot of time with his boy.

"Your son is Max, right?"

"Yeah."

"He seems like a sweet kid."

"He's the best. He gets it from his mum."

Laura figured that Dan must have an ex of some sort.

"Does he see much of her?"

"No, not anymore. She passed away three years ago."

Dan stared into his lap and hoped that Laura wouldn't turn and run. She didn't. Instead, she gently placed her hand on his, the warmth of her touch calming his need to restlessly fidget.

"I'm sorry."

"It's okay."

"Is that one of the reasons you didn't say anything to me?"

"Mhmm. One of them, yeah. I don't want to be a sob story. I've never wanted other people's pity. It's a horrible feeling knowing that people are looking at you like some kind of wounded animal. But I've still felt guilty for how I feel about you. Like I was betraying her somehow."

"I can understand that. I'm sorry that the past few months haven't been easy."

"It's fine. Like I say, I don't want to be a sob story." Dan let go of her hand and stood, turning back to look at her for the first time that afternoon.

"Look ultimately I just want you to be happy Laura and if

a part of that means we can be friends then I'd like that a lot. But I totally get it if that feels like too much."

She looked up at him, "Dan, I..." she said gently.

"My head isn't like most people's, Laura. This stuff is really hard for someone like me."

"Someone with ADHD you mean?"

Her question stopped him in his tracks. No one really ever knew about his condition without him talking about it first, which was something he rarely did.

"How did you know?"

"A friend of mine is just like you, a head full of everything. She stims a lot too. just not with her hands as much as you do; it's more that she has to hold something. She's always playing with her AirPods case or keys without realising she's doing it. And when she's struggling with something, she doesn't like eye contact either." She stood as she spoke.

Looking at her was too hard and he was grateful that she kept her focus on his chest and not on his face as she spoke.

"I understand, more so now I've read your book. It's okay. I see you. But I'm engaged, all we can ever be is just friends. I'm really sorry."

Even though she knew it was hard for him to look at her, Laura felt her own anxiety stopping her from looking up at him. She felt if she listened hard enough, she'd be able to hear his heart breaking.

"It's okay. I get it."

Dan couldn't help but feel worse. While she hadn't come out and directly rejected him, she had put the final nail in the coffin of the whole sorry situation and it left him with an empty ache in his heart.

"I just needed to get the words out of me. I'm sorry. I never meant for it to become all of this." It was a lie but trying to put some sort of brave spin on it was all he could think of doing as she stood in front of him, her head hanging low.

"No no. It's alright. I can see how this happened."

A frosty silence began to grow between them as they stood awkwardly; a cool breeze whipping around them as time seemed to drag excruciatingly on.

Finally, she spoke. "I should go."

"Yeah."

"Sorry."

"Don't be, it's fine."

"I hope we can be friends."

Dan nodded as she turned, gathered up her bag and left.

Watching her walk away was too much for him to bear. The crushing weight of expectation and hope he'd carried for months made him feel like he was being compressed from the inside out. It was only the thought of Max, waiting at Issy and Martin's that made him move from that lonesome spot in the park where for a few fragile moments, they'd shared time and space together.

Turning to walk back to the car, the cloud drifted across the afternoon sun and everything instantly felt cold.

* * *

IV

Part Four

Four months later...

Part Four

Laura closed the door behind her.

After everything that had happened, coming here was starting to feel normal again and she'd stopped dreading awkwardly bumping into him; months of not seeing him had eased those worries, eventually.

Since the day in the park, she had seldom spoken to Dan and even then only ever via text message. It had always been pleasant but she suspected that he was holding back on her; most likely not wanting to overwhelm her, especially while she was in the middle of trying to plan her wedding.

But still, she felt bad.

Laura really had hoped they might become friends but while it had been amicable enough the few times that they had messaged, the friendship she thought might grow between them had never materialised.

It had been an odd few months.

Thankfully, Sarah had been there for her the whole time, the two of them spending long hours talking about the situation via text message or on walks when Chris was working. But neither of them had seen Dan in months, and like Laura, Sarah had only been in touch with him briefly on the phone; always short conversations.

Gazing around the coffee shop, a small part of her hoped to see him, awkwardly smiling at her. He wasn't there and so the accompanying dread of a difficult conversation with him was avoided.

But as she looked she spotted something else.

The fluffy brown hair of a boy she had met before.

Max.

At a table with someone that Laura didn't recognise, Max was sitting quietly, subdued, with his feet up on the opposite chair. Laura had never seen him like that before. Whenever she had seen Dan's son, he had seemed so full of life. His ever-present big, toothy grin plastered across his face. But that was gone now, replaced with a heaviness that seemed to visibly weigh on him.

Max looked up and saw Laura. It took a moment for him to register who he was looking at but when he did, his shoulders slumped and he looked away. The movement caused the lady with him to turn to see what had caused it.

After the briefest of glances, she turned back and Laura watched as she placed her hand on Max's shoulder, saying something to which the boy nodded.

Laura made her way to the counter as Sarah finished up serving a customer.

"It's the first time I've seen him since Dan left." She realised that Laura had already clocked Max.

"He seems sad."

"Yeah. He does look unhappy."

"Hey. It's Laura, right?"

The unfamiliar voice pulled her attention to the woman she'd just seen with Max.

"Erm, yeah. Hi?"

"Could I have a word? I'm Issy, Max's aunt."

"Yeah. Sure."

Laura felt on the spot and didn't care for it. A horrible sinking feeling grew in the pit of her stomach and it didn't matter that Sarah was trying to give her a reassuring smile, something was wrong. She could feel it.

Walking over to the table, following Issy, she realised she was gripping the shoulder strap of her bag a little too tight; the knuckles on her hand turning white.

"Maxxy? Can you give us a minute, please? Why not go and say hello to Sarah? When I ordered our drinks she told me she'd love to catch up with you."

The boy looked up and simply nodded before trudging away.

Laura's heart ached for him as she sat down, watching him walk to the counter.

"He's not been himself for a while. He's had to deal with a lot in the last few months," Issy explained.

"I haven't ever seen him without a smile." *Something felt very wrong.*

"To be honest, he's not had much to smile about."

Issy paused. This wasn't going to be an easy conversation but

207

she felt like it was imperative, if life was ever going to return to normal again.

"What's wrong with Dan?" Laura knew something wasn't right. An uncomfortable sense of panic was rising in her. "Is he okay? What's happened?"

Issy sighed.

"Dan has gotten himself into a bad place. He'd hoped that writing those poems would act as some sort of exorcism and get you out of his system. But it has had the opposite effect, unfortunately."

Shame washed over Laura as she realised that it had never once occurred to her that Dan's general absence might be down to him struggling with what happened.

"Look, none of this is your fault and I'm not here to play the blame game but I care deeply for my brother-in-law and he's stuck in a place I can't bring him back from. I've kept him with us once before..." she trailed off.

It didn't need to be said. Laura knew that losing his wife would have been devastating to Dan, and despite Issy's reassurance she couldn't help but feel as though she was somehow to blame for this.

"It's okay. Whatever it is. Just tell me."

Issy thought back over the last few months and how it had pushed the family to their breaking point. She could have been mad at Laura but knew it wasn't her fault. She was just caught in the middle of it all.

"After you last saw him, Dan spiralled. I think to begin with he'd hoped that you'd see his actions as some sort of romantic gesture and you two would walk off into the sunset together. But I think he knew deep down that that wouldn't ever happen so he wished for the next best thing. That writing about you would exorcise you and the feelings from his heart and he'd be able to move on.

However, what was left was a profound sense of emptiness that he couldn't cope with. Before we knew it, an odd glass of wine at night to ease the pain had turned to a bottle of whiskey a day.

Bless him, Max did his best to hide it from us and look after his dad but one day Dan was too hungover to take him to school and his teacher called us, rightly concerned."

Laura sat dumbfounded. She listened, horrified, as Issy explained how Max had ended up living with her and her husband for the time being, so they could make sure he was being looked after and getting to school on time. That they'd managed to get Dan into a couple of AA meetings but the fight was a hard one and he was struggling desperately with it every day, meaning there were more failures than there were successes.

Laura could see the toll it was taking on Dan's sister-in-law. She looked exhausted, both physically and emotionally.

"Max will be okay. He's a resilient kid. But he's been through so much already in his short life. He lost his mum. We couldn't let him lose his dad too."

Issy turned to watch Sarah trying to make conversation with her nephew, who to his credit was trying to smile as best he could.

"Oh, Max." A tear rolled down Laura's cheek as she looked over at him.

"Look Laura, I know this is a massive ask of you, but I think Dan needs you."

"Me? Why me?"

"I don't think anyone can pull him out of this but you. I'm not saying you need to be with him as a couple or anything like that. Please don't think I am." Issy spoke quickly to reassure the woman in front of her who looked stunned. "But I think you might be the only one to reach him. We've tried everything. Please."

"I..." Laura's mind was reeling. Dan was in trouble. Max was a shell of the boy she'd talked to on his birthday. Issy and her family were struggling. "I don't know. What if I make things worse?" Panic set in. "I'm sorry but I'm going to need to think about this."

"Honestly, please. Just think about it. You don't need to do anything right now. I know you're engaged Laura, I really don't want that to get messed up but right now I feel like I'm out of ideas and you're fast becoming our last option."

The pair sat together while Issy explained everything that had happened. Dan had been devastated that Max was leaving though he understood it was for the best but for a few weeks that in itself drove him even further into the bottle. How, on one occasion, Martin had needed to break down the front door when his best friend had failed to check in and they'd found him unconscious on the sofa. When the door was repaired and the lock replaced, they'd been sure to take a spare key and sadly they'd needed to use it not too long afterwards when the same situation occurred again.

On his better days, Dan tried hard to pull his life back together but the emptiness seemed to creep back in as the evenings approached and time after time he lost the fight to stay sober.

Laura listened, feeling more and more guilty.

They were only stopped in their discussions when Max came back to their table carrying a piece of cake wrapped in a napkin, Sarah having exhausted all possibilities of keeping the boy occupied.

"Sarah says I can take this home. I don't really feel like it at the moment."

"Sure thing little man. You can have it after dinner if you want? Fish and chips tonight, yeah? Your favourite."

"I guess."

He turned to look at Laura who fought against every guilty feeling she had to look at him in return.

"Hey."

"Hi, Max."

"Aunty Issy, can we go please? I just want to go back to your house now."

As they made to leave, Issy gave Laura her phone number and told her to call anytime if she wanted to talk. And then they were gone, Laura watching them walk arm-in-arm slowly as if they were leaving a funeral.

"Jesus! I broke them, I broke Dan *and* Max!"

She cried onto her friend's shoulder as the dam that had held back all the emotions of the afternoon finally gave way and she told Sarah what she'd been told by Issy.

"It's not your fault, Laura. It sounds to me like he just emptied so much of his heart into his work, that afterwards there was nothing left for him to have hope for, so he chose

211

to hide in a bottle."

"What do I do?"

"Babe, I don't know, but you need to be careful. You need to think about Chris and the fact that you're getting married in a few months. Do not lose yourself to this!"

Laura's head felt heavy with everything she needed to consider. The last thing she wanted to do was to make things worse; seeing her might cause Dan to retreat further into his problems. On the other hand, she didn't want to give him any kind of false hope; hope that in a few months, on her wedding day, she would ultimately take from him, sending him right back to square one.

She needed time to figure out what to do.

* * *

An ambulance raced down the street, shattering the silence in the house with the sound of sirens. Neon blue lights reflected around the dark room, igniting all the glass surfaces, including the half-drunk bottle of Jack Daniel's held loosely in Dan's right hand.

Sitting on the floor, huddled in the shadows next to *Lucille*, he hid from the world. The shaking in his hands had at least stopped for the evening as was usually the case by the time the second fiery mouthful slid down his throat.

It was a sick kind of certainty that he both craved and hated.

Some nights when he'd drink, he'd hold his composure and drink just enough to take the edge off his pain. On other nights, like tonight, his eyes would be full of tears, the alcohol doing nothing to fade the edges of his aching heart.

I'm a fuck up.

The full thud of those words went round and around his drunk mind, sounding more and more vile, the less that remained in the bottle.

Why did that car hit Natalie and not me? Everyone would be better off without me.

Sobs racked his body as he struggled to fight the pain that was yet again consuming him in the darkness. His head slid along the wall and came to rest against the bookcase, full of the words he'd spent a lifetime writing, including his copy of *Endlessly*, which now seemed to be imprisoning him.

I love her so much and she won't even talk to me.

A car's headlights streaked through the blinds that hung in the front windows, flashing across the half-empty packet of paracetamol he'd started working through earlier that morning. The unwelcome light drew his eyes to the part-finished Lego set that Max had been building the morning Issy and Martin had come to collect him. Dan hadn't had the heart to move it from where it had been left.

I miss him so much.

Of this whole fucking mess that his life had become, he felt that his failure as a father to adorable Max was the worst part. Natalie dying had broken his heart. Everything with Laura had taken his legs from under him. But losing Max? That had taken away his last reason to go on. Just thinking about him not being there any more brought on another wave of tears.

He sunk another slug of bourbon from the bottle. It burned his throat all the way down, causing him to wince but it did the trick of numbing him a little more to the futility of the world around him.

Lifting it to his lips again without thinking, he saw that the mouthful had been the last the bottle would relinquish. Another night where he had finished a whole bottle of whiskey without even realising.

That fact alone should have caused him shame but it didn't. It just prompted a mental note to buy more tomorrow. He was out of food anyway and couldn't face more of Issy's sanctimonious leftover lasagne, so he would need to go out into the world again, if only for an hour.

Life has gone to shit and I'm the only one to blame. Everyone knows it. That's why they're not here and why I'm alone.

Letting his head rest on the bookshelf, he closed his eyes, allowing drunken tiredness to take him for a while.

Drifting in and out of consciousness, he dreamt of Laura. She was playing at Sanctuary. Her familiar white guitar resting in her lap. When she saw him, she smiled.

It felt like warm summer sun on his face and her smile quickly turned into a laugh; the kind you share with someone over a silly joke. But when he tried to smile back he couldn't and her laugh turned from playful and friendly to vicious and cruel, as if she was mocking him.

I could never love you. You'll never be enough for me.

Dan woke with a start, pain flaring in his neck from where drunk and asleep, he'd slid down the bookcase and now his body resembled a 40-year-old pretzel in trackies.

I can't keep doing this.

Pulling himself up from the floor, he stumbled to the stairs and somehow managed to make it up to bed before he blacked out.

When he woke, it was well past 11 am and there were two texts from Max on his phone.

Since they'd been separated, they'd started texting in the morning before the boy went to school; Max's way of checking in on his dad to make sure he was up and awake. This wasn't the first time he'd missed morning messages with his son but it hurt all the same.

Dan: Max, I'm so sorry. I had a really bad night's sleep and slept through my alarm. Hope you have a good day at school. I miss you, Maxxy. Love Dad x

He had to read it through four times to check it made sense; the effects of drinking a full bottle of bourbon hadn't fully been slept off.

Hitting send, Dan laid back and pulled the covers over his head, hiding from both the world and from the shame he felt.

* * *

Laura meandered down the bread aisle in her local Tesco and turned right to pick up a bottle of wine to go with the evening meal.It had been a long day and she was looking forward to getting home, to her fiance Chris, eating something good and sinking a glass of red with some mindless TV.

She had spent the better part of the past few days trying to figure out what to do about Dan and replaying the conversation with Max's aunt in her head.

Dan needs you. I don't think anyone can pull him out of this but you. I think you might be the only one to reach him.

In reality, she barely knew the guy but something was pulling at her in a way she hadn't expected. She knew full well that pretty much anyone else in her situation would say *thanks but no thanks, not my problem.* But with Dan, it felt different. She didn't know him, but she wanted to. She didn't know how to help him, but she wanted to.

Flashes of seeing him writing, engrossed, in Sarah's cute little coffee shop had been coming to her mind all week. The few times she'd seen him, lost in words, she'd not known what he had been working on and yet now, those beautiful lines seemed to stick in her head, like flies to honey. No matter what she had tried to do over the past few months, Laura had been unable to shake those words and the effect they'd had on her.

As she turned and looked down the aisle, she saw a man rubbing his temple, standing distressed in front of a vast array of bottles of whiskey. He looked like he was struggling. Not deciding which bottle to get but rather whether to get one at all. A pained expression spread across his face as he seemingly fought against an urge he had no control over.

He was wearing grey trackies and a hoodie that did little to hide the scruffy stubble and messy hair which wrapped around his tired-looking face. Dishevelled wasn't quite the right word for the appearance of the man, but she sensed he wasn't doing so well. Feelings of pity sent a shiver down her spine.

It took a moment for Laura to realise who she was looking at.

She watched as Dan finally made his mind up, quickly reaching for a bottle from the shelf in front of him and adding it to his basket. As he turned slightly, she noticed that the whiskey was accompanied by a small selection of ready meals for one and two packets of paracetamol.

Her heart sank.

When she'd spoken to Issy, Laura had been unable to visualise Dan as anything other than the man she'd sat on the park bench with, months before.

He certainly wasn't the kind of guy to be over flashy or to look polished. That afternoon, he'd worn a pair of blue jeans and a black t-shirt, his hair tidy on his head as it always was whenever she'd seen him and his beard sitting neatly around the lower part of his face. He'd looked nice without her feeling like he'd made a huge effort on her account.

Now his appearance seemed very different. While he didn't

look destitute, he certainly didn't look like the man she'd met before. He looked tired, his head down low as if he was carrying the weight of the entire world on his shoulders.

Watching him trying to fight the urge to buy a bottle of whiskey was painful. She'd watched him struggling internally for a few moments and could tell that he desperately had wanted to just walk away but hadn't been able to.

Laura's heart broke as he slunk off down the aisle away from her.

I think you might be the only one to reach him.

Issy's words rang in her head as she struggled with her own internal dilemma. She just couldn't understand why she was unable to walk away and accept that this wasn't her issue.

Taking her phone out of her bag, along with the crumpled-up card with her number on it, she called Issy.

"Hello?"

"Hey Issy. It's Laura."

"Oh hey. You okay?"

"I'll help."

" Erm...are you sure?"

"Very sure. I have no idea if I'm going to help at all; we need to understand that I could possibly make everything much much worse but I can't see him like this".

"What do you mean? You've seen him?"

"I've just seen him in Tesco buying whiskey. Issy, he looks a mess." Emotion caught in Laura's throat as she spoke.

"Fuck sake!" Issy couldn't hide her frustration.

"What? What's wrong?"

"He must be having another bad day. Fuck sake!"

It hadn't occurred to Laura that while she watched, Dan might be struggling to stay on the wagon right in front of her as he picked that bottle of amber liquid up off the shelf. She felt less than useless.

"Shit! Sorry Issy, I didn't think!"

"No, don't be sorry. It's not your fault. One of us will go over and help him through it and get rid of whatever he's bought. Look, it's great that you want to help him but right now I need to go and get to his house before anything bad happens. Can I call you tomorrow, Laura?"

"Yeah, sure. I hope he's okay."

As she ended the call, a wave of guilt rushed over her and she wished she'd gone over and slapped the fucking bottle right out of his hands. Visions of him sitting somewhere, drunk and alone, surrounded by discarded bottles ran through her head making her feel sick.

Abandoning her own basket of shopping on top of a pallet of fresh produce next to her, Laura left the store empty-handed. Rushing out of the main doors, she scanned the car park in the hopes that she might see him, wondering if she might be able to talk him out of whatever he was planning on doing. But Dan was nowhere in sight.

While everything felt like a mess, she still didn't know if seeing him would be the right thing to do but at least now she'd made the decision to try and help.

* * *

Dan sat steeped in exhaustion; a cup of strong black coffee on the table in front of him. He felt bone weary, the mental toll of fighting his rapidly growing dependency sapping nearly every ounce of strength from his body.

Staring into nothing, his mind seemed to slowly churn through random thoughts that didn't link together in any sort of meaningful way, so he just let his mind wander. The weight of his head on his shoulders felt heavier than anything he'd ever carried. He was tired. So very, very tired.

He'd fully intended to be nursing a hangover or even to maybe still be drunk by this point of the morning but had been surprised to find Issy waiting for him on the doorstep when he returned from the supermarket the evening before. She'd looked sympathetically at him as if he was some puppy in a cage at a rescue centre.

"Do you want some company?" She'd asked, her eyes saying that she knew where he'd been and what he was carrying in the bag in his hand.

She had a weird way of making him feel exposed and vulnerable while also giving him the security to be open and honest.

Knowing that she saw him and the struggle he was going through, broke him and for a moment he had cried on her shoulder on the doorstep as the world moved around them.

"It's alright. Let's get inside and we can just go from there, okay?"

A knock echoed through the house, pulling Dan's gaze away from the black abyss of his coffee. But it was another second knock moments later, a little louder than the first, that caused him to come fully back into reality.

His body ached.

After a night's broken sleep, desperately trying to fight the urge to ransack the house for alcohol, he was left physically exhausted and two coffees had barely scratched the surface. Rising from the kitchen table, he shuffled uncomfortably to the front door, stretching his arms above his head as he went. The movement caused a loud cracking in his neck, the pressure of a crappy sleep being relieved.

The translucent glass fitted into the top half of the front door didn't give away much of the identity of his morning caller. All he knew was, he wasn't in the mood for guests. Had he been nursing another raging hangover, he'd have ignored the intrusion and stayed in bed, hidden from the world. But given the fact he was sober, he felt more sociable, at least enough to tell whoever it was to go away.

He took a deep breath and turned the handle.

The face that greeted him was like a punch in the soul.

"Hey, you."

Laura stood on the front step with her hands in her jacket pockets and tried to look relaxed. Inside though, she was anything but. The rational part of her brain was reminding her that this was a really stupid idea; that even though she was a nice person this was way out of her wheelhouse. Her heart though, and a feeling she just couldn't shake, were keeping her on the doorstep.

"Hey, you," she said again, as Dan stood staring dumbfounded back at her.

He looked tired. The stubble on his face that was usually groomed nicely was ragged, which matched the fluffy unkempt bedhead look he was sporting. He had at least managed to get dressed in different clothes this morning; she'd been worried he'd be in the same clothes he'd worn in the supermarket.

Standing there, Laura thought back to sitting with Sarah at the coffee shop weeks before.

"I don't think he's doing too well but I can't really tell to be honest." Sarah had said, as they sat in Sanctuary sharing a slab of lemon cake.

Laura had looked troubled.

"Hey! It's not your fault. He's a grown man, capable of working through his stuff himself. You have nothing to feel guilty about."

"Yeah, but I still feel bad. I really hoped we could be friends, you know?"

"I know."

"A part of me misses him, oddly. Like he wasn't ever really in my life, not like he was for you, he was just in the periphery but it still seems strange that he's not around anymore."

Now she could see for herself that he wasn't in the best place.

"Erm, hi." *What was she doing here?*

"May I come in?"

"Laura, what are you doing here?"

"Issy came to see me."

Of course, she fucking did. Dan's head sank on his shoulders in exasperation.

"Hey. It's okay. She's just worried about you. I'm worried about you. Please, let me in and we can talk."

"Sure. Okay."

Laura stepped nervously across the threshold and was struck by what she saw. She had no idea what Dan's house would be like but a part of her had expected the home of an alcoholic to be messy and uncared for; this was anything but. It was clean. Tidy. And every bit a family home.

Pictures of Dan with his son adorned the mantelpiece above the fireplace. His guitar, *Lucille* rested gently on her stand by the window and there was even a half-made Lego set (*Max's, presumably*) on the low coffee table in the centre of the room.

It all looked normal. *Maybe things weren't as bad as Issy had made out?*

He led her through the living room to the kitchen at the back of the house. Dan looked uncomfortable as he moved, she observed, his body seemed to be stiff and unwilling to move the way he wanted.

"You have a nice house."

"Thanks. It's not much but it's home." He paused by the table. "Take a seat."

"Thanks."

"Can I get you a coffee?"

"I'd prefer a tea if you have one, please?"

"Yeah, okay."

Dan hadn't bought tea since before Natalie had died. It was her drink of choice but he'd never really taken to it. It just wasn't a taste he liked. Panic struck him as he searched the cupboards, realising he probably didn't have anything remotely resembling a tea bag in the house.

Laura watched as the panic seemed to build in him.

"Don't worry if you don't have any tea."

She'd come wanting to reassure him that everything would be okay but having him stress over tea bags wasn't the start she'd hoped for.

"Sorry."

"Dan, it's okay. Come sit down."

He dragged out the chair opposite her and instinctively pulled his half-drunk cup of coffee to him; the desire to have something in his hands too strong to fight.

As she looked at him, she could see the cracks that had grown around the edges of his personality. *He looked tired, long nights and hangovers most likely accounting for that* she thought. There also seemed to be little life in his eyes now. Even though they'd only been around each other a handful of times, she realised that a spark had always been there. Not now.

But it was the shaking of his hands gripping onto the cup that made her feel most sad. Dan's body language gave her the impression that if she were to pull out a bottle of whiskey and hand it to him, he would drink from it without question, like a man stranded in the desert who finally finds water.

Issy was right.

"So Issy seems to be quite worried about you and…"

"I'm fine. Whatever Issy told you, she's just overreacting." he interrupted, not wanting to hear the end of that particular sentence.

"Okay you're fine. But she's still worried and so am I."

"There's nothing to worry about Laura. I'm fine."

She hadn't expected him to be so dismissive of her concerns but could see in his face that he hated the scrutiny. She tried again to reassure him.

"Dan. It's okay."

"Look, I said I'm fine. Honestly."

The shaking in his hands seemed to amplify as the focus on him seemed to intensify, so Dan let go of his mug and crossed his arms. His skin was on fire; a sickly combination of his body needing alcohol and his ever-increasing anxiety at having Laura unexpectedly sitting in front of him. He had to close his eyes to stop his whole body shaking.

Seeing his discomfort, she got up, took an upturned glass from the drainer beside the sink and poured him some water.

"Here. Sip this."

Steadying his hand as best he could, he took the glass and drank. It wasn't whiskey but the cold liquid briefly took the edge off.

"Sorry. Must just be tired."

"Dan! Enough! Please, I know how things really are, Issy's told me everything!"

Dan sat quietly as he processed the notion that Laura knew about all of his failures. How he'd lost himself to drink after she had rejected him. How Max had had to move in with his aunt and uncle purely to ensure he made it to school each day. And how his whole world had seemingly imploded in only a few months, the combination of losing first Natalie and then the love he never had with Laura.

"You should leave."

He spoke calmly but inside his emotions were raging.

"Dan..."

"Please. Just go."

She knew pushing the issue would drive him further behind his defences, which had been erected to keep the world out.

"Okay. I'm sorry. I was just worried about you. I'll leave you be."

"Thanks."

As she collected her bag and walked out of the kitchen, Laura paused briefly and looked over her shoulder.

"I saw you. Last night. At the supermarket."

Dan didn't answer.

And so, without anything else to say, she left, quietly shutting the front door behind her, leaving Dan to carry on hiding.

Tears streamed down her face as she realised she'd fixed nothing and instead made everything so much worse.

* * *

For the better part of an hour, Dan deliberated about hitting send. It had been several days since he had pretty much thrown Laura out and everything about her visit filled him with self-loathing. The idea that she knew everything, that Issy had been telling tall tales about his sad descent, and that his shame was clear for her to see, made him feel sick. Every part of him wanted to just hide away in a bottle and ignore it all. But he also felt like he owed Laura an apology. He'd been short with her, abrupt verging on rude; she hadn't deserved that.

Dan: Sorry.

Not the most eloquent of messages he'd ever written but he just didn't know what else to say.

For the first time ever; she replied almost immediately.

Laura: It's me who should be sorry. I should have messaged you beforehand, not just turned up at your door unannounced.

He sat staring at her reply, trying to engage his hungover brain enough to figure out what to do next before she took the choice out of his hands. After she'd left, he'd hit the bottle hard over the ensuing days and this morning his head ached badly.

Laura: I really am worried about you though Dan. Can we meet somewhere so we can talk? I'd like to see you if you feel up to it.

Dan: I don't know if that's a good idea.

Laura: It would just be two people meeting to talk. That's all.

Dan: Okay.

Laura: Want to meet in the park? It's a nice enough day. Say after lunch? 1pm?

Dan: Sure. Okay.

A wash of anxiety flowed over him as he realised that many uncomfortable things would now have to happen. First, he'd need to leave the house; something he'd seldom done recently. Second, he'd be going back to the same spot where he'd been rejected by her; the site of the beginning of his downward spiral. And third, he'd be purposefully meeting her in person, not unexpectedly like the last time he'd seen her.

Dan rested his head in his hands and tried to slow the racing thoughts that were running amuck through his mind. People describe time slowing down at times like this but he was experiencing the complete opposite.

Everything seemed to be spinning around him and he was glad to be sitting down or he felt like he might have fainted. Dragging himself from the table and into the shower, he resolved to get himself out of the house at the bare minimum by lunchtime.

By 12:50 pm, Dan was sitting on an all too familiar park bench regretting ever agreeing to come. A cool breeze was whipping around the park, picking up empty crisp packets and pieces of paper, tossing them around. Even his big coat wasn't enough to keep the cold from his bones. A sickening thought spun in his mind as he sat waiting. *She's not coming.* As soon as the idea had formed, it was all he could think. *She's not coming. She's not coming.*

While he'd not made an effort to be early, he had still arrived with almost 15 minutes to spare and had half-heartedly expected to see her there already waiting. But she wasn't. Sitting alone on the bench, Dan made his mind up that she wasn't going to show. *This is a mistake.* He watched an old man with a ratty little dog shuffling up along the path to his right and wondered if that would one day be his fate.

"Hey you."

Laura's soft voice caused him to breathe in sharply without turning to see her. A wave of relief and an odd sense of comfort washed over him. Holding his gaze on the man and his dog, he spoke.

"I thought you might not come."

He felt her sit down beside him.

"I worried you might not either but I'm glad you're here."

He turned and caught her eye for the briefest of moments before looking away again.

"Hey."

"You doing okay?"

"I'm fine."

A silence grew between them for a moment. Laura was the first one to break it.

"Look. Before we start talking about anything else, I'm not going to keep asking you all the time if you're doing okay. It's not fair on you to keep having to answer that. Let's both correctly assume you're not doing okay and leave it at that. Yes?"

Dan thought about all the ways he could say he was fine and quickly realised her suggestion was a good one.

"Sounds good. I really am okay though."

"Moving on to point two of the agenda. Don't bullshit me over stuff. Please."

"I…"

"Dan, please. I know what's happened. I know my part in it. I know where you are right now and how I put you there. Please let's not do this."

"You can't fix it."

"I don't want to fix it."

"So why are you here?"

"Because I want to help make this right. I want to be there for you when it feels like you have no one."

"But why?"

Dan watched the ratty little dog sniffling at the grass ahead of him, his mind trying to focus on something present in an effort to hold his nerves rather than wanting to run and not look back.

Laura sighed. "Because after the last time I was here with you, I really did want us to be friends and now I know why we…" Her voice fell away as she thought about how she'd hurt both Dan and Max, sending their world spinning out of control, tears starting well in her eyes. "I didn't mean to…"

He couldn't find the words to reply. Everything he wanted

to say seemed hollow before he could form the words, so he let the idea of them drift away. He wanted to be able to tell her he was glad that she was there, that she wasn't to blame for any of his mess and that he still loved her. But instead, he said nothing. Before long, five minutes had passed with them sitting in silence.

Laura dried her eyes. "Point three on the agenda, I promise not to cry about this all the time."

Their eyes met briefly.

"You've caught me on a good day."

"What are the bad days like?"

"Bad." He paused, not sure how much he should say. "Some days I wake up having drunk so much the night before that I could have actually drowned myself."

"Dan..."

"It's a crutch that I can't rid myself of. One bad thing happens and I'm right back there, bottle in hand. It's the only way I can cope at the moment."

"Issy said you've been going to meetings?"

"Mhmm, in town. At the church hall."

"What are they like?"

"Embarrassing. It feels like I'm on show and everyone's judging me in my shame and misery. I know it's meant to help but I just can't seem to see it yet."

"Maybe I could come with you one day? For moral support?"

"No. They don't let people in like that."

"Oh okay."

Dan cursed himself quietly for shutting her down so quickly. He hadn't meant to but the idea of her sitting with him while he sat in a place with the sole purpose of seeing him so tragically vulnerable, panicked him and he'd rejected the idea without much thought for the gesture she was making.

"Sorry."

"It's okay. I guess this is all just going to take some time isn't it."

"Mhmm."

He really couldn't understand why she was even here. If she felt guilty then surely avoiding him at all costs would be the better course of action. He'd told her she couldn't fix it. Dan just couldn't make sense of it.

But the pull on his heart, whenever she was near him, was a force greater than he had the power to work against. Like a tug-of-war competition with one person against a team of eight; there was only one way his heart would go when he was with her. Even after all these alcohol-soaked months of misery, he still loved her even if he'd told himself repeatedly that he was moving on and past it. He just couldn't let her go.

For a while, they made small talk and watched the world go by before it was time for Laura to leave, with a lesson booked and a pupil expecting her.

As he walked in the opposite direction, Dan could feel a weight in his chest and a sense of sadness starting to overwhelm him. While the sickening habit of his drinking problem had taken hold, he had for the last few weeks, felt like he was getting over her; but he knew deep down he hadn't. And probably never could.

Passing the corner shop at the end of his road, he fought the urge to buy a bottle for the night, his fists screwed up tight at his sides. Yet by the time he'd reached the second front gate along the street, his feet had literally stopped him in his tracks without him even realising what was happening. For a moment he just stood in the middle of the street, desperately willing his feet forward.

Eventually, he was closing in on his own front door halfway down the street, clutching a blue plastic carrier bag and promising himself he would try again tomorrow.

* * *

A week or so had passed and Laura's mind wandered to Dan and how he was doing, so she decided to tentatively take the first step and text him.

Laura: Hey. How's things?

Dan: So so. Not the best few days but doing a bit better. Just back from a meeting actually.

Laura: It's good that you went. How do you feel having gone?

Dan: Like shit truth be told, but I always do afterwards cos each time I go I'm starting over and it's exhausting being back at the beginning and having to tell my whole life story for the umpteenth time.

Laura: Do you fancy a walk in the park today? We could grab a coffee?

Dan: Honestly Laura you don't have to do this. It's fine. You have your own life to lead.

Laura: You're right. I don't have to do this and I do have my own life to lead but I'd also like a coffee and a walk with you too, if you're up for it. So I'll be in the park on the bench at one o'clock with two coffees. If you're there, great. If not that's okay too.

Dan: Okay. I'll see.

Laura sighed as she put her phone down on the sofa cushion. He was such a frustrating man. She could understand that he was struggling but she was just trying to help and spend some time with him. *Why can't he just see that?* Then it hit her.

"Huh!" She said out loud.

This is exactly how he would have felt months earlier when he was trying to get to know her and she'd been too busy with her own life to even notice or see what he wanted. Guilt flared in her as she realised she was now living an alternate version of what Dan had lived through for the last few months. The shame made her heart ache.

Sitting on what was rapidly becoming their bench in the park later that afternoon, she checked her watch. He was late. The two cups of hot coffee remained untouched in their cardboard carrier next to her. He hadn't been late the previous times they'd met; maybe she had the time wrong. She checked her watch again. She had a sinking feeling that he really wasn't coming this time. Something in her gut told her that his head had gotten the better of him and he was now avoiding her.

She couldn't leave without at least checking he was alright, so bringing out her phone, she messaged him.

Laura: Hey.

Waiting for him to reply, she picked one of the coffees up and sipped it. By the time she got to her third mouthful, the phone rang. Dan's name flashed on the screen. *At least he was alive!*

"Hey, you. Did I get the time wrong?" She knew she hadn't but she needed to get him talking somehow.

"I'm sorry if I worried you. I just…"

"Didn't want to come out of the house?"

"Yeah. Couldn't face anyone else today. Sorry. The meeting this morning took more out of me than I realised, I guess. I should have messaged you to let you know though."

"It's okay, I get it. We didn't say it was a definite thing anyway." She tried to keep her tone light and cheerful. She didn't want him to feel attacked and if she was being truthful, she really didn't mind, she was just glad he was alright.

"I'll pay you back for the coffee."

"No you won't. It's fine, honestly. Do you have time to chat while I walk?"

"Yeah okay."

Reaching for her AirPods, she slipped them into her ears, automatically connecting the call and placed her phone back in her pocket. Then, collecting the coffees, she stood and began walking around the park in the sunshine.

"Do you want to talk about it?"

"About what?"

"About today. The meeting. Why you felt you didn't want to come out again." Dan's sigh was audible and it made her feel guilty for pushing.

On the other end of the phone, he felt the sting of regret; for not showing up without telling her and for missing an opportunity to be in the company of someone who he had longed to spend time with only months before.

"Just feel emotionally exhausted I guess."
  "Okay."
  "Being sober isn't easy."
  "Yeah."

The phone call cracked as both of them listened to the silence; neither of them quite knowing what to say next.

"Have you heard from Max?"
  "Yeah, this morning."
  "That's good right?"
  "Yeah."

At home, Dan pinched the bridge of his nose and closed his eyes. This was making his brain hurt. He shouldn't have called. He inwardly cursed himself for not texting to tell her he wasn't coming. That would have prevented all of this. Now all he wanted was to hide away and remove himself from what felt like her judgemental attention but he didn't want to just end the call. That would be rude and he'd already been too rude to her recently.

Laura walked slowly around the park feeling sorry for the whole situation. Maybe she should have never told Issy that she'd try and help. She had no idea what she was doing, Dan didn't really want to talk to her, she wasn't making anything better, it seemed.

"Look Laura, thanks."

His comment surprised her.

"Thanks for what?"
   "For giving a shit."
   "I'm just…"
   "Worried about me, I know." He paused for a moment to collect his thoughts. "I know I'm not being very forthcoming and stuff with you. I know I'm in a bad place. I know you're only trying to help. And while it might seem at times like I'm not, I am grateful."
   "It's okay. I just don't know what to do, Dan, that's all."
   "You don't have to do anything."

An incoming call alert chirped through the AirPods and pulling out her phone, she saw it was a call from Chris. She knew she couldn't really ignore it.
   "Dan, look I'm really sorry but I got another call. Can we chat another time?"
   "Yeah sure, whatever. It's fine."

Saying their goodbyes quickly, she connected her fiancé's call.

"Hey babe. All okay?"
   "Yeah. The florist called, they said you haven't been to look at the floral samples they were going to show you today?"
   Fuck! I completely forgot.

"Don't worry, on my way now. Just stopped to get a coffee as I needed a little pick-me-up."

"Sure. See you at home later then, shouldn't be late back from work."

"Okay babe. Love you."

Chris clicked off the call without saying *I love you* back. She was used to it; he'd never been very good at being forward with his feelings. Once they'd settled down into their easy relationship, a lot of the cute sweet moments when he'd tell her how he felt about her, had dwindled.

She put her phone in her pocket and headed back to the car; it was time to get back to her life and focus on that for a bit. She could check in with Dan again another day.

* * *

After talking to Laura, Dan felt like he ought to make some changes if he was ever to get better. The fact that she seemed to care, along with the support of those closest to him in his life spurred him on to try and turn things around. He was getting sick of starting over at meetings time after time.

He spent the next little while tidying up the house and cleaning. He hadn't quite descended into squalor yet but uncharacteristically for someone who loathed mess, he'd let the dishes build up in the sink and hadn't cleared away the last few days' worth of half-eaten food containers. It felt good to keep his mind and hands busy.

When he'd straightened the sofa cushions for the fourth time, he realised he actually had nothing else to do. Feeling the familiarity of habit drawing his attention to the kitchen and the bottles of whiskey hidden in the cupboard by the sink, he pulled out his phone as a distraction. In his notifications, of which there were precious few these days, was a message from Issy.

Issy: Hey. How are you doing today? Did you go to the meeting?

He knew it was more than just a casual enquiry, she was checking up on him but after months of this, it was beginning to wear thin although he knew that she was only doing it out of love.

Dan: Hey. Yeah, I'm okay. Went to the meeting, yeah, it was alright.

Issy: That's good. If you feel up to it do you want to see Max? He's missing you. It's been about a week or so since you last saw one another.

Dan knew this was exactly what he needed. His heart leapt at the thought of seeing his son again, even if it was only for a few hours. The distance between them was vast and he hated it.

Dan: Yeah, please. I'd love that if he'd like to.

He'd not had the energy to meet Laura, but he would crawl through fire if he had to, to see Max, he was so desperate for time with his boy.

Dan: I can take him out for tea maybe? To the chip shop at the end of your road? He still likes that one right?

The uncertainty of knowing what Max did and didn't like anymore troubled Dan so much that the self-doubt would threaten to overwhelm his fragile sobriety, had the thought of seeing his son not put him in such a good place.

Issy: He says yes. Come over tomorrow around five if you want?
Dan: Yeah great! Thanks Issy.

Dan punched the air.

At five minutes to five the next day, he rapped gently on Issy and Martin's front door, anxiety burning in his stomach. What greeted him filled his sore heart with joy.

"Dad!"

Max yanked the door open and rushed into his dad's arms.

"Hey, Maxxy. You okay? Missed you."

"Missed you too Dad. I'm okay."

Max didn't ask how Dan was. He didn't want to know. It was too hard, even for a boy of his age.

"You okay, mate?" Martin wandered casually through the hall towards them, causing Dan to look up. Martin could see the tears in his best friend's eyes, the emotion of a few moments with his son clear to see.

"Yeah. I am."

In recent weeks, it had become hard for Dan to visit Martin and Issy in their home. He felt so much guilt and shame for the whiskey-soaked disappointment he'd become that looking them in the eye and making small talk felt overwhelming.

Martin just smiled and nodded. "Right, Max take your coat

240

mate," handing it to his godson as he spoke.

"We won't be too long."

"Take your time. Enjoy your dinner together."

With that, the boys said their goodbyes and headed off down the street.

They spent the next hour or so talking about school and Lego and how Aunty Issy always made Max brush his hair before school, while eating their fish and chips.

"Go easy on that."

Max took a huge slurp from his can of coke and burped loudly.

"Sorry." His cheeky grin made him look anything but apologetic.

They both giggled at the silliness of it.

When the laughter died out, Max spoke quietly.

"When can I come home, Dad?"

Dan sighed and looked lovingly at him; his little face was trying hard to mask his desperation, his eyes pleading.

"Soon I hope. I need a few more days to get better and then I can talk to Issy."

Max stared at his empty chip tray. "You said that last time."

Dan felt like his heart was being crushed by his son's brutally honest words.

"I know. And the time before that. But Max, you have to trust me, I want to get better. I do. I want to be well again and have you back home where you belong. It's just…"

Max looked up and held his dad's gaze.

"It's just what?"

Dan felt the shame of all his broken promises wash over him.

241

"It's just hard to break this habit."

They fell silent as the chip shop bustled around them. Max reached across the table, putting his small hand on his dad's wrist.

"You can do it. I believe in you."

"Thank you." His heart caught in his throat as he said it. Where his son's strength and positive outlook came from he really didn't know but he was forever grateful for it.

When he dropped Max off with Martin and Issy a little while later, he walked away with bruised ribs from his boy's not-so-gentle goodbye hug and a renewed sense of determination that this time he could do it.

* * *

Laura dunked her tea-bag into her cup, squeezing it out between the teaspoon and her fingers while she waited for Sarah to join her.

She'd come to Sanctuary to see her friend. She needed to talk, just needed someone to help her work through everything, as holding onto it all in her head was becoming too much.

Sarah finished up, handing over to Jules, her part-time waitress and came over to join the troubled Laura.

"Sorry babe. All yours."

"It's okay."

"How is he?"

Laura was unsure what to say. She exhaled slowly and tried to find an answer to the question. Truthfully, she didn't know.

"Erm...okay I think? I don't really know."

Sarah looked at her quizzically.

"I mean, he's alright I think. When I last spoke to him he was sober and had just been to a meeting. But we were meant to meet for coffee at lunchtime that day and he never showed. We talked briefly on the phone and he said he couldn't face coming back out. So in the grand scheme of things, I don't really know if he is okay or not."

Laura's head throbbed from the confusion of it all. "One thing I do know? I understand now a little bit of what it must have been like for him for all that time before you gave me the book."

"How do you mean?"

"I just want to help him, Sarah. But he's keeping me at arm's length. It's fucking frustrating sometimes. I just want to talk to him and spend some time with him but he doesn't let me in easily."

"That must be shit."

"Mhmm it is. I'm guessing I'm not one to talk though. It's exactly how I was with him, isn't it? He just wanted to talk to me and I..."

Sarah thought about how her friend must be feeling, torn between what she could have done differently had she known the truth and what she could do now the situation had changed. She had always wondered how Laura, who was a really nice girl, had seemed so indifferent towards Dan. Curiosity got the better of her.

"Why were you like that with him?"

Guilt caused Laura to look away.

"I just never saw him. I hate myself for it. I was too wrapped up in myself and the wedding to see him for who he really was. The irony of it being that had I actually noticed him, he'd not be in this mess and I think we'd have gotten on really well, you know, been friends. Despite the state he's in now, he still seems like someone I'd actually really like to spend time with."

"Can I say something, babe? And it's said with love."

"Mhmm sure." Laura knew some hard truths were coming.

"You're not responsible for where he is now. That's on him. But...he's a really good guy and you should have noticed him. He was kind and gentle, and wickedly creative. You two would have probably had a laugh together if you'd just paid attention to who and what was around you for once."

Laura knew her friend was right. She'd become really self-absorbed in recent months, focused on sorting out the wedding and keeping the work coming in. It wasn't a side of her that she particularly liked.

"Do you think he's not any of those things anymore?"

"I dunno babe. I really don't. I'd like to think those aspects of his character are still in him but it's been a long time since I've seen him so I don't know the damage he's done to himself, or how lasting that might be."

Sarah softened as she saw Laura's head sink on her shoulders. She continued, "look, you didn't destroy him. He did that to himself. Maybe just pay a little more attention to the world around you in future? Take a breath and look up once in a while. You never know who or what this universe will bring into your life if you do."

Laura nodded. She knew Sarah was right.

"So what do I do now?"

"Just keep trying to follow your gut. If you want to help, then help, as much as he will let you. If you want to talk to him, call him. Just do what you feel is right."

* * *

In an effort to be a functioning human being, he decided that a home-cooked meal would be a good alternative to nutrition-lite ready meals for one. During these past few months, his microwave had seen as much action as it had while he was at university. Now as he was sobering up, his body was craving nutrients and something good to eat.

Having spent the day texting with Max after their trip to the chip shop, Dan was feeling like he could actually do it this time; he really could get this monkey off his back and return to normal life, riding on the wagon.

Realising he had no proper food left in the house, he made his way to the supermarket picking up a steak and vegetables. For a fraction of a second, his gaze turned to the aisle at the end of the store where his drug of choice sat adorning shelves from floor to ceiling. Taking a deep breath, he moved away, paid for the items in his basket and headed home.

Later that evening, the Muir family kitchen was a scene of devastation. The basic act of making of a simple meal for one had proved too big a challenge for the recovering Dan and with the timing apparently too hard for him to fathom, he sat on the floor drinking Jack straight from the bottle; a cremated sirloin steak going cold in the pan and boiled-dry peas on the hob above his head.

He felt useless. It shouldn't have been that hard but when one thing going wrong led to another, he had quickly lost control of the situation and had eventually given up and reached for the reassurance of the bottle.

Issy called, pulling him from his self-inflicted sorrow.

"Hey. How you getting on?"

She sounded cheerful. The last thing he needed.

"Not good. Burnt my steak."

"Huh? What steak?"

Dan slurred his way through a confusing explanation which Issy struggled to keep up with but she understood the end result.

"It happens, Dan. You're not the first person to burn a meal."

"Yeah." He took another swig of whiskey.

"Okay. I'm coming over to help you get cleaned up."

He knew she was talking about the kitchen but the implication that she also meant him and the sickly state he was in, stung.

Hanging up the call, he kept the phone in his hand and loaded up his messages with Laura. The devil on his shoulder willed him on, while the rational part of his brain tried in vain to fight.

Dan: Can't even cook food for myself. Not sure why you bother with me. Bottoms up.

Hitting send, he tossed his phone away, skittering it across the kitchen floor where it came to rest under the table.

When Issy arrived, she went straight to work. Disconnecting Dan from his bottle, she sent him to go have a shower and freshen up before she poured the remaining whiskey straight down the sink, for what felt like the hundredth time. By the time Dan returned, less inebriated and changed into clothes that didn't smell of burnt steak, she'd blitzed the kitchen and was making herself a cup of coffee; his phone returned to the top of the dining table.

"Sorry, Issy."

"It's okay."

"No it isn't. I know it's not."

"Dan, today is the first time in a long time that you've not only been sober but you've tried to take care of yourself. That's progress. Yes, I know that it didn't go to plan and…" She didn't finish the thought, instead added "I'm proud of you."

"I'll try again tomorrow."

"I know."

"Thanks, Issy. For tidying up and stuff." He felt ashamed not only for his behaviour but for his inability to even care for himself at the most basic of levels.

"It's okay. We'll go again tomorrow."

Kissing her cheek as she left a little while later, Dan felt like he'd failed her again. He shut the front door and looked across the living room. It was horribly empty without Max; the weight of his absence was crushing. Resigning himself to another disappointment, he trudged despondently to bed.

* * *

Issy was relieved when Dan opened the door, that he seemed to be doing okay. He looked as though he'd had a shower and had tidied himself up, along with the front room behind him. It was a reassuring sight after a rough few weeks.

"Hey you!"

"Hey."

They hugged, as they had always done on meeting ever since Natalie's death.

"You okay?"

When she used to ask immediately after losing her sister, Issy always did it out of sympathy and a desire to help. Now, she dreaded asking; it meant more problems if he said no. She was exhausted from trying to hold her family together by her fingernails.

"I'm okay. Having a good few days. No more burnt steaks."

"Sure?"

He stepped back and smiled.

"I'm sure. Haven't had a drink since the other night. Managing to sleep more like a normal person. I even managed another meeting yesterday."

"Ah, I'm pleased! Want me to tell Max?"

"Erm just give me a little longer? I just want to get a few more days under my belt before I tell him. I don't want him getting his hopes up again. What's in the bag?"

Dan looked pointedly at the carrier bag that she held.

"I made lasagna again last night and there are leftovers. Max wanted you to have it. So I figured you'd appreciate a home-cooked meal, y'know, something other than a ready meal, and you said you liked the last one."

"Thanks, Issy. I really appreciate it." And he did, but he'd had months of her trying to be the perfect sister-in-law, trying to fix everything and it was starting to wear thin as he scrambled to control his drinking problem on a day-to-day basis.

"Ah, you're welcome. It's no trouble at all, you know that."

They wandered through to the kitchen where she placed the bag containing the pasta onto the counter, before they sat at the table.

"I'm glad you're doing okay. I really think you can do it this time."

"Thanks."

He really did look better. She was relieved that he seemed to be turning a bit of a corner. They talked about his recent meeting and how he'd felt it was time to pull himself together.

"Why don't I make us a coffee?" She asked, feeling as though she'd be staying a while.

"Yeah, sure." Even as Dan said it, he panicked. "It's okay! Let me." He stood quickly and tried to beat her to the kitchen counter but it was too late. She'd already spotted it tucked away behind the kettle.

He watched in horror, as she looked at it, defeated. A half-drunk bottle of whiskey he'd not poured away, just in case he needed it, if he couldn't stay on the wagon. He'd been sober for a few days, it was true but hadn't been able to get rid of that last bottle; the alcoholic in him not wanting to let go just yet.

"You fucking arsehole!"

"Issy. Let me explain."

She grabbed it from the side, knocking the kettle off its

stand as she did so.

"This is sober, is it?"

She was so tired of it all. For months she'd been trying to keep him from destroying himself for the sake of her nephew and her deceased sister. Night after night having to care for a grown man who just didn't want to fight to keep his life intact. Sleepless nights. Long days. Never sure what to tell his son about why his father was like this. She'd had enough.

"I kept it just in case I got in a really bad place. I haven't touched a drop for days, not since you were last here. I promise."

"It's all fucking lies, Dan!"

"Issy, you have to believe me!"

He was desperate for her to understand but he could see the hurt in her eyes. He'd let her down again. He'd let them all down again.

"My sister would be disgusted in you if she could see you right now, you know that right?"

The words hit him like a baseball bat to the stomach.

"You don't deserve to have Max back if you're going to keep this up. That boy shouldn't have such a shit father in his life. You know my mother is questioning why we're even bothering to help you?"

Dan thought about his mother-in-law, sat on her high horse sneering at his mere existence, telling everyone that she'd always said he was a waste of space.

"All of this fucking bullshit over some girl, Dan! She'll never be interested in you like this. Why would anyone want to be with a man like you?"

He was speechless; unable to do anything but listen to the verbal abuse pouring out of the angry woman standing in front of him, bottle in hand.

"And you'll never write another book if you keep this shit up. Your career is basically over, you know that, don't you? You're wasting your life and I'm fucking sure as hell that I won't keep my family around to see you destroy yourself! You want to mope in a bottle?" She brandished it at him, "be my fucking guest! But I'm done with you!"

She slammed it down on the counter and stormed out, shouting over her shoulder as she wrenched open the front door. "Keep the fucking lasagna!"

The bang of the front door against the living room wall reverberated throughout the house and was soon replaced with a deafening silence, leaving Dan alone with his darkening thoughts, staring at the bottle of golden liquor in front of him.

She was right. Natalie would be disgusted by the man he'd become. Max did deserve a dad who was better than he'd been. And his writing career was over; no one would want to read the words of a drunk.

She'll never be interested in you like this. Why would anyone want to be with a man like you?

It suddenly hit him that Laura was hanging around him out of pity, not compassion. She didn't care.

A dark feeling of resignation descended on him as Dan instinctively grabbed for the bottle and opened it, downing the remnants in one. The alcohol hit his system hard, blurring the lines between pain and hurt.

He grabbed his keys and headed to the corner shop for more bottles. Tonight he was going to lose himself to the darkness and for once he didn't care if tomorrow came or not.

* * *

Laura's Voicemail:

Dan: I don't want you coming round anymore. My life's a mess and you're just adding to it. Go bother someone else. You don't fool me, I know it's guilt keeping you around. You don't care. I don't need you. Leave me to my whiskey

* * *

Issy picked up her phone even though it was the last thing she wanted to do.

"Issy? It's Laura."

"Hey."

"Sorry to call late, but Dan's left me a really bad voicemail and I think he's gotten himself in a mess again."

Laura heard Issy sigh in resignation on the other end of the phone.

"Laura, look. I can't do this with him right now. I'm exhausted. We had a big fight and the last thing I want to do is to go round and save him again. I don't have it in me. I'm sorry."

"It's okay. I'll go. You just take a few days."

"Thank you. There's a key under the flowerpot on the left-hand side of the doorstop. Martin hid it there a while ago in case of emergencies. Sorry, but I have to go."

Laura's hands were shaking as she ended the call. He was alone. Everyone had given up on him as he destroyed the world around him. *Everyone but me. I'm not giving up on him.*

* * *

Laura closed the front door behind her and tentatively walked through the front room, feeling anxious about being in someone else's house, uninvited.

"Dan? It's me. Are you okay? I got your message."

Silence.

She began searching through the lower level of his house and

253

quickly found him slumped at the kitchen table, a spilt glass on its side in front of him, next to a two-thirds empty bottle of Jack.

"Dan!"

He awoke with a start and looked at her.

"What are you doing here? Don't you have a set at Sarah's?"

"That was hours ago. What happened? You were doing so well."

He'd managed nearly three days sober, but had fallen off the wagon yet again after Issy had unloaded all her annoyance at him.

"I'm a fuck up, might as well drink. Nothing better to do."
    "Dan, please you're nothing of the sort. Come on, let's get some coffee in you."
    She reached for the bottle.
    "No!"

He didn't shout but she knew that he wasn't in the mood to argue about it. His eyes were red raw from tears and emotions. Nervously, she covered his hand with hers as it gripped the glass bottle beneath.
    "It's okay Dan. I'm here. I'm not going anywhere."
    He laughed but there was no merriment in it.
    "You don't fool me."
    His hand slid out of hers and off the bottle as his head

dipped.

Laura gently moved the bottle away from him, realising he'd drifted out of consciousness briefly. Quickly, without looking back, she moved to the sink and upended the rest of his whiskey down the drain. She noticed another already empty bottle left carelessly on the side to her left.

"What are you doing here, Laura? I don't want you here."

"I'm here to help. I don't want you to go through this alone."

"Yeah, right."

"Please, Dan?"

She sat down opposite him at the table and tears formed in her own eyes. She hated seeing him like this, broken and a mess, the responsibility for his troubles weighing heavily on her.

"Let me help you."

"Why? It's not like you've ever cared anyway."

His words slapped Laura across the face, stinging all the way down to her heart as she stared back at him.

"Of course, I care about you! I wouldn't be here if I didn't!"

"Oh now you care now, now I'm ruined. But back then you didn't care about me."

"What are you talking about?"

"You! I'm talking about you, Laura! I was right there in front of you the whole time!" A whiskey fire burnt in his eyes as he glared at her.

She thought back to the moment she'd found out that he'd written a book of poetry about her and how she couldn't believe she'd not seen him. His words had wrapped themselves tightly around her consciousness and she'd not been able to stop reading them or thinking about them since.

"I'm sorry, Dan."

He didn't want to hear apologies. He was on a roll and nothing was stopping him.

"I was right there, hopelessly in love with you and all you ever did was look at me like I was shit on your shoe, unless it suited you."

Even though he was slurring his words and struggling to hold eye contact, Dan knew he'd opened up the one part of his heart he never wanted her to see; he'd regret it in the morning but right now he didn't care.

"You fucked with my head for months. One day you'd smile and say hi, then the next, you'd blank me or worse. You couldn't even hold a conversation with me. All I wanted to do was to talk to you."

The whiskey had made his head heavy, meaning he had to make a conscious effort to stay awake. Laura might have poured the rest of his bottle away but it was still swimming around sweetly in his body. Had he not just started having a go at her, he might have had a good little buzz going.

"Dan I'm so..."

He cut her off before she could finish. "Don't. I don't want to hear another apology."

They sat quietly at the kitchen table, each lost in their own thoughts. Laura just wanted to cry. Everything he'd said was correct from his perspective and while not necessarily true, she was acutely aware that she'd not really noticed him for months; too wrapped up in her own life to pay attention.

During the few weeks they'd spent together trying to get him through this mess, she'd always left his place regretting that they hadn't been able to find a sense of friendship before all this. He might have his problems, but he really was a lovely guy. He was just struggling to cope with the trauma of the last few years. Her next words came out of her quietly.

"I didn't see you."

Dan sniffed, drunkenly swatting at the tears in his eyes.

"It wasn't that I didn't want to be around you or didn't want to talk to you, I just..."

Laura didn't know how to finish that sentence in a way that wouldn't hurt.

"I just didn't see you. I was too caught up in my life. You were just around in the background. I was too busy thinking about work. And the wedding."

"Yeah."

"I didn't know it would cause this."

Dan wiped away more tears and took a deep breath; the whiskey in his addled brain starting to slide away.

"You wouldn't have known what it was doing to me. I didn't until it was too late."

She cast her gaze down at her hands, spinning one of the rings on her fingers, feeling ashamed.

He continued, "I don't blame you. There's just a tiny part of my heart that's mad at you."

Dan watched her wipe away her own tears.

"But it's a small part. The rest of my heart still feels the same, no matter how much whiskey I try to drown you with."

He rose and stumbled to the sink.

"Dan. Don't please." She panicked as she watched him. "We can get you through tonight. Please."

Rather than hunting for alcohol, which she assumed he was going to do, Laura watched as he poured himself a glass of water and downed it. He spoke with his back to her as he placed the glass back on the counter.

"I still love you, Laura and I hate it. It kills me every day. I'm past wanting you to love me back; I just want you out of my head. No amount of whiskey has done it. I just want this to stop."

Dan turned and slid down the front of the kitchen cupboard, his legs weak from everything he was feeling and the poison in his veins. He sobbed openly, now making no effort to hide it.

"Please, just get out of my head, let me be."

Laura's tears streamed down her face as she watched him pleading with her. He loved her so much that the only way out of his feelings was to drown himself in whiskey and hide from the world. He loved her so much that it was breaking him from the inside out. She had never witnessed a love so deep, so consuming. Compared to this, Chris's affection for her seemed purely surface-level. Dan's seared him straight through to his core.

While she hated what it was doing to him and that she had partly caused the damage he was now trying to wash away, she knew that he truly loved her. These weren't just words he was saying, they were words he was feeling deep in his soul.

She moved across the floor to sit next to him.

"I don't know how to fix this. What can I do?"

He whispered, alcohol-fuelled sleep starting to take him.

"Just get out of my head."

And with that, his head dropped onto her shoulder and he was asleep.

Laura pulled her knees up to her chest and cried. Weeks before when she'd come to see him she felt like she could have easily walked away, now she knew that she couldn't. She cared too much for him.

Sitting there shoulder to shoulder, she thought about what she should do. She definitely couldn't leave him like this, asleep on the kitchen floor. She knew she should probably let him sleep it off and go home but she didn't want to leave him alone. The only place she really wanted to be tonight was here with Dan, making sure he was okay.

She pulled out her phone and messaged Chris.

Laura: Hey babe. Gonna stay at Sarah's tonight, had a few too many glasses of wine. I'll be back in the morning.

She hated herself so much for the lies she was having to tell but right now sitting on Dan's kitchen floor, she didn't want to be anywhere else. He was her priority.

After a struggle, with him slipping in and out of a drunken, sleepy haze, Laura managed to get him upstairs and into bed. As she turned out the light and made to leave his room, she heard Dan mumbling.

"I'll always love you."

Padding quietly downstairs, her heart felt heavy. It wasn't just words said in a drunken stupor, he meant it even if he would break himself apart in the process.

She sat down on the sofa, pulling a blanket off the arm as she did. It wouldn't make a bad bed for the night, she'd slept on worse in her uni days but she wasn't tired yet; one ear listening out in case he needed her.

She glanced across at *Lucille*, resting on its stand covered in a thin layer of dust clearly unplayed in a while. Laura remembered the first time she'd seen the beautiful guitar on Dan's Instagram story. They'd spoken briefly about it before she'd got pulled away by a phone call and had cut the conversation short.

She'd never seen him play this guitar, only the one at Sanctuary during the Open Mic day. He was actually pretty good. Laura had watched him play one of her favourite songs but hadn't been able to fully appreciate it, her head full of thoughts of the wedding and where she'd sit everyone.

Her eyes fell on a picture on the dresser of Max and someone she assumed was his mum. Natalie. Dan's wife, his first true love. She couldn't begin to understand the hurt they must have both felt when she died. Max was such a lovely little boy from what she knew. Dan must have been a wonderful father, guiding his son through the grief of losing his mother while managing his own pain at the loss of his wife. She felt for them both and the lives they were living now, separated from each other after all they'd been through together.

Laura spotted a laptop on the desk in the corner of the room, under the window and recognised it as the one she'd always seen Dan using at Sanctuary. She hadn't known it at the time but he'd been writing poems about her, ones that months later still moved her whenever she remembered them.

Her phone chirped on the coffee table in front of her. It was his sister-in-law checking in.

Issy: Hey how is he? Do you need us to come over?

Laura: He's okay. He's asleep now. I'm gonna stay though, in case he needs me.

Issy: Okay. There's a duvet and pillow in the cupboard under the stairs. Martin left them there for when he needed to stay over. Call me if you need anything.

Laura: Thanks Issy.

After claiming her bedding for the night, she tried to settle down and sleep but she couldn't stop thinking about everything; her head full of thoughts she couldn't seem to grasp.

Waking in daylight, hours later, she couldn't remember when she'd fallen asleep but was grateful for the duvet as the house felt cold first thing in the morning.

"I don't want to do this anymore."

The voice startled her and she looked around to see Dan, sitting on the edge of the coffee table, holding out a mug of hot tea for her.

"Hey. You okay? How are you feeling?"

"I'm feeling like I want to go to a meeting today. I don't want to be this person anymore."

"Okay. You can do that."

She took the tea from him as she sat up.

"I'm sorry about last night Laura."

"It's okay. I'm just glad I was here." She assumed he was talking about getting drunk again.

"You didn't deserve to hear those things I said about you."

"I..." Laura wasn't sure what to say; she didn't understand how he could remember how the night had unfolded.

Seeing her reaction, he explained. "Part of being a high-functioning alcoholic is knowing what I've said and done after the fact. I just have no real control over it at the time. I'm sorry. None of this is your fault. You didn't do anything wrong. This is on me. But I don't want to be this broken person anymore."

She put the mug of tea down and moved to the edge of the sofa, taking his hand. It wasn't shaking anymore.

"You can do this. I'll be here the whole way; I promise."

"Thank you. You don't need to do anything really, this is for me to fix, but..."

"Dan? What is it?"

He sighed. "Will you take me to a meeting today please? I think I need that and I'm not sure I can go alone."

"Of course."

"There's one after lunch in town, at the church hall. You can't come in with me, but if you could just help get me there... "

"Okay, let me go home to shower and change, then I can come pick you up and we'll go, okay? I can wait in the car until you're done."

"Are you sure? I don't want to steal any more of your time."

"I'm sure. And it's only stealing if I'm not freely giving it."

As she drove away a little later, Laura wondered if he'd reached a turning point; if pouring the hurt out of his heart the night before had somehow helped him find some light.

* * *

She turned the key in her front door and relished the prospect of a hot shower, a change of clothes and a bit of breakfast. While she had slept last night, she still felt exhausted but also relieved that maybe he'd finally turned a corner after so long. Stepping across the threshold, she felt buoyant for the first time in a little while.

What greeted her, deflated her instantly.

"I thought you were staying at Sarah's?"

Chris was sitting on the sofa, brooding, not even looking at her.

Her mind scrambled as she tried to think of an explanation.

"Erm...I...I did. I texted you, didn't I?

Laura panicked. *What did he know?*

"Yeah, you texted me."

"So yeah, you knew I was at Sarah's."

"It's funny though," he said, rising from his seat, "that Sarah rang the house phone last night when she couldn't get an answer on your mobile. She wanted to know if everything was okay."

"Chris..."

"Why would she ring here trying to get hold of you when you told me you were staying at hers?"

"Look...let me..."

"Where were you, Laura?"

Fuck! Her mind ground to a halt under the stress of the situation. She couldn't think clearly no matter how desperately she needed to.

"I..."

"Well?"

Chris stood in front of her, towering over her smaller stature, anger raging through his veins. There had been too many times in recent weeks when Laura had been absent, disappearing for hours at a time when she was meant to be either at home or teaching. At first, he'd put it down to her being busy with the wedding but as time went on he'd begun to suspect a more sinister reason.

When she didn't answer, he moved back to the sofa and reached for the book he'd left under a cushion, out of sight.

Laura recognised it instantly and subconsciously moved her hand to her bag.

"I think you forgot this yesterday before you left for the cafe."

He waved it in front of her like it was some kind of winning lottery ticket. She could only wait as he toyed with her, knowing the final blow was yet to strike.

"I remember when you told me about this. That Sarah had lent it to you, that a friend of hers had written it. It's well worn, Laura, seems like you must've been reading it a lot."

"Chris, you don't understand. Just let me…"

"I had a little read of it myself last night. It's mostly sentimental bullshit if you ask me. It doesn't even rhyme."

"Don't you dare!"

Chris ignored her and kept talking.

"Then I did a little digging. Seems this was written by someone who you follow online. You two seem to be sharing a lot of likes on your posts too which I found fascinating really. Then I noticed that this guy knows Sarah too, I'm guessing you met him at her cafe?"

"You don't understand."

"The internet is a wonderful thing, isn't it? After I found that out, I managed to find an address for him and would you believe it? Your phone's location for the past ten hours has been at the same address! This is that same sappy piece of shit from Sanctuary isn't it? The one who couldn't keep his eyes off of you?"

"Don't talk about him like that!" She'd been found out but she wasn't prepared to let Chris talk about Dan like that.

His rage finally boiled over. In a split section, he was on her, grabbing her arm and shoving her hard against the living room wall.

"Don't fucking tell me what to say!" His hand gripped tightly as he pinned her.

"Chris, stop! You're hurting me!

"You spent the night in another man's bed! You're lucky it's not worse."

"I didn't sleep with him!"

"Don't fucking lie to me!" Using his significant height and weight difference he pulled her by the arm, throwing her into the centre of the room and rounded on her. She scrambled to get away.

"I'm not lying! He needed me. He's my friend."

"Bullshit!"

Holding her hands up in surrender she tried to reason with him. "Chris, he's an alcoholic, he got in a bad way last night and I went to help and make sure he was okay. That's all. I fell asleep on his sofa."

"You're lying! That's why you lied last night."

"No, I swear, I'm just trying to help him!"

"It's not your place to help him, Laura. Your place is here!"

His words irked her in a way she'd not expected. Rather than cowering away from his anger, she felt defensive.

"Of course it's my place to help him!"

"No it's not! You don't owe that loser anything!"

"Don't call him that!"

"Why? That's what he is!" Chris leered at her, almost baring his teeth.

"NO, HE ISN'T! IT'S MY FAULT CHRIS! I BROKE HIM!" She screamed at him.

For a moment there was silence between them before Laura spoke, this time quieter and calmer.

"He loves me, Chris and when I turned him down, it drove him to drink. It's broken his home and his family. I'm trying to help fix it. Please, at least try to understand."

Chris closed his eyes as the skin on the back of his neck crawled.

"He doesn't love you, Laura. He's just a sad sap who needs to get a life. But that doesn't excuse you sleeping at his house!"

Laura stared in disbelief at Chris.

"Doesn't love me? Doesn't love me? You're blinded by your vanity. What would you even know about love in comparison?"

"We're getting married."

"So?"

"So what? He doesn't love you, Laura."

Now it was Laura's turn to be angry. She grabbed the tattered copy of Endlessly from the floor where it had been discarded during their fight.

"This is how much he loves me." She held the book up to his face. "He poured his heart onto these pages in a way that you could scarcely imagine. Then he began to tear himself apart piece by piece, soaking himself in whiskey so he could cope with it all. What have you ever done that's even come close to that? Told me you loved me maybe four times total and bought me an engagement ring because it was in a sale?"

"So you love him now then?"

"That doesn't fucking matter Chris! What matters is you accusing me of the worst thing imaginable when I've been devoted to you for my entire life!"

"Didn't answer my question though, Laura?"

They weren't lovers anymore. They'd teetered over the edge of the love hate divide moments before and hadn't even noticed.

As if seeing him properly for the first time, Laura realised that she actually hated him. His judgement. His lack of support for her life choices. How he never stuck up for her. The way he ate food was like he was some kind of fucking animal. She could barely stand to look at him and seeing him glare back at her, she knew the feeling was mutual.

"Get out." He said it calmly but she knew he meant it and if she didn't go now, things could turn even nastier. "Get out and don't come back."

Laura stood tall, the feeling of his grip on her arm still throbbing, along with the rapidly growing bruises on her back. Holding her head high, because the lie about where she spent the night was the only reason she had to feel guilt and shame, she stalked past him and wrenched open the front door.

It wasn't until she was driving away that the tears and the shakes found her, causing her to pull into an empty bus stop. Rushing out of the car she dashed to the curb and vomited into a bin, her legs feeling weak beneath her.

"You okay, dear?"

Laura looked up to see the concerned, gentle face of a little old lady who was waiting at the bus stop.

"Mhmm. Sorry." And with that, she drove off speeding towards Sarah's flat. She needed someone who understood. She needed to cry and scream and rage. And she needed a shower.

* * *

For the short drive she pretended that she was just tired. Dan commented that she looked as white as a sheet and maybe she was coming down with something but she played it off as the fault of his lumpy sofa. She even managed a fake wink as she said it.

Mercifully he was deep in his own thoughts, so she was able to fly her problems under the radar. Laura needed him to be focused right now; the shitshow of her life could wait a couple more hours. If he slipped back now then last night would have all been for nothing; wasted like the last few years of her relationship.

"Well, here we are. Sure you're okay?" She asked, trying to concentrate on him rather than letting her bubbling emotions get the better of her.

Dan sighed and looked across at the church hall entrance. "Yeah. I will be. This needs to happen."

She studied him closely as he watched the doors opening and closing with members making their way in. Laura realised how proud she was of him, both for coming back and for being ready to push through. He looked lighter. She knew some form of emotional ballast had shifted in him and now he was ready to move forward. It all just added to the emotions she was fighting to hold at bay.

"I'll be right here."

"Thank you. Time to do this first meeting for the last time."

Her tears began to fall when he'd only taken a few steps from the car. She stared intently at his back as he moved across the car park and towards the main entrance, holding back as much as she could while silently willing him on.

When he finally stepped into the building and disappeared from view, her head dropped onto the steering wheel and her body began to shake with the sobs she was unable to contain any longer.

For the duration of Dan's meeting, Laura sat in her car, parked up opposite the church hall and mourned the loss of her previous life, her relationship and her lost years with Chris. She raged against the guilt she felt from ending their relationship with a lie, her shame at hiding her support of Dan from her fiancé and for the way his poetic, lyrical lines gripped her heart. The sting from Chris's bruises on her arms and back ached as she replayed the last twenty-four hours in her mind.

Churning it all over, she realised that Dan had turned his anger and emotions inwards on himself, burdening his own heart; while Chris's first thought was to lash out and hurt her. The memory made her shudder.

As the clock ticked further through the hour, Laura began to realise she was feeling something akin to relief. Only now that she was out of her relationship, she was aware that deep down, she hadn't really want to get married at all. It just felt like an inevitable part of life and their relationship; the logical next step. A speeding train that she couldn't get off.

Before she could work her way through her feelings on it though, she spotted Dan walking back out into the sunshine. Quickly she dried her eyes and wiped her face, using the mirror on her sun visor to make sure she showed no signs of the tears that had flowed so freely.

"Hey! How was it?" She asked, forcing herself to sound bright

271

and bubbly.

He held up a bunch of leaflets and smiled. "Day one done. Again."

"How does it feel?"

"For the first time, it feels like the start of what's to come."

She threw her arms around his neck and hugged him; more for her own benefit than his. "I'm so proud of you!"

After getting over the initial shock of her body against his, something he still wasn't accustomed to, Dan gently held her. "Thank you. You helped bring me back, Laura. I can't thank you enough for that."

She cried on his shoulder, knowing that saving Dan had cost her her relationship.

"Hey, why are you crying?"

She sat back, drying her eyes. "I'm just happy for you." It was a lie she needed to tell but one that didn't feel good leaving her mouth. "Come on, let's get you home. I think some food will do us both some good, don't you? Why don't we get some bits from the shop on the way back and I can do us a fry-up?"

She was thinking with her stomach; she hadn't eaten since leaving for her set the night before and hoped that cooking would distract her for a while.

* * *

"Jesus, that was good!" Dan sat back happily and patted his stomach.

After getting back, they'd cooked together and talked about the parts of his meeting he was able to share with her. He'd explained that a form of detox was likely to come in a few days no matter how good he felt to begin with. It would be hard and he'd need to be strong. Laura promised she would check on him every day to help him, until he was through the worst of it.

When they'd cleaned up the kitchen and put pots away, Dan poured two glasses of juice and Laura nodded towards the living room "Shall we have these in comfort?"

They settled into opposite ends of the sofa and there was a pause before Dan spoke.

"It's okay, you know? You don't have to stay if you don't want to."

"Kinda want to stay for a bit if that's alright with you?" She didn't have the heart to tell him that now she technically had nowhere to go. While Sarah had promised her a bed at her house until she got back on her feet, she still for all intents and purposes, was homeless.

"Well, you might be keeping me company while I sleep in a minute. That lunch has finished me off!"

Dan wasn't lying and within a few moments was snoring softly on the sofa next to her. She took the moment of solitude to curl herself into a ball and hug a pillow for comfort. It didn't take her long until she too was fast asleep; the emotions and exhaustion of the day finally winning over.

When she woke, Dan was looking at her.

"Hey. Sorry. I didn't mean to fall asleep." She rubbed her eyes, wondering what time it was.

"It's fine, but after the night you had on this sofa last night, don't you think your own bed might be a little better for you?"

Laura looked sheepishly at him as she rested her head on the cushion.

"I guess."

273

"Don't you want to go home?"

She looked away, afraid that if she maintained eye contact he'd see right through her.

"Laura? Don't you want to go home?" The repeated question was one of concern.

"It's fine."

Dan hesitated. He felt as though it was very much as far from fine as it could get. Something was wrong, he could tell.

"It's not though is it? Does he know?" He couldn't bring himself to use Chris's name, "that you stayed here last night?"

She got up from the sofa and walked towards the kitchen. "I said it's fine."

Dan followed her. "What aren't you telling me?"

"It's okay, Dan. Please."

"Laura, talk to me!"

She kept her back to him. She didn't want him to see her face or the tears streaming down her cheeks. "We need to focus on you right now. I need to help you stay strong." Her voice wobbled as she spoke.

"Why don't you want to go home, Laura?"

Her shoulders slumped. He wasn't going to let this go. "Because I don't have a home to go to."

"What?!"

"Chris ended things with me this morning. I had to leave"

The weight of her words made Dan stagger back against the side of the sofa, where he steadied himself. In an instant he realised she was still dressed in the same outfit she'd been wearing when she left earlier that morning.

It hadn't occurred to him before; too wrapped up in his own shit to realise something was gravely wrong. She'd not been able to go home and change as she'd planned; more than likely walked indoors to her life being upended.

"Fuck."

Laura turned and made her way back to him. "It's not important. What's important is you and keeping you sober right now."

"Is it because of me?"

"Dan, don't do this, please? Let's stay focused, yeah?"

She was fighting through her tears trying to keep him steady. He sat down hard on the sofa looking away as he slumped.

"I'm so sorry."

"You have nothing to be sorry for," she said softly, sitting down next to him. "He was mad because I lied about staying here. It's my fault."

"It isn't, Laura, it's mine. I should never have put this on you."

"He just doesn't want to understand that you needed me or that for my part, I needed to be here last night to help you. He said and did some terrible things."

Dan began to shake. "What did he do?"

"It doesn't matter. I'm okay now."

He turned to look straight at her, dismay on his face. "What did he do?"

Looking at her hands, she began to explain everything that had happened; how Chris had been waiting for her when she returned home, how he'd known she'd lied and how he discovered the truth about where she'd been all night.

Dan listened carefully as best he could, hoping it wouldn't get any worse. She was able to hold back most of her tears but when she began to explain how he'd grabbed her and shoved her against the wall in anger, her voice broke.

"Fuck!" He wanted to riot and smash things, to rush to her now ex-fiance to defend her honour. Dan felt his mood darkening and for the first time in months, it was nothing to do with alcohol.

Laura saw him tense. "It's my fault. I made him angry."

Dan took hold of her arms and looked into her eyes. "His behaviour is not your responsibility. Don't enable him by taking the blame for this."

When she winced, he realised he was inadvertently hurting her, his hands igniting the bruises where she'd been grabbed by that low-life piece of shit, Chris. Dan let go of her instantly.

"Shit. I'm sorry." He looked mortified.

"It's okay. It's just a bit sore, that's all." She moved closer, savouring the warmth and the comfort of his proximity, while also trying to calm him. "I'm okay. I promise. It's just all very raw right now."

"Why didn't you tell me?"

She owed him honesty. "Because I didn't want this to derail you so early on. When you woke me up this morning, you seemed like a different person entirely and I really didn't want my problems to be the cause of you going backwards."

Dan thought about his situation. He was devastated for her, that his actions had caused the breakup of her relationship and that she'd been physically hurt in the process. He wanted to rage against Chris and show him how a real man communicates with a woman. He wanted to hold Laura until the tears stopped and to protect her from everything that sought to do her harm. But the one thing he didn't want to do was drink.

It was, in the middle of all the chaos swirling around them, a curious feeling. Had he been going through a personal trauma alone, he could have easily given in to an urge. But now? All he wanted to do was keep Laura safe.

"Honestly, I think I'm okay. The last thing I want to do right now is drink. I might want to kill him but I don't want to drink." He pulled her into a hug.

"Dan, don't be like that. It isn't you."

"Sorry."

"Listen, if you have the urge to drink, you don't have to hide it from me. It's better we talk about it."

"I promise I'm not. All I want right now is to make sure you're okay."

"I will be." She closed her eyes against his chest and knew that while he might be fragile, he really didn't want to see her come to any more harm.

"Look, stay here tonight. Stay as long as you need. I can make the spare room up."

She pulled herself from him and smiled. "That's not a good idea Dan."

Her response made him look away, worried that he had said the wrong thing.

Placing her hand on the side of his face, she made him look at her. "It's not that I don't want to take you up on the offer. But you're recovering and you need to focus on yourself, not me. Both of us are emotionally fragile right now, that's not a good combination. And if I stay, we also run the risk of fuelling the fire that Chris is feeling right now and that's the last thing I want."

He knew she was right. "Okay."

"I'll be fine."

"Where will you go?"

"Sarah's. I saw her this morning and she has said I can stay there, while this all gets sorted."

Dan nodded.

"But I'll be on the end of the phone, you can text me if you need me and I can come back tomorrow if you want me to."

* * *

Dan's body was racked with pain and tension as he tried to stop the shakes overwhelming his system. He now understood why his mind had never let him go longer than three days without concocting some reason to drink; it was protecting him from going through this torture.

The first few days had been okay. Laura had stopped by every day to make sure he wasn't going through it alone and with her help he'd managed to focus on getting his life in order. He'd known this was coming, it had been spoken about at his meetings.

It had begun with a bad night's sleep, Dan spending the entire night tossing and turning, unable to fully fall asleep. By the time he'd dragged himself out of bed the following morning, his head had been pounding like an over-excited toddler with a drum.

After he'd been to his morning meeting, Laura had arrived with coffee a little after 10 am and even though he badly needed the caffeine hit, the smell turned his stomach. They'd sat together for a while talking and watching mindless daytime TV but he couldn't focus and she could see he was struggling.

"Hey, why don't you go and lie down for a bit? I can come and wake you up in a little while so you don't wreck your sleep for tonight."

It pained Laura to watch her friend trying to fight against the shakes; the most obvious visual cue of his body beginning to go into detox.

"Mhmm yeah, okay." If he didn't know better, Dan would have sworn he was coming down with the flu', an unholy mix of feeling hot and cold and achy all at the same time. This was no flu though; there was no medication that would fix this.

The first hour in bed had felt like a lifetime as he desperately fought against his body and what it was craving. The only way to stop this was with alcohol. He knew that but while Dan's body felt like it was coming apart at the seams, his mind stayed resolved. He had to do this. He couldn't be that person anymore.

Laura muted the TV when she heard him cry out. For a moment she wondered if she should go and check on him or wait to see if he quietened down. Another muffled moan minutes later made the decision easy for her and without even turning the TV off, she climbed the stairs to his bedroom.

Waiting at the door a moment, she steeled herself, pushing it open against the silence inside. Tentatively she looked in, he seemed to be sleeping, a fever breaking on his face.

Turning back, she headed to the bathroom to find a flannel, soaking it in cold water, before wringing it out. Moving back to Dan's room, she knelt beside him as he writhed unconsciously in a feverish dream. She dabbed the cold flannel on his

279

forehead, tender and gentle.

After a few seconds, the coolness began to work on his headache and he began to relax into a quieter sleep. Relieved, Laura placed the damp cloth onto his nightstand and stood up. A part of her didn't want to leave him; even though he was now asleep she didn't want him to be alone.

Intending to sit on the floor next to the bed, she took a step back and as she did, a white wooden rocking chair in the corner of the room caught her eye. Simple and unobtrusive, a slender frame with two plump pillows; one to sit on, one as back support; a folded grey blanket tucked underneath.

Deciding that it was probably a way better place to sit than the floor, she sat down and settled herself. She ran her hands over the arm rests as she rocked gently, sinking into the softness of the cushions. It was one of the most comfortable chairs she had ever experienced. Resting her head back, she watched through half-closed eyes as he slept and relaxed enough that within a few minutes, she was asleep herself.

"How's your book?" Dan asked groggily from the bed, still very much in the throes of sleep.

Laura had only been awake a few moments herself and hadn't noticed that he'd started to stir. It seemed like an odd question and it surprised her.

"Huh?"

"The book you were reading the other day?"

Aside from her copy of *Endlessly*, she hadn't read a book in a while and definitely hadn't been reading in front of him. *Maybe he was still delirious.*

"Dan, I haven't been reading anything?"

Rolling up onto his elbows, he focused again on Natalie reclining in her favourite spot. She loved to read in the afternoon, sitting with him if he was napping. As he looked harder, he realised it was Laura who was in the room with him.

"Sorry, I thought you were..."

Realisation dawned on her as he looked away. This must have been his wife's chair. She felt like an intruder.

"Dan, I'm so, so sorry." She started to get up.

"No. Don't. It's okay. Just, no-one has sat there since..."

Laura was trapped. Caught between his request not to get up and her desire to not be sitting in a dead woman's chair.

"Honestly Laura, it's okay. It's just a chair. How long was I out for?"

"Erm a few hours I think. You had a pretty bad time of it but you seemed to settle after I came up. I didn't mean to fall asleep, sorry."

"Hey, it's okay. That chair has an innate ability to make anyone that sits in it fall asleep."

"This was Natalie's chair, wasn't it?" The words rushed out of her before she paused thought about what she was saying and left Laura feeling sick as she heard herself.

"It was. She'd spend hours reading in that chair, even slept in it a few times when she was pregnant and couldn't easily lie down."

"Oh."

Dan could see the discomfort written across her face.

"It's just a chair, Laura. Sorry, I wasn't with it when I woke up. Someone needed to sit in it eventually." He gave her a half-smile.

"It is bloody comfortable, I'll give you that."

He chuckled. "She found it years before Max was born at some car boot sale. I was adamant I didn't want it in the house because back then it looked like a piece of shit. But she didn't listen and brought it home anyway - typical Natalie. She spent a summer sanding it down and repainting it before she gave it a new home here in the bedroom."

Laura smiled. She adored stories like that, where things weren't just objects but memories.

"If you look on the left arm, you'll find little notches in it."

She lifted her hand and soon found small indentations in the wood, which looked oddly like teeth marks.

"Max. Went through a phase of biting things; that's his handiwork."

There was a comfortable silence for a moment and then Laura spoke.

"How are you feeling?"

"Better."

"Seemed pretty rough there for a bit?"

"Mhmm. But my head's clearer now. I just ache."

"You should think about eating something."

As if on cue, his stomach gurgled. "Yup I think you're right. At least now the idea of food isn't making me feel sick."

* * *

Dan cleared away the plates and came back carrying a drink in each hand; a tea for Laura and a decaf coffee for himself.

He was not about to replace one bad habit with another.

He noticed her staring at the mantelpiece.

"I'm guessing that's Natalie?" Laura nodded towards the photo of Natalie and Max, a happy image of them both laughing. "Max has her eyes but he's like a mini you." She sighed, quietly adding as he sat down, "she was very beautiful, Dan."

"She was; inside and out. You would have loved her. Everybody did."

He paused. He could have seen Laura and Natalie getting on like a house on fire and it left him with an uncertain, uneasy feeling.

"She had this way of putting everyone at ease," he shook his head wryly. "I have no idea how she managed that with me some days but she did. From pretty much the moment we met, my heart was hers. For someone who makes money coming up with words, I've always found it hard to find any that would explain it. It was just as though my heart knew hers. I felt compelled to talk to her. Like I couldn't have fought the urge to approach her even if I'd wanted to. It was the right thing; like some cosmic pull I had no control over or desire to fight against. She just understood me. She saw me. She was my safe place."

Laura sighed. "I don't think I ever felt completely safe with Chris. Wait, that sounds bad," she added hurriedly. "Like I didn't feel unsafe. I wasn't scared of him, well not until the

283

end. But I never felt that sense of... I'm not sure what the word is? Permanence, maybe? I loved him but he didn't feel like forever."

She lost herself to her thoughts for a moment wondering why she'd never vocalised that with her former fiancé, even though she'd been aware of feeling that lack for a while.

Dan nodded. "Ah, it was the opposite for me. I never imagined my world without her. I was in it for life. I guess when we said, 'till death do us part', we meant it. Neither of us thought that would come around quite so quickly though, you know?"

Laura stuttered, "Dan I don't know what to say... it must..."

Reaching for her hand, he reassured her; the warmth of her soft skin against his felt like comfort rather than something to make him recoil. Months before, he'd never really imagined he'd ever be in a place where he'd be sat opposite Laura Gray in his own house, let alone holding her hand.

"It's okay. No one ever does. Least of all me at times, but it is what it is." He paused and considered his words carefully.

"In life and in love I'm an all-in kind of guy. For me, it's got to feel right. In my work, in my friendships, in love, I know it's something special if it touches my soul. It's like ...I know the universe will bring the things and the people into my life that are meant for me. So I trust it. Yeah, it's thrown some tough shit my way but it's also given me the best of the best.

I am incredibly lucky to have had a life with Natalie. She gave me Max and he is the most amazing thing ever. I'm glad to have loved her. It taught me a lot. Love isn't something I give away lightly or easily and if I'm honest I struggle to accept it too. I can't do casual, I don't have it in me. If I fall, it's deep and all-consuming; my heart doesn't seem to know any other way. My heart always seems to know what I need..."

Dan's voice fell away, the two of them silently contemplating what he'd said and what that meant.

When Laura had first read his poems, she'd thought that it was some sort of simple infatuation and while it was very sweet, it probably wasn't all that deep or serious. In recent days though, seeing Dan tear himself apart trying to cope with his emotions, she'd wondered if she had underestimated the strength of his feelings. Now, hearing him talk about how he loved, she started to understand that Dan wasn't the type for casual flings or passing fancies. He trusted his heart when it pulled him to someone even when he didn't understand it and that meant that his love for her was something tangible and lasting.

"I've never experienced that," she said, quietly.

"I don't think many people do, to be honest."

"The last few months must have been horrible for you."

He could see where she was going and wanted to stop this before it gathered pace.

"Laura, don't torture yourself. Let's just leave the past in the past. Maybe now I'm on the road to recovery, we can just be friends?"

She nodded. "I'd like that." She took a breath, glancing around the room. "Feels like a new day doesn't it?"

* * *

Over the following weeks, Laura and Dan struggled individually through their own personal battles.

While he was through the worst of the detox, his cravings for alcohol at times were intense. Having made amends with Issy for everything he'd put her and Martin through, he'd ended up spending time with them at their house as a distraction from the habit he was so desperately trying to break. While still wary of the possibility of him sliding backwards, Issy had wanted to try and keep him moving forwards as best she could. If having Dan sat on their sofa while he tried to keep himself focused was the way to do that, then it was something she was prepared to go along with.

Knowing his dad wasn't well, Max had taken to sitting with him as they watched TV together. Whenever Dan felt the shakes or an urge for alcohol coming on, he would pull his son close and wait for it to pass. Together they worked through some tricky moments.

Dan made sure he attended his daily meetings, wanting to replace the habit of drinking with the new habit of sobriety. He'd even taken to walking to the church hall when the weather was nice enough. By the end of the first week he'd even gone with Issy to collect Max from school much to the delight of the boy.

He kept in contact with Laura via text as they both seemed to need that connection while times were rough.

She was doing alright for the most part; staying at Sarah's in her spare room while she reclaimed her stuff from the house she had shared with Chris and trying to look for a new place to set down roots.

It wasn't easy for her. Many evenings had been spent crying on the sofa, as they talked about everything that was happening with Sarah beside her and Buddy, Sarah's dog with his head on her knee.

On the first night, her friend had offered to open a bottle of wine but Laura had declined. Drinking didn't feel fair to Dan and the journey he was going through. And if she was honest with herself, alcohol had lost its appeal.

Her now ex had turned from a half-decent fiancé to a complete and utter arsehole in the space of a few days as he railed against the hurt he felt over losing Laura.

When she'd gone back to collect some things days after the breakup, she had found that he'd carelessly dumped some of her stuff in a pile in the front room. Some of her possessions had even been damaged in his anger, including a cherished copy of her favourite book, *Alice in Wonderland*. Seeing it ripped and torn as a result of his fury had broken her heart and she'd sat on the floor crying quietly, surrounded by her possessions as she contemplated her new life.

With a stroke of luck, Sarah had come home from work one afternoon to tell Laura with some excitement that she knew someone with a flat that was ready for a tenant to move into straight away if she wanted it. "Not that I don't love having you and you're welcome to stay as long as you want, but I know you'd prefer your own space."

Feeling a little hopeful, they'd gone to see it that same evening and decided it was perfect, accepting it on the spot.

As they left, Laura had paused, pulling out her phone. Sarah had watched as her friend had taken a picture of the flat's front door. Seeing her curious look, Laura explained.

"I'm gonna send it to Dan. He'd like that."

And he had done. Knowing that she was going to be okay and had successfully removed herself from the life she had with Chris had been a huge relief and a positive note to the end the week on. Dan promised to visit when she was all settled in and they'd both found themselves smiling at their phones.

* * *

Laura straightened the flowers on the windowsill again. While she'd only been in her new flat for a few days she was already house proud and wanted it to look nice when he arrived. Not that there was any importance to him visiting her new place, but she wanted him to see she was already settled and that she would be okay after all the mess of the last few weeks.

"It's going to be fine." She said to herself and now she was actually starting to believe it was.

Her phone vibrated merrily on the coffee table. Dan was lost.

Dan: Hey. Which one is yours? I can't seem to find your door.
Laura: Hang on. I'll come down.

The entrance was confusing; a multitude of flats with buzzers and Dan wasn't the first person to be muddled by it. She quickly grabbed her keys; she didn't fully trust the door to her flat yet not to lock her out. She bounced down the stairs to find him. As she made it down to the main hallway, she saw him through the glass doors looking bewildered.

When she opened the door it made him jump.

"Hey, you!"

"Hey!"

"That for me?" She looked curiously at the green leafy plant he carried in one hand.

He seemed surprised that he was even carrying the pretty blue pot. "Oh yeah. Erm, it's for the flat. It's a Japanese Peace Lily."

He handed it over to her.

"Dan, it's beautiful. You really didn't have to."

"I thought it might help brighten the place up a bit."

"It will. Thank you. I promise I'll try my best not to kill it." She grinned. It was nice to see him again. Laura had been so busy moving in that they'd only had the chance to talk over text, so it had been a while since they'd seen one another. "Come on. Come up."

He followed her along the hall and up the two flights of stairs to her new flat.

"Welcome to Casa de Laura."

She proudly waved her arm around the flat. Seeing that she seemed settled in and she'd made herself at home allowed him to relax; the tension of worrying about her having to find a place to live eased as he looked around the room. The flat had a decent living room area which she'd filled with a big comfy-looking sofa, a coffee table and a TV. He also spied her white guitar on a stand in the corner by the window. There was a small kitchenette to his right and he watched as she placed the potted lily on a plate and set it down on the counter, turning it till it looked right.

She looked good. The stress of the past few weeks seemed to have lifted from her shoulders and she was smiling again.

Wearing blue denim dungarees and a white t-shirt with her hair tied up in a loose ponytail, he watched as she flicked the kettle on and started to make hot drinks. The part of his heart he'd hoped to drown and suffocate with whiskey stirred and it was only when she asked him if he wanted sugar that he realised he'd been lost in thought.

"Erm, yeah. Two please."

Laura smiled as he returned his focus to her; wondering where his mind had drifted. He looked like he was doing well. Although his hair was longer than it had been when they first met, it was tidy. He'd gone back to keeping his beard trimmed too. It looked good on him. His ever-present simple black shirt and jeans combo hadn't gone anywhere. She felt as though she was blushing a little as he looked at her.

Realising she too had gotten lost in thought she nodded and turned back to the kettle. "Yeah, coffee. Two sugars. I should know that by now."

They chatted for a while over their tea and coffee, perched on stools, elbows leaning on the kitchen counter. She told him how she'd got to wait a few weeks for the internet to be installed and set up so she was having to watch regular TV like it was the 80s, while Dan had explained that he'd made a meeting every day since going sober and it wasn't feeling like an imposition anymore.

He tucked his hair behind his ear and drank the last of his coffee.

"Your hair has grown so much," she commented, her words making him look sheepish, "It suits you longer."

"Oh. Really? I was planning on getting it cut this week."

"And ruin your new rockstar image? Why would you do that Dan, why?" Laura winked at him.

He felt himself blushing and feeling conspicuous. She'd never commented on his appearance before and he was unsure if she was just being kind or if she was flirting with him. "Maybe I'll leave it then."

"Yeah, you do that." She grinned as she cleared their empty cups away.

"So I got you a little something."

Laura looked at him confused. "Yeah, the lily?"

"Well, that too. But that's for the flat really. This, erm, is for you. It's just a small gift."

He reached into his bag and pulled out a small parcel wrapped in brown paper, handed it over the counter to her and waited as she opened it.

As she carefully removed the wrapping, she stared down at the book cover, her heart in her throat. Tears began to spill onto her cheeks as she covered her mouth with her hand.

"I hated what he did to your book, so I wanted to replace it for you."

"Dan...I don't know what to say."

She looked lovingly at the copy of *Alice in Wonderland* she held. It looked like an old version, the ornate cover with gold leaf looked beautiful. She'd been heartbroken when she'd discovered that Chris had spitefully destroyed her book and that was one much plainer than this.

"I didn't want you to be without your favourite book, Laura."

She rushed around the counter, flung her arms around Dan's neck and cried. "Thank you. It's a wonderful thing

291

to do."

Standing so the force of her embrace didn't shove him off the stool, he held her gently and tried to breathe. He could feel her trembling against his body.

When she finally detached herself and dried her eyes, she removed the rest of the paper wrapping from it.

"You need to look after this one though, 'cos it's a bit special."

"Dan, it's very special. Thank you."

"No. I mean the book itself is very special." He picked it up and opened it, showing her. "It's a first edition. I have a friend who deals in rare books and with her help I managed to find this one. They're pretty rare!"

Laura was gobsmacked. "Dan!"

Her eyes spotted a white card tucked inside the front cover. Turning it over she saw that he'd written something for her. *He has beautiful handwriting.*

The secret, Laura, is to surround yourself with people who make your heart smile.
It's then, only then, that you'll find wonderland.

She sat down on the stool next to him and wept openly.

"I'm sorry. I thought you'd like it. I didn't mean to upset you."

"No no. I love it, Dan. These are happy tears."

"I'm glad you like it."

"It's going to be okay, isn't it? All this? Me living on my own and stuff?"

He took her hand in his, trying to portray an air of calm while inside he was actually feeling terrified.

"It will. You'll see. If I can live on my own, you can too." He was thinking about Max and how he really didn't want to live alone anymore and she seemed to read his mind.

"He'll be home soon."

"Well, I actually have some news on that."

"You do?" Laura's spirits rose. He'd been doing so well with his recovery, she felt like maybe he was ready.

"I talked with Issy and Martin yesterday and we're going to see about Max coming back at the weekend."

"Permanently?"

Dan nodded and scrunched his face up awkwardly not knowing whether to smile or cry but Laura did it for the both of them.

"That's wonderful news!"

And it really was. She felt like things were moving into a good place after weeks of darkness and upset. She hadn't expected the turns her life had taken when she first encountered Dan sitting awkwardly in Sarah's coffee shop and while they'd been through the wringer both together and individually, she could see a brighter future on the horizon for each of them.

* * *

"Are you buying a new guitar, Dan?" Laura looked curiously at the webpage full of acoustic guitars on the open screen of Dan's laptop.

He walked back from the kitchen with a cup of tea for her.

"No. Not me. I was thinking about getting one for Max as a welcome home present. He's always wanted one. I promised him lessons before..."

"Awww that's lovely. But you can't buy it online for him!"

Dan sat down next to her and handed her the tea. He looked guiltily over at *Lucille,* perched on her stand in the sunlight. "That's how I bought her."

Laura smiled. "Well that's different. She's a classic and you wanted her specifically. But this is different. This is Max's guitar. You need to try it out and get something that'll be right for him."

"Yeah I guess. You sound like you know what you're talking about."

"You know guitars is literally what I do for a living, right?"

"Funny. I thought you just hung out here every day."

He nudged her with his shoulder and they both giggled.

"Seriously though, you should buy it from a shop. Support local businesses and all that."

"Yeah that's true."

She had an idea. "You got a travel mug?"

He looked puzzled. "Erm no. But there's a few takeaway cups in the back of the cupboard I think, why?"

Laura stood and held out her hand. "Because we're going guitar shopping and I'm taking this tea to go!"

Forty minutes later they walked into Douglas Music on the high street and Dan felt overwhelmed by the array of guitars hanging on the walls all around him.

"Hello there, Laura. What can I help you with today?" An old man shuffled out from behind the counter to welcome her.

"Hey Ted. We're guitar shopping for a ten-year old. Can we have a look around and have a play?"

"Be my guest. Let me know if you need anything. You know what you're doing."

She turned back to Dan who was looking around nervously. Laura took his hand and stroked her thumb over the back of it.

"Hey. It'll be okay. Trust me?"

"Mhmm."

They spent the next while looking at and trying different guitars out. Many were discounted from the selection for being too big or too expensive.

"He probably will want a three-quarter sized guitar so that he's not struggling to play it but we need to be careful because they often have quite thick necks and he probably doesn't have very big hands."

Dan nodded, reassured that she knew what she was talking about.

Looking through the smaller sized guitars, he saw a blue one that looked really cool. He spotted the price tag; it was in the right price bracket for him.

"What about this one?"

Laura wandered back to him and took it from his hands.

"Yeah that'll do it."

They sat on the battered leather sofa in the middle of the store and as she tuned the guitar up, Dan watched her intently. She looked engrossed in what she was doing; it was beautiful. She was beautiful.

She looked up and caught him watching her. Smiling and tucking her hair behind her ear, she handed the guitar over. "Go on then, Dad. Try it out."

From nowhere, Dan was struck by shyness. "Ah I don't know. It's been a little while."

"I know but you play well. That's not something that ever

goes away." She smiled sweetly at him.

He melted. That that look would almost certainly be the death of him.

Dan took the guitar from her and sat it in his lap. It was perfectly in tune and he was impressed that she'd done it by ear with not a tuner in sight. Nervously he began to play.

Laura sat and watched as he strummed chords and played through riffs on the small nylon string guitar. He was no pro but she couldn't deny as he played, there was something attractive in him that she'd not seen before. She felt her cheeks flush. She was getting lost in his movements on the fretboard, his big hands fretting notes and strings with ease; all the while his face bore a look of determined concentration.

When he stopped it took her a few seconds to be present in the room with him again.

"Yeah it's okay that. I think this'll do nicely."

She met his eyes. "Mhmm yup. This'll do very nicely I think."

Laura stood up quickly to take her focus elsewhere. "Shall we?" She pointed to Ted who was reading his newspaper.

"Let's do it."

* * *

Pacing the living room wasn't doing the trick, even though he'd been doing it for the last half hour.

"Dan, he'll be here soon. Just try to relax."

He checked his watch again; still not time. "What if he changes his mind? What if he wants to stay at Issy and

Martin's?

"Hey! He won't. He wants to come home to his dad."

Ever since waking up that morning, Dan had been full of doubts and anxiety. Max was coming home for good but until the boy walked through that front door, he couldn't allow himself to believe it.

Waking around 6 am, too full of nervous energy to lie in bed any longer, he'd gotten up and gone around tidying the house. Not that it had needed tidying, as with Laura's help he'd cleaned it top to bottom the day before. He just needed something to do, anything.

Laura had arrived just before 9 am with two takeaway coffees in hand.

"I figured you'd appreciate a big, strong coffee this morning," she'd said, as she handed it over. He'd been hugely grateful for it and for her taking the time to come over to see that everything was okay for the big arrival.

"I'm not staying long, just wanted to make sure you had coffee in you and check that you didn't need anything else before he gets here."

"Thanks, Laura. You really didn't have to."

"I know but I wanted to."

Sipping his coffee while they talked, he'd constantly checked the time, she had seen the nerves oozing from him, his body posture tense.

The weeks leading up to this had been hard for him as he'd tried to get back on his feet but to his credit, Dan hadn't touched a drop of alcohol since the night Laura slept on his sofa. Not every day had been easy, and he'd had to fight harder some days than others, but he'd stayed on the wagon and for that, she was hugely proud of him.

She checked the time on her phone; fifteen minutes to go. Her cue to leave.

"Right you, time for me to go and get out of your hair."

Dan reluctantly walked towards the front door with her as she made to leave.

"You don't have to go. Please stay."

Laura thought back to seeing Max with Issy in Sanctuary. The way his face had fallen even further when he'd seen her at the counter. This was too important, she couldn't risk it, not knowing how the boy would react to finding her in his home.

If his excitement at being back dissolved into disappointment at her presence, it would be more than she could bear and she didn't want to steal that joy from Dan.

She turned back, stepping in close to him and resting her hands on his chest, smoothing out a crease in his T-shirt.

"This is your moment with Max. You don't need me here for that."

"I wouldn't have gotten here without you."

Laura smiled and slid away, pausing at the door.

"Message me later, let me know how it goes."

She really didn't want to go; lately when she visited she'd started to hate having to leave. But this was a special moment, Dan had earned it and she didn't want to be getting in the way of that.

The few minutes between her leaving and Max showing up felt like forever. Dan sat at the foot of the stairs and watched the door intently. Every movement on the street, vaguely seen through the translucent glass, made his heart stop. He just wanted to see his son again and know he was back to stay.

He knew that Max leaving to live with Issy and Martin was the right thing to do in the circumstances but it had been the hardest thing he'd been through after losing Natalie. The shame Dan felt at letting himself get into such a mess that it was better for his son to leave still burned like acid in his throat. But he was eternally thankful to Martin and Issy for everything they'd done in that time. He'd taken them to hell and back when they'd already been there beside him once before. Dan knew there was no way he could ever make amends for everything he'd done.

The black door handle turned and drew Dan out of his reverie.

There stood Max, rucksack slung over one shoulder, cheeks glistening with tears. Dan didn't see Martin and Issy walking up the path behind him, only his son's beautiful face.

For a moment they looked at each other, both of them trying to figure out if this was real or some sick, twisted dream, one which they'd wake up from in despair. But it was real.

Sliding off the bottom step of the stairs, Dan fell on his knees as Max dropped his bag where he'd stood and rushed to his Dad, arms outstretched.

Neither said a word as they crashed into each other. No words were needed or could have ever done the moment justice. He was back. After months of dark self-inflicted horror, Max was back and Dan didn't even try to hide the emotion of it all.

"I love you, Dad," Max whispered and his words drowned out everything in the world as he said them.

"I love you too, son. I'm so, so sorry."

Max squeezed him tighter, almost crushing his father's rib

cage. "Dad, I'm just glad you're back!"

* * *

Max clutched onto his dad's red 30-day chip and wondered what the future would be like. Sitting opposite him, his dad looked like the same person he'd always been but tired, like maybe he was just getting over the flu or something like that.

Even though his dad seemed cheerful and happy, Max knew that he could tire out easily and although he tried to hide it from him, some days were difficult. Turning the plastic chip over and over in his palm, he knew that things were already much better than they had been.

Sitting next to his aunty, he half-listened as they chatted easily about grown-up things that didn't really interest him. Sarah, sitting by his side, was keeping him topped up in cookies and hot chocolate and he was glad of her company.

The door to Sanctuary jingled and the gathered private party looked up and fell silent.

Standing in the doorway he saw Laura uncomfortably looking at where they sat, all eyes resting on her. No one spoke. Max recalled hearing his dad on the phone the morning before, asking her to come with them all.

"Please. I want everyone that's important to me to be there. And that includes you." He had been gentle but persistent.

Now as she stared back at the table, Max could tell she felt like an intruder and probably wanted to turn and leave, when Issy rose from her seat and walked over to her. "I'm glad you came," he heard her say.

"Dan wanted me to but it's okay, I can go if..."

Issy didn't let her finish the sentence and pulled her into a hug.

Max saw his aunty say something else that he couldn't make out, but whatever it was, it caused Laura to smile a little.

Pulling out of the hug, Issy had taken hold of Laura's hand. "Come on, let's get you a drink and you can have some cake too, or a cookie if Max hasn't had them all."

His dad had looked awkward but happy as she had pulled out a chair and sat down next to him. He was leaning close to talk to her. The rest of the table had resumed their conversations around the table, but Max could still hear his dad and Laura talking.

"You came then?"

"Mhmm, against my better judgment."

"It'll be okay."

She looked right back at Max across the table.

"I feel like I don't belong here, Dan."

Max sat listening to everyone talking around him and studied Laura. The last time he'd seen her was here when things with his dad were really bad. Seeing Laura that day had made his heart hurt. Now he didn't know what he felt.

Issy had told him that she was really nice and that she was helping his dad a lot but everything had been okay before she'd come along. He felt conflicted and he didn't like it.

As he worked his way through another cookie, Sarah kept him involved in the conversation around her. He'd missed her a lot. She always made time for him and never made him feel like a kid, unlike a lot of other adults; and she made the best hot chocolates.

"She's okay you know," Sarah said leaning into him gently.

Max had glanced across the table, uncomfortable.

"I know but…" He didn't know what to say.

"But what?"

"Everything was okay before."

Sarah felt for him. He'd gotten caught up in the middle of a difficult situation around adult emotions and some things he didn't fully understand yet.

"She's trying to fix it, Max. I promise."

"Mhmm. I know. Dad says it wasn't her fault."

"It wasn't."

Max looked across at Laura, who was talking with Issy. She did look like a nice person.

"If you give her a chance, you might find you two become friends."

Max spent the next little while thinking about what Sarah had said. He knew that Laura wasn't really to blame for what had happened. Soon after he'd come back home, his dad had talked to him about everything and had explained as best he could how things had gotten so bad. While Max didn't understand a lot of it, he did know that his dad was trying his best to get better and that Laura was helping. She seemed nice. Everyone said she was. But Max didn't know her and was scared that things would be different now.

Excusing himself, he went to the toilet. Rather than returning straight away, he sat on the step to the back kitchen and tried to work through how he felt about it all.

He remembered one of his favourite bedtime stories; *Max and the Loud Lion*. Laura wasn't shouty like the lion was but maybe she was frightened too. This couldn't be easy for her. Max was wondering if he needed to be gentle like he had been with the Loud Lion.

The sight of Laura coming round the corner on the way to the bathroom herself, caused him to look up. For a second they just stared at each other, not speaking, neither sure what to do, until Max took a deep breath.

He stood and walked the few steps over to her, looking up. He could tell she was definitely scared.

"I know it wasn't your fault."

She wiped a tear from her cheek as he spoke.

Max searched for the words in his head that he wanted to say.

"Thank you. For helping my dad."

She crouched to eye-level in front of him, and he saw that she looked sad.

"I'm sorry for everything that's happened, Max. I really am."

He fished a screwed-up tissue out of the pocket of his jeans and handed it to her.

She seemed to laugh but also cry more at the same time.

"It's not your fault. I just want my dad to be okay."

"Me too."

He watched her dry her eyes.

"We could help him together if you want?" He asked.

Laura sniffed more tears away. "I'd like that, if you'd let me?"

Max nodded and smiled at her.

Laura stood and made her excuses to use the toilet. As she started to push open the door to the Ladies, he stopped her. There was something important he needed to know.

"Laura?"

"Mhmm?"

"Do you like hot chocolate?"

"Yeah. I do." He could see she was confused.

"Me too!"

And with that, Max spun on his heel and headed back to the table smiling.

"Sarah? Please can I have another hot chocolate?"

"Sure you can. Extra flake?"

"Mhmmm please and can Laura have one too?"

It was going to be okay.

* * *

V

Part Five

Part Five

Stepping from the shadows of the entranceway, Dan flipped his 90-day chip into the air and watched it spin in the afternoon light before catching it with ease. Looking at it as it landed in his palm, he knew the weight that this small, seemingly insignificant object carried.

With a mixture of pride and relief, he understood that while this wasn't the end of his journey, it was a major point in his recovery and one he hadn't thought he'd ever reach. Grinning smugly to himself, he flipped it in the air again.

"You know if you lose that, they won't give you a replacement, right?"

Laura was sitting on the low wall by the church hall's main entrance.

"Ha! Well, that's true. Maybe I should just take better care of it." He slipped the token into his pocket. "What are you doing here? I didn't think I was seeing you today."

She stood as he moved towards her and slipped her arm into his. They walked down the path and into the car park. "I can count, Dan."

Even without him making a big deal of the day to anyone, she had been paying enough attention to know its significance.

"Thank you. I had no idea you knew."

"Well, I did. I've been keeping a note of your milestones as you've been going along. I was worried that you might be so focused on getting through each day that you'd lose track of how far you've come, so I wanted to make sure you knew when it mattered. But from that frankly quite blasé display as you walked out just now, I'm guessing you were well aware."

"Yeah. A few weeks ago I realised how many days I'd put behind me and I've been looking forward to getting this one. Means a lot. I just didn't want to say anything to anyone else or make a big fuss about it, this time."

"You don't need to. It's your day. It's not for anyone else. I'm just here to tell you I'm proud of you. And to give you this."

He stopped as she pulled something silver and shiny from her pocket. He frowned and gave her a curious look.

"What's...?"

"Do you trust me?" She grinned briefly. It made her eyes sparkle in the sunlight.

"You know I do."

"Chip please." She held out her hand.

He pulled the chip from his pocket and tentatively handed it over.

Taking it from him, she held it between her fingers along with the silver thing and he watched as she pushed it into place with a snap, before handing it back to him.

As he looked more closely, he realised what she'd brought him; it was a chip holder so he could carry this milestone with him all the time. His green chip sat snugly inside the silver hoop. It meant the world to him.

"You can replace it with your other chips as you go along. And maybe if it's attached to your keys it'll stop you launching it into the air." Laura winked at him.

"Thank you. It's really special."

He went quiet. She felt like something was wrong.

"Dan, what is it?"

He took a deep breath. "Can we talk?" They'd reached his car and he leaned against it.

Laura could feel her hands trembling as she sat next to him on the bonnet of his car. She couldn't look at him, scared to hear whatever it was he was about to say.

"So, a crucial part of my recovery is to apologise and make amends to the people I hurt as a result of my drinking."

"Dan, you don't have to…"

He stopped her, taking her hand in his.

"Please. I need to do this."

She looked out over the carpark.

"I'm sorry Laura, for everything I put you through. I should never have put you in the position I did, even before I started drinking. All of the hurt and trauma you've gone through is because of me and I am truly, truly sorry for that. I just hope in time you can forgive me and find some happiness."

Tears welled in her eyes and spilt gently down her freckled cheeks as she squeezed his hand.

"You don't understand." Her voice shook as she spoke through her tears.

"What do you mean?"

"Dan, you see what's happened as this huge mess of hurt and destruction left in the wake of your drinking. You're looking at it as if it's something that needs to be fixed. Because you feel and have felt broken. But I don't see it like that at all. It's taken me a while but in the last few weeks I've started to view this whole thing differently."

He sat quietly next to her, not sure where she was going with this.

"When I first read your poems, before I knew that you had written them, I felt like the author had looked into my soul and had written down how I saw love. Without me realising it at the time, it knocked off the blinkers I'd been wearing for so long. Had I been single when I found out it was you, this whole situation would have been different but I wasn't and back then I felt like I was on the path I was supposed to be on, with Chris. But your words have left an indelible mark on my heart ever since that day. When we met in the park that first time all those months ago, I told you I wished we could be friends. And I meant it. I really did. And that's why I don't see this as a mess. It's brought a wonderful friend into my life who I can't imagine being without now and it's helped to free me from a life that deep down I now know I never actually wanted. You don't have to apologise to me. Ever." She squeezed his hand again and rested her head on his shoulder.

"We're going to be okay, right?" Dan was fighting back his own tears as they sat in the carpark together.

"Mhmm we are. Promise."

* * *

Max aimed high and launched the ball as far as he could, Buddy racing off across the field to get it, making the boy giggle to himself, the same way he had the last hundred times he'd done it. It was a happy sound, one that Dan had missed over the last few months and one he was eternally grateful to be hearing after so long. Having his son back at home was one of the reasons Dan was starting to feel whole again.

He glanced at Laura, walking next to him; the other reason he had started to feel complete. She had become his rock, somehow helping him escape the dark abyss he'd found himself in. Their friendship was a blessing and one he was thankful for every day. While they were only friends, he knew that just having her in his life was enough.

Between the pair of them, Dan was beginning to feel a calm he wasn't used to and hadn't known for a long time.

Laura sighed. "I could get used to this."

"What? Max tiring Sarah's dog out for you?"

She laughed. He liked making her laugh.

"No, silly. The three of us."

"Four. You're forgetting Buddy."

"Right, are you going to be a dick all over my nice sentimental moment?"

He laughed. She liked hearing him laugh.

Dan held his hands up in mock defeat. "Sorry. Carry on."

"The point I was trying to make, before you were a complete dick..." It wasn't said with menace, the smirk on her lips told him so, "is that I could get used to the three of us like this."

"Me too."

Laura looped her arm through Dan's as they watched Max trying to wrestle the half-chewed ball from Buddy's mouth. This wasn't the life she thought she'd have a year ago when she was still engaged to Chris but walking with her friend and his son across the fields in the quiet of a Sunday morning was just where she wanted to be.

Dan had come so far in the past few months. He was staying sober. Going to meetings. Max was back and he and Dan were closer than ever before, according to Issy. And amongst it all, the laughter, the tears and the difficult conversations, she'd realised that her heart felt different when she was around this man.

"Max! Go left through the gate! Buddy knows where he's going!" She watched as the boy marched off with his new best friend, ahead of them along the path.

In the brief pause that followed as they walked, there was no awkwardness, just a quiet and easy contentment as they watched Max turn left and disappear from view with Sarah's border collie, Buddy.

Laura stopped. "Hang on. Think I have something in my welly."

Dan held out his arm for her to support herself as she removed, then upended her boot to eject the offending stone. Footwear replaced, as she stood back up she smiled at him.

"My hero."

"You're easily pleased aren't you?"

"Maybe I am Dan, maybe I am." She laughed.

They stood in the middle of the path as close as they had been before, not touching, but smiling at one another.

"What's on your mind, Laura Gray?" He could feel the anxiety building and the urge to look away was almost overpowering, but Dan held himself there, looking at her.

"Why does anything need to be on my mind? Can't I just stand here, smiling with my friend?" She dropped her voice slightly the more she spoke and he could have sworn she fluttered her eyelashes at him. It made Dan's mouth feel dry.

"Do friends stand this close?" He dropped the register of his own voice as she moved slightly closer.

Laura ignored his question as her hands found the sides of his body, "I'm thankful I have you in my life."

"Laura..."

Before he could say anything else she closed the final few inches between them, her lips finding his.

It wasn't a deep passionate kiss, but rather a soft, gentle one that only lasted a few heartbeats before they eased apart. As Dan looked down he saw her slowly opening her eyes.

"Sorry."

"Laura, you have nothing to be sorry for. It's just..."

"I know. I know. You don't need to say it." She was smiling.

"Hey, you two! Come on!" Max hollered from the gate a way down the path.

Laura felt a pang of guilt at the idea that Max may have seen her kissing his dad. While she didn't regret the kiss, something about that moment had just felt right, she did wonder if it was the wisest thing to do given the circumstances. She didn't want to muddle Dan up while he was on the road to recovery and she wasn't yet sure of her feelings for him, let alone if he still had feelings for her.

Dan walked in silence next to Laura, his heart hammering in his chest. He had gone to hell and back over the last few months but her hold on his heart had never wavered, he'd just gotten used to living with it. Now she'd kissed him and he was confused as to what it meant. It hadn't been a 'fuck me, I love you kiss,' more of a gentle kiss between two friends who liked each other; one that left a lot unsaid. But the last thing he needed to do now was go backwards after weeks of recovery.

By the time they got back to the car, the moment had been forgotten and things had gone back to how they had been when they started their walk an hour earlier.

"Laura? When will we see you again?"

Max beamed at her from the back seat as his dad backed the car out of the parking space.

"I think that's up to your dad, Max."

"You hungry?" Dan asked.

"I could be. Why?"

"Well there's a chicken roasting back at home if you fancy joining us for lunch? There's plenty 'cos I bought one that was big enough to feed a small army."

Laura glanced sideways at him. "He cooks?!"

She was impressed. *The most Chris had ever cooked was Pot Noodle.*

Her appraisal made him chuckle as he pulled the car out onto the main road. "Of course. I'm raising a hungry kid. Eventually you run out of ideas for simple meals and have to actually learn to cook stuff. Plus home cooked things are good for recovery, so I'm told. What d'you reckon Maxxy, think we should let her come back for Sunday lunch?"

"Yeah!"

"Looks like you're joining us for lunch then."

Dan smiled as Laura stroked Buddy's head, who was sitting between her feet in the footwell.

"I don't want to impose."

"You know we love having you around. It's up to you though. Don't let us change your plans."

"Well let's drop Buddy back to Sarah and then I think a nice afternoon with you two is just what I need to round off the weekend."

* * *

As she followed them into the house she was met with a glorious assault to her senses.

"Holy sh..."

She didn't finish the sentence as Max spun round quickly, open-mouthed, excitedly expecting her to say a dirty word. He giggled loudly as she clamped her hand over her mouth before shooting straight upstairs, kicking his wellies off as he went.

"Max!"

"I'll pick them up when I come back down Dad! Promise!"

Dan did what he knew his son wouldn't do and tidied the discarded boots away, before rounding gently on Laura.

"You were saying?" He cocked his eyebrows at her, which made her blush.

"Holy shit. It smells amazing," she whispered.

He turned, calling over his shoulder. "Should be about done. Just got to sort the veg."

Pulling off her coat and draping it over the back of the sofa, she followed him into the back of the house. When Dan had been caught in the struggles of his drinking problem, the house had seemed barren; as if the inhabitants had left in a hurry due to an emergency.

Now, like a symbol of rebirth, there was life again, in the large kitchen particularly. A large bunch of flowers in a cut crystal vase sat in the centre of the six-seater pine dining table. Placemats had been set on opposite sides; one for him and one for Max.

Everything looked clean and tidy but with a lived-in, homely vibe. The last of a loaf of white bread sat on a wooden board, scattered with crumbs; an open jar of strawberry jam with a knife stood up in it, not far away.

Laura smiled, remembering Max having a jam-stained face when she'd first seen him that morning.

What caused her the most intense joy was that smell. It was like heaven; casting her mind back to being around Max's age, helping her grandmother make Sunday dinner for the family. Her memory conjured up images of Blue Willow pattern plates, an old, floral apron that was too big for her and delicious apple crumble. It gave her a warm, comforting feeling deep inside.

Her attention was pulled back into the present as Dan opened the oven door, releasing steam and chicken aroma that wafted all around them. It made her mouth water.

"I think that'll do it." He carefully pulled a skewer from the meat and watched the juices run clear.

"Dan, that looks and smells amazing!"

"Thanks! Not just a pretty face I guess." He set the roasting dish to one side and proceeded to turn on the hobs under the already prepared pans of vegetables.

Laura peered over and saw more mouth watering delights. Peas and carrots. Potatoes set to boil for mash. And broccoli.

She turned to remark on his ability to whet her appetite, when she noticed him pulling a jug from a cupboard and setting it next to a bag of flour. Her curiosity was clear to see.

"You make your own Yorkshires?"

"Yeah, of course."

His face showed signs that it sounded like an odd question. The image of a lacklustre Pot Noodle flashed in her mind.

"You like yorkies right, Laura?"

"Definitely!"

They talked about their favourite foods as Dan prepared the remainder of the meal. He seemed at ease, quietly confident in his kitchen skills.

While he carved up the chicken, she made repeated attempts to steal small pieces of meat from the plate where he was depositing it. After the fourth attempt she was successful, smiling as she licked her fingers clean; it tasted incredible and she liked the happy look he gave her.

"You're worse than Max!" Dan shook his head. "Speaking of my son, can you go find him please and tell him lunch is ready?"

Returning minutes later with Max, she found Dan plating up.

"Want a hand?"

"No it's okay, thanks. Sit." He nodded his head to the table. She watched as the boy noisily dragged a chair out from under the table, and noticed that Dan had already set a place for her at the very end of the table, seating her between himself and

317

his son.

Laura sat and waited with Max, both eagerly anticipating the imminent meal.

When Dan set the plates down in front of them she knew if she died now, she would do so happily. On the table in front of her was a vision of pure, edible delight. Had she been asked to speak at that exact moment, she wouldn't have been able, due to the fact she was salivating so much.

Dan had piled wedges of thick white breast meat on one side of her plate over which he had poured a generous helping of goopy brown gravy. Next to that was a dollop of creamy mash potato nestled together with a mound of vibrant orange and green veg. But the cherry on top of this feast of wonder was the large homemade Yorkshire pudding. Rather than the regular shape of a shop-bought version, the one presented before her looked as though it had exploded from its tin; with a perfect brown top and fluffy centre, filled with yet more steaming gravy.

"Dan! This is amazing! I don't know where to start."

"Mhmm fank fad!"

Laura turned to see Max with a disproportionately large mouthful of Yorkshire pudding and gravy running down his chin. She giggled.

"You feed him, right?"

"You know, I'm starting to wonder myself because people keep asking me that."

The trio ate heartily, filling their bellies until they couldn't take any more.

Max looked up from his empty plate as Laura groaned in

satisfaction. "What's for pud, Dad?"

Dan pushed his similarly empty plate away and smiled. "Cheesecake. It's in the fridge."

As Max rushed off to claim his sweet treat, Laura turned to Dan. "You made a cheesecake?" She looked stunned.

He merrily blew air out his nose. "No. That's shop-bought I'm afraid. Meals I can do. Desserts? Not so much."

"Hmm okay then. Have to say I'm a little disappointed, unless it's strawberry cheesecake because that's my favourite."

"You and me both!"

Max put a large glistening red dessert down on the table, along with a carton of double cream.

The cheesecake was the fattest thing she'd ever seen. It was at least three inches tall, with a thick, buttery biscuit base, a generous amount of solid cream-cheese filling, glazed with a near-perfect jam layer and scattered with plump strawberries.

Laura pulled the plate towards her and looked at them both. "So what are you two having for dessert?"

An hour later, with the cheesecake long gone and all the dishes washed and put away, the three of them were sprawled on the big sofa in the front room, watching a random film on the TV. Laura watched out of the corner of her eye as Dan and Max cuddled up together; Max laying his head on his dad's chest contentedly. They looked inseparable and it pained her to remember the time they'd spent apart but simultaneously made her joyful that they were back together where they belonged.

She also felt a slight pang of jealousy that she wasn't herself relaxing into a warm embrace for the afternoon, though she would never want to separate the two of them for anything in the world.

With the day turning to early evening, she knew that it would be soon time for her to head back home. She really didn't want to leave.

As Sundays go, it had been a good one; the kind she'd happily repeat regularly given half a chance. Her cheeks flushed as she remembered the kiss she'd shared with Dan earlier in the morning but looking at him she knew it would all be fine.

"You okay?" He asked quietly, looking over the top of Max's fluffy head.

"Mhmm just thinking how lovely today has been. Thank you."

* * *

"'Night Max."

She hugged him and tried to breathe as he near enough crushed her.

"'Goodnight Laura."

"Go brush your teeth, I'll be up in a minute." Dan smiled. The worry he'd had, that Max would be wary of Laura given everything that had happened, had never come to fruition and now their easy friendship was lovely to witness.

"You hanging around?" He asked as he turned to her.

"I can if you want."

"It isn't about what I want. It's about what you want. Do

you want to?"

This playful banter between them, where neither of them quite came out and said what they wanted had become more frequent in recent weeks. While they both knew they were enjoying their time together, neither of them seemed to want to say so and jinx it.

"Do you want me to?"

Laura's smirk had the same effect on him every time she did it.

"Tell you what, I'm going to go up and tuck my son into bed and grab a quick shower, if you're still here when I come back down, I'll know you want to stay a while longer."

Laura grabbed the TV remote and sunk further down into his sofa, surrounding herself with cushions and smiled.

"Yeah, you do that."

Flicking through the channels as she heard the shower running above her, Laura realised what day it was. Checking the time, she quickly found the right channel and was relieved that she still had a few moments to spare.

Twenty minutes later she was engrossed in the season finale of her favourite show of the moment, *The Sanctuary of Nine*, hiding behind one of the big sofa pillows that smelt like Dan's aftershave. She watched in horror as the King's head was cleaved off his neck and rolled sickeningly across the forest floor.

"I didn't realise you liked this show."

The voice behind her made her jump.

"Fuck sake!"

"Sorry." Dan chuckled.

"You will be. And yes, I love this show! It's brilliant!"

He just nodded as he sat down next to her.

"Do you ever watch it?"

"Erm sometimes." In truth, it was something Dan rarely put on the TV at home for a multitude of reasons.

"Dan! It's amazing, you should watch it!"

"Meh, the book was better."

"I heard it was based on a book but I've never read it."

Aware that he still had a pretty big secret that she didn't yet know, he rose and moved to the bookshelf. As he placed his fingers on his copy of *The Sanctuary of Nine*, his life quickly flashed before his eyes.

The long hours turning Max's bedtime story into something for an adult audience. The first time he saw it on a shelf in the local bookstore. Natalie crying happy tears when they found out it would be made into a TV show.

He took a deep breath as he pulled the book clear of the bookcase and crossed the floor to Laura; it was about time she learned who he really was.

"Here. Have my copy."

"Aw. Thank you."

She took it from him and turned it over to read the back cover as Dan sat quietly on the sofa next to her and waited.

"It looks good! It might take me a while to read it though, it's a big book isn't it? Have you..."

Laura paused as she turned it back over in her hands and looked at the front cover. For a moment, what she was seeing didn't register. *That can't be right.* She looked again. *But that would mean...* Her brain was quickly trying to connect all the dots. *The Sanctuary of Nine. A Novel by Dan Muir.*

Dan waited patiently as she pieced it all together. Even though he felt exposed, he knew that being in her company was a safe refuge and it was time for her to know the truth about that side of his life.

"I don't understand." Laura was shocked and although she fully understood, the words had tumbled out of her mouth as soon as she had opened it. "You wrote this?"

"Mhmm."

"And the TV show? That's yours too?"

"No, not quite. It's based on the book. But yeah, my book."

"Wait. Hold the phone. You're a famous author?!"

"No. Not really. If you go ask Max, he'd tell you I am. In fact, I'm surprised he hasn't told you himself already. He has a habit of doing that. But in reality, I'm not famous, I'm just a guy who caught a lucky break, that's all."

"Dan! This show is huge!"

"I know. But it has very little to do with me these days. I sold the rights to it a long time ago; I just get a royalty cheque every six months that keeps the roof over our heads."

Laura sat stunned, looking between him and the heavy book in her lap.

"I'm sorry I didn't tell you."

She hadn't thought about the fact that he hadn't told her any of this. She knew he was a writer obviously, it was literally the thing that had brought their friendship to this point, but stupidly she'd never considered how he made his money. Now she thought about it, he must have had book deals that paid the bills, but she would never have guessed that one of her favourite TV shows would be his main source of income.

Dan continued, "you have to understand Laura, very few

people know who I am or that I have anything to do with that book, and that's the way I've always wanted it. I've always been scared that people would like me because of that show and not for me as a person. That's hard for someone with a brain like mine. But you liked me for me, even after everything..."

Laura smiled. "So you're telling me I kissed a famous author?"

"Again, I'm not famous."

"I'm not sure I would have if I'd known! I would have been too nervous." She spoke more to herself as if lost in thought.

Dan fell silent. A wave of doubt rushed over him as he began to feel as though she would change her opinion of him now she knew the truth.

Sensing what was going on in his head, Laura placed the book on the table in front of her and shuffled closer to him, sliding her hand into his.

"You are brilliant. But you have to understand, this doesn't change how I feel about you. I'd still be your friend even if you hadn't written this. I just think it's very cool and I'm immensely proud of you."

"You're not mad at me for keeping it a secret?"

"God, no! I get it. You're not one for fame or glory. I'd be the same in your position, I think."

"And you don't regret...anything?"

She thought back to their kiss. It was still making her smile.

"Not even a little bit. Do you?"

He shook his head.

"I'm not saying I want us to change this thing we have going on right now, Dan. You're in a good place and so am I. There's a lot of good stuff happening right now for both of us. But I can't lie, there's something there that wasn't before. And I'm not saying that because you're this wildly famous author."

She was playing with him and it made him smile, breaking the tension a little.

"I just need this to be a slow thing if it goes further, Laura. I lost myself to the speed of it all last time. I can't do that again; I won't make it back this time."

She gently rubbed her thumb over the back of his hand. The shakes he'd had the first time she'd been in his house were now long gone.

"Slow is good."

Dan smiled as he looked at her. "Thank you."

"So, do I get a signed copy of your book, or is that for special fans only?"

"I think you're probably classed as a special fan."

"Thank you. I'm honoured. So how does this work then? Max knows, obviously. And Issy and Martin I'm guessing."

"Yeah, aside from Sarah, the only other people who know are people in the book world, like my agent and stuff."

"Sarah knows?" Laura was surprised.

"Yeah, Max outed me to her the first time he met her as they were talking about my writing."

She thought about her friend, and how much she too loved the show. "No way! That's why Sanctuary is called Sanctuary isn't it?"

"Mhmm."

"That one must hurt the brain!"

He laughed. "Yeah, you could say that."

"Right, okay. I'll keep your secret on two conditions."

"Fine. Go on then, lay it on me." Dan relaxed back on the sofa, keeping hold of Laura's hand as he did so. She followed his movement and fell gently back with him.

"First, I get a signed copy one day."

"That's fine. I have some signed ones left over in a box somewhere."

"Oh no no, smart guy. I want a special message just for me, as your friend."

"Fine. And the other condition?"

She let go of his hand. It caused him to feel a small sense of loss as he watched her move away; his rejection sensitivity hadn't been drowned permanently with alcohol as he'd once hoped. Laura grabbed the remote and settled back down next to him.

"Next, you let me finish watching my show without any spoilers."

For the next forty minutes, they sat watching the series finale together.

Laura couldn't stop smiling, even during a furious and bloody battle at the end of the episode where one of her less favourite side characters had his arm cut off and was hit in the face with it.

Things felt good and she was glad that they'd come through everything they had together over the last few months, as it had led them to this moment. Dan next to her on the sofa, with Max upstairs sleeping soundly, she couldn't feel more content if she tried. The possibility of it always being like this quickened her pulse, which only made her smile more.

* * *

When Max walked into the kitchen the following morning he

was surprised to see his dad sitting alone at the table sipping his coffee.

"Where's Laura? Didn't she stay over?"

Dan looked up. "Well good morning to you too! No, she went home last night."

"Oh."

"Something wrong, Maxxy?" His dad couldn't hide his curiosity.

"It's just...I thought she'd stay."

"No, mate. She's got her own flat, hasn't she? No point sleeping on our sofa when she's got her own bed not that far away."

"Yeah, I guess. It's just I didn't say goodbye, that's all only goodnight because I thought she would sleep over on the sofa or something." The boy was confused. *Adults,* he decided, *were confusing.*

Recently their Dan and Laura's friendship had grown stronger and more intimate as her feelings for him had deepened. They weren't a couple but the lines between friendship and what lies beyond it had blurred, so much so that even Max was cottoning on to something happening, even if the two of them hadn't quite figured it out.

"She's playing at Sanctuary on Friday if you want to go watch? It would mean a late night, but it'll be the weekend so..."

"Yes! Please Dad!" He rushed to hug Dan before sitting down and reaching for the cereal.

"Don't be all day eating that, you can't be late for school." Dan glanced up at the clock. "We need to get a move on."

327

* * *

Friday evening came around and Max felt very grown-up as he stood with Sarah at the counter in Sanctuary, while Dan and Laura chatted at a table near the small performance area. It was too far away for Max to hear what they were saying but he could tell it was a happy conversation because they were both laughing and smiling at each other over their drinks.

"So Max, you've been spending a little bit of time with Laura lately; what do you think of her?" Sarah's question was gentle and caring, wanting to be sure her little friend would be okay with what she felt was inevitable, if it actually happened.

"She's really cool! I like her a lot and she's fun to be around."

"Your dad says she's teaching you a bit of guitar too."

"Mhmm. She says I'll be better than her soon!"

"I'm sure you will Max, I'm sure you will."

The boy glanced at Laura who was resting her hand on his dad's arm and laughing at something funny he must have said.

"She's nice," he continued. "She's different from my mum. But she's really kind to me and helps me with my homework and stuff."

Sarah felt for him. Other than his aunt, Laura was really the only other female to play any significant part in his life since losing his mum and she was the first woman to have captured Dan's attention. She knew it probably wasn't easy for him to share his dad after everything they'd been through.

As Max watched, it was clear to him that they should be boyfriend and girlfriend but he couldn't understand why they didn't say anything to each other about it. He hoped being an adult wasn't always going to be this confusing.

"Why don't grown-ups just say stuff to each other?" He wondered aloud.

Sarah laughed. "It isn't that simple, Max."

"Seems pretty simple to me."

He noticed Laura crossing over to where her guitar rested at the far side of the coffee shop.

"What are you two gassing on about over here?"

He looked up to see his dad in front of him.

"Ah, just friends catching up," Sarah said with a wink to the youngster who grinned back.

"Can I go watch Laura get ready please?"

"Yes. But don't be a nuisance, please. She needs to concentrate."

"Dad! I don't know *how* to be a nuisance! Oh and can I have another hot chocolate please?"

Without looking back, he skipped over to see Laura, leaving Dan and Sarah to chat.

"Hey, little man. You okay?"

"Yeah. Just wanted to come and wish you luck before you play."

"Aww thanks, Max. That's very kind of you."

As she went back to tuning her guitar using an app on her phone, she noticed him lingering in front of her.

"You sure you're okay?"

"You like my dad, don't you?"

"Of course I do, he's my friend."

"But you like him more than as a friend, don't you?"

She thought about his question. He was looking curiously at her, waiting for her answer and she felt like she owed him the truth. Only moments before, sitting with Dan, she'd felt all too familiar butterflies in her stomach when he'd looked into her eyes while they laughed at some stupid joke. She knew how she felt, even if Dan didn't.

"I think I do like him, yeah. Would it be okay with you if I did?"

"Mhmm. I'd really like that."

They smiled at each other.

"Me too. If I did and if he liked me as more than a friend too Max, nothing will change between you and your dad. I promise."

"You make him really happy."

"I do? Do you think he still likes me?"

Max rolled his eyes.

"God, why don't grown-ups just say stuff to each other? If I see someone at school I want to play with I just say 'Hey shall we be friends?' And then we're friends. It's easy. Why don't adults just do that?!"

Laura's adoration for the young man standing in front of her grew, as she realised how clever his simple way of thinking was.

"That's a very good question and very good advice. So Max … do you want to be my friend? I really like hanging out with you and your dad…"

Excited, he nodded and rushed in to hug her, not caring that her guitar still rested on her lap. The instrument twanged as he wrapped his arms around her neck but Laura didn't care. She wouldn't change this moment for anything in the world.

* * *

Sarah waved goodbye at the door, before closing it and turning back into the room.

"Things with you two going okay?"

She looked at Laura sitting with her feet under her on the sofa, nursing a cup of tea.

"Yeah, she's wonderful. I'm really into her and I think it's mutual? But enough of my love life, let's hear about yours."

She sat down and grabbed her own drink from its coaster on the little table at her side.

"I don't have a love life, Sarah. Single, remember?"

Her friend raised her eyebrow questioningly at her.

"Don't give me that look either."

"What look?"

"That look. Right there. The one that's dripping with the suggestion that I do have a love life."

"Well, it might not be as far along as mine but that doesn't mean you aren't interested."

Laura looked coyly away and picked up a biscuit from the packet on the coffee table.

"Don't know what you mean."

"So there's been no more doggy walk kisses then?"

"No."

"But you want there to be?"

"I didn't say that."

"You didn't have to. This is me you're talking to. So are you going to tell him?"

"Tell him what?"

"You know what to tell him, Laura. You don't have to create a big issue of it, just say that your feelings are changing."

Laura nodded at the serious change in the conversation. Having told Max a few weeks before that she might have feelings for his dad, she'd been hesitant in wanting to explore the situation any further, nervous about what it would mean and worried about Dan's sobriety.

"And what if it doesn't work out? What if we ruin our friendship and he goes back to drinking?"

"I know babe but you can't live in what ifs forever. These things might happen, but equally they might not."

"Yeah, I know."

"How much do you like him?"

"Ah," being under the spotlight was making her feel un-comfortable. "probably more than I should."

"What do you mean?"

"Not enough to write a book about it but enough that I'm having dreams about him."

Her freckled cheeks flushed red as she remembered dream Dan kissing her in the rain and how he'd done things to her no man had ever managed to do before.

"Laura Gray! You saucy little minx!"

"Don't!" She was dying of embarrassment wanting the sofa to swallow her whole.

Sarah winked at her. "Was he good?"

"Shut up!" Despite her acute embarrassment, she laughed with her friend.

When the laughter died down and they'd caught their breath, Laura admitted that she wanted to tell him. "I'll do it. Just not today. It needs to just happen when it happens."

* * *

Max pressed the button under the number for Laura's flat making it buzz aggressively. A moment later she opened the main door to them, surprised.

"Hey! What are you two doing here?"

"We're off to watch the meteor shower in the park. It starts in an hour. You coming?"

"What my over-excited son is trying to say is: *Hello Laura, how are you? Would you like to come and watch the Perseid Meteor Shower with us?*"

Max lifted a thermos up triumphantly. "We made hot chocolate!"

Twenty minutes later Dan pulled up in the car park and checked the time.

"Should start soon. Do we want to stay here in the warm until it starts or shall we go stargaze for a bit?"

Laura and Max were out of the car before he could even finish the sentence.

"Stargazing it is then..."

For an hour they looked up at the heavens, watching and waiting. While they did, Dan attempted to point out various constellations including the Milky Way.

"I literally have no idea where you're pointing!"

Laura was struggling to see the Big Dipper as he waved a finger around. He then moved behind her so that she could follow where he was pointing. She wasn't sure she could see what he was talking about but the closeness felt nice.

A little while longer and Max began getting bored: that, coupled with the plummeting temperature was enough to make him grumpy. Even a cuddle with Laura didn't shift his mood any.

"Come on, Max. Let's get you back in the car for a bit. Maybe if you shut your eyes and warm up a little you'll feel better."

"Yeah." A tired and fed up Max trudged back to the car with her, leaving Dan to wait with their stuff.

"I just really wanted to see them."

"I know you did, little man and you might still yet, but you're cold and you're tired, so just have a little rest and get warmed up. We can come and get you when it starts."

"Do you promise?"

"Promise."

She felt for him. Dan had mentioned that Max had been super excited all day for the meteor shower and when nothing had materialised after being out in the cold for a couple of hours, he'd quickly gotten fed up.

"You gonna be okay?"

"Yeah." He stifled a yawn as she reclined the seat a little for him. "I can still see you both from here. I might just close my eyes for a bit."

"Yeah, you do that. Text me or your dad if you need us?" Laura brushed his hair out of his face and let him snuggle down before walking back to Dan.

"He okay?" Dan asked, when she got back.

"He'll be fine. He's snuggled up in his big coat now, won't be long till he's asleep I think."

"Thank you."

"It's okay. You know I love being with him so that means

as well as the happy, fun Max, sometimes I get his mardy side too."

"I'm not sure where he gets it from."

"Sure you don't, smart guy."

"He loves you, you know? He told me as much last night after you headed home."

"I love him too," she smiled.

Laura was right. Max was dozing quietly in the warmth of the car within a few minutes of her being welcomed back by Ben handing her a plastic mug of hot chocolate, poured from the thermos in her absence.

"When do you think it'll start?" She looked up at the night sky expectantly.

"No idea. Although I reckon it should have started by now."

"I don't mind. I could stay out here all night." Between the hot chocolate and her big puffy down jacket she would be quite content to stand with Dan under a canopy of stars.

"Wait till the hot chocolate runs out and then you might think differently." Even in the dark she could see his smile.

For a while they just stood together in silence looking up, waiting for signs of the meteor shower starting. After a few minutes of waiting Laura spoke.

"Which one's the Big Dipper again?"

He pointed high up into the sky and drew his finger along the constellation. "There, look."

"No...I can't see it." Laura glanced sideways at him. "I think you need to show me again like before."

Dan shook his head ruefully and moved behind her. As he did so, she leant back gently against his chest and looked up trying to hide the huge smile on her face. She didn't care about the Big Dipper, she just wanted another excuse to feel him next to her; like Max, she'd gotten bored of waiting for tiny rocks to fall from space.

He pointed again into the sky, his arm coming over her shoulder to guide her line of sight. "See that one? See how there's a few nearby that form like a curvy line? That's the han...Laura you're not even looking!"

She wasn't. She'd stopped following the direction of his hand and had turned her head up to him to watch him explain; a smile on her face.

"Sorry. Sorry. You were saying." She looked back to his finger trying to feign seriousness.

"See how the handle then drops down a bit here...Laura!"

She'd become distracted again, her head leaning gently on his arm and reaching for his hand with her free hand.

"For someone who teaches for a living, you're not very good at being taught!"

"Yes. Sorry." She cleared her throat and stooped to put her cup down on the ground next to them. As she stood up she turned and stepped closer to him, sliding her hands inside his jacket for warmth. "You were saying something about a handle?"

"Erm, it's behind you!"

"Is it?"

"Laura, how am I meant to get your attention?"

"Oh, you have my full attention!" She fluttered her eyelashes at him.

Weeks ago they'd kissed briefly while out walking Sarah's dog, Buddy with Max and now as he glanced down, all he could think about was how soft her lips had felt that day.

"The Big Dipper..." he began, but was distracted from his repeated explanation, as she moved even closer to him, murmuring, "don't you think it's romantic?"

"What is?"

"Being out under the stars like this? Together."

He couldn't take his eyes off her. *Who gives a fuck about the Big Dipper!*

They hovered less than inch from each other, the tension building, both knowing what they wanted to happen.

"Mhmm very romantic."

And then it happened. They were kissing. Neither of them made the first move or instigated it; both had gone in for it at exactly the same moment. Their lips met softly and each of them lost themselves to it, Dan's hand finding its way into her hair at the back of her head. When Laura would retell the kiss to Sarah later the following day, she would simply describe it as *perfect.* She never wanted it to end.

Max stirred in the passenger seat, waking to see tiny flashes of light streaking across the sky through the windshield and was grateful he hadn't missed it. As he began to settle down again, his eyes fell on his dad and Laura who had not even noticed the stars raining down above their heads.

"Yes!" He fist-pumped in joy as he watched them kiss for a second longer before rolling onto his side and closing his eyes again.

"Hey! It's starting!"

Dan looked up, wondering if it was his vision that was creating shooting stars; or maybe the result of Laura's lips on his but she was right, the meteor shower was underway and was filling the sky above their heads.

"Let's wake Max up so he can see some of it."

She tugged his hand back as he began to move away causing him to bump back into her.

"Okay, just one more..." He dipped his head down and kissed her again.

"Mhmm one more."

There were actually four more smile-inducing kisses before they made it back to the car to fetch Max, who sat on the bench in awe, watching the meteors burning up in the atmosphere overhead, with Dan and Laura flanking him. By the time it all ended a short while later, he was yawning so violently that it looked like he was trying to swallow a boat.

"Right Maxxy. Let's get you home to bed!" His dad swung him up and over his shoulder as the trio made their way back to the car; tired, cold and happy.

* * *

"He all tucked in?"

Dan padded gently down the stairs as Laura waited by the front door.

"Yeah. Still fast asleep. Are you going?"

He looked concerned and disappointed. The evening had switched from what was a simple night of stargazing to being near enough perfect.

"Not yet but I was about to book a taxi; it's getting late and you need your sleep."

She really didn't want to leave but it felt like the right thing for her to do.

He crossed the floor to her and took her hand. "Or you could stay? I kind of don't want you to go."

He looked at her, almost holding his breath in an attempt to quell the nerves rising up inside him. "I can make the sofa up for you?"

Laura stepped closer to him and kissed him, her free hand finding his T-shirt, pulling at it harder than she intended.

"I'll stay but I'm not sleeping on the sofa." She moved past him, keeping hold of his hand and led him slowly upstairs.

* * *

"Morning, Dad." Max stumbled and yawned his way into the kitchen and sat down at the table opposite his dad, who was stirring sugar slowly into his coffee.

"Morning mate. You okay? Sleep good?"

The boy yawned a second time and rubbed sleep from his eyes. "Mhmm just tired."

"It was good last night, wasn't it?" Dan smiled.

"Yeah, it was."

"Want some breakfast, little man?"

Max spun around in his chair following the new voice to see Laura leaning against the kitchen counter, holding a cup of tea. He rushed over to hug her.

"You stayed!"

"I did." She kissed the top of his head and smiled as her eyes met Dan's across the room.

"I didn't realise you were staying. I didn't see the duvet on the sofa." Max looked up at her as he spoke.

She was exchanging a look with his dad and half-smiling like adults do when they know something you don't know and they're not saying anything.

"I've just been up for a while, that's all."

As Max stepped back he noticed that she was wearing one of his dad's old T-shirts and her legs were bare except for a pair of socks.

Watching his growing realisation as he added up all the new snippets of information, she tried to divert his attention before he could ask any more pertinent questions.

"So what do you want for breakfast?" She asked, clearing her throat.

"Erm toast and jam please."

"Coming right up!"

As Laura busied herself over the toaster, Max went and sat back down.

"So what do you fancy doing today, Maxxy?"

"We could go for hot chocolate?"

"I like that idea."

Laura joined them at the table, placing a plate of sticky jam-covered toast in front of Max. He realised that as she sat down, his dad had placed his hand on hers and that her chair seemed closer to his dad's than to his.

"You two kissed last night." Typical ten-year-old. Straight to the point from nowhere, a bolt that hits out of the blue. He watched their hands fly apart.

"I think you must have imagined it, mate."

"No I didn't. I saw you!" He wasn't cross or upset, he was just stating a fact.

"Max…" Dan began to try and head him off again but was stopped by Laura gently holding his hand. She looked at Max and smiled.

"Shall we tell him?"

The fluffy-haired boy nodded.

"You still sure it's okay?" She wanted to check.

He nodded again, this time even more enthusiastically.

"Anyone care to tell me what's going on?" Dan was bewildered.

Laura turned to him. "Your very intelligent son knows that I like you."

"Of course you like me, we're friends."

"No Dan. He knows that I *like* you."

The penny dropped. "Ah. Right."

"We spoke about it a little while ago and he told me he'd be happy if we ever became more than friends."

Dan looked at his son. "You sure you're okay if we try this, Maxxy?"

"Mhmm. Definitely!"

Laura took the little boy's hand. "Remember what I told you? It won't change anything between you and your dad. And we're going to take things very slowly." She turned back to Dan. "Aren't we?"

"We are. Nothing's going to change between us Max. I promise."

Max got up and moved around the table to his dad and hugged him. "I know."

"Love you mate. Thank you for understanding this. I know grown-up stuff can be confusing."

"Love you too, Dad. And I'm ten now, I understand grown-ups!"

Laura watched as they hugged. Their relationship was a beautiful thing to behold and she cherished being able to see it.

"Can I go watch TV while I eat my breakfast?"

"Sure thing. Just this once." Dan kissed his son's forehead before the boy moved to hug Laura, then claimed his breakfast and moved to the front room.

Dan looked at Laura and smiled.

"So this is us now?"

She smiled back and stood, moving to sit sideways on his lap.

"Mhmm seems to be."

"I meant it, you know. We'll take it all very slowly."

"I know." She stroked the side of his face. "You okay about last night? That we didn't..." she let the words hang, not wanting such a special moment to become awkward.

Dan thought back to how they'd spent most of the night talking quietly together before falling asleep in the early hours, and then had woken up a tangle of limbs. He could still feel the heat of her body against him. The fact they hadn't had sex was irrelevant. It had been everything he could have asked for and more.

"We're taking this very slowly right? And that means all of it. Of course I'm okay with it. I got to wake up with you and that makes me a very happy man."

He gently leant forward and kissed her nose causing Laura to bite her lip.

"If you do stuff like that, things won't be all that slow, smart guy."

"Noted." He winked at her as he moved back. "You gonna come for hot chocolate with us?"

She let out a small sigh. "No. I'm teaching today. Plus, slow right? It sounds lovely though."

Dan knew she was right. Spending every waking moment with each other in the beginning of this new phase of their relationship could backfire, so temperance and patience were called for.

"Want me to drop you back home this morning?"

"Please. That would be lovely. But first I'm going to borrow your shower." She slid off his lap, finished the last mouthful of her tea and set the cup on the side by the sink before turning with a smirk. "And don't get any ideas."

He grinned as he watched her go. She was right. He had ideas.

* * *

Dan slammed his laptop lid. The words still seemed to be imprinted on the inside of his eyelids as he closed his eyes and held his head in his hands. Surely even she couldn't be this petty?

Max's grandmother had always held a distinct dislike for Dan and had blatantly distanced herself from both him and Max after her daughter had died. This latest stunt, posting pictures of herself with her friends and their family on Face-Book with the caption: *Family is everything,* really took the piss.

She had a family of her own and she actively ignored them for three hundred and sixty three days a year. The slight contact she had with her only grandson was limited to a card at Christmas and one on his birthday where she insisted on using Maximus, never Max despite knowing that Max was what he preferred to be called.

He knew what he needed to do but it was late and much harder to manage now Max was back home from school. There was an opportunity in the next ninety minutes, though if there was a way he could... *Laura!*

Picking up his phone from the desk next to him, he messaged her.

Dan: Hey! Can I ask a huge favour?

Twenty-five minutes later he was zipping his coat up and thanking her profusely for being a lifesaver.

"Don't thank me. You know I'm happy to help."

"I'll be back as soon as it's done."

"Go. Or you'll be late for your meeting."

He opened the door to leave.

"Dan?" He turned back. "I'm proud of you. You're doing the right thing. Don't worry about Max, I'll make sure he's okay."

He flashed her an awkward half- smile and he was gone. Heading to the church hall to focus himself as he'd been told to do countless times when he was having a bad day.

Laura headed back into the kitchen where Max was finishing his homework.

"Is Dad okay?"

Even though Dan was much better now than he'd been, Max

was acutely aware that his dad's problem hadn't gone away, but was something that he needed to manage regularly and sometimes there would be hard days.

Laura tousled his hair as she passed him on her way to turn on the kettle.

"He's fine. Just stressed and annoyed about something and knew the best thing to do was to go to a meeting rather than sit and work himself up all night."

"Grandma's never liked him, you know."

For a moment they stared at one another. Laura, shocked at his candour; Max, sure that she hadn't expected him to say anything like that.

"Uncle Martin said that she never liked that my dad was a writer, even though now he's way more successful than anyone else."

"That can't be easy for you."

"It's fine. I've got Dad, Uncle Martin and Aunty Issy. And now you. I don't need much else. Grandma isn't a kind lady. Dad's always said that not everyone is going to like you in life and that's okay." He closed his school book. "Right, I'm done."

She checked her watch. "Okay, nearly bedtime. Go brush your teeth and stuff and I'll be up in a minute to tuck you in."

"You know I'm nearly eleven right? I don't need tucking in anymore!"

"Don't you take this away from me, Max! Don't.You. Dare!"

They both laughed before he rushed off upstairs to get ready for bed.

A few minutes later with a freshly brewed tea in hand, Laura stepped into Max's boy cave of a bedroom to find him sitting on his cabin bed, already changed into his PJs.

His bedroom walls were adorned with an array of posters of superheroes of both the human and the Lego variety and the floor was like a trip maze of toys and half-built brick sets waiting to be trodden on.

"Sorted?"

He nodded.

"So if I'm not tucking you in 'cos you're ten or whatever, am I doing a bedtime story or are you too cool for those too?"

"Don't worry. Haven't had a bedtime story in a while, not since I went to stay at Aunty Issy's, so you're good. Plus it's only Dad's that were ever any good."

"Your dad reads you his stories?" She was shocked. *Surely he wouldn't?*

"No, silly! Dad used to write me my own bedtime stories."

Laura wanted to melt into the floor. Something deep inside her ached and she craved this man, a father who would write their child their own personal bedtime stories.

"Seriously?"

"Yup. About me! I'm in all of them." Max crawled along the bed to his bookshelf and pulled down the ring binder and handed it to her.

"He used to write loads for me, then after Mum died, he sort of stopped but we still used to read them sometimes."

She leafed through the loose pages, marvelling at the words in front of her.

"He's a pretty good writer, your dad."

"He is." Max beamed at her.

"Max? Please could I borrow these? Just to have a look at tonight? I'll pop them back in your room before I leave."

He started to snuggle down into his bedding. "Yeah of course. The one with the loud lion is my favourite and that was the first ever one."

After kissing him goodnight, she headed back downstairs, mug in one hand and a clutch of bedtime stories in the other and proceeded to make herself comfortable on the sofa.

For an hour she skimmed over each story. They were wonderful. Dan had crafted them beautifully, weaving together fun adventures for Max with important morals for him to learn.

She turned to the page to find the story of *Max and the Lion* and began to read.

The lion looked even angrier and roared again, louder, lunging forward trying to reach what he thought would probably be a good snack in yellow wellies.

"ROOOARRRR!!!"

But for some reason, the lion wasn't able to get to him. It seemed stuck.

Max watched as the ferocious beast struggled and fought, snarling and snapping his fangs.

"You're stuck! That's why you're shouty."

The lion looked at Max. And Max looked back. All his anger seemed to fade and the lion whimpered a little, turning so Max could see that his back paw was trapped in the fence behind

347

Dad's shed.

Max realised that he didn't need to shout back to scare the lion away but instead, he needed to be brave and calm and more importantly, be gentle to help the lion get free.

He took a step forward. The lion snarled.

"It's okay," Max said, holding up his empty hands, "I'm going to help you, okay?"

The creative in her stirred and wondered why Dan had never done anything with these; she could see the potential staring up off the page at her. Quickly she pulled out her phone and frantically started typing in her Notes app to make sure she didn't forget any of the plan that was rapidly formulating in her head. *This could really work.*

When she was done, she'd opened the rings in the binder and had, with care, pulled out the pages of *Max and Loud Lion*, before climbing the stairs back to his bedroom. Making sure not to wake him, she pushed the ring binder back onto his bookshelf and quietly went back to the sofa.

Dan opened the front door as she was slipping the pages carefully into her bag. "Hey!"

"Hey, you! How'd it go? Feeling better?"

"Much, yeah. Thanks again for looking after Max for me. I needed that."

Laura walked over to him and kissed him, wrapping her arms around the back of his neck. It was a surprise to Dan, but one he was more than happy with.

"Mmm what was that for?"

"For being you."

With one hand he pulled her to him at the waist and with the other, tucked a stray strand of blonde hair behind her ear.

"You eaten?"

"Not yet."

"Fancy staying and getting a takeaway? My shout."

"Keep saying all the right things, Dan. Keep saying all the right things."

* * *

"So you think you can do it?"

Laura nodded to herself as the person on the other end of the phone was speaking.

"Yay! Okay okay. Right. Can I drop it round to you so you can take a look at it?"

Another answer brought another nod from Laura.

"Fab. Thanks, James! You're a gem!"

Ending the call, she clapped with excitement and glee.

* * *

A week later, Laura clutched her bag tightly to her side and tried to contain her excitement as she stepped up the path to Dan's front door. She hoped he wouldn't be mad for what she'd done, but the outcome was so good that she knew at least Max would love it, and anyway she was too excited to worry too much.

Rapping three times on the wooden door, she waited, bouncing gently on her toes.

She watched through the translucent glass as Max bounded through the front room and swung the door open.

"Hi!" He said, smiling bright at her.

"Hey, you. Where's your dad?"

"In the kitchen. Why?"

" 'Cos I've got something to show you both."

Laura saw Dan making his way through the house to see what all the fuss was about.

"Hey, you."

She grinned broadly. She had such a good feeling about this.

"Hey! Got something to show the pair of you."

"Okay? Best come in then."

Once they were all seated at the kitchen table and Dan had put a freshly brewed cup of tea in front of her, she decided the time had come to share her secret.

"Okay. So two things. Firstly, please don't be mad at me."

Dan quickly cocked his head to look at her, his skin prickling, worry immediately building in his chest.

She carried on before he could say anything.

"Secondly. I'm really excited about this." Drawing the folder from her bag, she continued.

"So, the other week, when I came over to keep an eye on Max while you went to your meeting, he showed me the stories you used to write for him."

"Okay?"

"And they're so lovely, Dan. Truly. So I kinda borrowed one as it gave me an idea."

"Ooo which one?" Max's excitement was growing at pace.

"*Max and the Loud Lion.*"

Laura pulled open the folder and slid three sheets of A3-sized paper out, unfolding them onto the table.

What lay before them was a beautifully illustrated version of Max's story in gloriously rich colours. It was stunning.

"So a friend of mine, James, is an illustrator and..."

"Dad, look! It's amazing!"

"You like it, Max?"

"Yeah!"

Laura looked at Dan as he stared at the pages, trying to take it all in.

"When I was reading it the other night I could easily see it as a book. So I asked my friend to do some drawings for it. Just to see."

He turned the pages around and looked down at the artwork mixed with his words that were spread on the table.

"You're not mad are you?"

Dan looked up and smiled. "Not at all. It's wonderful."

Laura relaxed. She'd hoped he wouldn't be too upset but a part of her was unsure because essentially, she had intruded on something personal between him and his son. She noticed his focus softening, as though he was becoming lost in his thoughts; his gaze drifted away slightly.

"Dan?"

She felt Max's hand on hers.

"It's okay. Just give him a minute. You'll see."

Dan's mind exploded with rapidly moving ideas. Colours. Words. Characters brought to life that hadn't been given faces before. A book. A collection of stories. His words. James's pictures. All of it swirling around in his head.

Laura desperately wanted to speak, to check he was okay, his recovery an ever-present concern but she trusted Max so held back and waited.

After a moment, Dan focused back on her before turning to Max.

"Maxxy, how would you feel if we turned your stories into an actual book?"

"Dad! Really?"

"Mhmm really!" He turned to Laura who looked gobs-macked. "You think your illustrator friend would like to work with us on this?"

"Us? Dan, it's your work."

"It's my words. It's your friend's pictures. And it's your idea."

She didn't know what to say. As she'd devoured his short stories the previous week, she knew they had potential but now he was sitting opposite her smiling that cute little half-smile he had and watching her intently. Whenever he did that she could feel her cheeks starting to flush.

"I think this has got something, Laura. I didn't really see it till now but I think we could make something really special out of this, if you'll help me."

"What help can I be?"

"I'm good with words. But you've seen something I hadn't. Along with James, I think we could make something really good out of this."

Laura felt the buzz of excitement growing in her belly as Max's fingers squeezed her hand.

"Please, Laura. Say yes. I know what it's like when Dad has a good idea. This could be really cool!"

She looked back at Dan who was watching her as she thought it over. There was something about his sparkly blue eyes that she was starting to have trouble saying no to but the look he gave her was one she'd not seen before. It was a look of possibility.

"Okay. I'm in!"

"Woohoo!" Max punched the air and his dad's half-smile turned into a fully-fledged grin.

"Maxxy, go grab me my notebook from my desk, please. We have some planning to do."

* * *

"That's it! It's a tricky chord change but you just have to relax and let your fingers do the work."

Dan listened from the front room as Laura continued teaching Max how to play a song they'd been learning together. Their little shared moments playing guitar were something that made his heart happy.

"Dan? You still there?"

His publisher's voice crackled through the little speaker of his phone.

"Yeah, sorry mate. Right here. Just lost in thought. Where were we?"

"Well, I think this short stories idea really has something. It'll be a totally different market for the most part but one that's really open and excited for things like this. Plus you'll probably get some cross-over readers from *The Sanctuary of Nine* who have kids and stuff. Your name still pulls a lot of weight so I think this could work. When do you think you could have a first draft ready for us to look over?"

"Erm, well the words are already there, it's the illustrations that we need time to pull together now."

"And you're sure you want this James to do it?"

Dan turned his head towards the kitchen and watched Laura as she chatted to Max with her white guitar in her lap.

"Yeah. That part is important to me. Sorry."

"Don't be sorry Dan. He's good, as long as you're happy, I'm happy and I can convince management to go with your decision. We can get a part payment set up for him this week too so he's not working for free."

"Thanks Rob. I appreciate that."

"So this Laura? The one who had this idea, is she...?"

Dan knew what his old friend was asking. Rob had been his publisher since the early days of his literary success and had been devastated to hear of Natalie's death.

"Yeah, she is. But it's very early days."

"Well, I'm happy for you."

"Cheers mate."

"Right, let me talk to management and get this money for James sorted. If you can get him to work up some drawings as soon as possible and work out a first draft layout, then we can chat again and get a proof printed."

"Will do. Thanks Rob."

As he ended the call, Dan realised that the thought of having a new project to work on was exciting. It had been a long time since he'd been in this position. The sound of a familiar chord progression sung out through the house as he heard Laura and Max playing *Faithfully* by Journey from the kitchen.

Smiling, Dan rose from his desk and headed to join them, picking up *Lucille* as he went.

* * *

Martin opened the door to the delivery lad who was struggling to see him over the stack of pizza boxes in his arms.

"Cheers mate!"

He shut the door, leaving the young lad to get back into his beaten-up Corsa and marched triumphantly through into the kitchen.

"Pizza's here!"

Issy mocked him, saying he should stop puffing his chest out like a hunter-gatherer while she grabbed some paper towels for each of them as well as a big bottle of ketchup.

"You want another tea, Laura?"

Laura sat quietly on the stool at the breakfast bar and smiled politely. "Please."

While she'd spent time with Dan's family once before at his 30-days sober get-together at Sanctuary, this was the first time they'd been all in one place since she and Dan had moved their relationship on.

She knew that being with him would mean spending time with his family too but it was all still very new and she was acutely aware of everything that had happened, as well as the fact that she was currently seated in the kitchen belonging to Dan's dead wife's sister.

Sitting beside Max was a gentle comfort though as they all ate and carried on their conversation about Dan's new book.

"It's okay, you know?"

Issy turned, as she and Laura folded the empty pizza boxes into the recycling bin outside, at the back of the house a little while later. Laura looked at her unsure of what to say.

"You two. It's okay."

"Thanks, Issy."

It felt like a heavy conversation and she didn't know where to start as so much had been left unsaid already.

Issy shut the bin lid. "We don't blame you, Laura."

"You'd have every right to."

"Not really. He got himself into that mess, you didn't do anything to cause it. That was on him. He never really mourned losing my sister because he was too busy being strong for Max. I think his feelings for you just made it all too much. But he's through it now. We're just glad he's better."

Laura turned to look through the patio window at Dan, Martin and Max who were watching rugby on the TV; the yellow glow of the lamp behind the sofa they shared feeling somehow warm through the glass.

"He's doing so well."

"Now, *that* you can take responsibility for."

Laura half smiled, not knowing what to say.

Issy continued. "He's got you to thank for that. I'd all but given up on him and God knows what would have happened had you not been there." She paused. "Can I ask you something?"

"Mhmm." Laura felt the grip of nerves tightening her

throat.

"You really do like him, don't you? This isn't just about you wanting him to get better?"

Laura looked back at Dan and smiled. This wasn't an awkward answer to give. She didn't need to hedge around the truth and make it sound like anything other than what it was.

"I really do like him. I've seen him differently these past few months. To start with I just wanted to make sure he was okay and that he had a friend. But as time went on I wanted to spend more and more time with him because of who he is and how he made me feel. Now he's the first person I want to talk to when I wake up and the last thing I think of before I fall asleep."

Issy looked at her. "I'm very glad to hear that."

"We're going slowly though for his sake and for mine and of course because of Max. I'm not in this for a fun few weeks with a nice guy, Issy. I want this to stick."

Dan's sister-in-law pulled her into a hug. They didn't need to say anything, but the moment cemented their own relationship.

A cheer went up from in front of the TV.

"Right, guess we better go back in as someone's obviously done something exciting with a ball. Do you understand this game?"

Laura laughed. "A little yeah. My dad used to watch it when I was a kid."

"Good, you can explain it to me then because Martin has tried and I still don't get it."

357

* * *

"I come bearing coffee."

Laura dramatically held out a takeaway coffee cup from Sanctuary and grinned at him. She'd surprised him, turning up unexpectedly on a Saturday morning laden with coffee and doughnuts and no plans ahead of her except unbeknownst to Dan, to spend some time with him and Max.

He raised his eyebrows at her and stood aside. "Best come in then."

After he had graciously lightened her of her sweet, heavy burdens, she walked into the kitchen with him in step behind her. It was a sight he knew he could get used to. As she took off her coat, he pulled her to him and went in for a kiss.

"Erm...excuse me? Don't you think coffee and doughnuts are enough?" Laura ran her fingers through his hair and shot him a coy expression.

"Don't you want to kiss me?"

"I didn't say that."

Giggling like school children they kissed as she leant up against the kitchen table. It wasn't a moment of raw passion, just a warm kiss because they were happy to see each other.

"So why the surprise visit today?"

"Do you want the real reason or the excuse I was planning on giving you?"

"Hmmm excuse first please."

"I've got the day off and I wondered if Max would like to do some baking with me today."

"Well, aren't you sweet?" He leaned in and kissed her nose. "And now the truth?"

"I missed you."

"Missed you too." She bit her lip, looking up at him through her eyelashes as he smiled at her.

They stepped slightly apart at the sound of Max thundering down the stairs but kept a hold of one another's hand not wanting to break their comfortable physical contact.

"Laura!"

"Hey, little man!"

He rushed to her for a hug.

"What are you doing here?"

Glancing at Dan, she smiled. "Well I have the day off today so I wondered if you fancied doing something? Maybe some baking with me? Something like that?"

"Yeah, please!"

"Well I'll let you two have fun, I have some bits to do for the book, so I'll jump on a video call with James and let you both destroy the kitchen." Dan stuck his tongue out as he grabbed a sticky chocolate doughnut from the box and left with his coffee in hand.

* * *

"So, how are we cutting this dough, Max?" Flour puffed into the air as she dropped the malleable mixture to the pre-dusted counter.

"Mum used to do circle ones with me."

Laura's heart sunk a little. She'd not considered that he might have memories of baking with his mum when she'd thought he might like to spend the day with her. She hoped she wasn't trampling on his memories.

Max was smiling at her. "Maybe we could do Pac-Man

shaped ones? I could cut the mouths out by hand?"

"Yeah! That's a great idea. I like that."

"And it's okay you know?"

"What is, little man?"

"You can call me Maxxy like Dad does. I don't mind."

Her heart lifted. "Are you okay with that?"

"Mhmm." He nodded. "I'd like it."

"Do you want to know a little secret that your dad doesn't even know?"

The boy's eyes lit up like headlights in the dark which she took as a resounding yes.

"My nickname when I was your age was Muffin. My dad used to call me that all the time at home.

"That's so cool!"

"Just don't tell your dad." She winked at him and he winked back as they conspired together.

For the next hour, they carefully rolled out the dough, cutting it into perfect circles before working carefully with a knife to create the computer game shapes which were then transferred onto a large baking sheet ready for the oven. As they baked they chatted easily about anything and everything, the sound of Dan working on his laptop and talking with James providing gentle background noise.

Max squidged the last of the yellow icing onto the cookie as Dan walked in and looked around the tidy and more importantly, clean kitchen.

"Blimey, I thought you two would have destroyed the place. I'm impressed!"

Laura looked at him in mock displeasure while wiping down

the kitchen side and Max moved to wash his hands.

"It's called tidying up as you go along, Dad. Maybe you should try it when you cook."

Max's delightful honesty made Laura laugh out loud. "Yeah, Dad. God!"

Dan shook his head, laughing along with them.

"All sorted?" She asked, motioning towards the front room where he'd spent the morning working.

"Yup think we're done now. James has a few revisions to make for the cover, but it's ready to go when he's done. He'll send it back over later this week and then if you want, we can go over it together and send it off to the publishers."

"Sounds good!"

The rest of the day was spent pleasantly with the trio relaxing in one another's company. Laura and Dan even managed to find a few minutes to carry on their earlier affections when Max went off to find something in his room to show her.

"Don't worry, he'll be gone for a while, I haven't seen that thing in years." He spoke softly as he worked his lips over the soft skin of her neck.

"You're terrible!" She smiled as she pulled him on top of her, back onto the sofa.

Only the sound of Max's pounding feet hitting the top step caused them to pause.

Later that night after they'd dropped her home, Max was unusually quiet in the car on the ride home. Dan could sense that he wasn't happy about something and the anxiety that his son might be unsettled by his growing closeness to Laura made him feel hot and uncomfortable.

As the car pulled up outside the house, the boy got out without saying a word.

"Max? You okay?" Dan sounded worried as he followed his son up the path to the front door.

"I'm fine."

It wasn't reassuring, said with all the energy of a moody teenager.

Dan shut the door behind them and locked it for the night. "Mate, what's wrong?"

"Nothing."

"Well, something's up. You're really quiet."

"I said I'm fine."

He noted that his son wouldn't look at him.

"Did I do something?"

"No."

"Are you not feeling well?"

"I'm fine."

Dan swallowed, nervous to ask.

"Is it Laura?"

Max didn't reply.

Dan's heart sank. They'd seemed to have had a really lovely day but maybe it was too much too soon for his son. Perhaps he was struggling with the concept that their life was now becoming a partnership with a plus one.

"I thought you liked her?"

He watched his son's nose twitch as he looked uncomfortably away.

"I don't like it when she goes. She should be with us."

"What do you mean?"

"I wish she was here all the time." His head dropped as he spoke.

Moving to his son, Dan pulled Max into a gentle cuddle that enveloped him.

"Me too Maxxy. Me too."

He'd been thinking about it for a few days. It just seemed right whenever she was with them in the house. He'd always hated her leaving after he'd got clean, but the desire to wake up with her, spend the day with her and fall asleep with her in his arms every night was fast becoming all he wanted.

"Why can't she live with us?"

Dan sighed. "It's tricky mate. We can't rush into stuff like that because if it goes wrong she could get hurt and more importantly so could you. But that doesn't mean I don't want her here with us." He kissed the top of his son's head. "Knowing that you're okay with it is good enough for me for now though."

Max drew himself out of his dad's arms and looked up. "Why?"

" 'Cos when the time is right for me to ask her, I know you'll be okay with it and that really matters to me."

"I am. I wish she was here all the time."

As they hugged again Dan looked over to the mantlepiece to where the framed picture of Max with his mum smiled back at him. He never wanted to replace Natalie but something in her expression, frozen in time looking back at them, made him feel like she'd also be okay with someone like Laura moving in, one day.

* * *

Laura's finger hovered over the mouse on her laptop, poised perfectly to hit send.

"You sure?"

Dan didn't look at her and just nodded. "Mhmm. Do it."

She hit the button and sent the final proof of the manuscript and cover for *Stories for Max* over to the publishers.

They'd done all they could do for now. It would be printed and sent to book stores all over the country, with a Q and A tour starting in a few months' time. Six weeks' worth of hard work had turned a folder full of loose leaf pages into something wonderful.

Yet as she turned to look at Dan, sitting behind her on the sofa, she noticed he didn't seem to share her excitement.

"What's wrong Dan? You don't seem at all happy about this..."

He looked deflated. Something she'd not seen in him for a while. It worried her. He stayed silent for a moment trying to find the right words.

"I hate this bit."

"What!? Why?" She moved quickly to sit next to him, concerned that she'd done something awful to him.

"'Cos it's out of my hands now." He looked at her. "Well out of our hands. What we think is really good, is now open for other people to pull apart."

"Dan! They're not going to do that. This book is wonderful."

"We think it is. But others might not. I hate it, but I can't help thinking that everyone will be disappointed in me."

She pulled him to her. "Dan, they won't think that at all."

"But they might."

Laura felt his shoulders slump. As she thought about it, she wondered if a part of his condition meant that he constantly worried how others saw him and how they'd feel about his writing, even though in reality he had nothing to worry about.

"It'll be fine. This is something wonderful and I won't be the only one thinking that. We've already got preorders and the tour is selling nicely. You'll see."

"Mhmm."

Laura paused. "Dan? Do you ever feel this way about me?"

She let him sit up and felt her own anxiety prickle. Laura's feelings for Dan were deepening every day and she couldn't imagine life any other way now but a part of her was worried about him not wanting her. She figured that his sensitivity to rejection must be like hers, but on steroids.

"Yeah I do. I always have."

"Why?"

He sighed.

"You, Laura Gray, are perfect. That's a hard measure to live up to. I'm always worried you'll realise that I'm not enough for you and that you deserve someone better. It's a fear that isn't easy to live with.

Not so long ago, when I was trying and failing to drink you out of my head, I thought I would be able to drown this side of me and extinguish the constant worry and fear and self-doubt. That didn't work and now although I'm in a much better place and you're a huge part of that, the fear never quite goes away. I don't think it ever will. "

Laura understood what he was saying and knew that the struggles he faced on a daily basis were hard ones. Her heart swelled with pride for the amount of control he had managed to find.

She climbed into his lap, taking him by surprise. "You, Mr Muir," she spoke while kissing his face, "are wonderful in every way. I can't take away your fear and worries but what I can do is show you every day how important you are to me."

Laura wrapped her arms around his neck and grinned at him. Dan relaxed and smiling back, slid his hands up her thighs.

"Thank you. I promise to try and not let it overwhelm me."

She leant in and kissed him, letting it linger.

"My love, you just do you. I understand you and that brain of yours well enough now to know that some days aren't as easy as others. Just promise me something?"

Concentrating was becoming difficult as his hands had moved from her thighs, over her bottom but he grinned at her as she tried to continue the conversation.

"Anything."

"Just keep talking to me. We can work through anything if we just keep communicating. You don't have to bottle things up."

She shuffled forward onto his lap, closer to his chest and let him kiss her.

"Promise."

"Thank you."

His lips found her neck and made her belly fizz.

"So how are we going to celebrate?" He asked.

"Erm not like that mister! That's for damn sure." Resisting was not something she wanted to do as her mind wandered to where she wanted his mouth but over his shoulder, she had noticed the time. "You have a son to collect from school."

"Fine." Dan's fingertips slid over the exposed skin at the bottom of her back and involuntarily, her hips bucked.

"Let's go pick him up from school and go out for fish and

chips." With that Dan spun her gently onto the sofa on her back and kissed her nose before getting off her with a smirk.

"Hmpf." She looked up at him, flustered.

"Hey! You said it's time to go." He laughed and held his hand out for her to pull herself to her feet.

"Yeah yeah yeah."

* * *

Laura looked across the fire pit, watching Dan show Max how to toast the marshmallow on the end of the boy's wooden skewer. His gentle and patient manner with his son made her feel like she was being warmed by something other than the burning logs, six feet away. She smiled as she saw Max giggling with glee as he tried to contain the rapidly melting confectionery he held at arm's length.

She had spent the day with the boys celebrating his 11th birthday and had shown up earlier that morning with a huge bag of presents for Max. They'd all sat together as he started tearing open wrapping paper at a staggering pace. When the boy had gone to add his new presents to the pile on the kitchen table, she'd slid a gift into Dan's lap.

"For you."

He had raised a curious eyebrow as he'd unwrapped it.

"It's wonderful Laura. Thank you. Not just for the gift but for everything you did you help turn it into a reality."

They'd stood the first copy of *Stories for Max* at the centre of the present pile for their guests to see, but not before Max took a multitude of selfies with both the book, his dad and with a very proud Laura. There had even been a lovely one of all three of them.

Now sat by the fire pit in Dan's garden, along with Max, Issy, Martin and Sarah she felt at home. Looking over the flames at the boys who had become the centre of her world, Laura knew this was what life was truly about.

They'd eaten stew from bowls, out in the cold evening. Dan had been slow cooking the hearty meal all day and it had been a perfect accompaniment to the evening.

With a mug of tea in her hands, she sat with Sarah, happy and content, lost in thought.

As Max licked sticky marshmallow from his fingertips, Dan's eyes had found hers and they'd smiled at each other like love-struck teenagers, with Laura even sticking her tongue out at him. She was looking forward to sleeping over tonight and getting time alone to gaze into his blue eyes once everyone had left but that could wait. For now, she was content to be surrounded by happy, familiar faces.

"You really like him don't you?"

Laura nodded, still half-lost in the narrative still playing in her head. "I love him."

She quickly realised what she'd said and that she'd in fact said it aloud for Sarah to hear. Her friend just nodded with a smug grin. "Knew it."

Laura had been feeling it for a while but hadn't quite vocalised it to herself, let alone anyone else.

"Just to be clear, we're not talking about Max right?" Sarah glanced sideways at her friend, whose eyes fell on the boy sitting in Dan's lap. Her heart swelled as she thought about how special Max had become to her.

"What's not to love about that boy? Look at him."

Sarah agreed, "he's a great kid."

"He really is." Her eyes drifted back to Dan. "I love him, Sarah."

Laura knew she'd fallen in love with Dan. The shy, quiet and slightly withdrawn man she'd first met had found a way into her heart and she knew now that she was completely and utterly in love with him.

"You two are so fricking cute together."

Laura thought back to earlier that evening when Sarah had stepped back into the kitchen to top up her drink, to find Dan feeding Laura marshmallows that were meant for the fire. They'd been locked in eye contact, as he had playfully made her work to take the sweet treats from his fingers. Laura had blushed when Sarah had loudly announced that they should get a room!

"Do you think he's ready? After everything?" Sarah asked.

Laura thought about all the hardships he had gone through and how far he'd come in his recovery. "Sarah, even if he fell apart again, I know that I'd fall through the devastation with him, just so we didn't have to be without each other."

Her friend made vomit noises into her mug of hot chocolate.

"Knobhead!" Laura nudged her and they both laughed.

"He still loves you, you know?" They both turned to see that Issy had moved behind them and was squatting down watching her brother-in-law. "He adores you."

"You think?" Laura couldn't help being unsure, even after everything.

"Are you kidding? Dan would walk through fire for you. He was the same with Natalie."

The trio fell silent.

"Hey, it's fine. My sister would be very happy that he makes you happy. You would have liked her, Laura."

"You sure you're okay with this, Issy?"

Issy reached forward and took Laura's hand. "Very okay with it. You make him happy."

The women shared a moment, both knowing they wanted only the best for him.

Issy's eyes drifted away. "Oh for fuck sake."

They all looked around to see that Martin had begun opening the box of fireworks and was passing the explosives to the wide-eyed birthday boy.

"Max!" Laura leapt from her seat to remove him from the imminent danger of holding explosives close to the fire.

"Martin!" Issy stepped around the fire pit at the same time to remonstrate with her unthinking husband.

Sarah just smiled and sipped her hot chocolate.

Watching the fireworks pop and fizzle above her head a little while later, Laura learnt back against Dan. He had his arms around her waist and was occasionally dipping his head to kiss her temple in between explosions.

Max and Martin were rushing around the garden, lighting fireworks, before running for cover much to Issy's frustration and everyone else's delight.

"You know we'll have to tidy this all up, right?" She surveyed the mess in the garden and wasn't even a little sorry, it would be worth every moment.

"Mhmm but it can wait till the morning."

"Oh? Why's that smart guy?"

He nuzzled his face into her neck causing the fire of lust to roar inside her.

"Because you feel cold and when everyone's gone and my son is in bed, I plan to warm you up."

"You keep kissing my neck and it isn't going to take long Dan!"

"Noted." He softly kissed her again in the same spot and she pressed back into him.

An hour later, with everyone gone and Max fast asleep, they laid in bed together, naked, much warmer and very happy; Laura catching her breath. Resting her head on his chest, she closed her eyes as Dan's fingers traced zig zag lines along the small of her back.

"Mhmm I could stay like this forever." She sighed contentedly.

"Then do it."

"You know we'd need to eat eventually."

"I didn't mean it like that."

Laura opened her eyes and was very much awake.

"I mean stay. With us."

She lifted her head and looked at him, bathed in the low light of the bedside lamp. He looked serious but there was a twinkle in his eyes.

"Move in with us, Laura."

* * *

Max bounded down the path to Dylan who was waiting in the car with his parents. Within less than a minute he was in the distance, gone for a day of trampoline parks and questionable fast food with his best friend.

Dan closed the front door and headed back into the kitchen.

Leaning against the kitchen counter was Laura, sipping a cup of tea. She was dressed in a strappy pyjama set, a pink vest top with thin straps and matching pink short shorts that rode high up her thighs. As the stone kitchen floor was always cold in the morning, she'd taken to wearing a pair of fluffy socks on her feet whenever she stayed over.

"Right, you gonna get dressed then? And I'll start tidying up?"

She just grinned at him. "No, I'll get a shower after we're done, I think."

"I'm not going to be able to tidy up if you're dressed like that Laura..."

"Mhmm. Yup. Mhmm."

He made his way to her, trying to slide his hands around her waist but she batted him away, the smile on her face growing ever more mischievous. "Nope. We actually do have tidying to do. Go on, you start out there," she pointed through the patio doors to the garden, "and I'll do in here."

"You really don't have to though. It's my place, I can do it all."

She leant forward and rising slightly onto her tiptoes, kissed his nose. "I want to help."

For the next half an hour they tidied, straightened up and cleaned. It was just surface mess really, not nearly as bad as it had looked the night before when the house was full of other people and their assorted coats and shoes. Soon however, they had it all sorted out and Laura was finishing up, washing the pots in the sink while Dan made them each a hot drink.

As the kettle boiled, he stole sideways glances at her. She had her hair up in a messy bun, wasn't wearing makeup and had just thrown on the pyjamas when they'd gotten out of bed earlier. And yet, she looked stunning.

He moved behind her, dropping the spoon that he'd been using to stir sugar into his coffee, into the bowl of hot soapy water in front of her with a splash. Two tiny drops of water landed on her vest top and while she tried to move backwards out of the way, she bumped into Dan.

"Knobhead!"

"Oops."

"I'll give you oops, mister!"

She brought her wet soapy hand back and wiped it unceremoniously on his face.

"Now now Laura, let's not start this."

"Erm, I think you started this with your careless disregard for spoons."

Soap-suds dripped down his face onto her shoulder and ran gently down her skin.

"You're right. I'm very sorry. How awful of me. Let me do it properly."

He moved his hand into the water with so much speed and force that it pushed a wave of liquid up into the back of the sink before it splashed back onto Laura.

The shock of having her midriff completely drenched caused her to jump backwards, in an attempt to move out of the way but again he didn't budge, so she was trapped against the sink. As the water settled, Dan triumphantly held up the spoon.

"Found it!"

"Dan, I'm soaked!"

She was laughing, as much in shock as at the stupidity of it all.

"Are you?"

373

"Yes!"

"Oh I don't think you're soaked really, it's just a bit of water on your top that's all. This is more soaked."

He quickly pushed his spoon-holding hand back into the sink, forcing another tsunami of dish water to slosh out over both of them, but Laura and her pink pyjamas got the worst of it.

She didn't speak.

She just stood in disbelief, saturated to the sink in disbelief trying not to laugh.

Dan turned away with a smirk on his face, going back to the coffee he'd left cooling by the kettle, his own t-shirt and trackies wet. But as he did so, he felt warm water explode over his back.

"Fuck sake!"

He turned to see Laura biting her lip holding an empty glass which suspiciously looked as it had been plunged into the sink seconds before.

"Oopsie."

She gently placed the glass on the counter and looked up to see him peeling off his drenched t-shirt.

"You're going to regret that." The look he gave her was one of pure lust and desire.

"Sure thing, smart guy. What you going to do about it?" Laura backed away, giggling, placing herself on the other side of the kitchen table.

He calmly dropped the t-shirt in front of the washer and moved around the table to get to her.

A game of cat and mouse ensued where he chased her around the table twice until he finally had his hands on her and she squealed. Dan pinned her against the table and kissed her. Heat and passion raged in both of them as they stood there wet in his kitchen, their lips locked together, their hands searching for one another.

"You're wet." He pulled at her straps.

"Mhmm very."

They rested their foreheads together breathing hard from the chase and the desire they were both feeling.

Laura thought back to the night before, watching him across the fire as she admitted to Sarah that she was in love with him. He was a wonderful man. She'd not set out to fall in love with him or his beautiful son, but she had and now she knew she never wanted to be parted from either of them.

When he'd asked her to move in with him the night before, she'd been hesitant. Not because she didn't want to, she did; but Dan's sobriety was really important to her and she wanted to be sure she would be doing it for the right reasons.

The soapy water dripped from them both and pooled at their feet. As their eyes met, she knew that she wanted to call this house, and this man, her home.

"Yes."

Dan pulled back and looked at her quizzically.

She smiled back at him and nodded. "Yes, I'll move in with you."

"Are you sure?"

"Mhmm. Very sure."

He sighed contentedly as he pulled her to him.

"I'd like that."

She rested her hands on his bare chest.

"Me too. I want this. Easy mornings together, having friends and family over at night, spending time with Max. I want to wake up with you every day and fall asleep in your arms every night. I want this life with you."

"It's not too fast for you?"

"I'm done going slow now, Dan."

He kissed her. His fingers snaking up into the back of her hair as he pulled her close. When the kiss ended he looked her in the eyes, resting his nose on hers.

"Thank you."

"You don't need to thank me. But you do need to let me get out of these wet things so we can finish getting *our* house tidy." She bit her lip for the thousandth time that morning and grinned at him.

Dan stepped back, pulling her by the hand across the kitchen to the living room.

"What are you doing Mr Muir?" She asked coyly.

"Helping you get out of those wet things and into a shower."

"Yeah, I could very easily get used to this life..."

* * *

She stepped down and sauntered over to him, grinning expectantly.

"You were amazing!"

"I was?"

"You always are!"

She'd hoped his reaction would be a little different. Picking up her drink she sighed inwardly, wondering if she'd been too subtle about the whole thing. He was usually so attuned to understanding her.

Looking at him, smiling back at her, she felt like she wanted to live in this moment forever.

But he'd missed her intention tonight and now she was left considering if she needed to show him in a way he would recognise; stepping into his world, rather than trying to pull him into hers.

Getting back to her flat a few hours later, she wasted no time. If she didn't do this now she'd lose her nerve and she knew it. The irony didn't go unnoticed; she now understood how he must have felt. Opening the top of one the packing boxes stacked up by the sofa, she reached in to find her copy of *Endlessly* and pulling it into her lap, leafed through the pages. It was worn and almost tatty from the number of times she had pored over its pages, drowning herself in the beautiful words. It meant the world to her.

Without pausing to even read her favourite parts, she turned to the blank page at the back.

* * *

Dan laced his fingers through Laura's, causing her to sigh softly, her head resting lightly on his shoulder. They'd been through so much in the last few months and yet here they were, back on the park bench sitting in the sunshine.

"Funny, isn't it?" She asked, smiling.

"Hmm? Enlighten me?"

"Months ago we sat here, you fidgeting like your pants were on fire, telling me you were in love with me."

"Oh yeah, I remember," his mocking tone making her chuckle, "didn't you tell me *thanks but no thanks*?"

"Hmm? No, I don't remember that. My memory is a little hazy."

Dan smiled and rested his head on hers.

"Sure it is."

"And yet here we are and you still love me."

Dan looked around behind him, making it appear that he thought she was talking to someone else.

"I didn't say that, did I?"

She moved and looked at him in mock surprise.

"You don't still love me?"

"I didn't say that either."

Laura relaxed back into his side as he pulled her to him.

"I do. Even after everything, my heart hasn't let you go. It seems to know what's inevitable."

She sighed. "You make love sound so poetic."

"You understand that's literally what I do for a living, right? Make stuff sound good?"

"Huh. Weird. I thought you just sat around all day until it was time to pick Max up from school."

"Yeah, well that too."

They laughed. It was a joyous, delicious moment shared by two people who cared deeply for each other and were comfortable just being together, regardless of where they were.

Laura looked out over the park, the people enjoying the fresh air and the open space. She'd tried to tell him how she felt in her own way the day before but the fool seemed to totally miss the point; Dan had a beautiful, creative brain but could easily miss what was right under his nose at times.

"What did you think of my set last night?"

He took a moment, trying to figure out what she meant. After she'd finished playing, he'd done what he'd done for ages, told her how amazing she was. Dan could have sworn he hadn't imagined doing it as usual last night.

"Didn't I tell you last night your set was amazing"

"Oh, you did." She slid her free hand around the inside of his arm, her body fizzing at the feel of his skin. "But I did a new song, didn't I?"

Dan smiled. The cover of *Making Me Look Good Again* by Drake White had been really good and she'd scarcely taken her eyes off him while she sang it.

"It was really good!"

She smiled ruefully as she watched the world go by. *Plan B it is then!*

Laura sat up straight.

"You okay?"

He wasn't concerned, just curious as to what she was doing, as he watched her reach into her bag. She pulled her copy of *Endlessly* into her lap and gently rested her hands on it.

"Mhmm. So there's something I wanted to talk to you about before I move in tomorrow. This book," she said nervously, "has literally changed my life."

She felt him recoil slightly next to her. While Dan had come so far on his road to recovery, seeing his book of poetry still caused him anxiety with the weight of everything those words had created still sitting heavy on his heart. He tried to listen quietly without fidgeting.

"It brought a man into my life who is both wonderful and beautiful and who loved me so completely that even now I struggle to wrap my head around it."

He made to turn around mockingly as he had done moments before.

"Don't even think about it, smart guy."

Laura knew it was time.

"Do you still love me, Dan, like you said you did on these pages?" She asked as she leafed through the book making her way to the final page.

He didn't need to consider anything.

While his love for her had nearly destroyed him, with her help, he'd managed to rebuild himself and find some balance in the world around him again. She was still at the very centre of his world and he knew he wanted to effortlessly spin around her for as long as the universe existed.

"Yes. My love for you hasn't faded, not even for a moment."

Laura smiled, gently nodding her head as she flicked to the last page of *Endlessly* over to show him what had been the blank page at the back.

Dan looked down and noticed the page wasn't blank anymore but was filled with her pretty handwriting.

"Now, I'm not as good with words as you and seeing as you totally missed my point last night..."

"What point?"

"Exactly. So seeing as you didn't get it last night, I've tried to tell you on your level."

Laura's nerves gone, she handed the book over for him to read. The moment had come.

Dan looked at the pages in his hands and tried to focus on the words in front of him. He had to read it three times before he realised what it was saying. She was right, she wasn't good at words *at all* but those words meant everything to him.

> *Even though some days are rough*
> *You will always be enough*
> *Time with you is always fun*
> *And I truly adore your son*
> *Roses are red.*
> *Violets are blue.*
> *You two make my heart smile.*
> *I'm endlessly in love with you.*

His breath caught in his chest as he raised his eyes from the page, his brain trying desperately to work out what exactly was happening. She loved him. After all this time, after all that had happened, she really loved him.

He felt his heart flutter, as it clicked into place with hers.

* * *

Dedicated to all the Lauras who were loved but never knew.

Epilogue

Max stood in front of her.

"I didn't forget anything and everyone even laughed at my jokes! Dad says he was really proud of me."

Dan pulled his son back against him slightly and kissed the top of his head. "I always am."

"My shirt collar was so annoying but I felt really grown-up with Dad and Uncle Martin. I wish you could have seen me, Mum. I miss you."

He stepped forward and gently placed his buttonhole on his mother's headstone, the pink of the rose accentuated beautifully against the smooth, white marble.

Laura drew him into a hug as he moved back. Max wrapped his arms around her and tried not to cry; something he always found hard to do whenever he came there. Laura kissed the top of his head just as his dad had done a moment before.

"You two head back to the car. I just need a minute." Dan spoke quietly.

She squeezed his hand before leading Max back down the path to the carpark.

When Dan was alone, he read the words delicately carved into the marble in front of him.

Here lies Natalie Muir.

Much loved mother, wife, sister and friend.

The world is a worse place without you

"It really is, you know?" The words caught in his throat as he said them. "Even with everything good there is in the world now, it would be all the better for you still being here."

The sun shone brightly across the ground where he stood.

"Max really did do great yesterday. He made me a very proud dad. I couldn't have asked for a better Best Man. Laura's not stopped telling him how handsome he looked."

Turning to look down to the car park, he saw his son waiting for him at the gates, holding his new wife's hand.

"I kept my promise, you know? You're still the only woman I've ever asked to marry me."

He thought back to Laura asking him to marry her; an excited Max bouncing on his toes behind her. Dan had stared in disbelief at the silver ring she held out in front of her.

"I picked out a pretty one with a big diamond, but Sarah said you'd want something a little less ostentatious."

"OMG, Dad! Say yes!"

"She makes me happy, Natalie. And Max. I hope you can see that. But you haven't been forgotten; we could never forget about you."

Back at the car, Max fumbled the small box in his pocket.

"Erm we got you something, Laura."

She looked at the boy curiously as she opened his car door. "You did?"

"Mhmm. It's from me and Dad."

He handed over the small box with the sheepish smile of youth.

Laura carefully opened the small navy jewellery box he'd given her. Inside it, sat a beautiful gold locket on a delicate golden chain.

"Max!" She breathed.

"Dad got one for Mum when I was little and she always wore it. And I wanted you to have one as well so Dad helped me pick it out. It has a picture of both of us in it, so we can always be with you."

Tears flowing down her face she lifted it from its velvet cushion and watched it spinning in the sunlight.

"Max, it's beautiful, thank you. I'll never take it off."

They hugged, as she held her gift carefully in her fingers.

"I love you, Laura."

"I love you too, Maxxy."

As he climbed into the car, she placed the locket around her neck and flicked her hair free before turning to watch Dan on the hillside.

He stepped back, holding his gaze on her headstone for a moment longer before turning away and heading down towards the gates.

"You okay?" She slipped her hand in his as he moved closer to her.

"Yeah, I'm good." He spotted the locket around her neck. "Looks good on you."

"It's perfect. Thank you."

"Ah, it was his idea mostly. But it's one I'm fully on board with."

He kissed her nose.

"Shall we get this honeymoon started then?"

He looked over at the car, bulging with suitcases, Max already in the back seat, excited.

"Let's." Laura smiled and hugged her husband.

As she leaned her head against his warm chest, she let her eyes fall onto Natalie's final resting place at the top of the hill and said to herself quietly, *I'll take care of them for you. I promise.*

* * *

About the Author

Born in rural Wiltshire, Eliza Hope Brown is a full-time writer of contemporary fiction. She studied English and Foreign Languages at DeMonfort University and was a primary school teacher and graphic designer before writing her first novel in 2022. She lives in London with her cat, Morley.

Also by Eliza Hope-Brown

Colours

Different universes. Different timelines. Different iterations of the same people.

You already know their names; it's time to meet the new versions.

Can Dan and Laura find their matching pieces in every world?

The same hearts, different lives. Will love find a way?

This time around Laura and Dan have been friends for a lifetime.

Their families have been close friends forever.

One of them falls in love with someone unexpected, one of them takes up a dream job on another continent.

If you liked Sanctuary, you'll love Colours, the second install-ment of the Sweet Inevitability series.

Sanctuary

A broken heart, a photographer fixated on his work and a chance meeting in an airport at 4am.

Laura, professional rugby player, strong body, shattered heart, unable to see an end to the pain caused by her former fiancè.

Dan, married to his job and haunted by an image from the past that he just can't shake.

A story that spans years and cities. Crossed paths and kept promises – does coffee really fix everything?

Find sanctuary in a book you won't want to put down.